SENTINELS OF TZURAC

RETALIATION

Books written by James Raven in the Sentinels of Tzurac saga

Terra Major Under Threat
Zarkwin's Revenge
Retaliation
Vengeance

International Film Festival Awards for
Script adaptations on first edition books:

Silver Award – Terra Major Under Threat
Gold Award – Zarkwin's Revenge
Gold Award – Retaliation

California Film Awards:

Gold Award – Terra Major Under Threat

James Raven

SENTINELS OF TZURAC

RETALIATION

Inspiring Publishers
P.O. Box 159, Calwell, ACT Australia 2905
Email: publishaspg@gmail.com
http://www.inspiringpublishers.com

A catalogue record for this book is available from the National Library of Australia

National Library of Australia The Prepublication Data Service

Author: James Raven
Title: Sentinels of Tzurac:
          Retaliation
Genre: Science Fiction

Paperback ISBN: 978-1-923449-04-6
ePub2 ISBN: 978-1-923449-05-3

*FOR her relentless help in editing my novels and for her
continuous strong support and encouragement of my writing,
I would like to express my deepest gratitude to my partner Julie.*

RESURRECTION

IN the silence and emptiness of space, a black scorpion-shaped battleship marked with a distinctive red-scorpion insignia had just dropped from hyperdrive to cruising speed. A thick set, long haired and unkempt figure was making himself more comfortable in the Captain's Chair when suddenly, his battleship was struck by a powerful force that reverberated through the ship's hull. He was jolted forward onto the console with his arms flailing, trying to buffer the impact. High pitched alarms screamed in the cabin and small coloured lights flashed wildly across the entire console. Dazed by the impact and with his eyes still trying to refocus, he struggled to regain composure.

Coming to his senses, the figure sprang into action. He reached for the controls, checking for signs of damage and scanning the monitors displaying the craft's perimeter. There was nothing to indicate the cause of impact – no asteroids, no space junk and no enemy ships.

Not taking any chances, especially in this treacherous, uncharted solar system, he immediately shouted commands in his accented native tongue, 'Computer, raise shields to one hundred percent and arm laser cannons! Assess damage and turn off those damn alarms!'

The screeching noise ceased instantly, and the flashing lights dissipated.

Within minutes a monotone simulated voice came over the Comms, 'Damage Report: All systems operational. Minor damage to hull. Cause of assault: Unidentified missile.'

The lone pilot realised he was under attack. But before he could take evasive action, the Comms unexpectedly crackled and came to life again, this time with a strident voice speaking with an unfamiliar accent in the pilot's native tongue, Treldarian. 'Attention, space voyager! We've fired a warning shot. You're about to enter a Treldarian zone. Identify yourself!'

The anxious intruder switched on his main screen and was shocked to see a massive, intimidating warship fast approaching and beginning to dwarf his vessel. 'Where the hell did that come from?' he blurted. 'Computer, magnify tenfold!'

The screen flickered to reveal a close-up of a heavily armed, black warship, unlike any he had seen before. Yet, it was bearing the unmistakable Treldarian insignia of a deadly-looking red scorpion.

The intruder knew he was out-gunned and, most assuredly, out-powered. Alone, he was at the mercy of these unfamiliar Treldarians. However, he had no intention of running. *This must be the remote Treldarian army he'd been searching for*, he thought. *The challenge now was to befriend them before being decimated.*

Before he had time to respond, another more threatening demand came over his Comms, 'Space voyager! Respond immediately! If you continue on your path, you'll be destroyed by the minefield you're fast approaching. If you try to escape, you'll be fired upon!'

He brought his battleship to a standstill at once and the screen flickered to reveal a larger-than-life image of his attacker. Before him was a mean-looking, solidly built Treldarian with a trimmed black beard, dark sunken eyes and the leathery face of a seasoned soldier. The slick Treldarian captain was dressed in a black uniform with blood-red epaulettes and matching sleeve cuffs. His jet-black, shoulder-length hair was pulled back neatly into a ponytail over a buttoned high collar and embedded on the helix of his right ear were three small gold studs. His face was stony as he glared intently at the intruder.

The lone pilot was not intimidated. 'Hold your fire!' he screamed defiantly. 'I'm First Lieutenant Ramlok, emissary for General Dranz, leader of the Treldarian Fifth Legion from the Northern Quadrant. I come alone and in peace on urgent business. I need to speak with your general!'

On board the threatening warship, the Treldarian captain tensed and leaned forward in his command chair. He was impressed by the stranger's defiance and curious to see the image of this audacious intruder which now flickered onto his screen.

Facing him was a thick set and dishevelled rebel whose face was marked with battle scars, his dark wild eyes staring with a haunting intensity. His straggly hair was greasy, long and matted and his beard ungroomed. He was wearing a well-worn, brown-leather battle-jacket over a crumpled, blood-red shirt with a wide, dull-yellow sash pulled diagonally across his broad chest. The Blader insignia of crossed daggers was emblazoned prominently on the lapel of his battle-jacket.

Recognising the guerrilla freedom fighter's outfit from descriptions in the annals, the captain addressed his captive with confident authority. 'I'm Captain Tarken, Commander of this warship. Our weapons are targeted on you. Give me proof of your identity!'

Ramlok's stone face gave no hint of fear, though he well knew Treldarians were inclined to shoot first and ask questions later. He reached carefully for his dispatch papers, slowly unravelling a dark leather pouch before holding the enclosed parchment up to the screen so it was clearly visible to the Captain. Ramlok watched Tarken's eye movements on the screen as he scrutinized the hand-written words and inspected General Dranz's signature sealed with an imprinted red wax crest.

After a tense moment, Captain Tarken raised his head and made direct eye contact with the rebel Blader as if searching for the truth. Finally, he spoke again with the same tone of control. 'Very well Lieutenant Ramlok, the document appears authentic, and our heat sensors indicate there are no other life forms aboard your ship. I'll escort you to my general on Planet Orkharn.'

Ramlok breathed a discreet sigh of relief. 'Thank you, Captain. I'll follow your lead,' he said with outward bravado.

'Be warned, stranger, we'll be monitoring your every move!' threatened Tarken, glaring at Ramlok through his dark eyes. 'You need to follow my route closely to avoid our space mines. Hold your course, Lieutenant Ramlok, or you're dead!'

* * *

'Comms, fire up the craft and follow that warship!' Ramlok instructed, thinking *so far, so good.*

As he trailed his new-found escort vessel, Ramlok reflected on the events that had brought him to this dangerous solar system and to his encounter with the assertive Captain Tarken.

On the orders of General Dranz, he had come on an urgent mission to find the long-lost Treldarian legions in the outer regions of the Eastern and Southern Quadrants of the Universe. He was carrying a message for General Khuram Vark of the Second Legion, and General Jelzad Rokan of the Third Legion. And, hopefully, he was about to meet one of them.

However, his mind was in conflict. These legions had deserted the Treldarian forces some five hundred years ago during a protracted interplanetary war with the Tzuracians over precious Xytrinium resources. Realising they were losing the battle against the enemy, Tzuracian Sentinels –who had superior qualities and an extended lifespan resulting from a secret process of infusing Xytrinium into their DNA – the Second and Third Legions had abandoned the fight and sought refuge in the far-flung outer regions of the Universe. The message from Dranz was requesting these deserters join forces with him once again in an all-out war to destroy their age-old archenemy the Tzuracians who had formed a Federation of Planets that now controlled most of the Xytrinium resources in the Universe.

Ramlok screwed his face up in disgust. Although he hated the Tzuracians with a vengeance, he was loath to side with traitors and he resented being sent begging on behalf of his General. He was a proud member of the defiant rogue Fifth Legion – a legion of Treldarians who had refused to surrender to the Tzuracians in the Grekadian Wars and had established a life of piracy as 'Bladers' plundering Federation transport ships carrying precious Xytrinium. The Bladers had continued their rebellious life for centuries.

Ramlok harboured a deep-seated animosity towards the Second and Third Legions who had deserted their brothers-in-arms in times past and he was sceptical they would now rally to support Dranz. But, if the Tzuracians and their Sentinel army were ever to be beaten, he had to put his pride and his prejudice aside. It was imperative that all those of Treldarian heritage come together again as one massive army.

Then, a devious smirk appeared on the Blader's face – he knew he was carrying with him the secret which would persuade these traitors to rally to the cause.

* * *

After travelling at high speed for several hours while navigating treacherous minefields, the two ships slowed to cruising speed as they approached the outer orbit of Planet Orkharn. Ramlok was astounded at what he saw before him – spectacular iridescent purple nebulae of swirling gases set against a black space void, thickly sprinkled with tiny white spots of stars.

Descending through the coloured haze to the surface of the pale grey planet, the rebel Blader could make out a thriving metropolis which stretched far and wide to the base of a distant, smoky-blue mountain range. Grey plumes of smoke belched from a number of tall stacks scattered amongst the congested buildings.

Ahead of the ships was a massive, almost-spherical hangar. It was constructed of thick heavy-metal girders interlocked to increase the structure's strength and stability, then overlaid with giant hexagonal panels.

'Lieutenant Ramlok, prepare to dock!' Captain Tarken demanded over the Comms. 'Shut down your thrusters!'

As his ship entered the hangar, tractor beams locked Ramlok's vessel in a fixed path towards the docking ramp leaving no margin for accidental collision or attempted sabotage. Ramlok spied several cannon batteries and mounted cameras positioned strategically around the walls of the giant hangar. The reason for the strong fortification was obvious. The hangar housed a large fleet of warships and battle cruisers coloured black or various shades of dark grey for space camouflage. All were silently resting like a pack of sleeping beasts in wait.

After disembarking from his vessel, Ramlok was confronted by ten armed Treldarian soldiers dressed in black uniforms. In an instant the soldiers seized his weapons and, under duress, Ramlok reluctantly handed over the leather dispatch binder. He cursed the traitors under his breath.

One of the escort soldiers delivered the binder to Captain Tarken who was striding towards Ramlok's ship after disembarking from his own craft.

'Apologies for the abrupt greeting, Lieutenant,' said Tarken in a conciliatory tone. 'You're an intruder to our sanctuary, and we don't take any chances. Follow me and I'll take you to General Vark's headquarters.'

Ramlok acknowledged silently by nodding. *He had made it to the Second Legion.*

The Treldarian escort remained cold and expressionless as they herded Ramlok to the General's headquarters. The entourage marched without a word through a maze of dimly lit, roughly carved, stone passageways barely wide enough for three abreast. Diffused bluish light emanated from large overhead panels, partially illuminating the rough, grey stone walls and floor. The passageways were cold and sterile.

After marching for several minutes, the Captain shouted 'Halt!' and the guards came to a standstill outside an entrance sealed by two thick metal doors. The doors opened leading into a spacious, well-lit and sparsely decorated room with a high ceiling. A collection of various weapons was mounted around the stone walls. There were large, long-bladed swords with intricate metal-sculptured hilts, metal shields with patterned emblems emblazoned with strange animal features, bows of both longbow and crossbow construction, and spears of different lengths with fancy designed hunting heads, as well as other unfamiliar spiked and bladed weapons.

An oversized wooden table, surrounded by several wooden-framed chairs padded with black woven material, stood in the centre of the floor. Seated on one of the chairs was a large imposing figure. His hair, tied back in the familiar Treldarian style, was streaked with silver-grey. It matched the colours of his moustache and medium-length well-groomed beard. From a distance Ramlok could discern a thinly grooved burgundy scar running vertically from the figure's forehead across his right eye and halfway down his cheek. *An old war wound,* he thought. Four gold studs were embedded into the outer ridge of the figure's right ear and like Captain Tarken, the figure was dressed in a black uniform with the blood-red trimmings of an officer on the collar and cuffs. He was also decorated with a gold-braid twine looped around his sleeve at the shoulder and a gold medallion pinned to the left breast of his high-collared jacket. *Impressive!*

As the escort arrived, the General rose from his chair. While gesturing with his right arm he spoke in a sharp guttural tongue, 'Bring the visitor to my table, Captain!'

'Yes, sir,' responded Tarken with a half-raised, stiff-arm salute, ushering his captive forward. 'Sir, this is Lieutenant Ramlok, emissary from General Dranz of the Fifth Legion, Northern Quadrant.'

Tarken turned to face Ramlok. 'Lieutenant, this is General Vark, Supreme Leader of the Second Legion.'

The introductions complete, Tarken handed the leather binder to the General, as Ramlok watched closely.

'Be seated, Lieutenant,' said the General, in what was more of a stern request than an order. 'And stand easy, Captain!' he commanded his subordinate, who was clearly a disciplined officer.

Ramlok slid a chair out from the table while watching this hardened, formidable pair and, as he sat down, the General seated himself directly opposite. Tarken stood behind his General, and both carefully scrutinised their unexpected and unkempt guest with the wild-looking, dark eyes.

'Like some wine after your long journey, Lieutenant?' Vark asked, waving his arm in the direction of a carafe and four metal goblets which had been placed on the table. As he did, Ramlok noted that the scar had caused a partial paralysis on the right side of Vark's face, giving him a villainous crooked smile.

'Yes, just what I need,' said Ramlok feeling more at ease.

'Captain, pour a drink for our visitor and one for me as well. It's a special occasion meeting our brother from the past.' He paused for a moment. 'It must be a desperate situation for General Dranz to send you all this way after all these years,' he said as he began to open the dispatches.

Ramlok sat silently watching the General stroke his beard carefully with his right hand while thoughtfully studying the dispatch in detail. The General's facial expressions mirrored his emotions, and his breathing became faster as he progressed through the pages.

When he had finished reading, General Vark leaned back in his chair and slowly raised his head. His furrowed brow indicated the gravity of General Dranz's request, and his cold, steel-grey eyes stared into the distance as he thought about the consequences. Then he reached across the table for his goblet and swilled a mouthful.

'Now let me see if I understand this request which has brought you to our far-flung region of the Universe … General Dranz is desperate to destroy the Federation and its Sentinels of Tzurac and gain control of the Federation's Xytrinium reserves. Nothing's changed in five hundred years!' He chuckled under his breath and Tarken joined in.

'And he's acquired the formula which gives the Sentinels their super-strength and longevity by infusing liquefied Xytrinium into their DNA. He's used it to enhance his own army of Bladers, including you I assume?' Vark raised the eyebrow over his scarred right eye. He was obviously surprised and impressed with this remarkable news. Captain Tarken, standing with his mouth agape, was also astounded.

Ramlok nodded in the affirmative and swigged his goblet of Treldarian wine in one gulp. 'Yeah, and I have it with me,' he said arrogantly. 'I have the formula and equipment which could transform *your* army into super-soldiers who could live for centuries.'

'You have it with you?' the General said with some scepticism. 'After all these centuries you're telling me we have the means of raising our powers to compete with the Sentinels on their own terms?' Vark eyed Ramlok up and down, noting his war-torn face and his dishevelled battle-jacket. 'You don't look like a super soldier, Lieutenant Ramlok,' he taunted. 'Why don't you show us what you can do?'

Without a word, Ramlok clenched his empty solid metal goblet and with a vice-like grip, squeezed it to a pulp with ease. Then he leaned forward and dropped the crumpled mass from shoulder height onto the tabletop. It landed with a solid thud and a resounding loud echo.

Vark and his Captain turned to each other clearly impressed. 'Not bad,' said Vark. 'You've got my attention … So, if Dranz had a super army, how come the attempted takeover of Terra Major's Xytrinium reserves and their mines on Terra Iota was foiled by the Sentinels of Tzurac? It says so in the dispatches.'

'The Sentinels were expecting us,' said Ramlok, raising his voice and clenching his fist. 'We were betrayed and walked into an ambush.' Vark could sense Ramlok's anger.

'Hmm … So now Dranz is determined to destroy the armies on Tzurac and Terra Major and he's offering *us* the benefits of Xytrinium infusion if we agree to join his army.'

Tarken's face instantly lit up. He was excited by the prospect.

Before Ramlok could respond, the General motioned to stop him from speaking. 'Why would I want to involve my Second

Legion in Dranz's war when we have everything we need in *this* galaxy?' He looked doubtful.

'When my Legion arrived here during the Grekadian War, we conquered five planets which now supply us with all our needs including Xytrinium from Planet Glantos. We've survived and prospered here, enslaving male captives to labour in the mines and the fields and females to serve for our pleasure. The Tzuracians have left us to our own devices in this isolated corner of the Universe. Yes, the promise of infusion is attractive, Lieutenant Ramlok, but would it be enough for us to disrupt the empire we've built for ourselves?' Vark pondered for a moment. 'I'm not convinced,' he said, shaking his head dismissively.

Vark was not easily persuaded. He was a highly intelligent soldier with a sharp mind, and he liked being in complete control. He was currently the Supreme Leader of his own empire in the Eastern Quadrant. Although tempted by the thought of taking vengeance against the Sentinels and controlling all four Quadrants of the Universe as well as the Xytrinium resources, he wanted to be sure of success before relinquishing his current position of power.

Ramlok took care with his response. He had to keep his resentment in check and avoid provoking the situation. He reached across the table for a fresh goblet and poured himself another wine without invitation. Then he leant back in his chair and throwing a leg over one of the chair-arms, took another mouthful as he considered his reply.

'Speak freely, Lieutenant,' said the General impatiently, pressuring Ramlok for more. 'Captain, sit down and pour yourself a drink. This is getting interesting.'

'Thank you, sir,' Tarken said as he sat down obediently and joined the party.

'Well, General,' said Ramlok, taking a deep breath, 'your peace and tranquillity is now under threat.'

Vark and Captain Tarken exchanged sceptical glances.

'How so?' Tarken asked defiantly.

Ramlok almost choked with emotion as he answered. His mood had suddenly changed. 'On my way here, I intercepted a Sentinel transmission announcing that General Dranz and our army on Steiros had been captured by the Federation and *executed.*'

Vark shook his head, almost in disbelief. 'What in the Gods' names! Dranz and his Bladers couldn't fend off the Sentinels on Steiros? Some super-soldiers!'

Ramlok shrugged his shoulders. 'Steiros was supposed to be our safe haven. I can only guess we were betrayed once again. Someone – and I have my suspicions – must have informed the Federation, and the Sentinels took my General and his soldiers by surprise.'

'So, you continued your journey here to ask me to join an army that no longer exists?' Vark was perplexed.

'Yes,' Ramlok said boldly. 'I came because I was following orders. I came because with your help I can avenge the death of my General and my comrades.' He paused for effect. 'And I also came to warn you that *you* may now be in grave danger.'

'In danger? What have I to fear?' Vark asked, confidently stroking his beard. 'On the contrary, Ramlok, *you're* the one in danger.' He glared at Ramlok. 'We could dispose of you right now and use the formula for ourselves.' Tarken concurred with a shake of his head.

Ramlok didn't flinch. 'You could, General, but you'd be losing all my knowledge and experience. And I suspect you will need it … *soon!* The Tzuracians have advanced techniques in mind-probing and it's highly likely they extracted information from General Dranz before executing him. It wouldn't surprise me if they know he sent me here on a mission to gather more forces and that I carry with me their formula for infusion. If so, the Tzuracians will be keen to strike quickly to recover their secret formula and prevent the development of more super armies. They could even be on their way to Orkharn as we speak.'

General Vark cursed under his breath as blood flushed his face in anger. He was livid. He sprang to his feet, sweeping the wine carafe from the table with a forceful blow, slamming his fist down and shouting at Ramlok.

'You idiot! You should *not* have come. You've jeopardised our sanctuary, trapping us into taking up arms against an elite force of Sentinels. I'll kill you for this!'

Vark reached for his blade, but before he could draw his weapon the seasoned veteran Captain Tarken placed a hand over the weapon's hilt to stop him. 'Let's wait and see what he has to offer, sir, before we dispose of him,' Tarken said firmly.

Although Vark respected the actions of his clear-thinking officer, the atmosphere in the room was tense.

'Shall I continue, General?' asked Ramlok with a smug calmness. He sensed he had the upper hand.

'Yes, Lieutenant, tell us more. Tell us everything!' said the General aggressively, removing his hand from his sword and reluctantly resuming his seat.

With Vark and Tarken gazing furiously at him, Ramlok casually took another swig of wine. 'Although General Dranz and my comrades are dead, the Tzuracian Sentinels have other enemies who would seize any opportunity to defeat them.

'When we attacked Terra Iota, we did so with the help of our allies, the Kyroni and Diunons. The Tzuracians have imprisoned the surviving leaders of both races and imposed martial law on their planets. You'd have the full support of these allies if you were to crush the Tzuracian overlords on their planets and release their leaders. They'd welcome the opportunity to take revenge.

With these reinforcements you could increase your Eastern and Southern Legions' armies to advance on Tzurac and Terra Major.'

The General and his Captain acknowledged the possibility somewhat reluctantly, tilting their heads to each other as Ramlok continued.

'I also think you can destroy the shield or Dome which has protected the Tzuracian capital of Khazor since the Grekadian War. General Dranz had been working on a scheme to build Xytrinium warheads capable of penetrating the forcefield. I have those plans. Together, your armies could take them by surprise and beat them at their own game.'

Ramlok sat back, confidently, and took another mouthful of wine, allowing time for the General to comment.

'Perhaps …' For a moment Vark seemed lost in thought. 'Clever … I can see why you were chosen by Dranz to be his emissary.'

'I was with my General for a long time,' said Ramlok. 'He was my mentor in battle tactics and war strategies, and a good one.' Vark could sense the admiration. 'Our attempt on Iota failed only because we were betrayed and our plans exposed to the Federation. This *will not* happen again!' Ramlok was now shaking with anger.

'I sense your anger and loss, Lieutenant. I also see you want your revenge. Anything else we should know?' asked Vark.

Ramlok contained his anger and lowered his voice. 'The Xytrinium deposits you have on Glantos won't last indefinitely. There are abundant stockpiles on Terra Major and more of this resource to be mined on Terra Iota by the Terranian owned company MERIC. Unfortunately, Terra Major is now a member of the Federation of Planets and is under the protection of the Tzuracian Sentinels. We need to destroy the Federation so all the Xytrinium will be under Treldarian rule.'

Ramlok knew General Vark and his Captain were becoming more interested. The Blader's words seemed to have aroused their warring instincts. Deep-seated hatred towards the Tzuracian Sentinels, which had been buried for centuries, was beginning to resurface. As they drank from their goblets, Ramlok could almost hear the wheels in their minds turning over the prospect of the Treldarians becoming rulers of the four quadrants of the Universe.

General Vark broke the silence, clearing his throat and speaking with authority. 'Alright, Lieutenant, I'm not overjoyed at you bringing this proposal to me uninvited, but I'll consider it. I'll summon my War Council.'

In spite of the strained atmosphere and his long-standing resentment of these Treldarian deserters, Ramlok was starting to feel some affinity with his brothers.

'Captain Tarken, escort the Lieutenant to his quarters and arrange a meal for him.' Vark turned to Ramlok. 'Be ready, Ramlok, when the War Council summons you in the morning. In the meantime, get some rest. That'll be all for now, Lieutenant. You're dismissed.'

'Thanks for the wine, General,' Ramlok said as he rose from the table and left the room with Captain Tarken. *His attempts to persuade the General had been successful. His next challenge would be convincing the War Council.*

WAR COUNCIL

RAMLOK was woken abruptly by what sounded like cannon fire. His eyes flashed open, his pulse thumping as he tried to recognise his strange surroundings. Instinctively, he reached under the pillow for his laser pistol. 'Damn!' he cursed. It wasn't there. He began to panic.

He was shaken into reality when he realised someone was bashing on his door yelling out his name.

'Lieutenant Ramlok! Lieutenant Ramlok! Are you awake?'

Ramlok sat bolt upright in bed, coughed to clear his throat and shook his head. The local wine was stronger than he was used to, and his head was fuzzy. He had no way of knowing what time of night or day it was as there were no windows, the room being illuminated only by artificial blue light coming from the ceiling.

'I am now,' he grunted loudly. 'What time is it? And who in the Gods' names are you?'

'Sir, it's midday,' came a deep husky voice. 'I'm Sergeant Krag and I'm here to escort you to the War Council!'

Ramlok gathered his thoughts. *This is Orkharn.* 'Hold fast, Sergeant!' he commanded.

Sitting on his metal-framed single bed, Ramlok surveyed the Spartan room which was devoid of artworks. The dull-grey stone floor and walls added to the drabness. Beside the bed was a wooden chest of drawers. Positioned against the opposite wall was a small, square, metal table with two metal chairs next to a doorway to a small bathroom.

The previous night Ramlok had tossed his battle-jacket on the wooden chest beside his bed before falling asleep fully clothed in his leather pants and still wearing his knee-high suede boots. This was not unusual for a Blader pirate. Ramlok had often woken in a strange bed, unwashed with a mild hangover and a body odour of stale sweat after a bout of drinking and wild women the night before.

So Ramlok did what he usually did. He quickly headed for the washbasin, splashed cold water on his tired face, ran his fingers as a rough comb through his thick, messy hair, and scrubbed his stained teeth with his fingers. He scooped a couple of handfuls of running water into his mouth from the metal spout and swirled the water around for a few seconds before spitting it out. Then he grabbed the nearest wine flask and took a quick swig. Throwing on his well-worn battle-jacket, he was now set for the day, or what was left of it.

On opening the door Ramlok was confronted by a tall and solid Treldarian in a black uniform with green flashes on his sleeve cuffs and a green sash around his waist. The soldier had a short-bladed sabre strapped on one hip, a laser pistol holstered on the opposite side, and a dagger sheathed in his black knee-high boots. His long, black hair was pulled back tightly, revealing a neatly trimmed, short, black beard that outlined a square jaw exuding a subtle smile. His face was weathered – *most likely from his years in the military exposed to the elements*, thought Ramlok. His most notable feature was his piercing, dark-brown eyes which stared with curiosity from beneath thick eyebrows. Ramlok sensed the soldier was wondering what had caused this stranger to travel so far to their world.

'Good afternoon, sir. Sleep alright?' There was a slight sarcasm in the soldier's husky voice.

'Yes. Thanks, Sergeant. Pity I was disturbed,' responded Ramlok, also with some sarcasm. 'Suppose there's no time for something to eat?'

'Sorry, sir, but the War Council has been convened for most of the morning and I have orders to escort you there immediately.'

The Sergeant set a brisk pace as the pair walked in silence through several wide, stone-built passageways throughout the expansive building, their footsteps echoing from the acoustics of the high arched ceilings.

Ramlok's own curiosity soon got the better of him. 'So, Sergeant Krag, where are we? What is this place?'

'This is the Administration Building, the planet Orkharn's seat of power. Along with the army barracks, armoury and military supplies, it's housed within a stone fortress. The rest of the city of Bharkaz is outside the fortress.'

No sooner had the Sergeant finished speaking when he announced, 'We're here, sir, at the Council Hall.'

The couple had arrived at two matching grey-metal entry doors guarded by two black-uniformed soldiers who were standing at attention on either side of the entrance. Both were armed with spears held vertically close by their sides. As the couple approached, the guards simultaneously snapped their upright spears into a crossed 'X', blocking the doors.

'No entry while Council is in session,' threatened one of the soldiers in a deep, guttural voice.

Krag stood his ground and placing a hand on his sabre's hilt, spoke forcefully. His intimidating height and angry facial expression added weight to his demand. 'Corporal, I'm Sergeant Krag of the 25th Infantry Battalion. Lieutenant Ramlok has been summoned by the War Council. Inform the Council he's here and don't keep us or the Council waiting!'

The straight-faced guard tried not to appear intimidated. 'Wait here, Sergeant,' he ordered in a stronger, higher-pitched voice. The guard opened one of the thick metal doors just enough to squeeze through and entered the hall, closing the metal door quietly behind him.

While they waited, Ramlok was intrigued by the seemingly ancient spears used by the guards. 'Those spears are fairly obsolete aren't they, Sergeant? They'd be pretty ineffective against laser guns.'

'Don't be fooled by appearances, sir. They're laser-spears.'

Ramlok raised a cynical eyebrow while the Sergeant continued with his explanation.

'At close range the tips yield a high voltage charge which can disable an opponent instantly. At long range, the shafts deliver a laser bolt which can kill or seriously maim the target.'

Ramlok showed increased respect for the guard barring the door.

One of doors opened wide as the straight-faced guard re-appeared. He signalled for his comrade to raise his spear, allowing Krag and Ramlok to pass.

Entering the hall, Ramlok's impression was again one of coldness. The hall, with its high, glass-domed ceiling, was lit by filtered sun streaking through grey skies, and small flames cradled in a dozen metal torches anchored around the grey, stone walls. This all contributed to an atmosphere of stark eeriness. There were no art forms and no painted ornaments or decorations of any kind to provide a feeling of warmth. The only relief from the drabness was a large map which covered half of one wall. It displayed the locations of five planets in the star system and each planet's topography and landforms were indicated by different coloured shadings.

Seated in large, high-backed metal chairs around an elongated oval table of polished, grey metal were ten figures who Ramlok assumed were members of the Orkharnian War Council. All were clothed in black uniforms with officers' insignias on their cuffs, gold studs in their ears, and wide sashes of various colours pinned across their chests. Most were males with silver-grey hair and matching beards while the two females amongst them wore their silver-grey hair swept up at the back of their head, displaying dark-patterned tattooed markings on their faces. All heads were turned in Ramlok's direction, the councillors looking surprised to see the dishevelled visitor standing before them.

'Welcome to our Council, Lieutenant Ramlok,' said General Vark who was sitting in command at the head of the table. He spoke sternly and his scarred face revealed no emotion. He turned to the Sergeant, 'Wait outside for Lieutenant Ramlok until he's ready to be escorted back to his quarters. You're dismissed.' He waved his arm, shooing the Sergeant away.

Sergeant Krag, who was still standing at attention, diligently saluted with a stiff, half-raised arm, about-faced and marched off through the entrance. The heavy doors sounded with a metallic resonance as they shut tightly behind him.

'Lieutenant Ramlok, take a seat,' Vark directed. 'We need some clarification.' He was focused on business.

Ramlok sized up his next challenge as he slid into the cold metal chair. *Obviously not built for comfort*, he thought.

'First of all, can you tell the Council more about the alliance between the Terranians or Earthlings and the Tzuracians? How is it they're in league together?'

'This may take some explaining, sir. It's a long story. Got some wine?'

The General was not impressed. 'Have some water, Lieutenant,' he said pointing to the jug on the table, 'and tell us the full story. We need a complete understanding if we're to consider a war with the Tzuracians.'

The members sitting around the table waited in anticipation.

Ramlok, now more alert, finished taking a sip of his water, wiped his mouth on his sleeve and proceeded to elaborate.

'Almost seven years ago, the Terranian mining company MERIC – Mining and Engineering Resource Industrial Company – discovered vast deposits of Xytrinium on Planet Iota in their solar system. The owner, Samuel Jensen, planned to report the discovery to the World Assembly and use it for the good of the planet. But, the owner's son, Jackson Jensen, who had more backbone than his father, tried to take over the company and the Xytrinium to build his own empire. He was a megalomaniac.' Ramlok chuckled. As a Blader, he admired rogues.

'Then some young do-gooder MERIC engineer, Kyron Shield, exposed Jackson's conspiracy. And would you believe it? He brought in the Sentinels led by Captain Ehrane Dakhar to stop the conspiracy. It turns out Shield had Sentinel blood in him. His father was living incognito on Earth under the name of Shield but was actually an elite Sentinel, Captain Ahrmon Tyros. He and Ehrane's father had served together on Tzurac centuries ago.'

General Vark sparked to life and raised his hand for Ramlok to stop talking. 'I've heard the name Dakhar before.' He paused while searching his memory, then frowned. 'Yes, yes, he's in our archives. Rhazon Dakhar was one of the decorated generals in the Grekadian War. He was a brilliant Tzuracian battle strategist. I read about his successful victories against our people. Might Captain Ehrane Dakhar be a descendant?'

The Councillors waited fervently for an answer, their eyes now focused intently on the Lieutenant.

'Yes, General, he's the grandson.'

'Ah! An enemy with real credentials.' General Vark seemed impressed.

Ramlok leaned forward resting his elbows on the table. 'You sure there's no wine?'

'Not until you finish the story,' said the impatient Vark. 'We're all waiting.'

'Okay. Well, one of Dakhar's Sentinels, Khaneera Zarkwin – a real nice piece of flesh – conspired with Jackson Jensen,' Ramlok said with a sleazy grin. 'Khaneera had her own agenda. She wanted to kill Kyron Shield because he was the son of Ahrmon Tyros, the Sentinel captain who'd destroyed her own father's career.

'In the end Dakhar and his Sentinel dogs proved too strong for Jackson and Khaneera.' Ramlok spat to the side in disgust. 'Khaneera and Jackson were imprisoned and Dakhar invited Earth to become a member of the Federation of Planets. That's how the alliance came about.'

'So how do you know all this?' Vark asked. 'Where do the Bladers come into it?'

'Well, I'm glad you asked, General. I was with Dranz on his warship around eighteen months ago when we encountered Jackson Jensen and his henchmen. They'd just escaped from prison on Terra Upsilon and asked to join forces with us, after Jensen convinced us he knew where to find the lost Xytrinium formula on Tzurac.

'We were just getting interested when Khaneera Zarkwin also turned up. You wouldn't believe it! She'd escaped from her lockup on Tzurac, and she actually *had* the Xytrinium formula and its infusion method with her. She'd stolen it.' He shook his head, laughing out loud at the coincidence. 'She offered Dranz the formula and the services of herself and her Sentinel partner-in-crime, Corporal Yarron Blandhar, if we agreed to all join forces against the Sentinels on Terra Major and Terra Iota. General Dranz couldn't believe his good fortune!

'So, after accepting the offer, we all got infused: Jensen and his men; our Bladers; as well as our Kyroni and Diunon allies. Then we planned a two-pronged attack – Dranz to take on Planet Iota and Khaneera, with Jensen and his crew to attack Terra Major simultaneously. While Khaneera was with us on Planet Steiros developing the plan, she told us all about Dakhar, Kyron Shield – the son of Ahrmon Tyros – and the history behind her Sentinel life.'

Then Ramlok, now becoming more angered, spat out in disgust again. 'We'd have succeeded in taking the two planets if we hadn't all been betrayed by that filthy sewer rat, Yarron Blandhar! Although he'd helped Khaneera escape from Tzurac with the Xytrinium formula, the traitor changed his mind and foiled our plans by letting Dakhar know we were coming.'

One of the rather intimidating female councillors interrupted, 'It's ironic that one Sentinel brought you the secret formula and another betrayed you. Who'd trust a Sentinel?'

'My sentiments exactly, lady,' said Ramlok.

'You can address me as Councillor Kurdarq, Lieutenant,' the councillor replied in a cold and condescending manner. 'So, tell me Lieutenant, did the infusion work effectively on everyone? Or were there side effects?'

Ramlok nodded in the affirmative. 'It worked well, Councillor.' Then he shook his head saying, 'Though not on everyone … According to Khaneera, while fighting Kyron Shield and Captain Dakhar on Terra Major, Jensen and his Terranian mercenaries began to age rapidly and die from the effects.'

'Are you saying Terranians are unable to survive Xytrinium infusions?' she questioned.

'That's correct, Councillor Kurdarq. Instead of slowing down the ageing process as it does for Sentinels and for us, Xytrinium has the opposite effect on Earthlings. So, the damn Sentinels won again on both planets. General Dranz was lucky to escape from Iota with some survivors including me, and Khaneera also escaped from Earth. Both eventually made it back to Steiros but, as I've already told you, they were eventually tracked down. I don't know how. I thought we were safe on Steiros. I reckon that lowlife Blandhar must have lived to inform the Federation about our hideout. End of story.'

The Council members seemed relieved Ramlok had finished his tale while Vark mulled over the implications. 'How well guarded is this planet Terra Major if it's under the protection of the Federation?' he asked, changing tack.

'I'm not sure about Terra Major, sir. I was never there and Khaneera didn't elaborate. But I know Terra Iota is heavily protected by the Sentinels, the planet being a main source of Xytrinium. Since I was there, they've probably transported more Terranians to continue the mining and most likely more Sentinels to give them increased security.'

'If we decide to go to war, how long would it take to infuse our soldiers?'

Ramlok took a moment to estimate. 'Once we get the infusion underway, we could handle around thirty soldiers a day. If we need to defend ourselves immediately, we could enhance your forces relatively quickly.'

Vark did some quick calculations. 'So, it would take us a couple of months to infuse our entire army. And we'd need to allow time for you to travel to the Third Legion in the Southern Quadrant and prepare their warriors, if they agree to join us.'

The Council members began shaking their heads and muttering to each other. Ramlok could tell from the worried looks on their faces they were seriously concerned for their future.

'Can I speak freely, General?' he asked.

'Yes, Lieutenant, go ahead.'

The Councillors were all ears as Ramlok seized the opportunity to convince them. He spoke with confidence and assurance, 'Councillors, it's critical you act immediately. You need to fortify Orkharn and infuse your army straight away in preparation for a possible Tzuracian invasion. If the Southern Legion agrees to join with your forces, you should take the initiative and form a strategy to strike first.'

A moment passed while the Council members absorbed the scenario, talking in whispers amongst themselves until General Vark stood, and the room fell silent.

'Councillors, do you have any further questions for Lieutenant Ramlok?' There was silence. 'Well then, Lieutenant, we have some serious decisions to make. We won't detain you any longer. Sergeant Krag will use this opportunity to acquaint you with our city. I trust your discretion. Avoid discussing these matters with anyone just yet. If you're asked why you're here, say it's a peace-making mission. We don't want to start any rumours, do we, Lieutenant?' he questioned, raising an eyebrow.

'I understand, General,' replied Ramlok rising to his feet. 'I've only one request …' There was silence. 'I want my weapons back.'

General Vark smirked with his villainous, crooked smile. *Ramlok was certainly of the same bloodline.* 'Yes, yes, Lieutenant. The Sergeant will see to it. However, I assure you there'll be no need to use your weapons here.'

'Thank you, sir. I'll be looking for that drink now.' Ramlok saluted the General in Treldarian style, acknowledged the Councillors, then turned and marched to the entrance.

As the door opened, General Vark called out to Sergeant Krag who stepped into the doorway, 'Sergeant, you can return Ramlok's weapons to him and show our guest the city before escorting him back to his quarters.'

* * *

When the doors closed behind the rebel Blader and the Sergeant, the Councillors broke their silence, and becoming more animated, turned to one another, looking for answers. There was much to debate.

Councillor Kurdarq was the first to approach Vark directly. 'General, may I speak freely?'

'No, Councillor!' the seasoned General said firmly, asserting control, 'I want to share *my* thoughts first … We've had no threats from the Sentinels for centuries since we arrived here and created our own empire. With the Blader coming here, this has now changed. By bringing the infusion formula to us, he has drawn attention to our empire and forced Tzurac's hand. If the situation was reversed, I wouldn't hesitate to attack to recover such a valuable asset.

'Ramlok has also reminded us that our Xytrinium supplies won't last indefinitely. Our alchemists suggest we have no more than five years before we exhaust our Xytrinium resource on Planet Glantos. This means we'll need to hunt for other Xytrinium sources soon, and most are now under the control of the Tzuracians. Either way, it seems conflict with the Tzuracians is inevitable.'

He paused for a moment to observe the effect his words were having on the other Council members, his scarred face intensifying. Holding a clenched fist in the air, and eyeing each of the Councillors in turn, he spoke with conviction. 'If we strike first with a surprise attack and with the support of our brothers in the Southern Quadrant, we might – no, we *will* – succeed in eradicating the Federation and its Sentinel army forever and gain control of Xytrinium. It's the only way.'

The General was stirring with excitement at the prospect of going to war with his own army of super-soldiers and all the Councillors, except for Kurdarq, were stirring with him.

She was more cautious and called for restraint, 'Our entire empire is at stake, so let's not make a decision in haste, comrades.'

However, in Vark's mind, the plan for attack was already taking shape.

* * *

When Ramlok emerged with Krag from the Council Hall, the impatient Sergeant turned to Ramlok eager to find out what happened. 'So how was it, Lieutenant?'

'Fine, Sergeant.' Ramlok quickly changed the subject. 'Now the General has authorised the return of my weapons, so when can we get them? And the General has suggested you acquaint me with your city. Perhaps you can show me what pleasures it has to offer?' Ramlok said with a glint in his eye, winking at the Sergeant.

Sergeant Krag was beginning to understand how this stranger thought. 'Yes, sir. We'll go to the Armoury first to collect your weapons. Then I know exactly where to take you after that.'

As he was escorted through the city, Ramlok was surprised to see how well established Bharkaz was. Solid buildings of reddish-grey ironstone covered with dull, slate roofs were spread along numerous cobblestone roads and alleys. These thoroughfares crossed over each other, leading in all directions. Noisy shops and street stalls selling an assortment of goods created colour and aromas amid the drab sooty structures which blended with the grey lifeless sky. Interspersed throughout these buildings were taverns filled with Treldarian soldiers drinking locally fermented wine, while attractive painted women danced and sold their womanly wiles. Every so often a patrol of Treldarian soldiers marched through the streets, keeping the peace.

'So, who are these beautiful women? And where do they come from?' Ramlok asked as they walked, and he leered. 'They're not Treldarians.'

'They're Ludaxians. When we came to this corner of the universe after leaving the Grekadian War, we explored five planets to search for resources and establish our empire. Planet Orkharn, where we are now, was uninhabited and, though it had vast deposits of minerals and metals which could be mined, there was little vegetation and poor soil for growing anything to sustain life.

'So, we went further afield and made our base on Planet Ludax. The inhabitants were non-aggressive peasants who grew crops and bred domestic beasts. As you can see, the Ludaxians have dark skin, dark eyes and black frizzy hair, making the women particularly attractive. We enslaved them, forced the farmers to produce food and fodder to feed our armies and used the women for pleasures of the flesh. Unfortunately, being closer to our sun, the planet was too hot and too wet. The heat was almost unbearable for Treldarians. We needed a more suitable climate.

'Planet Glantos, the planet furthest from the sun, was a frozen land of ice and snow and its inhabitants were small in size, with hairy bodies and grotesque features, living largely beneath the planet's surface. We couldn't live there either. The good news was, we discovered an old disused mine there containing large deposits of the blue crystal Xytrinium. It was a timely find. Our fuel supplies were becoming depleted, and the discovery enabled us to travel further afield and find the remaining two inhospitable planets in this galaxy. It also provided the energy source needed for heating, lighting and mining, enabling us to live comfortably back on Orkharn.

'Our mines are now worked by Glantosians and the peasant-farmers on Ludax supply our food. Many of the Ludaxian women now live here as well.'

'Yes, so I see,' said Ramlok, impressed by the women and amused by Krag's verbose historical account. As another patrol of Treldarian soldiers marched by, Ramlok pointed at them and asked, 'Can you explain your ranking system to me, Sergeant? Is it just the sashes that indicate rank? Or the ear studs?'

Krag was keen to show off more of his knowledge. 'It's both. The coloured sashes show whether the soldiers are non-commissioned or commissioned officers and what rank they hold.' He explained the colour-coding, and then went onto the ear studs, 'And the gold ears studs are inserted for commissioned officers only, the number of studs identifying rank, two for a lieutenant, three for a captain, and four for a general.'

Finally, they arrived at the city's hot baths, a half-enclosed, colonnaded, stone building enveloped in steam, teeming with Treldarian soldiers and painted women. It was an old-style building, reminiscent of ancient civilizations. Ramlok gave Krag an odd look.

'Not what you expected, eh Lieutenant? But I'm sure you'll like this,' said Krag, with enthusiasm. 'General Vark has a keen interest in history and has built the whole city in an old military style in honour of past successes. In the archives, he read about generals from an ancient race who rewarded their victorious gallant and fearless warriors in a special way. Upon their return from battle, they were indulged by beautiful women in hot baths. The baths rejuvenated the warriors' weary, battle-worn bodies while the beautiful women satisfied their sexual needs. It gave the soldiers more of an incentive to win battles, knowing what was in store for them on their return. Although we Treldarians no longer venture out to war, General Vark has provided his troops with the pleasures of our own hot baths – and with beautiful, Ludaxian females.'

Ramlok smiled in anticipation. 'I can't wait.'

After handing in their weapons, they changed into modified loincloths which just covered their bare essentials.

Sergeant Krag continued to show off more of his knowledge, enjoying the role of tour guide. 'The thermal heat comes from tapping into the planet's molten lava core. Heated water is kept on the boil in large wells and piped into foundries designed to smelt the ores. After passing through the foundries, and before cooling down, the water is piped through the buildings to provide central heating and to fill these hot baths, before being recycled back to the wells. Being rich in minerals the water makes the body feel rejuvenated, refreshed and invigorated.'

'No concerns about metal contaminations?' Ramlok teased.

'No,' laughed Krag, 'but if you stay in the baths for too long, a state of euphoria can disorientate the mind and cause hallucinations. In shorter doses, bathing here heightens sexual enjoyment, which is why the Ludaxian ladies frequent these establishments. It's a lucrative business as far as they're concerned,' he said, pointing out the private boudoirs towards the back of the baths.

'Well, Sergeant, I'll stay a short while. It's been a long time since I was in the company of such beautiful females. Let's get some wine and see what develops. I may even get to like this place.'

The Sergeant laughed raucously as he walked off to purchase some wine.

By the time the Sergeant returned, Ramlok was lounging comfortably in a corner of a large rock pool. Steam from the heated water created a natural sauna and Ramlok looked very relaxed as he admired the salacious Ludaxian females.

As the Sergeant slid into the pool and passed Ramlok a goblet of wine, he noticed one female in particular had caught Ramlok's fancy. She was slender, well endowed, and copper-toned with mesmerising hazel eyes. She was wearing almost nothing to show off her natural attractive assets. Her frizzy black hair was over-teased to emphasise her beautiful facial features. Two small, gold-coiled earrings dangled from her ears and a matching gold-coiled bracelet in the form of a snake, wrapped itself around her slender forearm. She started to walk towards Ramlok in a slinky, seductive manner, so Krag took the hint by quietly moving to one side.

'Hello stranger, you're new here. I'm Shanowah,' she said in her soft and silky Ludaxian voice as she knelt down beside the thick-set Lieutenant with the long-matted hair. Her sweet perfume wafted towards him. 'Where are you from?' She had a warm, fascinating smile with soft, pouting lips showing a perfect set of white teeth and subtle dimples in her high-boned cheeks.

'I come from the other side of the galaxy,' Ramlok said mysteriously, noting the distinguishing small black mole on her left cheek that was the only imperfection on her otherwise pleasant face.

'Are you here for business or pleasure?' she asked, seductively, raising an eyebrow.

'A bit of both, I hope,' he said invitingly.

She slipped into the water close beside him and they whispered quietly together as they enjoyed the soothing magic of the water, while sampling the local wine. Ramlok was captivated by her soft hands with bronze painted nails on her slender fingers.

Without warning a slurred deep voice bellowed from behind them, interrupting their intimacy. 'That's my property stranger! Hands off! You need someone to teach you some manners!'

As he slowly swivelled his head around, Ramlok was confronted by a tall, well-built Treldarian wearing only a loin cloth, standing with his arms folded across his broad chest. He was glaring stone-faced into Ramlok's eyes. The two gold studs on one of his ears denoted his rank as lieutenant. It was obvious the officer had consumed too much wine.

When the provoker's comrades jumped out of the rock pool and congregated around him, Sergeant Krag leapt from the pool and stood between Ramlok and the officer.

'He's a guest of the General. Go easy, Lieutenant. He means no harm.'

'Get out of my way, Sergeant,' ordered the burly bully, sweeping Krag aside with his arm. 'We'll see if this one has the guts to defend a lady's honour.'

Ramlok pulled himself out of the rock pool and faced the threat. He didn't want a scene, but his natural aggressive instincts had kicked in. He'd been a rogue pirate for years and wasn't afraid of a fight. 'Listen big boy, why don't you go and cool off before I embarrass you in front of your boyfriends and the lady.'

'You won't embarrass me, smart arse! It's me who'll embarrass you!' shouted the officer, suddenly throwing a right fist towards Ramlok's face.

Ramlok was too agile and quickly ducked before the fist made contact. In an instant he swept the burly drunken soldier off his feet and held him high above his head with ease, before throwing him with force against a stone wall some ten feet away. The officer tried to stand, wincing with pain, before slumping unconscious to the floor.

Everyone, including the Sergeant, was in shock, the onlookers whispering in amazement.

'Where did he get the strength to do that?'

'No Treldarian has that power!'

'Where does he come from?'

Shanowah was impressed. She sidled up to Ramlok and gently placed her soft hand on his broad, muscly shoulder. Proud of what this new stranger was made of, she extended her welcome, 'Would you like to come with me to escape this?'

Ramlok was very tempted by the seductive offer and smiled, but before he could answer, Sergeant Krag intervened. 'Lieutenant, we need to return to your quarters immediately.' Krag was instinctively protective of his new officer and was keen to ensure his safety.

Ramlok tilted his head in the direction of Shanowah. 'Thanks, it sounds very enticing. Perhaps another time ... soon?'

'I'll be waiting for your speedy return, handsome,' she said, smiling with anticipation and fluttering her dark, smouldering eyes. She knew how to exploit her looks.

The crowd was still in awe as Ramlok and the Sergeant quickly dressed and collected their weapons.

As they returned to the Administration Building, the curious Sergeant couldn't help but comment, 'Some show you put on back there. I guess you're not going to tell me who you really are or why you're here. Either the water worked miracles for you or it's some special tonic you've been taking.'

Ramlok smiled smugly at the Sergeant without offering an explanation.

DECISIONS

RAMLOK'S second day in the city of Bharkaz proved even more interesting as he was thrust into Treldarian army routine. At what seemed like the crack of dawn, he was rudely awakened by a regulation wake-up call, forcing him out of bed. A young corporal was rapping on doors, calling 'Mess Hall in 15 minutes!' Ramlok groaned at being disturbed for breakfast – *even as a guest, it looked like he was going to be treated as if he were living in the barracks.*

As he walked into the noisy Mess Hall crowded with uniformed Treldarian officers seated in groups at separate white square tables, the rowdy clatter and chatter instantly ceased. All eyes were fixed on the stranger with the super strength. Ramlok was surprised at how clinical the Hall was with its clean, white walls, bright lighting and sets of small, square food-dispensing boxes lined up along the servery counter.

Making his way to the servery, Ramlok's footsteps echoed in the peculiar silence. It was only when his meal had been automatically dished out and he had taken a seat at the only empty table in the hall, that the silence was broken and replaced with chatter and clatter once more.

After taking a couple of mouthfuls from his bowl of Treldarian gruel, Ramlok was pleased to hear the sound of a familiar voice.

'Morning, Lieutenant,' Sergeant Krag called out jovially as he approached Ramlok's table. 'Mind if I join you?'

'Not at all, Sergeant.' Ramlok was relieved to have company.

'You've made a name for yourself already.'

'It appears so,' said Ramlok. 'Or is this how you Treldarians treat all strangers?'

'The little incident yesterday at the baths has started rumours in the Regiments. The talk is why a renegade Blader who possesses super-strength has come to our world and whether there are more like you out there. They want to know who you are and why you're here.'

Just as Krag finished speaking, his eyes fixed on something over Ramlok's shoulder.

'What is it, Sergeant?'

'The lieutenant from the baths yesterday – he's coming our way.'

The room fell quiet once more and all heads turned in the direction of the approaching officer. It was as if everyone was holding their breath in anticipation.

Ramlok instantly rose from his chair and spun around to face the well-built lieutenant who was limping slightly and sporting a noticeable, bruised lump on his forehead. Ramlok clenched his fists bracing himself in expectation of another altercation. But the officer stopped at arm's length and spoke calmly in a deep voice.

'First Lieutenant Tykran Vark. I was out of line yesterday threatening a visiting Treldarian. Sorry. It was the wine and the euphoria that did it. I'll understand if you report me but at least accept my apology.' With a sincere look the Lieutenant offered an outstretched arm to Ramlok, inviting a handshake.

Ramlok was momentarily taken aback. Treldarian soldiers weren't known for apologising, especially in front of subordinates.

There was a sigh of relief from the soldiers in the room when Ramlok gave a wry smile and swung his right arm forward to clasp Tykran's arm. 'Apology accepted, Lieutenant. No need for a report. Soldiers need to have some sporting fun every now and then. You'll have to forgive me though – sometimes I don't know my own strength.'

'Thank you, sir.'

'Call me Ramlok. I'm a First Lieutenant with the Fifth Legion, Northern Quadrant.' Ramlok smiled. 'Did you say Vark? Are you related to General Khuram Vark?'

'Yes, sir. He's my father. He'd probably demote me if he heard about the welcome I gave you.' The Lieutenant sounded remorseful.

'Don't worry yourself, Tykran. You have my word. Let's move forward,' said Ramlok, gesturing for the Lieutenant to join him at the table.

'Thanks,' said Tykran as he seated himself. 'The Fifth Legion? Pirates, aren't you? I've heard about you Bladers. But *where* does your incredible strength come from?'

Before Ramlok could say anything, Sergeant Krag intervened again. 'Sorry to interrupt Lieutenant Ramlok, but we need to leave, *now*. You've been summoned by General Vark.'

'Well, Tykran, we'll talk some more while I'm here, perhaps over a goblet or two of your wine. Maybe at the hot baths?' said Ramlok with a wry smile and a wink. 'Come on Sergeant, let's go!'

The Mess Hall was buzzing as Ramlok and the Sergeant departed.

'You didn't tell me I'd assaulted *the General's* son,' said Ramlok, scowling at Krag. 'This could change things.'

* * *

When they reached the Council Hall, the Sergeant waited with the guards outside the heavy metal doors, leaving Ramlok to enter alone.

There was a cold atmosphere as Ramlok walked into the room to find the General already standing at the large oval table with his war councillors. Their cold faces matched the surroundings, and their emotionless eyes were fixed keenly on him as the General directed him to take his place. Ramlok dipped his head to them to acknowledge their presence. There was no reaction.

When the General spoke, his commanding tone of voice made Ramlok feel uneasy, and the General's facial scar seemed more prominent than before. 'We were informed you got yourself into a fight at the hot baths yesterday after you left this Hall. You picked up one of our soldiers, raised him above your head and tossed him against a wall with ease, like a small barrel of wine. Are you usually in the habit of making enemies so soon in a strange land? Especially when you're a guest? Well, Lieutenant, is this true?'

'If I may speak freely, General?' Ramlok paused and waited for a sign of approval.

Without naming his assailant, Ramlok explained how he was provoked by an officer who'd had too much to drink.

'Lieutenant, I'm sorry my soldier behaved badly, but did I not say to you yesterday you were to be discreet?'

'Yes, General.'

'And would you say you disobeyed my order by showing what the effects of Xytrinium infusion can produce?'

'No, sir, I would not.'

Angered by Ramlok's response, the General shouted impatiently, 'Then explain yourself, Blader!'

The Councillors waited keenly for Ramlok's response.

'Well, sir, with respect, the only thing I revealed was my strength and agility, which I might add, was in self-defence. The

Sergeant was with me and witnessed the entire event. I've told no-one, including the Sergeant, how I became this strong and agile. I realise the event has left your soldiers bewildered, but I've said nothing to anyone about our discussion.'

There was tension in the air and for a short moment the two stared intently at each other, both knowing Ramlok had kept his word and had not disobeyed the General's wishes.

'Alright, Lieutenant, you have a point. I won't pursue this matter any further.' The General seemed relieved to be able to let the matter rest and the icy atmosphere in the room began to thaw. It left Ramlok somewhat surprised there'd been no mention of the victim being the General's son. *Perhaps neither of them wanted to make an issue of it?*

'Now let's turn our attention to more serious matters. It's been a long night of debate, but the Council has finally come to a unanimous decision.' Vark glared sideways for a moment at Councillor Kurdarq who nodded somewhat reluctantly in agreement. 'However, before we sanction it, we need to know exactly what effects the infusions will have on our soldiers. You indicated the infusion will increase their strength ... as *you've* already demonstrated at the hot baths.' He couldn't avoid the dig. 'It will enhance their agility, speed and stamina and presumably, extend their life expectancy. Will there be any other changes?'

Ramlok settled himself in the cold metal chair before answering. 'The infusion will give them nocturnal vision, sharper day-vision, and enhanced hearing. It will amplify the volume of sounds and enable them to hear a wider range of pitch. There'll also be psychological effects, and these will be the hardest to adjust to.'

'It won't send them mad will it, Lieutenant?' the General asked with concern.

'No more than usual,' Ramlok joked, though everyone remained straight-faced. 'The crystal compound simply enhances the inherent personality and characteristics of the host. It will amplify the aggressive nature of Treldarians and Kyroni, making them fiercer and more fearless. They'll need to learn more self-control. Once your soldiers are infused, they'll need to be retrained to maximise the use of their enhancements.'

The General interrupted by addressing the Councillors, 'I'm not surprised the Sentinels won the two-hundred-year war with the advantage they had over their adversaries. No wonder the Tzuracians wanted so badly to prevent this formula from getting into the hands of their enemies.' Ramlok could sense the General's excitement at the possibility of facing the Federation army on equal terms.

Vark continued, 'We know the Tzuracians might come hunting for their best-kept secret, to stop at all costs a war with a race of enhanced super-soldiers. Matched with super abilities we'll have a chance, after all these centuries, to finally destroy our lifelong nemesis.' Ramlok could see vengeance in the General's eyes and hear hatred in his voice. 'When I look around the table, I can sense the renewed passion of my fellow Councillors.' The General raised his voice with defiant enthusiasm. 'This is the moment we've long awaited – the opportunity to restore our freedom throughout the Universe!'

The Councillors thumped the table loudly in anticipation of challenging the so-called, self-appointed 'Guardians of the Universe'.

Gritting his teeth in determination, Vark declared, 'Lieutenant, the War Council has decreed our Treldarian soldiers *will* be infused. We'll be prepared for a possible invasion by the Sentinels, and we'll also develop the Xytrinium warheads to annihilate the Tzuracians on their planet once and for all.' There was a sense of victory in the room even before the battle had begun.

Ramlok glowed internally with the news. *This was just what he wanted.*

'Ramlok, you'll be commissioned to oversee both the enhancement and retraining process. Then you'll go as our emissary to the Southern Quadrant carrying General Dranz's dispatch papers and our endorsement of the battle strategy. I'm hoping you have as much success in convincing them as you've had with my War Council of the Second Legion.

'We understand it will take some time for the Treldarian Legions to be ready to fight and more time to plan for an attack on Tzurac and Terra Major. Nonetheless, I'm sure our soldiers will be eager to do battle, to test their new abilities and their mettle on equal terms, and to demonstrate their might by becoming the fierce warriors they once were. We Treldarians were always destined to be feared throughout the galaxies.'

Around the table the Councillors called 'Hear! Hear!' in unison, while thumping their fists repeatedly on the table again in their traditional show of support.

Ramlok cut across the rumblings. 'When do I start, General?'

'At once. Here are your authorisation papers. I've assigned you to the 25th Infantry Battalion. You need to discard your old Blader leathers and replace them with a fresh Treldarian army uniform and red sash.' Vark paused before announcing, 'I'm officially promoting you to the rank of Captain.' For a third time the Councillors hammered loudly on the table.

Ramlok was speechless, but grateful. Although he would have to buckle down to military regimes, he was no longer homeless. He'd been accepted into the Second Legion and given more authority than he'd known previously. With a disciplined force behind him, he would be able to avenge the death of General Dranz and continue the fight against the Federation.

'What do you say to this, Captain Ramlok?' asked the General who was pleased to see Ramlok's expression of surprise.

'I'm very appreciative, General. It'll be an honour to serve in the Second Legion.' *He had forgiven his brothers for their past desertion.* But Ramlok hesitated. 'However, I'm concerned whether your soldiers will accept taking orders from a newcomer, particularly a rebel Blader from another Quadrant who arrived only two days ago.'

'When they're told you have brought with you the wonder drug to make them as powerful as the Tzuracian Sentinels and see you as living proof of this, they'll embrace you, Captain. They'll respect your past experience in engaging with the enemy and have confidence in your ability to prepare them for battle. I think you're well qualified for the role, don't you Captain Ramlok?'

'Well, when you put it that way, General, how can I not agree?'

Both Ramlok and the General smiled, Vark showing his villainous look.

'Welcome aboard, Captain! Take this letter of authority with you and go straight to Army Supplies to collect your new uniform. Keep our strategic plan 'under wraps' for the time being. Tomorrow morning you'll report to Colonel Murzak, Red Star Regiment, and be escorted to the alchemists to brief them on the infusion process. With the formula they can immediately start distilling the Xytrinium crystals. Your battalion of soldiers of the 25th can begin unloading the infusion equipment from your vessel. You have your orders, Captain. You're dismissed.'

Still grinning with his newly bestowed commission, Ramlok saluted the General respectfully and acknowledged members of the War Council before marching to the exit doors.

Sergeant Krag had been waiting anxiously outside the Council Hall for Ramlok to reappear and rushed over to him. 'How did it go, sir?'

'It went well, Sergeant,' Ramlok replied, deliberately keeping Krag at bay and testing his patience.

'Well? You've been in there for over an hour. Is that all you have to say? Did the General reprimand you over the altercation with his son?' Krag was curious.

'No, on the contrary, you need to escort me immediately to Army Supplies for my new uniform. I've been assigned to the 25th Infantry Battalion. I'm officially a Treldarian soldier now.' With a glint in his eye, Ramlok held up the authorisation papers to confirm it to the Sergeant before quickly tucking them away in his jacket.

'That's my battalion, sir!' exclaimed Krag. 'Well done! Welcome aboard.'

* * *

On arriving at the Army Supplies depot, which was detached from the main complex, Ramlok was impressed at the scale of the building and its surrounds. The main building was constructed from ironstone and fortified with a ten-foot-high, metal-barred fence with solid metal doors which were left open but were protected by two Treldarian guards shouldering long-barrelled laser guns. Seeing Ramlok and the Sergeant coming towards them, the guards quickly swung their guns into defence mode.

'Identify yourselves!' one of the guards called out abruptly.

'I'm Sergeant Krag, 25th Infantry Battalion, and this is Lieutenant Ramlok.'

'State your business, Sergeant!' ordered the guard, still anchored steadfast and pointing his laser weapon in their direction.

As Krag began to explain, Ramlok offered his papers to the other stern-looking guard now standing close by. After quickly studying the documents, and promptly returning them, this guard turned to his partner, saying, 'Let them pass corporal, they're here for a uniform fit authorised by the General.'

The corporal lowered his weapon, standing aside to let them through.

Ramlok and Krag continued through the main entrance of the building and marched to the front desk which was manned by a soldier sitting rigidly behind a sign on the counter marked 'Officer-in-Charge'. The starched-faced officer lifted his head and focused on the pair approaching. When they reached his counter, the OIC eyed Ramlok up and down with some suspicion. He was unaccustomed to dealing with scruffy strangers dressed in well-worn brown leathers.

Without speaking a word, Ramlok smiled confidently and thrust his papers towards the officer.

Snatching the documents from Ramlok's hand the straight-faced officer questioned the Sergeant forcefully, 'Who are you? And why have you come here with this unauthorised ruffian?'

'Sir, I'm Sergeant Krag,' he replied, saluting while standing to attention. 'I've been ordered to bring this Treldarian to Army Supplies for his new uniform.'

Somewhat surprised, the officer returned the salute, before lowering his head to read the document. After several moments, he spoke again with a query. 'Is this in order, Sergeant Krag?'

'Yes, sir, we've just come directly from General Vark. The orders couldn't be more explicit.'

Still shaking his head in disbelief, the officer scrutinised the papers once more to verify General Vark's signature. Finally, and somewhat reluctantly, he directed the Sergeant and his ragged friend to the fitting rooms down the passageway.

As they walked, Ramlok was impressed by what he saw both sides of the passageway and further in the distance of the complex. He was in a huge armoury containing a grand assortment of munitions stacked on shelving which reached right to the ceiling. There were numerous cupboards marked to identify their contents of uniforms, bedding, blankets and armour.

They were soon met by another soldier who directed Ramlok into a fitting room, closing the door behind him while Sergeant Krag remained seated outside.

When Ramlok finally emerged wearing his new black uniform with the red flashes, Sergeant Krag was clearly surprised. 'Wow! That looks very smart, sir,' he complimented. 'But they've made a mistake. You've been fitted for the rank of Captain!'

'No mistake, Sergeant,' Ramlok boasted, pumping out his chest and standing akimbo. 'The General has promoted me and given me a commission.'

Krag quickly saluted in respect of Ramlok's new rank, understanding now why the Officer-in-Charge had been so sceptical. 'Congratulations, sir. That *was* quick! Three gold studs!'

No sooner had the Sergeant spoken than a young fresh-faced corporal appeared with a sheathed, decorated silver-hilted sword in hand. He saluted the new captain, 'Here's your regulation officer's sword, Captain. If you'll take this sir, I'll escort you to have your hair cut and ear studded.'

Ramlok defiantly buckled his own weapon around his waist. 'You can keep your ceremonial sword, Corporal. I'll retain my faithful sabre.'

The corporal hesitated. 'This is highly irregular, sir.'

'Are you questioning my authority?' Ramlok glared at the soldier.

'No, Captain,' the soldier replied, feeling intimidated. 'I'm just following protocol.'

'Well, just follow *my* orders, Corporal, and lead on.'

* * *

With a smart military hairstyle, three small solid-gold studs embedded in his right ear, a tailored black uniform with a red sash, and highly polished black knee-high boots, Krag was amazed at the makeover. 'I hardly recognised you, sir.'

'I hardly recognised myself, Sergeant.'

Ramlok suggested to Sergeant Krag they celebrate his induction with a visit to the hot baths.

'You want to see the lascivious Ludaxian beauty Shanowah again do you, Captain?' teased the Sergeant with a big grin.

'There are several ways to celebrate eh, Sergeant? And besides, what better way than a relaxing hot bath, a full carafe of good wine and indulgence in the company of a wicked woman. There's only one drawback. As I've only just been drafted into the army I haven't been paid any credits. Can I charge it to the keeper?'

'I don't see why not,' said Krag. 'Most of the soldiers who frequent the place have large debts to pay back and now that you're a higher-ranking officer, your credentials should be guaranteed.'

'Quite right, Sergeant,' said Ramlok, slapping Krag forcefully on the back. 'Let's go have some fun. That's an order!'

THIRD LEGION

WITHIN days, the Second Legion had swung into action. Vark had advised his regiments of the proposed defence and attack strategies. In accordance with the formula, his alchemists had begun liquefying and purifying Xytrinium crystals and infusions were well underway. With the assistance of Sergeant Krag, Captain Ramlok had started training the soldiers who'd been infused, and once the first unit of Treldarians had been fully inducted, they too helped with the training.

Just as Ramlok had predicted, some negative side-effects were noticed soon after the soldiers were transformed into super-warriors. The Treldarian soldiers tested their new-found powers by challenging each other at every opportunity in hand-to-hand combat, weapons and hunting. Their pain threshold increased immeasurably, and their aggression became almost uncontrollable. They began to consume more and more wine which contributed to their belligerent behaviour. While the infusion process continued over the ensuing weeks, so did the incidents and altercations. The soldiers began abusing the Ludaxian women and eventually General Vark's intervention was crucial.

Vark summoned the leaders of all the regiments as well as Ramlok to the Council Hall. When they were all seated at the oval table, the stern-faced General began his lecture. 'The blue crystal infusion is going to plan, thanks to Captain Ramlok's efforts. However, the negative effects are *not* being controlled.'

Vark raised his voice, 'I won't tolerate unruly conduct. If we're to win this war, we must maintain discipline, with the one goal – to destroy the Federation for good. As their leaders, you must play your part in constraining the animalistic behaviour of your soldiers. We need to contain their aggression, so it's unleashed against our enemies, *not* against each other.'

The General rose from his chair and threatened with a tightly clenched fist, speaking slowly and deliberately to ensure that no word was missed by his audience. 'If you cannot control those you are responsible for, you'll be replaced! Do I make myself clear?' Vark's scar-face twitched with anger.

The leaders responded obediently in unison, 'Yes, General!'

General Vark sat down, taking a moment to compose himself. 'Although the outer patrols are still to be infused and the re-training of units continues, it's time for Captain Ramlok to travel to the Southern Quadrant to seek our brothers' support for our war strategy.'

Ramlok nodded in agreement.

'You're to leave within forty-eight hours. Take some of the soldiers with you for protection as well as an alchemist to oversee the infusions. You'll carry General Dranz's dispatches, as well as my own signed and sealed papers. All going according to plan, we'll expect your return within a few months. We now have the forces to defend Orkharn in the event of an attack by the Federation Sentinels. Should you happen to be intercepted by Federation ships, we'll dispatch backup urgently. Dismissed!'

* * *

On the day of his departure Ramlok presented himself at General Vark's office accompanied by Sergeant Krag.

'Enter, Captain,' commanded the General as the two soldiers appeared at his door. 'Ready for your mission?'

'Yes, General. My craft's been serviced and fuelled, and the galley stocked with supplies. I've selected the unit who'll be accompanying me.'

'Who have you chosen?'

'I asked for volunteers, and all were willing. Because my Destroyer can only accommodate seven, I've selected a unit of five soldiers plus the alchemist. I'm taking Sergeant Krag, Lieutenant Vark, and three other fully trained soldiers.'

Krag, who was standing beside Ramlok, beamed.

'My son volunteered?' Vark was obviously surprised and questioned the choice. 'This seems out of character for Tykran. I'm surprised he'd want to leave his drinking companions and the places of pleasure he frequents.' The General was thinking out loud. 'Why would my son volunteer? Does he want to escape my direct command?'

'General, if I may speak freely?'

'Yes, go ahead.'

Between conversations with Krag, visits to Shanowah's boudoir, and drinks with Tykran at the baths, Ramlok had learned more about Vark's son. Tykran's mother had died while he was still a young boy and Tykran had been raised in a strict, militaristic way by his ambitious father. Tykran had turned to drink and women, looking for relief from his father's constant high expectations and criticisms. But Tykran was a good soldier underneath his irresponsible façade and Ramlok sensed Tykran just needed some acknowledgment and an opportunity to prove his worth.

'Perhaps you underestimate Tykran's abilities?' said Ramlok. 'I understand he hasn't always led by example, and I know he enjoys the baths and the wine, as I do. But under my command, he's proven to be a competent officer and a fearless leader. The soldiers respect him, and I do as well.'

With his hands clasped behind his back General Vark silently paced the floor. He was contemplating the virtues his son had apparently acquired under the guidance of a rogue Blader – the virtues he himself, as an experienced general and a father, had tried unsuccessfully to instil. The irony was not lost on him. 'Very well, Captain Ramlok, I trust your judgement.'

Vark walked over to his desk and picked up Dranz's leather binder and a scroll bound with a red ribbon. He turned, handing them to Ramlok. 'Take these and guard them with your life. Present them to General Rokan who resides on Mankro, one of the three moons orbiting the uninhabitable planet Dunkor in the Clavistoq Star System.'

'I will, General,' responded Ramlok, placing the documents under his left arm and saluting the General with the other.

Sergeant Krag snapped to attention and saluted. Then they both turned and marched towards the exit.

'And bring my son back safely,' Vark called out sharply as the two disappeared from sight. 'That's an order!'

'That's out of character for the General,' Krag said. 'It's not like him to show any feelings.'

Ramlok grinned smugly to himself on his quiet achievement. He knew he'd been instrumental in strengthening the fragile bond between this father and son.

* * *

The signs of being trapped in an enclosed space capsule for an extended period of time were beginning to emerge. The three recruited soldiers were becoming irritable and more aggressive. Daily workouts, endurance testing, supervised sparring and weapons maintenance kept them occupied for most of the time. Yet every now and then the soldiers wanted to shoot at objects floating in space. When an isolated asteroid or a piece of space-junk glided by, they would head for the laser cannon turrets looking for competitive target practice. It was taking all of Lieutenant Vark's and Sergeant Krag's efforts to control them.

Thankfully, Ramlok's calculations of the time needed to reach the Southern Quadrant had been very accurate. It was exactly a month since the new Captain and his unit of elite super-soldiers had left the Orkharnian Domain and they were now entering the orbit of planet Dunkor. The soldiers would soon be more involved in their mission.

Suddenly and without warning, Ramlok's vessel came under attack. His ship was being used for target practice by someone else. Continuous blasting from laser fire battered the hull. Red emergency lighting and screeching alerts automatically switched on as spot fires and electrical sparks flared up from some of the panels on the Bridge. The soldiers covered their ears, their enhanced hearing amplifying the sound of the alarms. It was only the ship's shields – which had been activated in anticipation of rebel stalkers as they entered the Clavistoq Star System – that saved the ship from being destroyed.

There were no signs of foreign spacecraft on the ship's radar. Ramlok's mind raced. *He couldn't maintain shields indefinitely if the firing persisted. But if he switched to cloaking to hide from this unknown attacker, he'd leave the ship vulnerable having to power down the shields. He could try out-running them, but in which direction? There was only one thing left to do.*

Ramlok gave an immediate order over the intercom, 'Soldiers! Take your turret positions and hold your fire until I give the order!'

Then he activated the Comms system and started to broadcast confidently, in the hope that he was addressing fellow Treldarians. 'This is Commander Ramlok, Captain of the 25th Infantry, Eastern Quadrant. I'm an emissary of General Khuram Vark and you're firing on a Treldarian battleship. We come in peace!'

Suddenly the firing ceased. On the main screen two Treldarian warships bearing the red scorpion insignia de-cloaked. One was located directly in front of Ramlok's craft and the other on his starboard side.

The screen flickered and a face appeared. The Treldarian's thick black hair was unkempt, hanging raggedly down to his shoulders. His bushy beard was also uncombed, and his ears were pierced with three gold studs. Compared to the clean-cut Treldarian military on Orkharn, he was scruffy in appearance. His outfit was more in the style of a Blader pirate with a well-worn, brown leather jacket over a black shirt.

The Treldarian spoke over the Comms in a serious but hoarse Treldarian drawl, 'Commander Ramlok, I'm Captain Globak Chekhmar, Commander of the Treldarian warship, *Trigan*. You're trespassing in an unknown craft and asking for trouble. We're protective of our territory and trust no-one.

'Stand down and prepare to be boarded by one of our security units. You'll be under guard while we escort your ship to our base on Planet Mankro. Be warned, Captain, if any of my Security soldiers are harmed, you and your crew will answer for their injuries.'

'Yes, Captain, understood.' Ramlok was much relieved to hear the voice of Treldarians, but apprehensive about what was to come. He knew he was about to confront General Jelzad Rokan of the Third Legion.

The main screen flicked back to the outside environment and the emergency lighting and alarms ceased.

'Stand down, soldiers!' Ramlok ordered over the intercom. 'Prepare for a Treldarian security unit to board. Do nothing to provoke them. Captain, out.'

* * *

As they passed through the Clavistoq Star System, the crew members had a clear view of the huge and lifeless red planet, Dunkor. It was set in a stunning rainbow background amid the three surrounding colourful moons and a myriad of enormous, scattered asteroids. Mankro, the larger of the moons, was bathed in swirls of vivid greens and blues, while the other two moons, Ankrod and Nujhar, had distinct pastel-green tinges.

When Ramlok's vessel finally came to rest on Mankro the landscape they encountered was quite unique. The green valley floor was a carpet of tightly matted, low-lying grasses, surrounded by steep slopes covered with a forest of giant trees. So dense were these trees, no light penetrated them. Several Treldarian vessels were sitting idle further up the valley covered in camouflaged webbing.

As the Treldarian Security unit ordered them to disembark from the ship, Ramlok gave specific instructions to his unit, 'Leave your weapons on-board and do *not* do anything which might provoke these Treldarians! Our mission is to negotiate an alliance. We need this Southern Legion to help us destroy the Federation. Contain your aggression or you'll suffer the consequences. Understood?'

'Yes, sir!' responded all six in unison.

Waiting to greet them at the docking bay was a party of a dozen soldiers with weapons drawn. They were dressed in well-worn, brown-leather outfits and looked mean, battle-scarred and uncouth – a group reminiscent of the Bladers Ramlok had been accustomed to in his days of pirating. Although Ramlok sensed the similarity, it wasn't a friendly reception by those he would once have called his brothers.

Leading the group was Captain Globak Chekhmar, a figure who was even more intimidating in person than on the screen. With a condescending smile revealing a few missing teeth, Chekhmar stepped closer, raising his arms in an outstretched gesture. 'Welcome to our sanctuary, Captain Ramlok,' he said in a loud and gruff voice, reaching out with his right arm to offer a Treldarian arm-shake. His fingers were adorned with chunky, silver rings and his stinking breath was overwhelming, as was his body odour.

Ramlok responded accordingly and grasped Chekhmar's arm, giving it a firm shake while suppressing his disgust and mustering all the diplomacy he could. 'Thank you, Captain Chekhmar,' he said. 'It's good to see our brethren after all this time and to know you've survived in this strange world. But I'd feel more comfortable if your soldiers lowered their weapons.'

'Yes, of course. It was just a precaution.' Chekhmar sneered before turning to his soldiers and signalling for them to lower their weapons. 'Follow me and I'll take you to see General Rokan.'

Ramlok and his soldiers were led up a steep, narrow path carved out of the hillside. Rudimentary shallow steps covered in damp moss had been fashioned into the granite rock to prevent slipping. The overgrown path wound its way uphill for several hundred yards to a thick forest before levelling off as they reached the top of the mountain.

After another ten minutes' walk through the dense, shadowed woods and over mulched leaves covering the damp soil, they entered a ten-foot-high, log-fenced enclosure, populated with log huts of various sizes. Whispers of grey smoke were rising from a number of scattered charcoal-fire pits within the compound. Several wood-fenced animal pens reeking of animal manure held small odd-looking beasts, similar in appearance to wild boars, with elongated snouts. They were snorting noisily and wallowing in the mud and straw. And there were many civilian Treldarians, both male and female, preoccupied performing arduous chores.

The village indicated a primitive society compared with the more civilised one Ramlok had just left behind at Bharkaz. It was like going back in time to the way Planet Treldar used to be after the Grekadian War. Ramlok turned to his men and noted from the expressions on their faces that they were as shocked as he was. And as the newcomers marched through the village, the local inhabitants stopped what they were doing to return the stares.

Finally, the group reached their destination coming to a sudden stop when Chekhmar gave the order to halt. Before them stood a two-storey log hut smeared with dry mud, in an attempt to seal the narrow gaps between the stacked logs. The building was covered with a thatched roof. Two small, square windows flanked by open wooden shutters were positioned either side of a heavy wooden door. The door was elaborately carved with unfamiliar symbols.

'Wait here!' ordered Chekhmar as he stepped up to the entrance. He hammered heavily on the door shouting, 'General Rokan! You have visitors!'

There was a slight delay before the door finally creaked open and a beautiful young female cloaked in a black robe with matching hood appeared. She stood stiffly with a presence of authority and distaste. It was clear she had no affection for Chekhmar, who leered at her.

'Who is here to see the General?' she demanded coldly.

'Bhalar,' ordered Chekhmar, 'tell the General that Captain Ramlok, an emissary from our Treldarian brother General Vark, requests an audience. And be quick about it, woman!'

'Wait!' she ordered, slamming the door on Chekhmar, who now stood waiting impatiently with an indignant expression on his leathery face. Ramlok noticed the obvious friction between the coarse Captain and the beautiful handmaiden who opened the door.

After another short delay the door slowly opened again.

'You! Come with me!' Bhalar said in a more authoritative tone, pointing at Ramlok. 'The rest, stay!'

Chekhmar protested with a snarl, raising outstretched arms in a gesture of frustration. He didn't like being excluded.

Bhalar ignored Chekhmar's actions, beckoning Ramlok through the door and closing it quickly behind him as he entered.

Once inside, she led the visitor up a steep flight of roughly cut, wooden stairs. On the next level Bhalar ushered Ramlok into a large, dark and musky room while she lingered, almost inconspicuously, in the shadows near the doorway. She was intrigued to hear what this new visitor had to tell the General.

Covering the wooden floor was a thatched dried-grass mat which cushioned the sound of Ramlok's heavy-booted footsteps as he paced slowly towards the dark figure at the far end of the room. Seated in one of the far shadowy corners, at a round wooden table sliced from a huge tree trunk, was an elderly Treldarian wearing a black robe edged with a gold hem and gold cuffs.

'Welcome, stranger,' came a rather feeble voice from the shadows. 'Take a seat and tell me what brings you all the way from the Eastern Quadrant.'

Ramlok drew up one of the rudimentary wooden chairs and, pulling it to a position at the table directly opposite his host, sat himself as comfortably as he could facing the old General. In the subdued light coming from the window, Ramlok could scrutinize the General's face more clearly. His long hair was snow-white, as was his long beard, and his severe face was heavily wrinkled.

Was he wasting his time? The Treldarians on Mankro seemed ill-equipped for a war and their general was ready for the grave.

Putting his doubts aside, he continued as planned, knowing they needed the Third Legion to complete the dual invasion. *Perhaps there was more to this Legion than conveyed by first impressions?*

'General, I'm Captain Ramlok. As an emissary, I've been ordered to deliver these signed dispatches from General Dranz of the Fifth Legion, Northern Quadrant and sealed papers from General Vark Second Legion, Eastern Quadrant.' Ramlok placed the leather binder and scroll on the table in front of the General and slid them towards him.

As the General reached for them, he tapped heavily on the floor with his wooden walking stick and called out in a stronger voice, 'Bhalar! Bring some tea for our guest.' Then, opening the leather binder, he began to read.

Without hesitation, Bhalar rushed downstairs to the kitchen, quickly prepared the refreshments and returned. She wanted to hear more of the conversation. Re-entering the room, she placed the tray on the table, poured two cups of tea into the ceramic vessels and glided silently back into the shadows, remaining within earshot, out of sight, just behind the doorway.

While the General read, Ramlok sat quietly sipping the insipid tea and wishing it were wine. He watched with interest the General's changing facial expressions, imagining what was going through the aged Treldarian's mind.

After a time, General Rokan replaced the leather binder on the table, inhaled deeply and took a mouthful of the now-lukewarm tea. Raising an eyebrow while slowly nodding his head, he reached for the scroll, began to unravel it and, without a word, commenced reading once more. His tired, squinting eyes moved rapidly over the words. When he'd finished reading, he placed the scroll back on the table and sat silently in deep thought, staring out the window. Finally, he turned to Ramlok and began conveying his profound thoughts.

'I'm old and tired, Captain Ramlok, and my days of warring are finished. Over many years I've fought many battles with barbaric tribes, trying to subdue them. I've resigned myself to waiting out my remaining years on this isolated moon, in peace. I've only a thousand soldiers and our Xytrinium resource is fast being depleted. We use what is left sparingly to fuel our vessels and charge our laser weapons, resorting to animal oils and wood to provide for our basic needs. I consider we'd not be of much use in assisting to overthrowing the Tzuracians.'

There was another moment of silence as the General had second thoughts. 'Yet the thought of being infused with this powerful blue crystal to enhance our powers is an enticement, even for me. My Legion has remained hidden and undisturbed by the Federation for centuries, left to plunder the less advanced civilisations inhabiting the other moons of Dunkor. My soldiers still carry a deep-seated hatred of the Federation and the Sentinels of Tzurac who ousted us from our home planet Treldar all those years ago. Memories still smoulder like embers in their hearts and minds. They're restless and out for blood. Perhaps, with a new lease on my life, I too could rekindle the fire that burns deeply within.'

'May I comment, General?' Ramlok asked, motioning with his hand to interrupt.

'Yes, of course. You're free to talk.'

'How many barbarians on the other moons would join your cause if we enticed them?'

'Possibly a thousand, and maybe more.'

'Well, I understand the battle strategy proposed by the War Council under the seal of General Vark. The plan is for a two-pronged attack. General Vark and his army will lead the main assault on planet Tzurac. At the same time, you with your soldiers and barbarian reinforcements will attack the Sentinel base on Terra Major, which we believe is not well fortified. We have details of their major strategic defences from the information provided by General Dranz. While the Sentinel forces are preoccupied fending off your attack on Terra Major, they'll be unable to send reinforcements to Tzurac.'

General Rokan understood the reasoning, nodding his head slowly.

'If you agree to join us,' Ramlok continued, 'my crew will be stationed here for a month until all your soldiers have been infused and fully retrained. I've enough Xytrinium infusion solution and the necessary equipment on board my vessel to enhance your entire army. I also have an armoury of powerful modern weapons with which to re-equip and re-train them.

'When completed, I'll return to General Vark to synchronise the two-pronged mission, leaving you to recruit the barbarians. Of course, we won't be infusing them for obvious reasons. I also carry with me, and will leave with you, extra supplies of Xytrinium fuel to enable your vessels to reach Terra Major.'

The old General listened intently to what the young emissary had to offer and mulled over thoughts of his own. *The Xytrinium infusion was very tempting. His soldiers would embrace the promise of a four-hundred-year lifespan and the chance to prove themselves against their long-time sworn enemy. They'd be eager to use their newfound powers and their new weapons to be equally matched against the Sentinels of Tzurac. If victorious, the once-scattered Treldarian Legions would unite once more to become the most powerful force in the Universe. No more living in fear of the Federation. The Treldarians would finally have total control over the blue crystal Xytrinium. It was an opportunity too good to refuse.*

'Very well,' said the General, 'I'll consult the leaders of my Legion before I take a final decision to join forces, but I'm certain they'll be interested. Give me until the morning and in the meantime, enjoy what our village has to offer. There'll be a feast tonight to welcome you and your crew.'

'Thank you, General, I look forward to hearing what your leaders decide.' Ramlok was feeling more confident about the Third Legion's involvement, though he had his doubts. *He had helped persuade the General to consider going to war, but was the old general able to fulfil his role leading the attack on Terra Major? He had no choice but to make the most of what was available.*

Ramlok finished on a positive note, 'We appreciate your hospitality. I always enjoy a good party.'

The General leant across the table smiling and gave Ramlok a Treldarian arm-shake. Then, still seated, he called out loudly, 'Bhalar!'

Waiting momentarily, in order to appear as though she had come up from downstairs, Bhalar quietly entered the room.

'Bhalar, show our guest to the door and bring Captain Chekhmar to me!'

She did as instructed without a word.

Chekhmar was intrigued to know what had transpired between this newcomer from the Second Legion and General Rokan. The moment the door opened to reveal Ramlok with a confident smirk on his face, Chekhmar glared begrudgingly at him and barged past Bhalar, storming up the stairs.

The interaction between Rokan and his Captain was brief and cryptic.

'Captain, gather the leaders for a meeting tonight and prepare a feast for our visitors.' The General stood up and, without warning, slammed his fist down hard on the table. 'Tonight, Captain,' he decreed forcefully, 'will be the night our fate is decided for better or worse! The future has come looking for us, instead of us waiting for it!'

Chekhmar shook his head. He was confused. *There was something serious happening and he was anxious to know exactly what it was. He'd been his General's closest confidante for years and it was not like Rokan to keep him in the dark.*

He also had a deeper concern. *He'd been waiting patiently and loyally for Rokan's time to come to an end and the mantle of power of the Third Legion to become his. Rokan was old and his time imminent. This new-found zeal in his General was unexpected. Did it threaten his future ambitions?*

* * *

That night, Ramlok and his soldiers made friends with their Treldarian brothers while eating an unusual meal made from the planet's produce, quenched with the Treldarians' rough fermented wine. They drank and celebrated well into the night.

While the feast entertained the new arrivals outside his log hut, Rokan and his leaders debated the offer presented to them by the emissary from Generals Vark and Dranz, including the possibility of recruiting the Ankrodians and Nujharenes on the other moons in their star system. The meeting continued into the early hours of the morning, Chekhmar now understanding his General's changed behaviour.

The following morning, Ramlok woke late on board his ship with an all-too-familiar hangover. *The rugged Mankro wine was more potent than the Orkharnian brew.* He splashed his face with cold water before rallying his crew and then headed back to General Rokan's hut with his Lieutenant and Sergeant. *They needed to get down to business.*

'We've agreed to your terms, Captain Ramlok,' said the old, eager-eyed General. The gap-toothed Chekhmar was nodding enthusiastically by his side and exuding a devilish smile. 'When can you start the infusion and training?'

'At once,' said Ramlok, content with the outcome. *The Treldarian armies were growing, and the battle strategy was on track.* 'My alchemist will start the infusions and Lieutenant Vark and Sergeant Krag will lead the training.' He turned to his two offsiders, signalling their involvement and they smiled in agreement.

As they left the General's hut, Ramlok joked quietly with Tykran and Krag in typical Blader style, 'And I hope we can also find some more drinking time. I guess they don't have hot baths and beautiful women?' Captain Ramlok was still a rebel at heart.

A NEW DAWN

ON Terra Major (Earth) a tall, well-built Sentinel with short-cropped, fair hair and steel-blue eyes was returning home for the evening from the new Earth-based Tzuracian military citadel. Dressed in his dark-red cadet uniform and travelling in a sleek, silver, autopilot hovercraft, Kyron Shield was deep in thought. *How his life had changed!*

Born and raised on Earth, knowing only that he had some unique abilities and qualities, Kyron was now fully embracing his identity as a Sentinel. Under the guidance of his friend and mentor, General Ehrane Dakhar, who was now the Commanding Chief of Military Operations for the Western Quadrant, he had learnt so much over the last fifteen months of training. He was excited at the prospect of graduating as a Sentinel officer, following in his late father's footsteps.

During his training, Kyron had learnt much about Tzuracian military protocols, spacecraft and weaponry, astrophysics, navigation, chemistry and astronomy. He had become fluent in Tzuracian, and he had learnt about Tzuracian culture, history, religion, customs and his own ancestry. Cadetship for officers at the Academy was usually three years, but Kyron's previous studies as an engineer, coupled with the tutoring in Sentinel martial arts he received from his father in the past, allowed him to advance rapidly. Looking down at the Pledge ring his father had left him, Kyron felt proud to be a 'Tyros' about to join the first round of officer graduates trained on Earth.

As the hovercraft came to a standstill outside a magnificent sandstone mansion on the outskirts of busy New York City, Kyron took a moment to admire the home where he now lived with his own family, his wife Torri and their two young children. The sandstone mansion was a stark contrast not only to the country farmhouse in which he had been raised by his parents, but also to the Company accommodation he had stayed in when he first became a MERIC employee. The Company apartment had been modern, sterile architecture with fully automated service provided by a Voice-Activated Laser-Enhanced Response Interchanger, VALERI, modelled on the face and voice of the woman who was now his wife.

The mansion had been bequeathed to Kyron by his old mentor, Samuel Jensen, the founder and CEO of MERIC – the man who had given him his first and only job as a graduate engineer. Samuel Jensen had been like a father to him, especially after Kyron's own father passed away. When Samuel Jensen began to suspect his own son's conspiracy to take over, by force, MERIC and the newly discovered Xytrinium deposits on Terra Iota, Samuel Jensen had entrusted Kyron to uncover the plot and help protect the Company.

When Samuel Jensen was murdered by his heartless son, Jackson, Kyron was devastated. However, he was surprised and honoured to find that the CEO had bequeathed to him not only Samuel Jensen's Company but also his mansion, cutting his deceitful son out of the will completely. Samuel Jensen would have been surprised to learn that his protégé was in fact of

Tzuracian Sentinel blood. He would have been proud of the way Kyron had joined forces with Ehrane Dakhar and the Sentinels – not once, but twice – to fight off Jackson and his allies and protect MERIC, the Xytrinium and the future of Earth.

Kyron enjoyed living in the home of this man of principle who had mentored him, trusted him, and confided in him. He treasured the quality belongings and olde-worlde chattels Samuel Jensen had accumulated during his life. These included fine bone china, leather lounges, paintings by the classic masters, rich carpets and rugs, marble statues, solid wooden fixtures and lead-crystal glassware. Wherever Kyron ventured in the house he was reminded of the good person with a good heart who had worked hard all his life. Even the beautiful gardens with manicured lawns gave evidence of Samuel Jensen's caring nature. Kyron would never forget the man who had taken him under his wing and treated him like the son he always wanted.

'Hello, I'm home,' Kyron called out fondly as he entered the front door and removed his military cap. His two children, Zuri who would soon be seven and Ehrana two years younger, rushed to hug him. Rich aromas from the blending of exotic Tzuracian herbs and spices permeated throughout the house. He could smell something unusual and enticing coming from the kitchen.

'Hi darling, dinner's just about ready,' Torri called out to him, smiling. 'I've made something special and hope it's a pleasant change from your military mess hall meals.'

Kyron was a strong, principled and gentle person, keen to support not only his new-found Sentinel compatriots but also his biggest love, his family. He had some good news and was waiting for the appropriate moment before sharing it. He watched with pride as his family took their seats around the table and Torri dished out a home-style Tzuracian meal accompanied by a purple-coloured beverage.

While they indulged in this unfamiliar, but very tasty cuisine, Kyron admired his family. Torri was dressed in a dark green Tzuracian kaftan which defined her lithe, slender body and complemented her straight and shiny deep-red hair, striking emerald-green eyes and rose-coloured cheeks. *She was as beautiful as ever,* he thought, *and Zuri and Ehrana had grown into wonderful children. Little Ehrana was the image of her mother with the same dark-red hair and sparkling green eyes while Zuri had fair hair and steel-blue eyes, just the same as him.*

How situations had changed since they'd befriended the Tzuracians! A computer engineer by profession, Torri was not only managing MERIC while he studied at the military citadel, but she was also embracing everything Tzuracian. She'd become a close friend of General Dakhar's wife, Tajhira, and in her social life she now enjoyed swapping recipes with Tajhira, sharing traditions and shopping together for clothes in the latest Tzuracian and Terranian fashions. She was pleased that Zuri and Ehrana had also become friends with Tajhira's son, Kyrah. *Torri was happier than she'd ever been.*

'Torri, Zuri, Ehrana, I've some news to share with all of you,' Kyron announced.

Young Zuri couldn't contain his excitement, 'You've been made a captain, Daddy?'

Kyron grinned and chuckled softly, 'No, Zuri, not yet.'

Ehrana, who didn't want to be outguessed by her older brother, called out in her high-pitched voice, 'We're going to get a new kitten like you promised, Daddy?'

Kyron smiled again. 'Sorry sweetheart, not yet. No, I was told by your Uncle Ehrane I've now been accepted as a Sentinel officer and I'm to graduate as Lieutenant.'

'Oh, Kyron, that's wonderful news.' Torri leant across the table and kissed him. 'I'm very proud of you.'

The children were also thrilled.

'A lieutenant! Wow!' exclaimed Zuri, while Ehrana shook her head up and down enthusiastically.

'And now for the bad news,' he said, rather dramatically, looking more serious. Torri braced herself and the children's smiles were instantly replaced by frowns. 'General Dakhar has decreed all new graduates have to attend an official ceremony …'

'What's so bad about that?' Torri cut in.

'Well, the ceremony must be held in the capital, Khazor, on Tzurac.'

Torri and the children looked glum. *Would he be leaving them to travel to Tzurac?*

But Kyron was teasing them. 'Cheer up, it's not so bad. We're allowed to bring our families with us. How would you all like to come with me?' he said, grinning.

The children couldn't contain their excitement. They started jumping up and down in their seats, calling out, 'Can we go, Mummy? Please, please. We want to go on a spaceship!'

Torri was more cautious. 'Alright, calm down. I need to discuss this with your father. There's a lot to think about.'

She watched as the children played quietly with their meal, using their forks to brush their food around on their plates. Churned up with mixed feelings of excitement and disappointment, they had lost their appetite. 'Alright then,' she said gently, 'if you've had enough to eat, I think it's time for bed.' She offered them a glimmer of hope. 'It might work out we can all go on this trip, but let's just wait and see.'

Grinning with anticipation, Zuri and Ehrana excused themselves from the table and raced off upstairs.

* * *

Once the children were settled for the night, Kyron and Torri made themselves comfortable on the lounge with a glass of wine and resumed their conversation.

'So, my love, tell me what you're thinking?' Kyron asked sincerely. 'Ehrane needs to know our decision fairly soon so he can finalise arrangements for everyone.'

'I've many questions, Kyron. When would we leave? How long would we be away? Who'll take care of MERIC while I'm gone? What about the physical effects of space travel on the children? And how will we manage on a strange planet?'

Kyron well understood her concerns. 'Torri, we'd leave soon, and we'd only be away for a month. Lauren can handle MERIC temporarily while you're away – I have full confidence in her competence and abilities as I know you do. In fact, I think she'd almost insist you take the opportunity to go to Tzurac. The children will be fine, and you won't be out of place on Tzurac. Tajhira and Kyrah will be travelling with Ehrane and some of the new cadets will also be bringing their Terranian spouses.

'I understand you're anxious about leaving our home on Earth and venturing to a new world. Although you'll be experiencing something new, and you'll get a taste of what might become our home at some time in the future.'

Something else was worrying Torri. 'I'd like to be there with you Kyron, to see you fulfil your dream, but have you forgotten Khaneera Zarkwin is still locked up in Khazor's Citadel prison?' She looked at Kyron with deep concern written all over her face. 'I just don't want to be on the same planet as her. Remember, she still has a death threat on you. I can't stand the thought of her interfering with our family's safety again.'

Kyron put down his glass of wine, leant over and held Torri closely in his arms. 'I understand how you feel, my love, but Khaneera is safely locked away in a high security prison and we'll be protected by the Tzuracian Sentinels in the Citadel. There's no need to worry.'

Torri sat silently for a while, contemplating Kyron's words of comfort. 'I know how much it means to you to have us all go to Tzurac.' She looked into his eyes. 'Well, if Lauren agrees to manage things at MERIC while I'm away, we'll come with you.' She squeezed his hand tightly. 'Though I still wish Khaneera wasn't there.'

They hugged affectionately. 'Torri, I love you.'

'I love you too … And we'll tell the children first thing in the morning.' She turned her head to one side and added, light-heartedly, 'Of course once I've sorted out arrangements for the Company, I'll have to go shopping with Tajhira for some new travel outfits. What does a Tzuracian female wear to official functions?'

'Don't worry, sweetheart,' he chuckled, 'I'm sure Tajhira will help you select the perfect wardrobe.'

Kyron found it hard to get to sleep that night. His mind was a kaleidoscope of thoughts. *He was proud to be graduating as a lieutenant into the ranks of the elite Sentinel army, upholding the tradition of the Tyros family. He was also excited by the prospect of meeting his father's Tzuracian relatives for the first time. But would they accept him with open arms knowing his mother was Terranian and he'd been raised on Earth? And would they accept his Terranian wife and their children?*

After tossing and turning for some time, his mind finally settled, and he succumbed to sleep with Torri snuggled in his arms.

* * *

Kyron was woken abruptly by the jolting of the bed and loud high-pitched shrieks of delight from Zuri and Ehrana. Torri was up before him, and she had just told them they would be going to Tzurac. The excited children were now jumping for joy on the bed. Kyron noted the flashing digits on the wall screen – 5.00 a.m. The sunlight had just started creeping through the small crevices of the long, drawn drapes. Four hours sleep was all he'd managed. While Kyron tried to raise himself from the bedcovers, Zuri and Ehrana threw themselves onto him and started hugging him.

'Alright, children. Enough, enough!' exclaimed Kyron, laughing at their enthusiasm, cuddling them in turn and then shooing them off the bed. 'Zuri, if you want to be a soldier like me, we need to complete our martial arts training before breakfast and then get you and your sister ready for school. Go change and I'll meet you in the gym.'

Zuri saluted his father playfully.

As Zuri and Ehrana disappeared from the room, Torri appeared in the doorway and watched Kyron yawn and stretch.

'You were restless last night,' she said. 'Something you want to tell me, my love?'

'Nothing you should worry about – just feeling a little anxious about my first trip to Tzurac. I was wondering how the Tzuracians will respond to me. I want to embrace my heritage, but will *they* want to embrace me?'

'Don't be silly, Kyron. They'll respect you just as Ehrane does. You've already proven yourself a valiant and elite soldier. You can stand proud like your father.'

'I guess you're right. What would I do without you? I hope they soon discover a safe Xytrinium infusion for humans so we can grow old together.'

'Me too,' she smiled. 'Well, time is running away, and Zuri is waiting for you.'

* * *

Later that day Kyron arrived at the barracks. Located inside the towering walls of the Citadel and taking up almost half the grounds, the large, white-washed and thickly concreted complex was built to accommodate two thousand Sentinel soldiers, including officers and cadets. Rising three stories in height with four divided wings in the shape of a giant cross, it housed a fully complemented armoury, vehicle depot, uniform store, target range, gymnasium, swimming pool, mess hall and barracks. One of the wings contained the Administration offices with other rooms used for communications, simulator training and guests. Sleeping quarters for the officers and cadets remained separate but within the main barracks.

Walking down the corridor of the barracks where he had spent most of the past fifteen months as a cadet, his thoughts were abruptly interrupted by his commanding officer.

'Sub-Lieutenant Tyros, you're ordered to report to General Dakhar post-haste.'

Acknowledging his superior with a salute, Kyron was soon marching briskly through the Citadel passageways heading for the administration wing. There, he presented himself in his dark-red cadet uniform and military cap to the Lance Corporal stationed at the desk just outside General Dakhar's Office.

'Good morning, Corporal,' said Kyron in a disciplined tone, 'Sub-Lieutenant Kyron Tyros reporting to the Chief-Commander as ordered.'

Checking his appointment schedules on the large holographic screen hovering just above his desk, the Corporal acknowledged the appointment and tapped an intercom button at the side of his desk.

'Yes, Corporal,' came the response in a familiar voice.

'Sub-Lieutenant Tyros is here to see you, sir.'

'Send him in, Corporal.'

'Yes, sir.'

An electronic buzz sounded as the door unlocked and slid sideways into an opening in the wall cavity.

'You may go in, sir.'

Rising from his high-backed, chestnut-coloured leather chair behind the polished oak-wood desk, General Dakhar held out his arm for a Sentinel welcome. Dressed in the distinctive dark-maroon uniform of the Sentinel army with his fair hair pulled back in the Sentinel style, the tall, broad-chested General looked somewhat out of place in his surroundings.

There was none of the latest-designed contemporary furniture and fixtures. Ehrane Dakhar preferred to furnish his office with all the olde-worlde natural materials of Earth: polished, solid-wood bookcases; thick woollen carpet with a dark red pattern; brass 'n' glass lamps; and large richly coloured portrait and landscape oil paintings, which hung from the oak-panelled walls. Dakhar's office was very much in Samuel Jensen's style and made the atmosphere warm and inviting, especially for Kyron. It was a complete contrast to the harsh, sterile environment of the bleak, grey steel and concrete military academy. Ehrane and Kyron shared the same tastes.

'Welcome, Kyron, it's good to see you,' said Dakhar in a friendly, mellow voice. Kyron removed his cap and reached out to return the Sentinel handshake as the sliding door closed silently behind him.

As they clasped arms, Kyron returned the warm welcome, 'Thank you, sir, it's also good to see you.'

Ehrane Dakhar and Kyron Tyros shared a very strong bond. Their fathers had once been close friends in the elite Sentinel army on Tzurac until Ehrane's father, Rhyk Dakhar, was murdered by the Bladers. Kyron's father, Ahrmon Tyros, was framed for the crime and fled Tzurac. Centuries on, Ehrane and Kyron had been inadvertently united across the universe, becoming close friends and allies. Both had discovered the truth – another Sentinel, Khane Zarkwin, Khaneera's father, had been found guilty of the conspiracy.

Together, Ehrane and Kyron had protected Earth from attacks by the ruthless Jackson Jensen and the Sentinel traitor, Khaneera Zarkwin. They had, in turn, saved each other's life. And together, they had brought Earth into partnership with the Federation of Planets, guided by the noble principle of using precious Xytrinium only for good and not for evil. Ehrane had tutored Kyron through his training in the Sentinel Academy on Terra Major and, as he did, their families had developed a deep and sincere friendship.

'Please sit down, my friend. Now you're to become an officer, we'll need to maintain protocol in front of the other Sentinels. We can relax the formalities when in private, as we are and always will be, close friends. So, feel at ease in my office, Kyron.'

'Thank you, Ehrane, I will.'

'One of the reasons I called you here is to ask if you've had a chance to discuss your trip to Tzurac with Torri and the children. Have you decided?'

'Yes, Ehrane, we've talked about it and they're all happy to come. The children are more than excited to be on a spaceship with your son, Kyrah. Torri is making plans for Lauren Blake to manage MERIC temporarily and …' he laughed, '… she'll be asking Tajhira for fashion advice before we go.'

'Excellent,' Dakhar smiled. 'However, there's something else you need to know before we finalise things.' Dakhar paused and the expression on his face changed. Kyron sensed the seriousness.

'You know we've been receiving messages intermittently from the estranged Sentinel, Yarron Blandhar, informing us of the remaining Blader locations …'

Kyron nodded, listening intently.

Dakhar lowered his voice, 'Well the last message we had from him was quite disturbing.'

Kyron leaned forward in his chair, his eyes focused on the square jaw and intense, azure-blue eyes of Ehrane in anticipation.

'The Federation was under the impression we'd eradicated almost all the Bladers and Yarron was hunting down the few remaining stragglers. Yet, in his travels, Yarron recently heard rumours from bounty hunters and soldiers-of-fortune that a large army of Treldarians is gathering with intentions to destroy the Federation.'

Kyron was stunned. 'A Treldarian army! How can that be?' He shook his head in disbelief. 'I thought the former Treldarian army was destroyed hundreds of years ago in the Grekadian War leaving only the pirate Bladers. And that most, if not all the Bladers, have now been killed or imprisoned.'

'Yes, you're right in part, Kyron. I was under the same impression. However, during the Grekadian War, the Treldarian army split into two other factions. The Bladers were part of the faction we fought. The other faction of Treldarian soldiers fled and headed for the remote Eastern Quadrant. They've remained there ever since and because they've kept to themselves and have caused us no trouble, we've left them alone. I understand they're now regrouping, so I'm sending a warship to investigate.'

He touched Kyron's shoulder gently, as a friend. 'Look, I don't know for sure whether there's a real threat or not, but I thought you should know before we leave for Tzurac. If the Treldarians intend attacking Tzurac, I don't want any harm to come to you and your family. In fact, you may even want to reconsider bringing your family with you.'

Kyron sat quietly for a while pondering the unwelcome news. 'Ehrane, I appreciate your concerns for my family, although at this stage it's only a rumour. There's no telling where or when this so-called Treldarian army may or may not strike. If they happen to attack Tzurac while I'm there, I'd rather have my family close with me to protect them. I certainly wouldn't want them alone on Earth if an army strikes here while I'm away. With your permission, Ehrane, and I know this information is confidential, I'd like to discuss this with Torri, although I'm sure she'll agree with me.'

'Yes, yes, of course. Talk it over with her in confidence, as I intend to talk about it with Tajhira. I hope for all our sakes it's just a hollow rumour. So, my friend, assuming there's no change of plan, you need to start making arrangements for the journey. Help Torri put her MERIC affairs in order and inform the children's school. I'll keep you informed if we hear more from Yarron.'

As he returned to the barracks, Kyron was deep in thought. *Could there be any substance to this rumour?*

THE LONE CRUSADER

IN the dead of night, an unmarked, black battleship landed quietly on the isolated planet of Krima, on the border of the Eastern and Southern Quadrants. A tall, shadowy figure dressed in the forest-green suede uniform of an Urgellan soldier emerged from the hatch door. A matching cape was draped over the figure's shoulder to one side, partially hiding a holstered laser pistol. The broad-shouldered figure had short-cropped black hair, a black moustache and a small beard on his chin.

Planet Krima was well known as a lawless haven for criminals who congregated there from all over the galaxies. It was a thriving den for black-marketing where contraband goods including weapons, bootlegged alcohol, jewellery, spacecraft parts, and even valuable Xytrinium crystals were traded against a backdrop of debauchery.

As the strikingly handsome newcomer strolled into a crowded, noisy and smoke-filled tavern, he sensed all eyes watching his every movement with curiosity. Experience had taught him to be wary of strangers who would just as soon knife you in the back, or shake your hand as a diversion, while pulling a laser pistol and threatening your life for your purse. Knowing this was the very place this sort of thing would happen, he remained fully alert and prepared for the unexpected.

While ordering a drink from the ugly alien bartender whose features resembled something of a diseased reptilian creature, he was suddenly accosted by three strangers who flanked him. They were bare-chested, large-muscled and mean-looking, with tattooed leathery skin, pointy ears, and a single long and thick black plaited pigtail growing from the back of their smooth domed crowns.

The readily identifiable Kyroni were inebriated. The one on the right, the apparent leader of the pack, pushed his face up close to the newcomer, eyeballing him with inflamed, bloodshot eyes. He blurted out slurred words, his breath stinking of rotting fish and stale wine and it almost made the newcomer vomit.

'Where are you from, stranger?' the aggressive Kyroni asked with a deep menacing accent. He was clasping the handle of the broad-bladed scimitar hanging at his side.

Showing no fear, the newcomer took a slow sip from his glass which the bartender had just filled with green liquid and placed in front of him. The overproof alcohol in the shot-glass burned his throat as he swallowed. He screwed his face up. *It was rugged stuff.* 'I'm from all over,' he answered in fluent Kyroni.

'No, you're not!' the Kyroni yelled in anger. 'I recognise you.'

For a moment the newcomer's heart missed a beat. He thought his true identity had been discovered. Taking another mouthful from the glass in his right hand, he subtly moved his left hand onto the handle of the laser pistol hidden beneath his cape.

The Kyroni continued in a more boisterous voice, 'You're Urgellan, I recognise that uniform. You and your kind sided with the Tzuracian Sentinels and massacred my people on Planet Iota.'

At that instant, the whole place was deadly silent, the crowd waiting for a blood-letting outcome. The newcomer was relieved his true identity hadn't been discovered, but his life was under threat. He had to think quickly to escape the wrath of these three Kyroni. *He was not going to die in a cesspool of thieves and murderers. He would have to lie and deceive his way out of this to stay alive.*

'You're mistaken about me, my friend,' responded the newcomer in a calm and low tone, not wanting to further antagonise the situation. 'I took this uniform off the body of an Urgellan I killed. He'd also accused me of being someone I wasn't.'

'I don't believe you!' the Kyroni shouted as he drew his scimitar, the other two Kyroni following suit.

The newcomer was too fast. With lightning speed, he drew his black-and-silver laser pistol and before the Kyroni had a chance to swing their blades, fired on all three aiming to wound, not kill.

For a moment nobody stirred, except for the bartender who casually poured more green liquid into the newcomer's glass. The newcomer was still waving his firearm at all three attackers who were now lying on the dusty wooden floor. Their weapons were scattered, and they were clasping their injured arms while writhing in pain from the searing laser burns. The newcomer's eyes darted sharply around the room in case others had drawn weapons. No-one else seemed to care about the incident. The disjointed music started up again and the noisy chatter resumed.

The newcomer calmly re-holstered his pistol and offered a hand to help the injured Kyroni to their feet in turn. They accepted reluctantly, after collecting their blades and slipping them into their wide sheaths.

'Alright, stranger,' said the first Kyroni with a contorted expression on his face. He was in pain and struggling with his words. 'Why didn't you kill us instead of wounding us?'

'Because,' said the newcomer casually, 'you may be able to give me information and you're no good to me dead. Besides, I only kill those who have a price on their heads.'

'You're a bounty hunter?'

'Among other things. I'm also a blade-for-hire.'

'You work for the Federation?' the Kyroni said, drawing back.

'No way!' exclaimed the newcomer. 'Why do you think I'm as far away from them as I can get? They hate bounty hunters, and they usually hang soldiers-of-fortune.' His intention was to lull the Kyroni into a false sense of trust.

'Yeah, don't I know it,' agreed the lead Kyroni, his partners-in-crime leaning on the bar and shaking their heads in silence. 'We've seen what they do to their enemies. So, what do you want to know?'

'Bartender, give my friends a drink to numb their pain and quench their thirst,' ordered the newcomer.

The ugly bartender placed another three shot glasses on the counter and filled them with the same green liquid. 'That'll be four gold bits! We don't take credits here,' he demanded in a strange croaky voice.

The newcomer reached into a side pocket in his suede jacket, pulled out four gold bits and slammed them on the counter. He continued the conversation almost in a whisper. 'I've heard rumours about some general who's recruiting an army to fight whoever for the spoils. They might just need my skills in return for my share of the rewards.'

'Well, stranger,' the Kyroni leader began, looking interested, 'you might just be in luck.'

'Call me Armel,' interrupted the newcomer.

'Okay Armel, I'm Harjar and this is Sarkan and Kulbark,' he said, waving his hand in their direction. 'We three Kyroni escaped our planet just before the Federation declared martial law after the battle on Iota. We weren't chosen to fight on Iota because they thought we were too young.' He paused and raised his good arm towards the ceiling, calling out, 'We're warriors and we'll fight the Sentinels to the death!' He was incensed with hatred.

'Alright, Harjar, tone it down,' said the newcomer. 'There could be spies here who'd have you arrested for treason.'

'Yeah, you're right,' Harjar said more quietly, lowering his arm beside him while he cautiously surveyed the room. 'We must be discreet, or the secret might get out.'

Armel's ears pricked with interest. 'And what secret might that be, Harjar?' he said nonchalantly, confident he had now gained their trust.

'You say you're looking to join a rebel army to share in the spoils. Well, it just so happens we're on our way to such an army. It's not a rumour. There's a Treldarian general whose sanctuary is in the Clavistoq Star System in the far reaches of the Southern Quadrant. For some time now he's been actively recruiting soldiers and warriors who want to join him in destroying the Federation.

'We're planning on leaving tomorrow,' he said, pausing, 'if our wounds aren't too serious.' He gave a wry smile. 'So, if you want, you can come with us to find this general.'

'Thanks for the invite,' said Armel, 'and you *will* be leaving tomorrow as planned. Your arms will be sore for at least a week, but I deliberately aimed to miss your main arteries. Your wounds are only superficial. I have my own battleship, so I won't need a lift.'

'That's even better.' Harjar's eyes lit up with glee. 'The general would definitely welcome a mercenary with his own fighter craft. In that case, you can follow us.'

'So, where's this planet we're going to?' Armel asked casually, as he raised his glass and took another sip, his throat now accustomed to the coarse firewater.

'We don't know, but once we enter the Clavistoq Star System we'll send out broadcasts to attract the rebel army.'

Armel knew he didn't have much choice but to accept their offer. *If he ventured to this star system on his own the rebels would most likely try to capture him, kill him and take his ship. Travelling in partnership with the Kyroni, the Treldarians might accept him as a blade-for-hire with his own battleship.*

* * *

Two days into their travel deep into the Clavistoq Star System, Armel awoke from a nightmarish dream. A permanent laser scar on the side of his neck burned and he reached with his hand to massage the spot and soothe the pain. He had been reliving past events turning over and over in his mind.

With a warrant out for his arrest and a bounty on his head, the fugitive Sentinel, Yarron Blandhar, was on the run. He was travelling throughout the galaxies in a remodelled Tzuracian Destroyer battleship, avoiding any physical contact with the Federation. Travelling incognito under the name of Armel, he was posing as an Urgellan turned soldier-of-fortune or blade-for-hire. Ironically, the fugitive was now helping, not hindering his pursuers – hunting relentlessly for pirate Bladers and sending communiqués revealing their locations to Ehrane Dakhar.

It was the youthful desire for adventure and the foolish blindness of love that had led him initially to help the imprisoned Sentinel traitor, Khaneera Zarkwin, escape from Tzurac. He also stole for her the precious Xytrinium formula from his mother's laboratory. His reckless actions had allowed dark forces to invade Earth and Terra Iota with their new super armies.

Realising Khaneera's black heart and wrestling with his guilt-ridden conscience, Yarron had later disclosed to Dakhar, details to help foil the enemy's planned invasion. Risking his life to block a laser shot fired by Khaneera at Kyron Tyros, he then pursued Khaneera when she fled the scene, passing details of her whereabouts to the Sentinels.

Yarron was content to know that Khaneera Zarkwin was again locked behind bars on Tzurac, where she could do no more harm to the Sentinels or the Universe. Yet every time she appeared in his thoughts, the laser scar on his neck burned, reminding him of her deceptive ways, and his brush with death at her hand. He prayed the work he was now doing would bring him salvation in the spiritual eyes of the Ancients.

Recently, Yarron had begun to notice the numbers of Bladers in the Northern and Western Quadrants decreasing, and not necessarily through *his* efforts. His thinking was they had either gone into deeper hiding or travelled to the other Quadrants of the Universe.

The Southern Quadrant was too dangerous for isolated travellers. It was a rugged wilderness of dead planets and uncharted asteroids. Stories surfaced telling about numbers of space crafts never returning, their passengers disappearing without trace. Even the Federation stayed clear of the Southern Quadrant.

So, Yarron's hunt for the Bladers had brought him first to the outskirts of the Eastern Quadrant. Yarron knew that, centuries ago, some of the Treldarian army had travelled deep into the Eastern Quadrant, claiming their newfound territory and laying a border peppered with thousands of space mines. Their borders were regularly patrolled by Treldarian battle cruisers to prevent outsiders from entering their territory. Federation patrols steered clear of these borders, leaving the outlanders in peace. There, after visiting some of the hideouts of smugglers and corrupt business entrepreneurs, he'd heard rumours of a Treldarian army readying for war with the Federation. Immediately, he had forewarned General Dakhar via his Sentinel Pledge ring.

Now, travelling into the Southern Quadrant with the Kyroni for protection, he was trying to discover more …

* * *

Barely three days into the Clavistoq Star System, the broadcast signals sent by the Kyronis met with success. Two huge black warships with the Treldarian insignia of a red scorpion tag on their hulls suddenly confronted them.

Yarron was gripped with fear and hate when an image of a Treldarian officer exploded onto his main screen, tempting him to open fire. *He had to suppress his emotions if he were to infiltrate this rebel army successfully and discover their plans for battle.*

The Comms crackled to life with a deep accented voice, 'I'm Captain Chekhmar of the Third Treldarian Legion of the Southern Quadrant. Stop your crafts or you'll be fired upon!'

Simultaneously the Kyroni and Yarron cut their ships' power and hovered motionlessly, waiting in anticipation for the next command from the Treldarian Captain, or for cannon fire to obliterate them.

The screen displayed a scruffy looking captain with ragged, shoulder-length, black hair and a bushy unkempt beard. He was wearing a well-worn brown-leather jacket over a black shirt. When he spoke, the gaps in his teeth were evident.

'Who are you and what are you doing in our territory?' Chekhmar asked. 'Be warned, if I don't like what I hear, your lives will be in danger.'

Yarron left it to the Kyroni to explain while listening to his Comms.

'We come as allies,' responded Harjar in an uncharacteristically timid tone. 'We've heard there's a Treldarian general recruiting soldiers to fight against the Federation and we'd like to join the crusade. We're Kyroni and the other craft belongs to a blade-for-hire who also wants to join the cause.'

There was a pause before the captain spoke again, 'How do I know you're not spies trying to find our armies and the location of our hideout?'

'As you can see, Captain Chekhmar, we're Kyroni,' Harjar said, pumping his chest out and gesturing to his partners. 'We're sworn enemies of the Federation, looking for revenge to kill those who massacred our brothers on Planet Iota.' There was hatred in his words.

The captain shrugged his shoulders somewhat sceptically. Then, directing his comment to the unknown inhabitant in the other spacecraft, he asked, 'What about you, 'blade-for-hire'? What's your story?' His expression had changed to a cold stare as if he were reading Yarron's mind.

Yarron had to think quickly. 'My name's Armel,' he responded confidently. 'I'm an Urgellan fugitive wanted for murder. For the last four years I've been on the run from the Urgellans and their allies, the Tzuracians. So, if you're looking for soldiers to overthrow the Federation and reap a share in some of their spoils, then my blade is yours.'

On hearing Yarron's confession on his Comms, Harjar turned to his Kyroni friends. 'I *knew* he was Urgellan, even though he denied it!' he said through clenched teeth. 'I guess he's only covering his tracks – the murderous fugitive.'

The captain hesitated for an instant. 'Alright, I'll spare your lives for now and take you to my General. I'll let him decide your fate. But be warned strangers, if you try anything, you'll suffer the consequences. Follow us at Level 4 hyperdrive propulsion and *no* games!'

No sooner had he spoken than the Comms went dead, and the screen reverted to the picture of the two warships ahead of them, turning in readiness to head off in the direction of their planet. The Kyroni and Yarron hit their thrusters the instant the Treldarian warships' thrusters ignited.

* * *

On arrival at Mankro, Armel and the Kyroni were confronted by half-a-dozen armed Treldarian soldiers who confiscated their weapons, before escorting them to General Rokan's village, marching them through the crowds who gathered to see these strange looking aliens. They were taken direct to General Rokan's hut, where they were met by what appeared to be a servant woman who opened the solid, carved wooden door.

'Bhalar,' said Chekhmar, in a rough voice. 'I'm here to see the General and present these four captives – three Kyroni and one Urgellan.'

Yarron was struck by what he saw. Bhalar was beautiful. She had silken tanned skin and glistening black hair which was combed back into a long loose plait that was draped around the nape of her slim sleek neck. Her dark piercing eyes shone like polished onyx, and she had narrow lips that were a soft pink. Her tightly clinging sarong outlined a perfectly proportioned slender body. Never before had he been taken by the beauty of a Treldarian female.

Bhalar glared coldly at Chekhmar and then looked the strangers up and down. Her look was severe. 'Wait here!' she ordered in a strong voice, as she closed the door leaving them standing outside.

The crowd edged closer and closer, muttering and pointing at these strange folk. One of the older females in the crowd reached out to touch Sarkan's long pigtail. Before she could, he swung around grabbing her arm tightly and raising his fist to strike her. The Treldarian escorts raised their laser pistols but with speed reflexes, Yarron intervened and Chekhmar raised his hand, signalling his soldiers to hold their fire. Yarron grasped Sarkan's wrist, forcing Sarkan to release his hold on the female, then yanked Sarkan's arm back hard.

Sarkan yelped in pain. 'You're very strong for an Urgellan,' he snapped, holding his sprained shoulder. Chekhmar and the others were also impressed.

'Speed more than strength,' responded Yarron, trying to hide his Sentinel powers. 'We don't want to upset our hosts on our first meeting, do we?'

'Yeah, Armel, you're right.' Sarkan was still angry. '*No-one* is permitted to touch our plaited hair without permission. It's a sign of disrespect for Kyroni, and those who've attempted this in the past have had their hands severed.'

'Well, this is *their* world, and we *must* obey their customs if we're to become their allies and not worm fodder.'

Chekhmar acknowledged Yarron's 'wisdom', and then scowled at the aggressive Kyroni warrior. 'Next time, alien,' he said, 'you won't get off so lightly.'

The door opened again and Bhalar waved Chekhmar and the strangers into the hut. Chekhmar led them upstairs with two of his soldiers trailing closely behind. After a moment or two, Bhalar followed, remaining within earshot in the shadows outside the door to the General's room.

On entering the room, the captain spied his old General sitting in his usual spot in the corner at the rudimentary carved wooden table. Rokan's eyes glistened and his skin appeared remarkably youthful. Chekhmar was convinced the Xytrinium infusion had given the once-feeble General a new lease of life, filling his body with renewed vitality and super strength. Chekhmar had mixed feelings. *How many more years was his General to live?*

'Be seated my alien visitors,' commanded the General, waving his hand in the direction of the other wooden chairs around the table. 'So, you want to join our rebellion, do you? Why is this so?' The old Treldarian's now-sharp eyes were fixed on the Kyroni waiting for their answer.

'Well, General,' replied Harjar, as their leader, 'as we've already told your captain, we seek revenge for the slaughter of our brethren by the Federation on Iota.'

'Alright, if this is what you seek, I'll give you Kyroni the opportunity to seek your blood vengeance. Though I'm unable to offer you the Xytrinium infusion your brothers received to equal the odds against the Sentinels. It's miraculous stuff, but the Treldarian captain who travelled here to infuse my soldiers, has already departed with the formula and the equipment.'

Yarron stifled his surprise. *They have the Xytrinium infusion?*

Harjar and his companions weren't fazed. 'General, we just want to kill as many Sentinels as we can!' The other two Kyroni nodded with enthusiasm.

The old General then turned his attention to Yarron, 'Well Urgellan, what's *your* reason for rallying to the cause?'

Yarron hid his anxiety, as Sentinels can do, and acted calm under pressure. He responded in a casual manner, 'As I told your captain, I'm a wanted Urgellan fugitive and if the Urgellans or the Federation catch me, they'll execute me. So, I've nothing to lose and a lot to gain if there's bounty in it from the spoils. And I don't want anything injected into *my* body over which I have no control.'

General Rokan looked to his captain who was standing behind them, waiting for a verdict on these intruders who had come to join the ranks.

Chekhmar tilted his head, saying, 'The Urgellan has good reflexes and has his own battleship, sir.'

Rokan raised his eyebrow with interest. *An extra battleship would come in very handy.* 'Alright soldiers, welcome aboard. Captain Chekhmar will return your weapons and show you the ropes. As for your sleeping quarters, you can stay in your ships. And keep out of trouble! That's an order! My soldiers don't need much to upset them. You'll be joining our hunting parties when we start recruiting from some of the tribes who live on the other two moons. Captain, escort them out.'

Yarron sighed quietly in relief after being accepted into the Treldarian rebel camp, but he was shocked to hear the General's soldiers had been infused with Xytrinium.

That night his mind was racing. *How was this possible? He had destroyed the Bladers' base on Planet Agorra and after tipping off Ehrane Dakhar, the Tzuracians had retrieved their formula and destroyed the infusion equipment held by the Bladers on Steiros. All on Steiros, including Khaneera and General Dranz, had been killed or captured. So, who was this Treldarian captain who had the formula? And where was his next port of call?*

He had to discover who was helping General Rokan and uncover the General's plans for attack. To do this he would need to keep a low profile. Hopefully, he would find out soon when and where they intended to strike and with how many super-soldiers. Then he'd contact Dakhar to forewarn him. The sooner Dakhar knew, the more time the Federation would have to prepare a defence.

TRELDARIAN TACTICS

FOLLOWING a month-long mission on the moon of Mankro, Ramlok was enjoying a deep sleep back on Orkharn. Suddenly, he was woken abruptly by loud hammering at his door.

'Captain Ramlok! Captain Ramlok!' a voice bellowed. 'Are you awake, sir?'

Ramlok dragged himself out of bed and staggered to the door, semi-conscious and still groggy. He flung the door open and was ready to throttle whoever it was disturbing his peaceful slumber, when he saw the familiar face of Sergeant Krag with a big grin on his face.

'Good morning, sir,' said Krag in a cheery voice, while saluting his senior officer.

'Morning, Sergeant,' responded Ramlok. 'Why are you so lively? And why are you here at this time of the morning?'

'Sorry to disturb you, sir, but General Vark has asked to see you at the Council Hall in an hour to report the outcomes of our mission to General Rokan. I thought you needed time to prepare yourself and the report.'

'Thanks, Sergeant, what would I do without you?' said Ramlok, half-joking and running his fingers through his untidy, thick hair. 'I'll get cleaned up and meet you in the Officers' Mess Hall in forty-five minutes.'

'Very good, sir.' Krag saluted, about-faced, and marched off down the passageway.

* * *

After a satisfying breakfast, Ramlok was escorted by his Sergeant to face the War Council. As usual, Krag remained outside the closed metal doors while Ramlok entered.

The members of the Council were all seated, with Captain Tarken beside the General at the head of the table. They were all waiting anxiously to hear from Captain Ramlok.

One councillor muttered under his breath to another. 'What a difference a uniform and decent haircut makes. Quite a transformation compared to the first time we saw him.' Although his thick hair was still untamed, Ramlok looked slicker than before in his black Treldarian uniform.

Standing confidently with a sardonic smile Ramlok went straight to the point, 'General Vark, Members of the Council, it's been a successful mission. The Third Legion are now our allies.'

Holding up a document for all to see, he continued. 'Here's their signed and sealed agreement to join the Second Legion in the fight against the Federation. General Rokan and all of his one thousand soldiers have been successfully infused and trained. And during the month of my return trip to Orkharn, General Rokan was planning to recruit more warriors from the tribes who inhabit the moons of Ankrod and Nujhar. In return for his allegiance, General Rokan expects a share of the spoils. When our sun is in full eclipse of Orkharn, he will be leaving the Clavistoq Star System with his armada of five warships to head for Terra Major.'

'Thank you, Captain,' said Vark with his crooked smile. 'This is great news.' Vark rubbed his hands with satisfaction and the Council members hammered the table. 'We're pleased with your success in reuniting us with our Treldarian brothers. Bring the papers and leather binder to me so the Council members may examine the agreement for themselves.'

Ramlok strode confidently over to the stone table, saluted the General and handed the documents to him. Then he stood waiting at attention for further orders.

'Take a chair at the table, Captain. You need to know what role you'll be playing in this invasion.' Ramlok took a seat opposite the General who, after taking a quick look at Rokan's agreement, passed it on to the others to scrutinise.

While the members were busy reading and discussing the documents, Vark leaned forward across the table towards Ramlok and in a quieter voice asked, 'How's my son, Tykran? Did he live up to your expectations? Or did he disappoint you?'

'Your son performed well beyond his duties. You should be proud of him, General.'

Vark raised his eyebrows, 'Really? Well, that's welcome news.' He seemed relieved all round.

Vark took control of the meeting again. 'Members, I'm delighted the Third Legion has joined our cause. It's time to initiate our plan of attack.'

'Hear, hear!' the members of the Council called out, beating their fists lightly on the table in complete agreement.

General Vark's eyes were now on fire. 'As most of you are aware,' he continued, 'we've successfully manufactured several Xytrinium warheads which we'll carry with us to Tzurac. The first priority is to attack Planet Kyronis, dispose of the Sentinels, and free the Kyroni on condition they become our allies. We'll offer to infuse all who want to join us.'

Vark turned his attention to Ramlok. 'Captain Ramlok, your role is to oversee the infusing of the Kyroni using your battleship as a base. Make sure you have enough liquefied Xytrinium onboard your vessel. We leave in a week. I don't want any delays. Timing is everything! And if you were happy with my son's performance on Mankro, you're welcome to take him with you on board your ship.'

Ramlok acknowledged the suggestion. *It was a sign of progress.*

The General was now in full flight. His fists tightened on the table in front of him and he spoke louder, with more passion. 'Once we've defeated the Sentinels on Planet Kyronis, we'll move swiftly to invade Tzurac, just as General Rokan reaches Terra Major. The Tzuracians will be unprepared for our surprise attack and won't expect the Xytrinium warheads. Once Khazor's protective Dome is destroyed, our ships will land on the surface to mobilise our army. We want to take the planet, not destroy it, because it has all the resources we need, including Xytrinium deposits. Terra Major's military will be unable to come to their aid while trying to fend off General Rokan's assault.'

Vark was wringing his hands with great satisfaction, obviously proud that his plan was coming to fruition. 'Commanders, ensure you have sufficient amounts of Xytrinium on board to make the journey. Now if there's nothing further to discuss, we can all start our preparations. Do *not* disclose our destinations to your units. We can't afford any leaks. I want to catch those elite do-gooders off guard. Meeting adjourned!'

Ramlok followed the Council members as they quickly filed out of the Hall.

His loyal Sergeant was waiting patiently outside the entrance ready to escort him back to his quarters. With a sharp salute, Krag asked keenly, 'How did it go, sir?'

'All good. We're leaving again in a week and there's not much time to prepare.'

'Where are we going, sir, if you don't mind me asking?'

'Well first stop is the hot baths. While the others are preparing, I want to see my beautiful Shanowah. We deserve some rest and relaxation. What do you think, Sergeant? Will you be in that?'

'Sounds good to me, Captain,' Krag replied enthusiastically, 'you don't have to ask twice.'

'But after that, our next stop … Well, all I can say is we've got a long hard journey ahead of us.'

* * *

Relaxing in the hot baths for most of the afternoon was just the indulgence Ramlok and his returned soldiers needed after the long trek to and from the wilds of Mankro. After spending some time with the seductive Ludaxian beauty Shanowah in her boudoir, Ramlok returned to bathe with his unit in the euphoric waters and drink the tasty, fermented wine, the pleasures he had greatly missed.

He slid into the water near Tykran Vark. The young Lieutenant Vark had become a friend of Ramlok's, and the pair spent their time engrossed in conversations about war strategies, weaponry and of course, women – not necessarily in that order.

While Ramlok and young Vark were chatting, Ramlok noticed a group of soldiers at the far end of the baths talking amongst themselves and watching his every movement. He didn't recognise them individually, but he acknowledged their stares with a confident nod. He knew there were a few soldiers who still resented him as an outsider joining their ranks, but he figured they would eventually come around. As the group dispersed, he shrugged off any uneasiness, submerging himself in the healing waters.

Relaxed and a little tired, Ramlok soon decided it was time to head back to his quarters to ready himself for the evening meal at the Mess Hall. Leaving the young Vark in the baths, Ramlok and the Sergeant dressed hastily and donned their weapons.

It was nightfall by the time the captain and his subordinate left the baths. They were taking a short-cut to the barracks through one of the narrow back laneways when, suddenly, they were confronted by six hooded strangers who were blocking their pathway. The strangers were cloaked in unfamiliar attire with the lower half of their faces masked. Standing silent, with cutlasses in their hands, the strangers started walking slowly towards Ramlok and Krag.

The laneway was the perfect place to ambush someone in the dark. It was narrow with high walls and no windows, leaving no room to manoeuvre. Only those with superior skills would stand a chance of surviving an attack by six swordsmen in the confined space.

Without hesitation Ramlok and his Sergeant drew their blades instinctively. Then Ramlok raised his free hand in a motion to stop the approaching swordsmen.

'What do you want?' he questioned in a strong, fearless voice, hoping to force them to speak so he could identify them. Silhouetted in the semi-darkness, Ramlok could discern their tall physiques, but he was uncertain whether they were infused Treldarian soldiers or rogue Ludaxian males.

Out of the darkness their leader responded in a sinister tone, 'We want your death!' and the gang members began to charge at them two at a time.

Ramlok crouched and with his left hand, pulled the concealed dagger from his boot, and as he rose, unsheathed his sabre, giving him a combination of short and long blades. It was the technique he used in his past days as a Blader. Now standing defensively, he clashed with the leader on his right, while the Sergeant took the attacker on the left. Sharp metal blades clanged with defence and attack, as swords swung ferociously.

Although the burly leader fought with bravado, he was no match for Ramlok's freestyle. As the attacker thrust his sword towards Ramlok's chest, Ramlok instinctively swivelled to the left and in one swift single movement blocked the leader's blade with his Blader sword. He continued the circle, slashing across the leader's neck with the dagger held in his left hand. The razor-edged blade found its mark, severing the carotid artery.

Ramlok stepped back to avoid the spray of blood spewing from the wound as the shocked assailant clasped his hand over the slash in a futile attempt to stop the rapid flow of crimson liquid. Within seconds his body was swaying and then he collapsed heavily onto the cobbled ground like a felled tree. Death was instantaneous.

In spite of the life and death predicament he was facing, Ramlok was enjoying the thrill, spurred by the adrenalin rush. Judging by their speed and strength, as well as their reliance on traditional military sword patterns, Ramlok soon realised he was duelling with enhanced Treldarian soldiers – soldiers *he* had trained.

Fortunately, Ramlok's freestyle was making short work of his one-on-one confrontation. Sergeant Krag, however, was still battling with his first assassin, when the next assailant stepped forward and lunged at Ramlok with his outstretched sword. Anticipating the move, this time he pivoted to the right blocking the attacker's blade with his own blade. With the dagger still tightly held in his left hand, he plunged the short, sharp blade into the assailant's right shoulder, deeply puncturing the thick muscle. The serious wound forced the soldier to release his blade and drop to the ground in excruciating pain, desperately trying to stop the gushing blood with his other hand.

At the same time, Krag finally overwhelmed his opponent, leaving his cutlass half buried in the soldier's stomach and the soldier gasping for air. Seeing the state of their defeated comrades and knowing they were out skilled, the other three assailants turned and fled into the darkness of the night.

'Are you alright, Captain?' asked Krag with genuine concern, breathing heavily.

'I'm alright, Sergeant,' said Ramlok, catching his breath, 'but I see you didn't get out of this without a few scratches.' There were cuts to Krag's right arm and left leg where his attacker's blade had sliced through his uniform.

'If I wasn't wearing this uniform,' Ramlok cursed, 'I would've killed them all. I'd like to find out who they are and why they attacked us. We need to keep them alive to interrogate. We'll catch the other cowards later.'

Just as he finished talking, Ramlok spied one of the wounded attackers slowly raise his arm and point a pistol in their direction. With lightning reflexes, Ramlok swept the Sergeant out of the way and flung his dagger towards the assailant. The dagger found its mark, burying the blade into the victim's forehead and killing him instantly.

Shocked and dazed Sergeant Krag scrambled to his feet and dusted himself down. 'By the Gods that was close! You saved my life!'

'Well, Sergeant,' said Ramlok in a cool and calm manner, 'I'm not sure which one of us he was intending to shoot. Unfortunately, we won't be getting any information out of him now.'

The Sergeant stepped towards the unconscious soldier with the buried sword in his stomach and then bent down to remove his hood and mask. 'I don't believe it!' Krag exclaimed. 'It's Sergeant Jhamarz of the 33rd Infantry Battalion. He's a loyal soldier who's respected by his battalion and his senior officers. Why would he do this?'

Ramlok stepped up to get a better look at the assailant's face. 'I recognise him from the hot baths this afternoon. He was with a group who seemed to be keeping me under surveillance. Pull the hood off the other one, Sergeant. Let's see who he is.'

Krag moved to the other assailant lying on the stone floor of the alleyway and flicked off his hood and mask. 'That's Lieutenant Myzek from the same battalion.'

'He was another one in the group eyeing me off today,' said Ramlok. 'I'm betting the three who fled were from the same group. What's their problem, Sergeant?'

'Some didn't like an outsider being promoted above them, you know – especially a rogue Blader.'

'Well, we'll just have to help them get over it, one way or another.' Ramlok chuckled with dry humour as he pointed to the three assailants lying on the ground.

'What has me intrigued, sir,' said Krag, 'is that these soldiers lay waiting to ambush us. How did they know we'd be taking this particular route from the baths back to the barracks? It's not the usual route.'

Ramlok thought for a moment, searching for an explanation. 'Perhaps they just took a chance we might come this way? Although … I inadvertently told Shanowah we'd be staying longer this afternoon because you knew a shortcut back to the barracks.' Ramlok paused, his mind ticking over. 'But I trust Shanowah,' he said, trying to convince himself. 'She wouldn't betray my movements to other soldiers. What reason would she have to tell others what I was doing?'

'Be careful, sir. I know you're fond of Shanowah, but as much as they give us great pleasure, Ludaxian women aren't to be trusted. They make money any way they can by applying their seductive talents.'

Ramlok shook his head, dismissing the suggestion. He was confident – or at least *wanted* to be confident – that he had become one of Shanowah's favourites. 'Thanks for the advice,

Sergeant. I'll keep that in mind. But if Shanowah mentioned my movements to anyone in passing, I'm sure it wasn't intentional. Now let's haul the two surviving soldiers to the med centre and have Security deal with them. Leave the dead one. We'll have Security pick him up later.'

* * *

The following morning Ramlok was ordered to report immediately to General Vark.

'Come in, Captain,' the General called out to Ramlok as he arrived at the office door. The General waved his arm indicating for Ramlok to take a seat. Looking around Vark's room Ramlok was not surprised to find how sparsely furnished it was. It was similar to the rest of the building in appearance; bare dull-grey stone walls, basic table and chairs of metal with a tall grey metal cabinet standing in one corner. Only a large map spread across one of the walls added some colour to the bleakness. Natural light came through a wide window fixed in the wall behind the table which overlooked the expansive cobblestoned parade ground.

As he peered over the tabletop of neatly arranged military paraphernalia, Ramlok could see clearly through the window. A brigade of troops was engaged in a marching exercise, and he could just hear the faint sound of orders being yelled by a tough drill-sergeant, until his concentration was interrupted by General Vark's voice.

'How are you feeling after your altercation last night, Captain?' the General asked with concern. 'I'm sorry again for my soldiers' behaviour.'

'I hadn't expected drawing blades against my fellow soldiers – against soldiers *I* had trained,' Ramlok responded angrily. 'Sergeant Krag and I are lucky to be alive. It might have ended differently if we hadn't been in that narrow alley which prevented all the assailants striking at once.'

Vark shook his head in disgust.

'Did they catch the three cowards who ran off, sir?'

'No, Captain. Not yet. They managed to evade Security and commandeer a battlecruiser during the night. If we ever catch them, they'll wish they'd never been born!' The expression on the General's scarred face showed the depth of his fury and he clenched his fists tightly. 'But they have a ten-hour head-start on us and my immediate concern is that the Federation might catch the deserters first. If they do, these traitors might divulge details of our planned invasion. It's bad timing!'

'Can't we track their heatsink?'

'It would be difficult with them travelling at hyperspeed and, given our invasion plan is already in motion, I can't afford to waste time and resources tracking them down. So, I'm advancing our departure, Ramlok. We've no other choice. All troops have been ordered to speed up preparations. Captain, start loading the infusion equipment, fuel and food provisions, immediately! The Second Legion fleet of six warships and three hundred scout-ships will depart Orkharn as soon as possible.'

'Good move, General,' said Ramlok, feeling an adrenalin rush.

Vark spoke with a loud vengeful tone, tightening his right fist to white knuckles and holding it in front of his chest. 'The time has come, and I will *not* have this mission fail because of a handful of cowardly conspirators!'

'Damn right, General!'

ANKROD

CAPTAIN Chekhmar had been sent by General Rokan with fifty warriors to find and persuade the nomadic tribes on the other two moons of Dunkor to join the rebellion. Yarron and the three Kyroni were accompanying them. Chekhmar's intention was to lure the natives on Ankrod and Nujhar with the promise of a share in the spoils after the Federation was destroyed.

Their first destination was Planet Ankrod. According to the information Chekhmar had retrieved from the data records logged during the last visit to this planet two years ago, the bleak rocky planet hosted over a hundred widely scattered tribes. The Ankrodians were primitive hunter-gatherers who ventured out in small packs of about six, felling their prey with stones, spears and rudimentary tomahawks. Their axe heads and spearheads were made from ironstone. They also used coarsely fashioned bows and arrows constructed of animal bones. Even their knives were made from sharpened bone. The females gathered root vegetables, berries and wild fruits as well as fish from the lake, and the nomads camped in hidden caves amongst barren rugged mountains.

Physically, the Ankrodian males were six to seven feet tall, solid muscle, with thick-set brown eyes, long and scraggly brown hair and no facial hair. Their hand-woven clothes were usually dyed grey or bleached to a natural fawn colour and for protection against the bleak weather the Ankrodians wrapped themselves in animal furs and hides. They were fearless. What they lacked in fighting skills and weapons, they made up for with brute force and sheer strength. Yarron was intrigued.

After three days, Chekhmar's vessel, *Trigan*, approached the orbit of Ankrod. It felt very strange to Yarron entering the planet's coloured atmosphere – it was different from any other planet the Sentinel fugitive had encountered in his travels. Instead of the usual floating white and grey clouds laden with moisture, the moon was shrouded in a dense violet mist, like a blanket, making visibility difficult. Lightning from electrical storms flashed and thunder rumbled continuously around their craft, the vibrations shaking the warship violently.

Navigation and landing were performed automatically by the ship's computers and the vessel landed on a plateau spread across the top of a high mountain range overlooking a massive deep-blue lake. Very little vegetation grew on the craggy slopes. The sun was screened by the thick atmosphere, permitting only short grasses and mosses to grow in the trapped soil caught in the crevasses of the rugged grey-slate cliffs. An abundance of large jet-black birds with wide wingspans soared high over the water. Occasionally they plunged at great speed into the depths to retrieve strange-looking slippery grey fish in their prominent serrated beaks and long sharp talons. It was a cold uninviting planet with a brisk breeze constantly chilling everything and the air was thin, making breathing laboured.

Before disembarking the imposing gap-toothed Captain Chekhmar issued strict orders. 'The native tribes are primitive and fearless. They don't take kindly to Treldarians. Our task is to identify and note the locations of the tribes on your maps. You'll be working in pairs, some in scout ships and others on foot, in order to cover a wide area. We'll be travelling light, carrying only our weapons. Stay alert and keep your eyes open. Avoid contact with these ferocious Ankrodians. If attacked, they'll retaliate with brute force and most likely kill us all. We'll scout during daylight and return to the ship at end of day. Move out!'

To Yarron's relief, he was paired with one of the Treldarian soldiers and instructed to trek on foot to search for inhabited caves amongst the windswept terrain. He hoped this would give him the opportunity to glean more information about Rokan's war plans.

'Tarhaz? It is Tarhaz, isn't it?' Yarron asked his travel companion for the day.

'Yeah,' the Treldarian soldier grunted.

'I'm Armel.'

It was clear Tarhaz was not happy being paired with the Urgellan stranger.

Tarhaz's ragged appearance in his worn-out uniform gave the impression he rarely washed himself or trimmed his long straggly beard. It was hard to tell on his unintentionally camouflaged face where the smeared powdered dirt finished and his rough beard began. Thick black eyebrows shaded his dark eyes, and his full lips hid his yellow stained teeth. Yarron was pleased his burly companion didn't talk much as his rotten breath was overwhelming when he walked too close.

They trekked in silence for some time before taking a rest break, seating themselves on a couple of small boulders on the even sloping ground. Trying to gain the trust of his disgruntled partner, Yarron offered him a drink. Concerned about what he might contract drinking from the same flask, Yarron poured out a capful of water and handed it to Tarhaz. The Treldarian gestured a quiet 'Thanks' and Yarron began to disclose some details of his past.

'I guess you've heard I'm a fugitive Urgellan.'

Tarhaz gave no response, and kept sipping on the container of water, looking blankly towards the mountains in the distance.

Undeterred, Yarron continued, 'I was a guard in the Urgellan army and was accused of a murder I didn't commit. I hate the Urgellans and the Tzuracians who've pursued me like a hound.' He spat in disgust on the ground. 'I can't wait to start wiping out my enemies.'

'You won't have to wait long, comrade,' Tarhaz sneered as he returned the empty flask cap.

Yarron jumped at the chance to find out more. While rinsing out the cap and screwing it back on the flask, he asked, 'So what's the plan for this battle? Where will it be? Are we joining up with other troops somewhere in the galaxy? Or will it just be us and these natives?'

Suddenly Tarhaz grabbed Yarron by the sleeve and jerked him off the boulder, flinging him to the hard ground and diving with him. He pressed his finger to his own tight lips to indicate silence. 'Ankrodians!' Tarhaz whispered. 'About fifty yards north of us.'

Still lying low, Yarron and Tarhaz peered cautiously around a large slate boulder nearby to observe a hunting party of six Ankrodians strolling across the mountain range. From appearances, the hunters were returning with a fresh kill of a large beast. Two Ankrodians were carrying it by means of a wooden pole mounted on their shoulders, leaving the beast to hang upside down with its four legs strapped by their fetlocks over the pole. While they journeyed, the animal's blood oozed freely from its many wounds.

Keeping a safe distance out of sight from the hunting party, Yarron and Tarhaz followed the fresh blood trail for half a mile, which eventually led them to a communal cave hidden among jagged rock formations. As the hunters carried the bounty towards the cave, a horde of natives swarmed around the hunting party with their catch in a frenzy of excitement. Within minutes, a pit fire was roaring in front of the large cave and the beast was prepared for roasting.

'Tarhaz, do you want to mark this place on the map and continue searching for more tribes?'

'Yeah,' he replied, quickly unfolding the weatherproof compact chart and inking a black 'X' on the coordinates. 'Let's go.'

As they journeyed with more caution, Yarron started up the conversation again. 'So Tarhaz, you never got the chance to tell me more about the battle. Where and when is it happening?' Yarron asked eagerly.

'I don't know ... all I've heard is once we get these tribes, we're headed to Terra something.'

Yarron had to contain his shock. He couldn't believe what he was hearing. His mind was reeling. *It might be Terra Iota but more likely Terra Major, Earth. General Dakhar's fleet and the Xytrinium reserves must be the stronghold they were planning to conquer. The situation was serious.*

Yarron was engrossed in deep thought when Tarhaz leaned towards him and in his foul breath added, 'Yeah, and some of the soldiers said there's another Treldarian general across the Universe gathering an army to join us. It'll be big!'

Yarron rubbed his hands, feigning delight. *This must be the rebel army from the Eastern Quadrant – the army he had already forewarned General Dakhar about. He must send another message to Dakhar telling him about the second army – and soon. He would do this as soon as he returned to Mankro.*

Deep in thought, Yarron didn't see the spear streak past him from out of nowhere and skewer Tarhaz's right thigh. Tarhaz let out a blood-curdling scream before collapsing to the ground in excruciating pain. Yarron spun around to see a furious Ankrodian native bearing down on them at full running speed, wielding a tomahawk and shouting a war cry. With speed reflexes Yarron drew his laser pistol and fired at point blank range, the fatal blast felling the big warrior. The Ankrodian landed at Yarron's feet with a smouldering hole in his forehead.

'What have you done, Armel?' Tarhaz cried out, writhing in pain.

'What I do best, Tarhaz,' said Yarron clinically. 'I kill those who want to kill me.'

Tarhaz knew Captain Chekhmar and feared the repercussions. 'Captain Chekhmar won't like this,' he groaned.

'The Captain would have done the same thing in the situation. Better to save the lives of two soldiers than the life of a savage.' Yarron was calm and confident.

Tarhaz had to agree. Gripped by pain, he responded only with a nod.

'Let's look at this wound to see what the damage is. The savages will have heard your scream, so we need to get out of here quickly.'

Kneeling beside his partner Yarron saw a barbed bone spearhead piercing through Tarhaz's thigh and protruding out the other side of his leg.

'Well, Tarhaz, the good news is that while the spear is lodged in that position it's preventing blood loss.'

'What's the bad news?' cried Tarhaz, still writhing in pain.

'Well, the bad news is if we're to escape these barbarians, I need to remove it, *now*.'

'Alright, just do it,' replied Tarhaz gritting his teeth and forcing a brave face.

'Okay, Tarhaz, bear with me.'

Yarron ripped off one of the Treldarian's shirt sleeves and tore it into several long strips. Grabbing the short bone dagger from the dead savage, he wrapped one of the pieces of cloth around Tarhaz's leg above the wound and twisted the ends with the dagger to make a tourniquet.

'Brace yourself soldier, this will be painful. I'm going to laser off the spearhead and pull the shaft back carefully through the entry point. You might want to bite on your leather belt.'

Tarhaz awkwardly slid the thick belt from around his waist, folded it in three and clenched his teeth tightly over it.

'Ready?' said Yarron.

Tarhaz nodded his head several times in response while grimacing.

Yarron unholstered his pistol and blasted the shaft of the spear just above the spearhead, severing it from the shaft and simultaneously cauterizing the wound on one side. 'Now I'll pull the shaft out on a count of three. One …'

Yarron didn't wait for the full count. He quickly pulled the wooden shaft out from the other side, before Tarhaz knew what was happening.

'Aargh!' screamed Tarhaz, biting down harder on the leather strap, muffling sounds of agony as large beads of sweat dripped from his brow.

After pulling the shaft free, Yarron quickly wrapped the wound tightly with the remaining shirt strip. 'Right,' he said, 'let's see if you can stand.' As Yarron helped Tarhaz to his feet, he handed him the spear shaft. 'Use this to support yourself. Now let's get the hell out of here.'

Slowly and painfully the two hobbled back to the ship, Yarron supporting Tarhaz around his waist with Tarhaz's arm draped over Yarron's neck and shoulders.

Darkness had fallen by the time they arrived back at the Treldarian battleship, exhausted. The ship, a virtual mobile barracks and gunship, was essentially a metal hull stripped internally of all comforts to maximise munitions storage and increase its speed. Luckily, it was fitted out with a well-equipped medical facility or infirmary for the treatment of the seriously wounded.

Once inside, they were confronted by Captain Chekhmar and the other Treldarians who had all returned earlier from their reconnaissance. The captain noted the blood-drenched trouser-and-rag tourniquet on Tarhaz's right leg with displeasure. 'What happened to you two? I hope you haven't stirred up an ant's nest!' he said angrily.

Before they could speak, Tarhaz collapsed unconscious to the floor.

'Sergeant Kasell! Get this soldier to the Med Unit for treatment at once!' the captain ordered roughly. 'And *you*, Urgellan, sit down and tell me exactly what happened.'

By the time Yarron had told his story, Chekhmar was livid. He paced back and forth, waving his arms about, cursing and uttering unintelligible sounds of anger. 'You've jeopardised this mission, *bounty hunter*, by disobeying a direct order not to attack the natives.'

'We were attacked without warning by a stray hunter. I acted in self-defence to save our lives, sir,' said Yarron defensively.

'Don't interrupt me when I'm talking!' shouted Chekhmar who was now red-faced and fuming. He continued to analyse the situation, talking out loud to himself. 'We came in peace seeking a joint alliance. But, by the time the word spreads to the other tribes, they'll want to rise up against us to seek revenge. What a mess you've created *bounty hunter*. My soldiers have already identified five tribes, and we may have found many more tomorrow. Thanks to you, it's too late to convince these tribes of our offer now.'

Raising his voice and pointing his finger threateningly at Yarron he demanded, 'What are *you* going to do to resolve our dilemma, Urgellan, seeing as *you're* the cause? I should send you out alone to make peace with these tribes!'

The other Treldarians nodded, agreeing with the captain's proposal. 'Yeah, yeah, send him back!' they jeered.

'Well, sir,' Yarron said calmly, 'if you're asking me, I have a better idea.'

Captain Chekhmar stopped pacing and turned on the spot, folding his arms in a defiant manner while staring into Yarron's eyes waiting for his miracle answer. 'Okay, I'm all ears, *Urgellan.*'

'I wouldn't trust these savages at all. From what I've just experienced, they could turn on your soldiers in battle. I'm not sure what the Nujharenes are like, but I'd focus my efforts on them. They can't be as volatile as these backward Ankrodians.'

Chekhmar raised an eyebrow. Yarron could see he was seriously considering the possibility. Yarron also noticed the anxious expressions of the other soldiers – after seeing the blood-soaked injury to their comrade, they didn't want to risk their lives relying on these volatile primitives.

After a long silence the captain responded, 'You have a point, Urgellan.' He sensed the stranger's physical strength and mental insight. 'There's no guarantee we can recruit these savages to become our allies. They'll be unpredictable under battle conditions and it's better to be safe than risk the lives of my soldiers.' Then he laughed out loud, saying, 'Those savages wouldn't know what to do with the spoils anyway.'

He turned to face the others. 'I'm aborting our mission on Ankrod. We'll concentrate our efforts on persuading the clans on Nujhar. The Nujharenes are a far more advanced civilisation, and I think we'll have more success with their allegiance. Prepare for departure. We're heading to Nujhar.'

Yarron breathed a sigh of relief. *He'd avoided personal retribution and stalled the formation of a larger enemy army.*

NUJHAR

TRAVELLING at hyperspeed, Captain Chekhmar and his Treldarian army reached the moon of Nujhar within two days. Nujhar was quite a contrast from the moon they had just left. The upper swirling atmosphere was tainted with a green hue. Instead of lightning bolts striking with massive electrical intensity, the gases reflected a form of sheet-lightning which flared up intermittently throughout the swirling clouds. The ship's computer showed the moon's crust contained concentrations of various metals, a high percentage being copper with smaller amounts of tin, manganese, zinc and aluminium. The topographical landforms comprised both extinct and active volcanoes amid mountain ranges and numerous lakes of varying sizes in the valleys.

Nearing the planet, Captain Chekhmar prepared his troops by describing what he knew of the Nujharenes. 'Their skin colour has a pale greenish tinge due to centuries of exposure to copper metal and they have distinct mental, as well as emotional, capabilities. Nujharenes have the power to read thoughts between themselves and other species and they have a high tolerance for pain, making them formidable foes in battle.

'They have learnt to mix copper with other metals to produce light and strong bronze body-armour, swords and daggers. However, their long- and short-barrelled pistols are primitive and use highly inflammable black volcanic sulphur-powder to fire bronze pellets. The Nujharenes are yet to venture into the galaxies as their vehicles are powered only by organic fuel and they guard their moon with hostility towards uninvited visitors.'

As Chekhmar's ship approached the inner orbit of Nujhar the crew could easily identify from their altitude the carved contours of the planet. There were patches of bare and arid flat land where there were no signs of vegetation, most likely inhibited by the sulphur gases escaping from several active volcanoes.

Yet in other areas, there were lush forests and undergrowth probably thriving from the volcanic lava slowly eroded over eons of time by the rivers and washed downstream to build up rich, alluvial plains and valleys. It was certainly a planet of contrasting landscapes. The crew also sighted hundreds of villages, large and small, scattered amongst the forests and on the plains, some having paddocks growing grain or fenced in to contain livestock.

The battleship finally landed close to one of the large lakes surrounded by thick low-lying shrubbery. All those on board were fascinated by the lake's striking luminescent emerald-green colour.

Chekhmar gave similar orders to those issued on Ankrod for his soldiers to divide into pairs, find the locations of the Nujharenes and mark the co-ordinates on their maps. They were warned again not to engage the natives.

'I desperately need these fierce Nujharenes to reinforce our army. Anyone who disobeys this order will wish they hadn't been born, including *you*, Urgellan,' he stressed, glaring at Yarron. 'Now move out and return before sunset.'

This time, Yarron was paired with the Captain for obvious reasons, and it was an uncomfortable pairing. They made their way by foot over the rugged volcanic mountains and down into the heavily wooded valleys, all without exchanging a word. Shrills and shrieks of unseen creatures echoed every so often amongst the tall trees and thick undergrowth. Swarms of large bright-coloured insects buzzed fervently from treetop to treetop, while clouds of gnats flew close overhead, settling temporarily on the lush thickets heavily laden with small berries and wild fruits of vibrant colours.

On the slopes of the second valley, Yarron and Chekhmar needed to use their blades to slash through the dense foliage, while trying to maintain their stealth. Yarron sensed they were being observed by something hidden in the forest but keeping its distance.

Eventually they came to a sudden standstill as they reached the floor of the valley, and slowly lowered their blades to their sides. Standing before them were at least a hundred tall, solidly built, pale-green figures lined up in a semi-circle. They were armed with spears, swords and pistols, all aimed in their direction. Dull bronze breast armour with matching arm and shin plates covered the upper and lower parts of their bodies. Short leather tunics with plaited fringes hung loosely from their waists down to their knees.

Short, pointed noses matched their oversized tapered ears which sprang out from mopped heads of pure-white hair that trailed down to their shoulders. *More like an animal's mane,* thought Yarron. Some had faces streaked diagonally with ochre-coloured paint and Yarron was momentarily captivated by the Nujharenes' narrow, almond-shaped, green eyes which reflected the emerald-green colour of the planet's lakes. Their expressions were ruthless and cold. *Just as Captain Chekhmar had described.*

Yarron's mind was spinning with a defence plan. *They could try to outrun this war party, but they might encounter whatever was watching them from the forest. If they stood their ground, he would take out as many as he could before he was killed. But there was no way he and Chekhmar would survive an onslaught.*

Yarron slowly started to pull out his laser pistol with his left hand only to have it clapped frozen by Chekhmar.

'Don't do anything stupid, bounty hunter,' the Captain warned under his breath.

Chekhmar raised his left arm in front of him at head height and faced the palm of his hand towards the Nujharenes before speaking in a language Yarron had never heard before. Yarron was astonished not only by Chekhmar's knowledge with an alien language, but also by the fact that the natives all lowered their pistols.

Yarron was even more amazed when an older Nujharene, who was standing in the middle of the semi-circle, stepped slowly towards Chekhmar with his arms outstretched. The Captain responded by stepping forward to embrace him as they met. It was a remarkable sight; the rough Treldarian captain with his unkempt thick black hair and bushy beard clasping the tall solidly built pale-green figure with pure-white shoulder-length hair. A loud cheer of rejoicing resounded throughout the crowd. The Nujharenes raised their arms and held their weapons high in the air. *Obviously, this was a friendly welcome.*

When the noise subsided, only Yarron and Chekhmar were led through the shadowed valley, while the rest of the soldiers remained guarded by the tribe of Nujharenes. They travelled up a steep slope along a pathway winding through a heavily wooded forest, bathed in filtered sunlight. All the while they were treated to the constant sound of exotic whistles and shrieks from the menagerie of birds hidden in the treetops.

Upon reaching the top of one of the tallest peaks in the mountain range, which was set against a pale green sky, Yarron was in awe of what he encountered. Carved out of the volcanic rock was an enormous city which even the captain hadn't seen on his last visit to Nujhar. It was a hive of activity and, just like bees, large numbers of small vessels were entering and leaving tunnels hollowed into the sides of the mountains. Several tall towers sprung up from the rim of the mountains with large metal dishes affixed to their bases.

After another steep climb up a hundred or more wide, stone-carved stairs, they reached a large, flat area paved with stone blocks spread before a wide opening in the mountain. The entrance was supported by immense, towering rock pillars at least fifty feet in height and adorned with intricately-sculptured figurines in battle scenes – all holding shields and wielding swords, all bearing looks of anguish on their faces. Only a handful of the warriors escorted Chekhmar and Yarron through the wide opening and along a broad well-lit passageway.

After a short walk they were led into a huge cave converted into a throne room. A large and ornately decorated bronze throne-chair stood on a raised circular pedestal about twelve feet in diameter made of highly polished, grey-streaked volcanic rock. Rectangular panels of the same type of polished volcanic rock covered the floor and the walls. Large oblong panels of intense light embedded in the high ceiling, illuminated the room and gave the polished rock a reflective high sheen.

Surrounding the pedestal and facing the throne were twelve bronze chairs in a half circle. The two visitors were directed to be seated while the Nujharene escorts remained standing behind them. Seating himself on the throne-chair and clasping at his side a short staff with a sparkling green gemstone the size of a fist on the top of it, the leader of the pack issued instructions to one of his warriors. Then, smiling at Captain Chekhmar, he spoke in his native tongue and waited for the Captain to reply.

To Yarron's surprise, Chekhmar spoke fluently for some time before being interrupted by the return of the warrior who was carrying a tray of drinks. Both he and Chekhmar accepted a glass goblet filled with a dark-orange liquid and the conversation continued.

All Yarron could do was sit and listen while sipping on his drink, which was unexpectedly sweet and tasty, like some sort of nectar. As he scrutinised the leader's wrinkled face, Yarron detected five scarred parallel lines about a quarter of an inch apart running down each cheek and noted a small bronze ring through his pointed nose similar to the bronze rings in his pierced ear lobes. Yarron noticed every change of expression on the leader's face and was intrigued by the leader's glaring bright-green eyes and pointed ears that twitched intermittently and then flattened slightly like a wild hound's when he spoke in a louder voice.

After what seemed to be an hour of bartering, the conversation ended abruptly. The leader stamped his staff down hard on the stone floor beside his throne, rose from his throne chair and walked towards Chekhmar, smiling. In turn, Captain Chekhmar rose to embrace him. Then the leader shouted something to his warriors, and they all cheered with excitement.

Chekhmar leaned over and whispered in Yarron's ear, Yarron reeling from the rotten breath. 'Our mission has been successful. Stand up, Armel, we're off.'

Yarron was bewildered. He had no idea of what had just transpired.

Surrounded by pale-green warriors, Chekhmar and Yarron were ushered out of the cave and escorted back to their ship. As they journeyed, Chekhmar pulled a transceiver from his jacket pocket and opened communications to his troops. 'Captain

Chekhmar here. Return to the ship immediately! I'll be there in twenty minutes. Out!'

He returned the device to his pocket before filling Yarron in. 'The Nujharene leader, Kelfas, was reluctant at first to join our rebellion, not wanting to bring his planet and people to the attention of the Federation. However, when I offered shares in the Xytrinium reserves and assistance in building interplanetary space vessels and advanced laser weapons in return for their support, he pledged his allegiance. Kelfas has given us two thousand warriors. You were right, Armel, to advise me to disregard the Ankrodian barbarians and to focus on the more advanced Nujharenes.'

'Thank you, Captain, glad I could be of service.' Yarron was concerned by the growing enemy numbers and amazed at how straightforward the negotiations had been. 'I'm curious about one thing though.'

'What's that?'

'How come you speak fluent Nujharene and received such a warm welcome by Kelfas? I feared we were about to be slaughtered.'

The Captain grinned. 'When I first arrived here several years ago as a young lieutenant, there was disharmony amongst the now-united tribes of the Nujharene. Constant wars over territory were being waged and we Treldarians landed our ship right in the middle of it, unaware and unprepared. After leaving our ship to explore this new world we were captured by one of the tribes, led by Kelfas. They kept us hostage for a month deciding what to do with us. Kelfas knew if he killed us or let us go, more Treldarians might come and destroy their world.

'Kelfas was trying to make peace with the other tribes but had achieved little success. So, while being kept under guard, I learnt their language and offered to be an independent peace negotiator. Eventually I was able to persuade Kelfas I was on his side and would convince the other tribes to live as a united race, working together to build an empire. In time, I succeeded in bringing peace. Kelfas was forever grateful to me for saving his people from destroying themselves. Kelfas believes he's now honouring a debt his people owe the Treldarians.'

Despite his distaste for Chekhmar, Yarron was impressed. *There was clearly another side to Captain Chekhmar – or at least to the Chekhmar of old.*

'I asked Kelfas to have his warriors ready to board our warships when we return. I'm sure General Rokan will be pleased with the reinforcement of two thousand Nujharene warriors, though I'm not sure if we'll have enough laser weapons to replace those antiquated pistols they're presently using. Anyway, good advice, Armel. You may prove useful yet.'

On the flight back to Mankro, Yarron had a lot to think about. *He needed to warn General Dakhar, urgently. He would use his Sentinel ring with an ultra-high-pitched frequency to avoid detection by the Treldarians' less-sophisticated communication equipment. But how and when would he be able to escape from his captives without getting caught or killed?*

* * *

It was nightfall when Chekhmar's ship docked back on Mankro. Captain Chekhmar dismissed his soldiers and headed off at once to report to General Rokan.

Trying not to attract attention, Yarron strolled casually back to his Destroyer. He scanned the peripherals to make sure no one was watching, boarded his vessel, locked the entry hatch behind him and retrieved his Sentinel ring. Feeling apprehensive, he kept his high-frequency transmission to Dakhar short and sharp, ensuring he included all the crucial information.

'… That's as far as I know, General Dakhar. I'll be in contact when I have more,' he said as he signed off.

While trying to sleep that night, Yarron's mind was in turmoil questioning his future. *He was caught between the rebellion and the Federation. If he left Mankro, where would he go? To Terra Major? To Tzurac? Or should he just turn his back on them all and let them fight it out? After all, he was still a fugitive and there was no guarantee he would be pardoned by the Tzuracians if he survived the battles. Perhaps he could find a place to hide and live out the rest of his life in isolation? No, he had an obligation to help the Sentinels. He would decide in the morning when he would leave and in which direction he would head.*

Night passed and Yarron awoke after a short but deep sleep. He prepared himself for the day, ate a light meal and ventured out towards the village to find out more about when the Treldarian armada would be departing.

On entering the village through the tall open gates, he was immediately surrounded by at least twenty Treldarian solders, with their weapons armed and targeting him. They were led by Captain Chekhmar whose face appeared stone cold under his unkempt black hair and beard.

'Bounty hunter, you're under arrest! Hand over your weapons!' Chekhmar demanded with hatred in his voice, striking Yarron with a backhand across his face, his rings leaving stinging red marks on Yarron's cheek.

Yarron did as he was ordered. *Had they discovered his true identity? Or intercepted the message he'd sent?* As they bound his hands behind his back with chain-links and marched him to General Rokan's hut, Yarron now feared for his life.

Chekhmar pounded three times on the solid wooden door before the door slowly opened. Standing at the entrance was Bhalar, calm and aloof as always.

'We've brought the bounty hunter to see the General.'

As before, Chekhmar was told to wait outside with the door closed.

After a brief moment, the door opened again. Then Yarron and Chekhmar with his six soldiers were ushered upstairs. As they arrived at the doorway at the top of the stairs, General Rokan ordered all of them to come into the room. He was standing confidently, arms folded behind his back, glaring at Yarron with burning eyes. And, he had discarded his stick – thanks to the rejuvenating effects of the Xytrinium infusion, he no longer needed it.

'You traitor!' the General shouted aggressively. 'What was in the transmission you sent last night? Tell me now or we'll torture you for the answer and find out exactly who you are, where you're from and what your real intentions are!'

Yarron remained silent. He was willing to be sacrificed to save the Sentinels.

Without warning, Chekhmar struck Yarron's head from behind using the hilt of his sword. 'Answer the General, bounty hunter!' he yelled, as Yarron fell to his knees, semi-conscious.

The Captain was about to strike again when Rokan raised his hand. 'Stop, Captain, beating him won't help extract the information. We have better ways of making him talk. Take him to the lockup for now. We'll deal with him later.'

Chekhmar restrained himself, cursing under his breath, 'Yes, General! Alright soldiers, you heard the General. Move out!'

Two of Chekhmar's soldiers grabbed the groggy captive by his arms, lifted him up and started to walk him out the door, with the others following behind.

'Chekhmar,' Rokan called to his Captain, detaining him out of earshot from the others. 'Advance our plans. We leave in the next couple of days.'

Bhalar had heard every word while hiding, unnoticed in the shadows.

* * *

Yarron was thrown into a small hut with iron bars on the walls, ceiling and floor, which served as a primitive prison cell. Secured in binding chains, it was impossible for him to escape. His mind was racing again. *He couldn't believe the Treldarians had the technology to detect his ultra-high frequency transmission. How could he help the Sentinels now? And what torture did the Treldarians have in store for him? Even if they found out he was a Sentinel fugitive, they wouldn't hand him over to the Federation to collect the bounty. They'd execute him. He was doomed.*

OPPORTUNITY

THROUGH the bars of his cage Yarron could see the Treldarians preparing for their assault, loading weapons and supplies into their land vehicles in readiness to transfer onto their ships. As the afternoon wore on, the Sentinel fugitive prepared himself for torture and probable death, drawing on his basic psychological training. He went into deep meditation, numbing his senses, slowing his heart rate, and switching his mind into a semi-hypnotic state to feel no pain and to dispel all fear.

A few hours later something tapping on metal suddenly brought him back to his surroundings. Opening his eyes, all he could see was the blackness of the night and Bhalar's sweet face peering through the barred door of his cage. She was holding a finger to her lips, gesturing silence. Yarron was surprised to see her, and in the cramped space, scrambled over to her on his knees.

'Don't make any sound,' she whispered. 'I'm here to help you escape and also to help *me* escape. I've brought your weapons with me. Give me your hands so I can unlock your chains.'

Yarron was puzzled but responded quickly. His hands were secured behind his back. So, turning around with his back facing her he stretched his arms out towards her.

Before Bhalar acted, she added, 'I'll only help you if you promise to take me with you.'

Yarron needed no time to consider her proposition. 'You have my word.'

Bhalar unlocked Yarron's chains before gingerly edging the cage door open, trying to minimise the high-pitched squeaking of the partly corroded hinges. Yarron stepped through the doorway, quickly strapped on his laser pistols, then sheathed his short sword and boot dagger.

Crouching low, and under cover of darkness, the pair made their way with stealth towards Yarron's battleship. No soldiers were standing guard and there were no Treldarians roaming in the village. Everyone appeared to be congregating in one of the larger well-lit huts where rowdy music and frivolities were in full swing. Keeping to the shadows, they passed through the large gates that fortified the village and moved quickly towards the area where all the ships were assembled.

Reflexes brought Yarron to a sudden halt when he spotted the three Kyroni standing by their vessel barely fifty yards from them. They, in turn, sighted Yarron and his accomplice.

'Get behind me, Bhalar,' said Yarron abruptly, brushing her aside. 'This could get ugly.' In order to avoid the noise of his laser pistol, he drew his staff-sword, activating the double-edged blade.

As Yarron finished speaking, the Kyroni drew their scimitars and bolted towards him. The first one came charging with his outstretched sword in front of him, his blade aimed directly at Yarron's upper body. Just as the tip of his blade was about to pierce Yarron's chest, Yarron twisted sideways with incredible speed and dropped to one knee, drawing his dagger from its ankle-sheath with his left hand. The Kyroni's blade passed within a hair's breadth of Yarron's shoulder as Yarron sliced across the Kyroni's abdomen, his razor-sharp blade gashing the bared flesh. The assailant was dead before he hit the ground.

Yarron sprang to his feet and somersaulted over the oncoming second assailant, slashing his double-edged sword across the Kyroni's neck and shoulder. The blow severed the assailant's carotid artery, leaving him to bleed out as he collapsed heavily to the ground.

Landing steadily on his feet, the Sentinel set himself ready for the final encounter. To his surprise, this Kyroni didn't charge like the others. Yarron recognised Harjar as he paced slowly towards him with a scimitar in each hand, slicing the air in a rapid figure-eight pattern.

Yarron stayed silent and focused, planning his attack as Harjar bellowed, 'So traitor, you may have escaped your prison, but you'll not escape your death tonight. I suspected you were a liar when I first encountered you on Krima.'

Just before the moment of contact, Yarron sprang high into the air and with a twisting somersault knocked one of Harjar's swords from his grip, leaving a deep gash across the back of the Kyroni's hand. Yarron landed on his feet behind the wounded Kyroni and threw his dagger with incredible force as Harjar turned to face his opponent. The Kyroni's reflexes were too slow, and the fast-speeding dagger pierced through his bare chest and plunged into his heart.

Harjar stood motionless for a moment, in shock, clasping the dagger's handle, 'Ah …' He managed to pull the dagger free, but then started to sway, blood gushing from the wound. Yarron watched as his opponent collapsed and gasped his last breath of air. Then Yarron, showing no sign of emotion, sheathed his sword and retrieved his blood-stained dagger, wiping the blade clean on Harjar's leather trousers.

Bhalar ran out of the darkness and overcome with fear and emotion, threw herself instinctively into Yarron's arms. 'Thank you, thank you,' she whispered.

'You're welcome, Bhalar,' he replied, squeezing her tightly to comfort her. For a brief interval the two escapees embraced in relief.

'Now, Bhalar,' said Yarron, 'help me drag these Kyroni over to their ship. We don't want them to be discovered until we're well on our way.'

Working together they managed to haul the limp heavy bodies away from the scene of the fight and heave them into the Kyroni ship. Snapping a small leafy branch from one of the nearby trees, Yarron brushed over the area, smoothing away the loose blood-stained soil, the footprints and all signs of the scuffle. When finished, he cast the branch into the undergrowth and grabbed Bhalar's hand firmly.

'That should do it,' he said in a hushed voice. 'Let's get out of here.'

Aboard Yarron's Destroyer, the pair quickly strapped themselves into the pilots' seats in the front cabin. Through the wide front and side portals Bhalar had an unimpeded view of the clear night sky settling on the horizon of the distant shadowed hills. On this particular night, Mankro was bathed in full exposure by the light reflected off the dead planet Dunkor. Bhalar kept her thoughts to herself about their untimely escape knowing Yarron's ship could be easily seen departing from the surface by anyone lingering outside the huts. Yarron might well have drawn the same conclusion, but Bhalar could tell by his determination he was not letting anything or anyone interfere with their escape.

Sitting silently, surrounded by computers, screens and other electronic equipment, Bhalar watched in fascination as Yarron toggled switches, flicked levers and pressed buttons. As each control was activated, different coloured lights illuminated on the console accompanied by electronic sounds. Yarron switched to stealth mode before igniting the blasters – *the last thing they needed was to alert the Treldarians and be pursued by them in one of their warships.*

'Comms, set coordinates for Terra Major. Launch the ship!'

The craft silently lifted off the surface and within seconds it was cruising to the outer orbit. Once his ship was safely out of visual range, Yarron engaged hyperdrive, and the craft vanished with a streak of multi-colours into the dark starry void of deep space.

For a while the two fugitives sat silently, waiting anxiously to see whether a Treldarian warship was in pursuit. The silence was intense.

When their anxiety dissipated and they were sure they were not being chased, Yarron turned to his Treldarian passenger. He wanted answers. 'Okay, Bhalar, why have you risked your life to save my hide? And why are you escaping with me? I don't understand.'

Bhalar's head was bowed, and her glistening straight black hair fell loosely around her shoulders. She smiled and responded in a soft voice, a voice very different from the harsh tones she had used when she first greeted Chekhmar and Yarron at the General's hut.

'It was me who detected the ultra-high frequency transmitted from your battleship last evening. I was the one who reported you. I'm deeply sorry for risking your life, Armel, but ...' she hesitated for an instant, '... but I was desperate.'

Yarron was confused – he was both angry and curious. '*You* detected my transmission? How so? You're a servant, aren't you?'

'No,' Bhalar said firmly, looking directly at him, 'I'm General Rokan's daughter.'

Momentarily stunned, Yarron stared at her in disbelief.

'*I am General Rokan's daughter*,' she repeated slowly, emphasising every word.

'Bhalar!' Yarron exclaimed. 'Do you realise what'll happen now? Your father will send a warship to pursue *me*, but he'll send his entire army to get *you* back.'

'No,' Bhalar said bitterly. 'He won't come after me. Our relationship as father and daughter deteriorated years ago. He'll be relieved to see the end of me. He thinks more of Chekhmar and his army than he does of me.'

'I still don't understand,' Yarron said, shaking his head.

'My mother died giving birth to me and I was raised by a midwife. My father hated the sight of me because I reminded him of the woman he loved and lost. Every word, every look he gave me showed his resentment.'

For an instant, Yarron detected a tear in Bhalar's eyes and then she spoke more harshly. 'He drank a lot and sometimes after drinking he beat me. My midwife tried to protect me, but she passed away when I was only fifteen. Then I had to fight to protect myself from my father and from Chekhmar and his sleazy soldiers who attempted to have their way with me. I despise Chekhmar. For the last twenty years my father has treated me like a servant woman – his personal slave. There was no escape.'

Yarron felt her anguish. 'I'm sorry, Bhalar.'

'I was forbidden to step foot outside his hut. So, to channel my frustration and despair, I practised my fighting skills every day and immersed myself in learning all about electronics. Technical equipment which had been salvaged from alien spacecraft, was stored in our hut and, over the years, I was able to make much of the equipment operational and piece together some basic alien phrases. For the last ten years I've been secretly sending out distress signals on high frequencies hoping to be rescued.

'My hopes were raised when, several months ago, Treldarians from the Eastern Quadrant landed on our moon, only to find they had not come for me. Instead, they were on a mission to find reinforcements for a rebellion against the Tzuracians.'

Yarron was absorbed in thought as the pieces of the puzzle fell into place. *So, the Treldarians from the Eastern Quadrant must have brought the infusion formula to General Rokan.*

'My hopes were rekindled when you and those Kyroni arrived in our village. I thought my signals had been picked up this time, only to learn otherwise once again. I was disheartened but desperate, determined to make the most of this opportunity. I needed to find a way of having you captured. Then I could help you escape and take me with you. Without knowing, you presented the perfect opportunity sending that transmission last night.'

Yarron interrupted, 'If you were able to monitor my transmission, were you also able to decipher the message?'

'Some of it. I know you alerted the Tzuracians to the planned Treldarian invasion of the planets Tzurac and Terra Major. But I took a chance on you and kept your secret. I sensed you had a good heart. I told my father only that you'd sent a transmission and not what it said.'

Yarron was impressed that Bhalar had deciphered a coded Sentinel message. *She was obviously highly intelligent and very capable.* 'Why, Bhalar? Why would you want to jeopardise the Treldarian attack?'

'Because I despise my father and his army,' she said coldly. 'So, I waited tonight for all the soldiers to join in the celebrations for the impending attack. I knew they'd be too indulged and intoxicated to notice our escape.' She relaxed a little before adding, 'I hadn't anticipated the three Kyroni interfering. You fight very well for a bounty hunter, Armel, if that's your real name.' She reclined in her pilot's seat with a knowing smile and an entranced look in her onyx eyes. *Bhalar was clearly perceptive as well.*

For a moment Yarron's thoughts were confused. *Bhalar seemed to be a truthful person who was seeking safety after suffering at the hands of her father and his Treldarian army. However, he'd been betrayed before by a beautiful female with hidden motives.* The scar on his neck began to burn, snapping him back to reality. *He must be cautious about trusting her.*

Yarron turned to look at Bhalar who was staring at him, making him feel guilty about his thoughts. He deliberately avoided the question about his identity.

'Well, Bhalar, I thank you for helping me escape. I was preparing myself for torture and certain death until you freed me. I'm pleased I could answer your call for help, even if unintentionally. So, I guess we're in this together now.'

They exchanged knowing glances and a warm smile and Yarron began to relax. 'It's a long journey to Terra Major, Bhalar, so you'll have plenty of time to make yourself at home and explore the ship. We could even practise some martial arts together to hone our fighting skills. As a fugitive, I'll need to keep constant vigilance for Federation patrols. And next time I may need your help to fight off assailants,' he said, smiling. They both saw the humour in this. 'For now, though, are you hungry? Would you like a drink?'

'Yes, Armel, after what's happened tonight, I'm famished.'

Yarron was fascinated by her soft seductive voice.

'Maybe you could tell me more about yourself over a meal, Armel?' she prodded, talking with her eyes.

They climbed out of their seats and headed for the small galley towards the centre of the craft, leaving the ship on autopilot. While Bhalar refreshed herself in the cleansing compartment near their sleeping quarters at the rear of the ship,

Yarron prepared their meals from the well-stocked pantry. His mind was turning over. *He'd been attracted to Bhalar from the moment she first opened the door of Rokan's hut. Yet he must keep his emotional distance. After all, he'd let his feelings interfere with his logic once before in the company of a beautiful woman, with dire consequences.*

Sitting across from each other at the compact dining table in the galley after finishing their meal, Bhalar opened the conversation. She was curious. 'You say you're an Urgellan, Armel, yet you sent a transmission in Tzuracian code. We're in a ship which bears no insignia of origin, yet all the controls are labelled in Tzuracian symbols. I recognise them from some of the salvaged equipment I've worked on. So, I think …' she said, smiling, '… I think you're either a very good liar or you've stolen a Tzuracian vessel, or both.' She stared directly into Yarron's steel-blue eyes to observe his reaction, and she was struck by his handsome face and chiselled cheekbones.

Yarron felt slightly uncomfortable, and a smirk appeared unconsciously across his face. 'You're very observant Bhalar. This *is* a Tzuracian ship and the transmission I sent *was* in Tzuracian. For now, let's just say I have allegiance to the Federation even though I'm being hunted by them.'

Bhalar chuckled, 'Well, Armel, or whatever your real name is, you can trust me to keep your secrets. You're a very mysterious character – fascinating and likable – and I'd like to learn more about how you developed your extraordinary fighting skills. My skills are no match for yours.'

He was still taken by her beauty. 'Alright, Bhalar, in due course. For now, it's been a long day, and we need to get some sleep.'

As Yarron led the way to their sleeping quarters he added, 'I want to thank you again for rescuing me. I'm in your debt.'

'I'd like to thank *you* for rescuing me from a life of slavery,' Bhalar replied. 'I guess we're even,' she said with good humour and a sparkle in her eye.

Their rooms were well-appointed, each with a stylish, single bunkbed, infrared lighting for heating, an intercom system and airlock doors for security and privacy. After showing Bhalar how to operate all the devices in her room, Yarron bade her goodnight and retired to his room across the passageway. Their doors slid shut automatically, making an air cushioning sound.

Lying in bed in the darkness in their own quarters both Yarron and Bhalar were thinking of each other. They were wondering how the voyage ahead would give them an opportunity to discover more about each other's character, intentions and feelings.

GRADUATION

GENERAL Dakhar's flagship and his four escort Destroyer battleships arrived on Tzurac two weeks after departing Terra Major. It was an historic event for the Tzuracians. They were welcoming Terranian allies to their soil for the first time and they were about to celebrate the graduation of fifty Sentinel cadets trained off base, at the Terra Major Officers Academy. The occasion symbolised a handshake across the universe, strengthening the newly formed bond between Terra Major (Earth), and the Federation of Planets.

As the flagship descended slowly to the air base, Kyron had a clear view of the metropolis of Khazor that sprawled beneath a faint opaque dome-shaped protective membrane – the Dome. The city was not what he expected from the visions he'd seen in his dreams after first wearing his father's Pledge ring. The images in his mind were those viewed through the eyes of his father Ahrmon, who had grown up in the old city over three hundred years ago while Khazor was still being restored after the Grekadian War. The stone walls of ancient buildings had now been replaced by tall cylindrical structures of metal and glass that glistened in the bright sunlight. Eight huge, sculptured towers with clear glass lifts scaling them surrounded a massive multi-storied complex in the centre of the city. Sleek long-barrelled silver laser-cannons, mounted on top of each of the towers were all aimed in defence of the multi-storied complex which Kyron surmised to be the Citadel.

After disembarking from Dakhar's flagship, the passengers and crew were directed into hover-shuttles which took them directly to the Citadel. Although Kyron didn't say anything to Torri, he was feeling slightly disorientated, experiencing a sense of *déja vous* as if he had been in Khazor before. The only logical explanation he could think of was that memories imprinted on a Sentinel's DNA are passed on from the parents to their children.

While Torri was in awe of this modern metropolis, she noticed the bewildered look on Kyron's face as they stepped from the now-stationary shuttle outside the Citadel. 'Are you alright, my love? You seem a little pale.'

'Yes, I'm okay. I'm just a bit overwhelmed at being back on the planet where my father was born. It feels very strange.' Shrugging off the thought, Kyron firmly clasped hands with his two very excited children, one on each side, and strode proudly with Torri towards the entrance of the Citadel.

All the regalia was in place. Numerous maroon and blue Tzuracian flags were fluttering in the gentle breeze high atop the walls of the Citadel. The Citadel was built around an ancient, cobbled courtyard and a wide red carpet lined with one hundred Sentinel soldiers in full battle dress stretched from the entrance to the courtyard. General Dakhar, along with his cadets and passengers, had now assembled.

The twelve stately Senators dressed in their distinguished robes – some in crimson and others in purple – greeted the General. They were delighted by his return to Tzurac after a fifteen-month absence and to see he had completely recovered from a near-fatal stab wound delivered by the vengeful Sentinel traitor, Khaneera Zarkwin. Hundreds of colourfully dressed Khazor citizens turned out to welcome the cadets and the newcomers from Terra Major. It was a perfect spring day to celebrate this memorable occasion.

The welcome parade followed the General and Senators into a huge reception hall in the centre of the Citadel. The hall was jam-packed with hundreds of chairs facing in the direction of a raised stage which stretched from one side of the hall to the other. A formal address had been prepared by the Committee of Senators. When all the visitors and citizens had filed into the hall, were seated and the noise subsided, the Elder, Senator Ghalbrak, the oldest and wisest in the Senate, approached the dais to deliver the address.

To the crowd, his appearance was quite distinctive. He was donned in a dark purple, velvet robe and, slightly bent with age, was supported by a tall staff. His long snow-white hair and matching long beard which covered most of his furrowed features, made him appear almost wizardly. There was an air of authority surrounding him which compelled the crowd to give him their full attention. The noise of the crowd had subsided, and the room was now in complete silence awaiting Ghalbrak's address. He spoke in Tzuracian with an interpretation for the visitors projected simultaneously onto a large screen.

'Welcome cadets and citizens of Terra Major. We've waited a long time to embrace the safe return of our cadets and to meet some of the newest members of the Federation. The citizens of Khazor will be accommodating the Terranians who have travelled here with the cadets and will help them settle into their new surroundings. We look forward to sharing our hospitality, friendship and knowledge and to the official graduation for our new cadets.

'The Tzuracians have a lot in common with the people of Terra Major and where there are differences in our culture, it will give us the opportunity to learn from each other and increase our understanding. The Senators and I look forward to meeting all of you personally during your short stay and hope you enjoy our company as well as the celebrations.'

The audience broke into applause which lasted for several minutes. Then Senator Ghalbrak motioned with a wave of his arm for General Dakhar to respond. Dakhar rose from his chair on the podium and approached the dais to make his announcement.

'Thank you, Senator. We're pleased to be here. I'm sure the citizens of Khazor will make everyone feel welcome.' He turned to the Senator and gestured by placing his hand over his heart. 'Now let's organise ourselves. Cadets with family here on Tzurac may return to them today after reporting to Staff Sergeant Drahmel for a leave pass. All other cadets are to report to the barracks. All cadets will present themselves on the parade ground at 0800 hours sharp tomorrow morning. For now, please enjoy some Tzuracian hospitality, catch up with family and make some new acquaintances.'

During the welcome Tajhira had been seated next to Kyron and Torri and their children with her six-year-old son Kyrah by her side. As the crowd dispersed and began to mingle, Tajhira turned to speak to Kyron and Torri.

'Well, my good friends, we're finally here together on Tzurac. How does it feel?' she asked sincerely in her gentle voice. She was a beautiful royal Urgellan with angelic features, wispy flaxen hair, violet eyes and a slender body—a fitting partner for the handsome General Dakhar. Her son Kyrah had also been blessed with his mother's looks and violet eyes.

'I'm overwhelmed to finally be here on Tzurac,' said Kyron. 'I'd seen the Citadel in my dreams, but it's more amazing in real life. I feel as if I'm home.'

'I'm pleased to hear that.' Tajhira turned to Torri. 'And you, Torri?'

'I'm happy we've all arrived safely,' she said, smiling, 'although I'm suffering a little from what we Earthlings used to call jet lag.'

'You'll feel better when we get you and the children to our house. Stay here for a moment and have something to eat and drink. I'll tell Ehrane we're leaving.'

Before Kyron and Torri had a chance to sample the Tzuracian cuisine, Tajhira returned, beaming.

'Why the smile?' asked Torri.

Tajhira pointed to the tables of food and, when Kyron and Torri turned their heads in the general direction, they spied Zuri, Ehrana and Kyrah stuffing themselves with multi-coloured cakes. Their mouths and hands were covered with lime-green goo.

'I guess we should rescue them before they make themselves sick,' said Tajhira, laughing. 'And then we'll be on our way. Ehrane will join us later after he finishes his official duties.'

'I just need to report to Sergeant Drahmel for a pass,' said Kyron.

'No need, Kyron,' replied Tajhira, 'Ehrane's already arranged your pass. We're free to go.'

'Thanks, Tajhira. Let's get the children.'

They left the Citadel in a small hover-vehicle travelling at high speed along gullies carpeted in lush greenery, surrounded by hills of trees swathed in autumn-coloured leaves of orange, yellows and rust browns. Even the wide glistening river they crossed over was crystal clear and small schools of fish could be easily seen darting away from the mild turbulence created by the hover-vehicle.

Within ten minutes they arrived at a magnificent ancient mansion. It was set high on a hill overlooking another valley containing a forest of vivid dark-green trees divided by an azure-blue snaking river.

Kyron strolled out to the lower-ground balcony with Torri and Tajhira, while Zuri and Ehrana raced off with Kyrah to explore the big house.

The view from the lower ground balcony was spectacular. Before them was a picturesque landscape of natural beauty with blue skies blanketing rolling, green plains in the distance. It reminded Torri of England before it became polluted, as shown to her in images by her parents. Tzurac was like a new Earth with clean fresh mountain air, clear skies, lush vegetation and the sound of chirping birds – nature in all its glory. *Perhaps we would enjoy living here*, Torri thought.

Standing beside Torri and Kyron on the balcony, Tajhira explained the history of the mansion. She described how it had been constructed from blocks of sandstone salvaged from the ruins of the ancient city of Khazor, before the new city was reconstructed at the end of the Grekadian War. Ehrane's grandfather, General Rhazon Dakhar, had wanted to retain the heritage of Tzurac by building the mansion as a monument to remind all Tzuracians of their lineage and their great achievements, both in peacetime and in war. And the mansion had been passed on through generations of the Dakhar family.

Inside their beautifully-architectured building, a wide intricately carved wooden staircase wound its way from the centre of the spacious smooth-stoned foyer to the upper level. This level housed numerous bedrooms and bathrooms as well as other functional rooms. Apart from the modern designed bathrooms, most of the rooms were lined with dark wood panelling adorned with collections of life-size portraits in large, gold-leafed frames. These portraits depicted Dakhar's ancestry of Sentinel officers with stern appearances all looking proud and dignified in their smart military uniforms.

'You have a beautiful home, Tajhira. You must have found it hard to leave it to come to a strange planet light years away?'

'Thank you, Torri. Yes, it was hard to part from my home. But when married to a high-ranking officer, you must accompany them wherever and whenever they're ordered to go. Besides, I wanted to be with Ehrane and to meet you and Kyron and your lovely children. You're all Ehrane talked about each time he returned from your world.'

Torri and Kyron smiled graciously.

'So would you two like to see your bedrooms and freshen up before Ehrane arrives?'

Torri and Kyron both nodded a 'thank you' as they drifted inside through the sculptured stone archway.

* * *

General Dakhar arrived home later in the afternoon, looking quite worried.

'Something wrong, my husband?' asked Tajhira in a serious tone.

He dismissed her concern, saying, 'Nothing to worry yourself about, dear' and turned to Torri and Kyron with a changed demeanour. 'Welcome to my home, my friends. I hope you find your quarters, I mean rooms, to your liking.' Then, chuckling, he added, 'Don't get too comfortable Kyron. You may be spending more time in the barracks with the other cadets while we're here.'

After dinner, Zuri and Ehrana excused themselves and went off to play again with Kyrah. Torri and Tajhira went upstairs, while Dakhar and Kyron retired to the den for a more private discussion.

After pouring two glasses of strong fortified wine, Dakhar got down to business. Kyron saw an unfamiliar worried look cross his friend's face and sensed trouble as Dakhar suppressed his voice into a low whisper.

'Kyron, what I'm about to tell you is confidential. You mustn't say anything to anyone until the Senate makes a formal statement. Do I have your word?'

Frowning unconsciously, Kyron raised a curious eyebrow before answering in a quiet voice, 'Of course, Ehrane. What's worrying you?'

'Early this afternoon, I received another transmission from Yarron.'

Kyron stopped sipping his wine and listened intently while Dakhar spoke in the same low whisper.

'The transmission was brief, but alarming.'

Kyron was now even more intrigued and stared at Dakhar with set eyes and a clenched jaw, waiting to hear just how serious the communication from the Sentinel fugitive was.

'Yarron has just uncovered plans of the Treldarians who *are* intending to launch a full assault on the Federation, striking Tzurac and Terra Major.'

Kyron was shocked and took a moment to digest Ehrane's words. 'Are you sure about the accuracy of this information, my friend?'

Dakhar nodded solemnly in the affirmative, 'And that's not all.' He spoke his next words slowly and precisely. 'They have in their possession the formula for Xytrinium infusions.'

Kyron shook his head in disbelief. 'They have the Xytrinium formula? How in the Gods' names did they get hold of it? Did Yarron say where they got it from? Or who gave it to them? If it's true, we have to prepare for an onslaught of super-soldiers.'

Dakhar sat silent for some time, stroking his beard and searching his mind before continuing, 'No, he didn't say how they got hold of it, and you're right my friend, we *do* have to prepare ourselves for an invasion of a super-army. I've already dispatched a reconnaissance warship to the Eastern Quadrant but they're still *en route* and as yet, they've nothing to report.'

Kyron was still staring hard at Dakhar as Dakhar continued. 'I have a rough plan for a battle strategy, and I'd like your thoughts. I need to present it to the Senate Council first thing tomorrow morning. We have to act swiftly.'

'Fire away.'

'According to Yarron, we have a small window of time to organise ourselves in preparation for the invasion. Our enemies are still gathering forces and have a long distance to travel. I want to continue with the graduation. When my new officers are sworn in, there'll be more First Officers at my disposal.'

'That's if you can trust Yarron's word,' Kyron interjected.

'Well, his 'intel' hasn't let us down so far.'

'Agreed. And I know from personal experience, he's on our side.' Yarron had saved Kyron's life in the recent past.

'So, let's get started.'

Over some more strong nightcaps, Ehrane and Kyron worked late into the night, refining and honing an effective defence strategy. There was no sleep for the two Sentinels.

By the time they were satisfied with their plans, the morning sun was edging over the horizon and fingers of sunlight were creeping through narrow openings between the heavy drapes. Drawing on their reserve Sentinel energy, they prepared themselves for the day and left the mansion before the others had even woken.

Arriving at the Citadel just before 0600 hours, Kyron went to the parade grounds, while Dakhar headed straight to the Elder, Senator Ghalbrak, to request an immediate Senate hearing.

Within an hour, all twelve Tzuracian Senators dressed in their designated coloured robes were seated behind closed doors at a large translucent circular table in the Senate Room. The Elder signalled Dakhar to speak.

'Thank you for attending this meeting at short notice, Senators. The matter is extremely urgent. We're talking about the future of our planet and our people.'

Dakhar had gained their full attention. The Senators sat rigidly upright and listened intently. They looked distraught when he informed them about Yarron's message, and then resolute as he proceeded to outline his battle strategy.

'Senators, I believe the larger Treldarian force will be attacking Tzurac, while a smaller Treldarian army will be assaulting Terra Major. If we act immediately, we should have enough time to gather reinforcements from our allies, the Urgellans and the Armonusians. The combined forces should be sufficient to defeat the Treldarians who attack Tzurac.'

One of the senators interrupted, 'General, the Regiments stationed on Terra Major won't be enough to defeat the other Treldarian forces and their allies, even with the support of Terra Major's military.'

Senator Lhantar was one of the more senior members of the Senate who had been initially involved in the military arrangements for the establishment of the Citadel on Earth. He was familiar with the numbers of Sentinels stationed on that base and their military strength and spoke with some authority.

'You're quite right, Senator Lhantar. I agree.'

All the senators looked bemused. *What was General Dakhar thinking?*

'I've anticipated this,' Dakhar continued. 'I propose to activate the two thousand Diutrons we have hidden away on Planet Iota and send them to Terra Major under our control.'

There was a surprised hush. None of the senators expected that answer.

'You'll recall that the battle was won on Planet Iota after the enemy's giant robot Diutrons froze up during the attack. What some of you may not know is that, after the battle, I had Engineer Grant Thompson disable their electronic control circuitry and keep them securely locked in storage on Planet Iota. They can be resurrected if we request Thompson to reconfigure their circuitry for us to control. These eight-foot-high mechanical robots with thick Xytrinium amour plate and equipped with laser pulse cannons are almost indestructible. We might have lost the battle on Iota if we hadn't destroyed the ship controlling them. They're a perfect force to provide a strong reinforcement to our Sentinels and General Blake's soldiers on Terra Major. We can use what were once our enemy, as assets against the invaders. We won't stand a chance otherwise.'

Shocked by the threat of another major war on Tzurac, and the challenge of transporting the Diutrons to Earth, the senators began heated discussions.

Dakhar let them talk for a few minutes before raising his voice above the noise to silence them. He spoke with confident authority. 'I recommend we move our fleet of warships and Destroyer battleships to the hidden side of our closest moon, Jorhan. Our vessels will wait in that position in 'cloak' mode ready to surround and annihilate the Treldarian armada once they enter Tzurac's orbit.

'In the event that the enemy manages to evade our ambush, we still have the protective Dome, but the contingency will be to move our citizens and the visiting Terranians to our underground tunnel network for their protection. We need our armies in readiness for ground combat should it come to this. If the Senate sanctions this battle plan, I'll take immediate action.'

Before the senators could respond he added, 'I have one last request, if I may Senators. I want to continue with the graduation of the cadets and assign them as First Officers to their respective Fleet Commanders and their Destroyer battleships.'

'Do we have time for this?' asked the Elder, obviously concerned.

'Yes, Senator. According to Yarron Blandhar's advice, we should have just enough time to prepare.'

Senator Ghalbrak questioned Dakhar again with some concern, 'General, why are you putting your trust in a wanted fugitive who may be working with the enemy and giving us misleading information?'

Dakhar replied with more conviction in his voice. 'Because he has forewarned us in the recent past and proved without a doubt that he can now be relied upon to help save the Sentinels and the Federation from total destruction. He's the insider who's been giving us vital information about the intentions of the rebel Treldarian armies and who led us to the capture of General Dranz and the traitor, Kaneera Zarkwin. Yarron is trying to make amends for his past grave mistakes.'

After some debate the council finally agreed unanimously to implement Dakhar's plan, nominating Senators Volhardtz and Morzhan – the same emissaries who had undertaken a similar mission just over fifteen months ago – to negotiate with the Urgellans and the Armonusians. They were selected because of their language and diplomacy skills and their membership of the legal fraternity.

Volhardtz, a tall and slim Tzuracian, with trim short greying hair and beard and pale blue eyes, was proficient in speech of five different languages. He could speak eloquently and was 'a natural' in diplomacy. He projected a warm face with a discerning look which captured all those who engaged in conversation with him.

Morzhan, who was noticeably shorter in stature than Volhardtz, was clean shaven with slightly longer blonde hair.

He'd studied the laws of the Ancients and was familiar with the esoteric wisdom of the past. He was the perfect candidate for an emissary to the Armonusians, having a deeper understanding of their way of life.

'You'll leave tomorrow,' Senator Ghalbrak directed them, before turning to speak to the group as a whole. 'We need to act swiftly and decisively. Haste is on our side and surprise is our ally – we need to make the most of the small window of opportunity we have. There's no time to waste!' He paused for a moment before concluding, 'We also need to be discreet with our operations. We don't want to start a panic. Initially, it must look as though we're simply preparing for the graduation ceremony. May the spirits of the Ancients protect and guide us all!'

As soon as the meeting adjourned, General Dakhar headed for his office in the Citadel and activated his Pledge ring to holograph Captain Zawkon, the acting Commanding Chief of Military Operations at the Terra Major outpost.

The smoky holographic image cleared to show a ruggedly handsome veteran warrior with a six-foot muscular frame and broad chest. He had a well-kept full beard and long and thick fair hair pulled back into a tightly plaited ponytail and his face bore many faded battle scars. He was an admired and respected soldier whom Dakhar trusted implicitly.

In their brief exchange, Dakhar forewarned Zawkon of the imminent threat and outlined the battle strategy. '… So that's the plan, Zawkon. Use your discretion on the finer details. From here on, all communications are restricted to Sentinel Pledge rings. Out.'

In turn, Zawkon holographed one of his officers on Planet Iota. 'Captain Skarhdok, this is acting Commanding Chief Zawkon,' he said in his deep voice. 'Prepare your defences immediately for a possible assault by enemy forces. Tell your soldiers it's a drill and you have orders from me to test their efficiency. Find Engineer Grant Thompson, *urgently* and holograph me when you find him. I'll be standing by.'

'Yes, sir! Right away!'

Within minutes, the captain holographed Zawkon. He was standing with the Irish engineer beside him. Thompson was a reasonably tall and well-built man with a leathery face, green eyes, wild unkempt red hair and a rough stubble growth of red bristles.

'Hello, young lad,' Grant blurted out in his distinctive dialect, 'and congratulations on ya promotion. I s'pose this ain't a social chat.' The good-humoured Irishman had a beaming smile. 'Surely you'd be wantin' sometin' if I'm not mistaken?'

'It's good to hear your jovial accent again, Grant, and yes, I would be *wantin' sometin.'* This is an urgent request direct from General Dakhar.'

Grant replied more seriously, 'Okay, I'm listnin'. You've got me undivided attention, lad.'

'I want you and your engineers to re-activate the Diutrons and reprogram their memory for Tzuracian control.'

There was dead silence.

Zawkon was anxious for a moment. 'You still have them, don't you Grant?'

'Yeah, yeah, indeed I do,' replied Thompson, 'but they're under wraps.'

'Well, I need them here on Earth ready to go as soon as possible. Believe me Grant, it's a matter of life and death. I'm sending some of my warships to collect them. They should reach you within a fortnight, travelling at hyperspeed. Can you arrange this in time?'

'It's a tall order Cap'n, but I'll do me' best. We'll prepare as many as we can.'

'Thanks, Grant. I knew I could rely on you. Zawkon, out.'

As the holograph faded, the ever-optimistic Irishman turned to Captain Skarhdok, 'Well, I'd better get crackin' lad if we're to meet the deadline. Holy Mother Mary! Sometin' very serious is happnin'.'

KYRONIS & DIUNON

ON the other side of the Universe, General Vark and his armada of six heavy black warships were halfway to their destination of planet Kyronis. Vark was determined to expand his Treldarian forces by freeing the Kyroni from Sentinel martial law.

Suddenly, in the still of the vast empty space, a lone Tzuracian patrol warship was detected on the long-range sonar.

'General, see this!' Ramlok called out in surprise. It was unusual to see Tzuracians this far from their home planet and this far into the Eastern Quadrant.

'Incredible!' cried Vark. 'What are they playing at? You were right, Ramlok. They've come after us!' The General's hate and thirst for war flared within.

He acted immediately, ordering the release of one of the new Xytrinium warheads. *It was imperative he destroy the Tzuracian vessel before it discovered his armada.*

'Fire!'

Within minutes, a long-range missile armed with one of the Xytrinium warheads intercepted the Tzuracian vessel with devastating results. On the viewing screen the Treldarians watched the Tzuracian warship vaporise on contact, leaving no trace. Dakhar's reconnaissance ship was no more.

'Yes! Direct hit!' Vark gloated, raising a clenched fist as the crew cheered. *The secret of the Treldarians' surprise attack was safe*, or so he thought. 'Pity we can't thank them for giving us the opportunity to test our new weapon,' he said sarcastically. 'Imagine what our warhead will do to Khazor's protective shield.'

The crew laughed and bellowed at the thought, Ramlok laughing the loudest. They were hungry for action.

* * *

Vark's armada continued uneventfully – detecting no other Tzuracian vessels in the vicinity – until they finally arrived at planet Kyronis in the Northern Quadrant. There, orbiting in stealth mode, Vark's soldiers prepared for battle.

Vark broadcast his final orders to the other five warships over the Comms system. 'Attention, Captains, this is General Vark. Our mission is to eliminate the Sentinels who are controlling the capital city, Vexar. Take no hostages except for high-ranking officers I'll use for interrogation. Once the Sentinels are eliminated, free the imprisoned Kyroni soldiers and wait for my ship to land. If you find Kyroni volunteers who want to join our cause, bring them too. All will be infused with Xytrinium.

'As planned, select seventy soldiers from each warship and send them in scout ships to the chosen locations we mapped out on the planet's surface. From those locations, work your way towards the centre of the city, eliminating the Sentinels as you proceed. I want this operation to be quick and clean!

'Captain Tarken, you'll take command of the ground attack. Inform me when we've taken the city, and I'll land my warship to collect the Kyroni. Just before you descend, I'll be jamming all signals other than Treldarian transmissions from Kyronis. You have your orders. Now go!'

On the main screen, General Vark watched more than forty small scout ships dart like swarming wasps from the warships towards the planet's surface. Without warning, laser fire ignited from the Federation's ground defences as the ships neared the planet's surface. Most made it safely to ground, but two scout ships took a direct hit. They went into a spin with black smoke trailing behind as they spiralled and crashed onto the surface.

Vark cursed out loud, 'Damn these Sentinels!'

Captain Tarken's scout ship was first to land near the city. He broadcast at once to his other landing parties. 'This is Captain Tarken speaking. All ships report in immediately, in sequence.'

There was no response. He repeated his transmission.

Then the pilot from the first ship responded, 'Gharmox here. We've landed safely. Sentinel units are patrolling within the city limits and around the outer boundaries. I'll start leading my soldiers into the hub of the city and take out the Sentinels as we go.'

'Good, Lieutenant. We've lost two scout ships but continue your assault. Out.'

No sooner had the captain signed off, than a second transmission was received. 'Lukhan, sir! So far, so good. We're in the east corner of the complex and about to leave our vessel. I saw two ships take a hit and crash. I assume there'd be no survivors, but we'll check as soon as we've dealt with these Sentinels. Out.'

In turn, Tarken received confirmation from the other scout ships' leaders who had landed and were mobilising their soldiers in the pre-arranged areas.

On his main screen, Vark had a bird's-eye view as his rebel troops, all dressed in black, spilled from the scout ships and began converging on the city. He was keen to see how his 'super-soldiers' would perform with their new enhanced abilities.

To his great satisfaction, the advancing Treldarians were soon creating havoc. Bunkers and gun turrets, set up by the Tzuracians to maintain martial law, were being obliterated by grenades and laser pulse-cannons. Amid the grey smoke from incendiary grenades and fires from the burning buildings, Vark could see units of maroon-uniformed Sentinels darting through the streets, ducking and weaving to avoid the streaking green laser fire.

He could see some of his soldiers taking hits from the Sentinels' red laser fire and being defeated in close-quarter hand-to-hand combat. But their new strength and agility made them an equal match for the elite Sentinels, and outnumbering them two-to-one, Vark's soldiers were soon killing the Sentinels and taking prisoner only a handful of high-ranking officers. *The Xytrinium infusion had worked better than he'd anticipated and his confidence in defeating their old archenemy was growing.*

On the ground, the whole battlefront from the outskirts to the centre of the city was filled with the sounds of explosions, the noise of intermittent laser fire, and the screams of soldiers on both sides yelling in pain from their wounds. Yet the Treldarians were winning.

Within two hours of landing, General Vark received word from the assault leader on the ground. 'General, this is Captain Tarken. We've secured the city. All the Sentinels, except for three of their officers, have been killed. In our ranks we have fifty-five dead and ten wounded, including those in the crashed scout ships. We've destroyed all the Tzuracian communication equipment. There's an open field on the eastern side of the city for your warship to land. The Kyroni prisoners are yet to be released. I await your orders, sir!'

'Thank you, Captain. Leave the release of the Kyroni prisoners to me,' Vark replied. 'Good and bad news – though that's to be expected in battle. I was impressed with our new super-soldiers, weren't you?'

'Yes, I'm confident we'll be able to take back what belongs to us and have control of the Universe.'

They shared the same thoughts.

'While I'm landing my ship and organising the Kyroni prisoners to board, I want you to leave a unit of soldiers in the city. Take your scout ships to scour for other villages within a one-hundred-mile radius of Vexar, inviting Kyroni warriors to join our rebellion. We leave in two days. I'll use the time to extract as much information as I can from the captured Sentinel officers.'

'Understood, sir.'

It wasn't long before General Vark's warship had landed on the surface of the planet and Vark with his troops were heading for the prison.

As his troops opened the crowded cells they were confronted by a horde of bare-chested tattooed warriors, each with a single black plaited pigtail on their otherwise bald heads. They looked ferocious. The Kyroni cheered wildly on seeing their liberators, while the Treldarians stood back in awe.

There was chaos for a moment until the noise eventually subsided and Vark began to explain his intentions using his portable interpreter equipment. The Kyroni were eager to take up arms with their liberators against the Sentinels. They relished the thought of being reinfused to avenge the deaths of their comrades and share in the spoils.

* * *

After two days of intense interrogation, General Vark extracted valuable 'intel' from the Sentinel officers concerning Khazor's defences. Under extreme duress, the officers also divulged information about the impending graduation ceremony which would involve a gathering of all the Tzuracian dignitaries, including General Dakhar, the Commanding Chief of Military Operations in the Western Quadrant.

What a bonus, thought Vark, rubbing his hands in anticipation. *Here was an opportunity to kill off one of Tzurac's most senior military officers along with his crop of new lieutenants. The Gods must be with the Treldarians to have arranged this so conveniently. He couldn't have planned it better and felt even more confident about defeating the Sentinels.*

There was another revelation however, which caused him to call Ramlok to the Bridge.

'Sit down, Captain Ramlok. I have something to discuss with you.'

'Yes, General, what's on your mind?'

'First of all, Captain, how's the infusion progressing?'

'Good, sir, it's taking less time than I thought it would and the Kyroni are adjusting to their enhancements. It will take only another day to complete the process.'

'Excellent, but our journey to Tzurac may be further delayed. I have a change of plan.'

Ramlok was curious about what the General had in mind.

'The Sentinel officers told me the Diunons were allies of General Dranz and his Bladers when they attacked Planet Iota. And these Diunons had an army of mechanical robots which gave Dranz an advantage in the battle.' Vark glared at Ramlok. He was looking for an explanation. 'Why didn't you tell me about this when I was planning our war strategy?'

'Well, General,' Ramlok replied calmly, 'I'm sure I mentioned the Diunons before, but two of their ships, carrying a thousand Diutrons and most of their soldiers, were shot down and destroyed when they crash landed on Iota. Only one ship survived to release two thousand Diutrons.

'It's true that the robotic Diutrons did a lot of damage and killed large numbers of the enemy, but when the Diutrons reached the mining enclosure, they simply froze in their tracks. They just shut down. That's when Dranz and our remaining soldiers retreated back to the General's ship knowing the battle was headed for defeat. We had a very narrow escape.'

Ramlok could see the General was angry.

Vark thought for a moment before speaking again in a more irritated tone. 'Well, what happened to those two thousand robots, Captain?'

'I don't know, sir. I assume they were destroyed because they were no longer operational. All things considered, I believe the Diunons had little to offer us in our cause this time.'

'You should have let *me* do the considering, Captain Ramlok,' responded Vark sharply, waving a clenched fist inches from Ramlok's face. 'We need to go to Diunon to see what they *can* offer – to find out if they have more of these robots we can use.'

'Can't you just send them a transmission, sir?' enquired Ramlok, somewhat hesitantly.

Vark snapped back. 'I could, but a message might be intercepted by the Federation who are policing the planet. Besides, I want the Diunons to see the force of our armada.'

Ramlok nodded. He understood the General's reasoning.

'Computer,' Vark snarled, 'what's the shortest time to reach Planet Diunon from here?'

A simulated voice responded promptly over the Comms, 'The diversion from our initial trajectory to Tzurac will take five days, travelling with increased hyperdrive.'

Vark was thinking out aloud. 'We still have enough time to coordinate the simultaneous attack on Terra Major as planned with General Rokan, even allowing for the remaining Kyroni to join us. Computer! Set a course for Diunon. Inform the other warships of the change in coordinates. We leave tomorrow. Alright, Captain Ramlok, continue with the infusion process. You're dismissed.'

Ramlok rose from his seat, saluted and marched out, feeling as though he had been kicked out, rather than dismissed routinely.

By the following afternoon, all the Kyroni warriors were aboard Vark's warship, and the General was pleased to have five hundred new recruits plus five hundred from the prison cells, expanding his super-army by another one thousand soldiers. With the new coordinates, the Treldarian armada set sail for Planet Diunon, looking for more support.

* * *

As Vark's armada approached the volatile volcanic-red planet Diunon, the ships went into stealth mode and orbited while dispatching five scout ships. As expected, the planet was less fortified than Kyronis and the Treldarian scout ships landed without incident. After quickly disposing of the Sentinel guards, the 'all clear' was given and Vark's warship landed.

It took the General a while to adjust to the appearance of the Diunons who flocked around the alien visitors. They were a strange devilish-looking race, small in build with scaly reddish skin, beady red eyes and rusty-coloured hair. Their round ears were pinned tightly against their heads and their noses were wide and flattened.

General Vark was soon in negotiations with their leader, Kiken, using an electronic translator.

'We're grateful to you, General, for releasing our soldiers from their prisons and disposing of the Tzuracian usurpers,' said the red leader, 'but we're unable to supply you with any Diutrons. Under martial law, the Federation banned us from making war machines and, in any case, we no longer have the Xytrinium to manufacture them.'

'Understood. Do you know what happened to the two thousand Diutrons on Planet Iota when they seized up?' asked General Vark with keen interest.

'Our tracking devices on the Diutrons were disconnected,' Kiken replied, 'so we've no idea whether they're still in existence or whether they've been dismantled and their Xytrinium power pack salvaged for another use. We can't help you.'

The General was disheartened. *It seemed Ramlok had been right in playing down the potential for any possible support from the Diunons or their mechanical monsters.*

'Then we'll leave you in control of your own planet, free from Federation rule. We trust we might be able to rely on your allegiance in the future.'

Kiken agreed. He shared the same hatred of the Tzuracians.

So, after a day's delay on Diunon, the Second Legion Treldarian fleet was speeding to its intended target, Planet Tzurac, with an army of infused Treldarians and Kyroni but with no additional reinforcements. And as they travelled, Vark's respect for Ramlok was growing. Ramlok was proving his worth and value as a captain in the Treldarian army.

URGELLAN & ARMONUS

BACK on Tzurac, the deliberations over the battle strategy with the Senate and General Dakhar had concluded. Senator Ghalbrak summoned the two chosen emissaries, Volhardtz and Morzhan, to his Chamber to discuss their missions and final orders.

'Thank you for coming at such short notice, Senators. You've been elected to travel once again to the planets Urgellan and Armonus and request their support in the fight against the Treldarian threat. Obviously, you need to emphasise the gravity of the impending invasion. We don't want another Grekadian War. If we don't cut the head off this viper, all the Tzuracians who've worked so hard to achieve peace and tranquillity for the last five hundred years, will be lost and the Universe will be thrown into chaos run by cold-blooded warmongers.'

Volhardtz and Morzhan agreed wholeheartedly.

'Senator Volhardtz, you need to ask Queen Tarune if she would be willing to lend her support once again by giving us five thousand of her enhanced Urgellan soldiers. I'll leave the diplomatic plea in your very capable hands, Senator. You'll need to take three warships with a unit of Sentinels in anticipation of her kindness and generosity.

'And Senator Morzhan, you'll need two Destroyer battleships and a small unit of Sentinels. Don't delay, Senators. We must be fully prepared before the Treldarian armada reaches us. Any questions?'

Volhardtz spoke first. 'No, Senator, we'll impress upon our allies the urgency and the need for their support.'

Morzhan remained silent, eyes fixed on the Elder.

'Very well, Senators,' said the Elder, 'you have your instructions. Safe journey, and may the Ancient spirits protect you.'

* * *

Three days later, Senator Volhardtz was granted permission to land his three warships on sovereign Urgellan soil. Viewing the countryside from one of the portals on his ship as they glided into the landing area, the Senator recognised the familiar, ploughed fields amongst the expansive, dark green forests. On landing, he selected six Sentinels to accompany him for his audience with Queen Tarune and issued orders for all remaining crew members to remain on board their ships.

After disembarking, their entourage was formally greeted by twenty of the Queen's Royal Guards. The guards were all dressed in their colourful uniforms, just as Volhardtz remembered them from his last visit.

When the Captain of the Guards ordered the Sentinels to relinquish all their weapons, including their staff swords, they protested. 'A Sentinel never surrenders his sword!' So, after an awkward exchange of words the captain relented, permitting them to keep their staff swords but surrender their laser weapons.

Respecting their honour and maintaining diplomacy, the Royal Guards led their visitors through Urgellan's capital, Asram, towards the Royal Palace.

Visiting the city once again, Volhardtz still felt as if he was going back centuries in time. There were no towering multi-storey structures of metal and glass, but instead only single storey, and some double storey, cottages built of sandstone and wood, standing either side of a main thoroughfare made of well-compacted crushed gravel.

Sometimes the escorted Sentinels would pass by what the Senator considered to be workhorses, tied up to hitching rails waiting patiently for their riders to return. Occasionally a workhorse would turn its drooping head with an indifferent glance at the strangers, then flick its tail as if automatically shooing away the annoyance. It was a different reaction by the inhabitants who, together with the shopkeepers and traders, crowded along the sides of the road muttering amongst themselves while staring at the intrusion of alien soldiers.

The entourage eventually reached the Royal Palace which was surrounded by a high stone wall at the far end of the city, and the visitors were marched through the wide entrance shouldered by two large, ironstone pillars. Large and heavy wooden doors had been drawn back towards the inside of the walls.

Marching a short distance over the palace grounds they reached the entrance doors of a massive two-storey sandstone palace. The Sentinels were ordered by the captain to remain outside. Then, Senator Volhardtz led by four of the guards and the captain, was taken to Queen Tarune who was seated on her high throne in the huge hall.

The hall had not changed in appearance since Volhardtz's last visit. Huge rich-coloured tapestries draped on the surrounding high sandstone walls still overlooked the expansive black marble floor. The one difference Volhardtz noticed was that the tall white sculptured columns now displayed banners bearing coats-of-arms of the different clans.

Courtesans wearing elaborate costumes of assorted colours filled the hall and their incessant chattering and laughing ceased as the Senator and Royal Guards entered. They stood motionless, heads turned, and eyes fixed on the new arrivals. They recalled the last time the Royal Court had received an emissary from Tzurac – when there was imminent war in the galaxy. They waited in anticipation to hear what had brought the same Tzuracian emissary to their planet once more.

The Captain of the Guards halted the escort, then paced to the lower landing, ten feet from the throne. He removed his broad-brimmed black felt hat, adorned with a feather, sweeping it in front of him whilst bowing low, holding the hilt of his sword in the other hand. Then he rose, stood upright, and commenced his introduction. 'My Queen, I wish to announce the arrival of Senator Volhardtz, the emissary from Tzurac.'

After replacing his hat, the captain stood rigidly at attention. There was dead silence in the hall and all eyes were fixed on the Queen.

'Thank you, Captain Walkarm. You may return to your unit.' The captain saluted the Queen, marched back to the Guards, swivelled on the spot stamping his right foot on the floor and remained standing at attention.

'Welcome, Senator Volhardtz,' Queen Tarune said in her soft, feminine voice. She was smiling, 'I'm pleased to see you again, though I'm somewhat concerned about the purpose of your visit. Please come forward.'

As he approached, the Senator could see how beautiful and young Queen Tarune still looked. Her long gown was of deep red velvet with a high-laced collar and long flared sleeves. Her long auburn hair was no longer left falling in ringlets, but instead was tightly swept back into a bun. It revealed her long neck adorned with a rich gold necklace, draped around her smooth porcelain-white skin. Large gold earrings completed the set with a matching gold crown encrusted with large rubies balanced elegantly on top of her head.

Volhardtz walked slowly to the lower landing, bowed and returned to his upright stance. He was momentarily mesmerised by the Queen's sparkling emerald-green eyes complemented by pastel rainbow-coloured eye shadow.

His fixation was brought back by the voice of the Queen asking, 'What brings you to our world this time, Senator?'

'Thank you, Your Majesty. I'm also pleased to see you again and thankful you've allowed me this audience. My message is confidential, and I need to ask you if the Royal Court might be temporarily vacated?' The Senator was trying to be as diplomatic as he could.

The Queen remembered Volhardtz's previous visit and his comment, *'one cannot assume everyone is loyal to the cause'*. Without hesitation she raised her right arm and graciously waved it in front of her in the direction of the hall entrance, at the same time calling out sternly, 'All of you must leave!'

Within minutes the Royal Court was emptied of courtesans and Royal Guards. Queen Tarune rose from her throne and stepped down to stand closer to the emissary. 'Senator Volhardtz, you may speak freely without the presence of prying ears.'

'Thank you, Your Majesty.'

Whispering with haste, Volhardtz relayed news of the impending assault on Tzurac and Terra Major by the Treldarians and their allies. '… If they are not stopped, the rebels will crush every planet in their quest to rule the Universe and take control of Xytrinium reserves, enslaving those who survive. It will be another Grekadian War. We need your support once again.'

There was no hesitation in her decision. 'You will have my infused soldiers, Senator – five thousand of them – if it will help defeat this dark force. But it will take at least a day to assemble them if I dispatch my couriers immediately. In the meantime, you and your Sentinels are welcome to stay in my palace.'

'Thank you, Your Highness, for your support and your kind hospitality. We'll be most honoured.'

Within two days Senator Volhardtz's warships were on their way back to Tzurac with the promised Urgellan soldiers.

* * *

Meanwhile, after a three-day journey, Senator Morzhan arrived at the mysterious planet Armonus. Leaving the escort of Sentinels on board, the Senator was welcomed by the same young priest as before. Manku led the party through a semi-dark tunnel to the main temple. The familiar scent of orange blossom permeating the quiet atmosphere brought back refreshing memories. The Senator felt a calm reverence and knew he was in a holy place.

Entering the white temple with its vacant chalk walls, his eyes fell on the familiar gathering of the six high priests in their magenta robes, seated at the round stone table in the centre of the large room. The orange blossom scent was more pungent in this room. Subtle smoke was rising from a ceramic vase placed in front of the unforgettable huge bronze statue of their deity – a praying female. There was an eerie silence instead of the faint tantric chanting he had heard on his last visit.

Coming towards him with open arms and a warm smile was Master Tarq, who was still the Head High Priest. He was easily recognisable by the gold sash over his shoulder and the high priests still presented themselves as he remembered them, with shaved heads and yellowish skin and a small round dark-red gemstone, like a garnet or ruby, embedded in their foreheads. No other jewellery adorned their bodies. Master

Tarq's outstanding feature was his dark, almost onyx, eyes. They were mesmerising and hypnotic, appearing as deep wells which drew the gazer in.

'Welcome, welcome, my friend,' Tarq said softly in his native Armonusian tongue. 'It's good to see you again.'

'Thank you, Master Tarq. I'm also happy to see you and your priests,' Senator Morzhan responded in their native language.

They embraced and held each other for some time in silence until Tarq spoke again. 'We knew you were coming long before you sent your message to ask to see us, Senator Pyrham Morzhan. Come and sit at the table with us.'

As he walked to the table the Senator opened his arms and raised his open palms to the other high priests. Without a word, they returned the gesture of peace-welcoming and smiled gently. While the Senator was seating himself comfortably, Manku quietly placed goblets of fruit wine on the table for the group before slipping away almost unnoticed.

While Morzhan sipped on his drink, Tarq continued. 'Our premonitions, although not totally clear, showed to us the coming of a destructive force – a force which will disrupt the balance of the Universe unless there is a greater force to prevent this from happening. We believe the Tzuracians are the only ones who have the power to end this invasion with the help of allies.'

The other priests nodded in agreement then bowed their heads.

The Senator spoke once more. 'Thank you for your vote of confidence, Master Tarq. From what we've learned, the Treldarians will be launching a simultaneous, two-pronged attack on Tzurac and Terra Major within two weeks. General Dakhar is now at Khazor leading the defence. My people have also sought help from the Urgellans to help defend Tzurac and we'll be resurrecting the two thousand Diutrons left by the Bladers on Terra Iota fifteen months ago. They'll be transported to Terra Major before the battle begins, to become part of Earth's defence.'

Tarq sat deep in thought for some time with Senator Morzhan, observing the facial expressions associated with the telepathic conversations amongst the other high priests. The movements ceased and Tarq turned to the Senator, saying, 'Pyrham, we have all agreed to help in any way we can and invoke our spiritual powers to maintain the stability of the Universe. The High Priests have suggested we accompany you on your return to Tzurac and three of us continue on to Terra Major. We know time is of the essence and we're ready to leave Armonus when you are.'

'Thank you, my friends, we're most grateful,' replied Morzhan. 'Will it be too soon if we leave tonight?'

Tarq turned to his priests who were already indicating their agreement with the arrangements. He turned back to the Senator to answer his question. 'We can leave immediately after our evening meal which is already being prepared for you and your Sentinels.'

'Thanks again, Master Tarq. I'm sure my soldiers would very much appreciate your invitation.'

Soon the Senator, accompanied by his six Sentinels and the High Priests, were gathered around the table enjoying a basic meal of bread, grains, fruits and nuts. Conversation between the Armonusians and the Tzuracians was limited. In fact, the only ones involved in discussion were Master Tarq and the Senator.

'So, Pyrham, can you tell us exactly what happened after the Tzuracians defeated the rebels on Terra Iota?'

'Yes, of course ...' The Senator explained about the capture of General Dranz on Planet Steiros, his execution along with all his rebel Blader soldiers, and the imposition of martial law on planets Kyronis and Diunon. He explained how the Tzuracians had failed to contain the Xytrinium formula, allowing the Treldarians in other Quadrants to be infused.

'Now, with an army of super-soldiers, the Treldarians obviously believe they can compete on equal terms and retaliate against the Federation again. But thankfully, we've been forewarned once more by the same fugitive Sentinel. We have time to prepare and surprise our enemies.'

Master Tarq could not resist telling the emissary how he felt. 'As you know, my friend, we Armonusians are people of peace and harmony. However, we cannot ignore what the consequences might be if these warmongers inflict sorrow and pain on all those who live in this Universe. We can't turn our back on the chaos they'll create and see a repeat of the devastation that resulted during and after the Grekadian War. We'll do all in our power and teachings to maintain the balance.'

MOBILISATION

ONE week after the three warships left Terra Major for Terra Iota to collect the Diutrons, Acting Chief-Commander Kal Zawkon received a holographic transmission from Terra Iota.

'Commander, Captain Skarhdok here. Mr Thompson needs to speak with you.'

'Go ahead, Grant. What's the problem?' responded Zawkon in a strong, if somewhat anxious, voice.

'It's not really a problem, Commander,' said Thompson in his unmistakable Irish lilt. 'I've some good news and some bad news and I need a decis'n.'

'Well, I'm listening, my friend. Tell me what's needed?' questioned Zawkon with keen interest.

'Well, the good news is, me engineers have all the robots up an' runnin' – two t'ousand of 'em. The bad news is, those crafty little Diunon red devils who configured the controls didn't install a main overriding toggle switch in the units. These war machines can only be controlled using a ship's main control *or* a soldier on the ground manipulating 'em. You can't do both at the same time. It would take time to manufacture and install overridin' switches in all the units. So, the t'ing is Commander, do ya want me to

162

delay gettin' these robots to ya? Or make it a fixed control for a ship or for a soldier?'

Zawkon didn't hesitate. 'Okay Grant, make the controls operational for a soldier to use on the ground. My warships are already on their way to you. There's no time to spare.'

'Very good, sir. It'll take me engineers only a day. I'll have 'em ready when the ships arrive.'

'Thank you, Grant,' replied Zawkon, sounding much relieved. 'You've done a great job. Now, let me talk to Captain Skarhdok again.'

'Yes, Commander, I'm here.'

'Captain, you need to start setting up stronger defences around the mining complex and increase sentry duty in case the Treldarians attack Iota and mobilise their soldiers on the ground. Our information tells us that Iota may not be involved, but have your troops prepare the underground accommodation facility in readiness for the miners and their families, just in case it's needed for their protection. I'm not taking any chances.

'I also want you to cease immediately all mining transporter movements to and from Planet Iota until further notice. I'll inform General Blake I've overridden his authority. Communication from now on will be by Sentinel holographs only. That's all for now. Zawkon, out!'

* * *

Stationed in the Central Administration Offices of the newly built Citadel, Zawkon had finally completed his plan in preparation for the forthcoming Treldarian invasion. His immediate priority was to liaise with General Blake, the Earthling in charge of the Aeronautical Space Program for Exploration, Colonisation and Transportation (ASPECT). Blake was also responsible for the Space Academy and all its jet fighters.

General Blake had been a long-time business associate of Samuel Jensen after MERIC joined forces with ASPECT to transport Xytrinium from Terra Iota to Earth. Blake was the epitome of a typical military officer – a short back-and-sides regulation haircut, neatly trimmed moustache, pressed navy-blue uniform with polished black shoes and belt, shiny silver buttons and buckle. He carried a short swagger stick and was always punctual. He was also a dedicated and caring soldier who took pride in his men and his responsibilities, and it was these traditional traits Samuel Jensen had admired.

Zawkon had included in his battle plan, security and defence measures for MERIC, the company responsible for the mining and storage of Xytrinium reserves. He knew Sentinel Kyron Tyros and his wife Torri, who owned the company, but he hadn't met General Blake's daughter, Lauren, who'd been left in charge to run the Company while the Tyros family were away on Tzurac. Zawkon needed to contact her to set up an immediate meeting with all parties.

He made a call. After introducing himself and exchanging pleasantries, it was time to get serious.

'Ms Blake, as much as I'm enjoying our conversation, I need to ask for your help to arrange an urgent meeting with yourself and your father. Also invite your Security Chief. I'll explain everything when we're all together, perhaps in one of the secure boardrooms in the MERIC Building?'

Lauren was fascinated by the Sentinel's deep rich-sounding voice. It had strength in it, yet she sensed compassion. 'Yes of course, Commander. I'll arrange it immediately and get back to you.'

'Thank you, Ms Blake.'

'Please call me Lauren, Commander.'

'Alright, Lauren, thanks again for your help.'

* * *

Arriving at the MERIC Building the following afternoon, Commander Zawkon was escorted to Ms Blake's Penthouse Office by two burly Security guards.

As he arrived Lauren looked up from her desk and peered at him over her black-framed reading glasses which were balanced precariously on the end of her nose. Zawkon was taken with her appearance. She was a slender woman in her early forties dressed in a tailored dark-grey corporate pants suit, her long crimped dark hair trailing over her shoulders.

She was taken with his appearance too. Before her, was a magnificent figure dressed in a smart tight-fitting maroon uniform with a midnight-blue velvet cape clasped over his broad shoulders. The outfit clung to Zawkon's solid muscles, and his gleaming fair hair was pulled back into a long-braided ponytail. Lauren had heard from Torri about this battle-scarred war hero who had fought to save Earth and capture Khaneera. And here he was, in person. She smiled at the Sentinel standing tall and proud in the doorway.

'Come in, Commander Zawkon,' she said, gesturing to him as she moved from her seat behind her desk. She walked over to shake his hand. 'The others have only just arrived and are waiting in the board room.'

The Commander's hand was twice the size of Lauren's, and when they clasped, she felt his firm but gentle grip which sent a mild tingling throughout her whole body. On his hand Zawkon wore a gold Sentinel Pledge ring, similar to Kyron's. It was the first time she'd been close enough to a Sentinel to examine a ring's details. It was intricately engraved with unfamiliar symbols, the sides studded with small dark-blue crystals.

'You can call me Kal,' said the Commander, as he slowly withdrew his hand. He caught the scent of the fragrant Jasmine perfume she was wearing. 'Just between us, I think we can dispense with the formalities, don't you, Lauren?'

Despite Zawkon's tough invincible exterior, Lauren was drawn to his penetrating azure-blue eyes and the sound of his rich soft voice. For a moment she was stunned, and the silence soon became very obvious. Then, snapping herself out of it, she started the conversation again. She was blushing like a schoolgirl with a crush and feeling a little faint. 'Yes, I agree, Kal. We don't need to be formal. Well, we best go so as not to keep the others waiting.'

As they entered the softly lit boardroom, Zawkon was impressed by the room's smart décor. Pastel olive-green fabric covered all the walls and the tilted wooden blinds on the corridor window matched the large oval mahogany table at which two men were seated in oversized high-backed dark brown leather chairs.

When Lauren closed the door behind Zawkon and herself, the two men rose to greet them. After formal introductions with the Chief of Security, Richard Hammond, and Lauren's father, General Blake, Commander Zawkon proceeded to brief them about the Treldarian invasion.

By the time Zawkon had finished they were in partial shock. They couldn't believe it was only fifteen months since the last attempt by the Blader rebels, Earth would once again be under attack.

With a puzzled look on his face, General Blake, challenged Zawkon with scepticism, 'And you know all this, Commander, from information transmitted to you by only one source? Corporal Yarron Blandhar? He's a wanted criminal for God's sake! A Sentinel deserter who betrayed the Tzuracians, stealing their infusion formula to create an enemy with super-powers! He's also a traitor who conspired with another Sentinel traitor, Khaneera Zarkwin, to join forces with the Bladers who intended conquering the Federation and stealing our Xytrinium reserves!

'I know he had a change of heart and ultimately helped us fend off the last attack, but can we still trust him? What sort of madness is this? With respect, Commander, I thought you Tzuracians were a race of highly advanced intelligence. So, tell me why you trust anything this fugitive is telling you? How do you know it isn't an elaborate tactical hoax to create a diversion while these Treldarians attack some other undefended planet?'

Zawkon thought for a moment. *He understood General Blake's reservations, but his Sentinel instincts told him an attack was imminent. He needed to gain the trust of the General and the Security Chief.*

'I understand and agree with all you've said, General,' Zawkon replied calmly. 'It might seem foolish for us to believe the word of a treacherous Sentinel deserter. However, General Dakhar and the Senate are certain Corporal Blandhar genuinely regrets the mistakes he made in the past. Over the last fifteen months, he's proved his loyalty to Tzurac by hunting down Blader rebels and transmitting to us details of their hidden sanctuaries. We believe he's repenting for his past sins, trying to earn forgiveness, not just from the Tzuracians, but also from the spirits of the Ancients and his Maker.

'If we believe what he's telling us is true, then we'll be prepared in time to surprise and defeat the rebel force. And, if his information is false, the only real damage done is the time we'll have taken to organise ourselves. It'll provide a practice run at mobilising our troops and fleets in case something like this does happen in the future.'

Zawkon waited patiently for their verdict and, after some deliberation, General Blake was first to comment.

'I see your logic, Commander. As you say, it's better to be safe than wear the consequences if we're wrong and not prepared. Do you have some kind of battle plan for us to consider, Commander?'

'Yes, of course I do, sir.' *His words had worked.* 'General Dakhar has asked me to arrange the defence of Terra Major and

Terra Iota in consultation with your military, including the air force. Although it's obvious, I must emphasise confidentiality here. We need to maintain as much secrecy as possible and keep the element of surprise to our advantage.'

All three gestured their agreement while Blake and Hammond verbally reinforced acceptance of the Commander's request.

From his Pledge ring, Zawkon projected a holographic three-dimensional chart displaying the earth's orbit and its moon. 'Here's what I suggest we do immediately for our defence so we're ready within the week. Please feel free to contribute any other ideas to improve the plan.

'I believe the Treldarians will concentrate their forces on New York City and the World Assembly in Washington DC, where the sources of power reside. They'll try to destroy the defence forces at ASPECT and the air base. The rebels will then attempt to take control of the Xytrinium resources stockpiled at MERIC. They'll also hit the Tzuracian Citadel to destroy my ground forces.'

While outlining his strategy, Zawkon informed General Blake he had contacted Engineer Grant Thompson on Terra Iota and requested all mining operations and all flights by the load-transporters to and from Earth to cease. 'I hope you don't mind me overstepping your authority, General, but this was urgent.'

'No, Commander, I agree with your quick actions. You did the right thing.'

Zawkon explained about the resurrection of the Diutrons on Terra Iota and the plan for them to arrive soon at the ASPECT Air Base.

The General looked shocked. 'The Diutrons that were used by the Bladers against us?'

'Yes, they've been re-programmed for our control. General Blake, may I impose upon you to receive these robots and keep them hidden in the underground bunker in readiness to mobilise them at the appropriate time.'

'Yes, of course. Your plan seems quite ambitious, but I'll prepare for their arrival.' The General hadn't encountered a Diutron before. *He was curious to see what they looked like and how they operated.*

Zawkon turned his attention to Richard Hammond and Lauren. 'Chief Hammond, I was told last time you had to fortify the MERIC Building against Jackson and his rebel soldiers, placing gun batteries on top of the building and patrols near the basement of this building. I suggest you do the same again. What do you think, Lauren, since you are currently in charge of MERIC?'

'Yes, I think it would be our best defence. What's your take on this, Richard?'

Hammond, who was deep in thought absorbing all that had been discussed so far, instantly snapped out of it. 'I'd also like to place a gun battery manned with several units of your Sentinels at the front of the building.'

Zawkon could tell by the looks on their faces that the reality of the impending catastrophic event was beginning to sink in. *They had been attacked before by Khaneera Zarkwin, Jackson Jensen and his thugs but they had never had to deal with a full-scale invasion by aliens. They were a planet of Terranians who had lived in relative peace for centuries without any inter-planetary forces interfering in their tranquil lifestyle – a race which was vulnerable, exposed and inexperienced. They were now potentially fighting for their very lives and the protection of their planet against an alien army of super-soldiers using advanced weaponry. They needed the help of the Sentinels if they were to survive.*

'Well,' said Zawkon, 'I think that just about covers it. I must forewarn the World Assembly of the coming dark forces. I'll be leaving in the morning. Is there anything you'd like me to include in my address to them?'

There was a short pause before Zawkon spoke again. 'If there's nothing more to add, I'll call this meeting to an end. Let's start moving on our plan straight away, shall we?'

As General Blake, Chief Hammond and Lauren stood from the table and headed for the door, Zawkon called to Lauren, 'Can you stay behind for a minute, Lauren?'

She stopped and turned to face the Commander as the other two disappeared into the passageway and out of hearing range.

'Can I ask a favour of you?'

Lauren blushed as her body tingled with anticipation, wondering what the Commander had in mind.

'Would it be possible for you to arrange through your contact in the Assembly, a time for me to address all their members? Tomorrow if possible? Preferably without telling them what I'll be speaking about. We don't want to start a panic.'

'Yes, Kal. I can do that for you,' she responded with a smile. 'Is there anything else you need from me?' she added with provocative undertones and a flutter of her eyes.

The Commander was left somewhat speechless. He'd never been in this situation before. For the first time in his life, he felt powerless as mild electricity surged through his muscular body. 'No, no,' he stuttered. 'I think that's all I needed, Lauren.'

'Please join me in my office for some tea, Kal, while I call for Security to come and collect you.'

The Commander felt comfortable in Lauren's presence and although he didn't say much while waiting in her office, he felt an immediate fondness for her. Lauren felt the same way. She was attracted to the Commander, even though they had only just met.

* * *

Later that afternoon Lauren contacted Commander Zawkon back at his station in the Citadel to inform him she had arranged an afternoon appointment for him the following day at the World Assembly.

'Thank you again for your assistance, Lauren. Perhaps we could catch up for dinner when I return from the World Assembly?' He was somewhat nervous suggesting it.

There was no hesitation on Lauren's part. 'I would very much like that, Kal. Hope you have a safe journey and please stay in touch.'

DECEPTION

TWO weeks had passed since Yarron and Bhalar's narrow escape from General Rokan's campsite on Mankro. They had left in haste, their course set for Terra Major, not having any time to take stock of the fuel and food reserves on Yarron's Destroyer. Travelling on hyperdrive, their fuel was depleting rapidly. Yarron was now concerned whether they could make it to Terra Major before their supplies ran out. They were in the uncharted south-west region of the Western Quadrant. They needed to find a planet with Xytrinium reserves – and they needed to find it soon.

During the journey Bhalar and Yarron had become very close emotionally, mentally and physically. Yarron was teaching Bhalar the Tzuracian language and they practised their fighting skills almost daily. Yarron had sworn he would never trust another female, but Bhalar was sincere and honest and spoke with a true heart. His feelings for her had grown as she confided in him about her home life living under her father's rule.

'My midwife, Jelkah, was more like a mother to me. She was the wife of one of my father's favoured captains who was killed in a tribal battle on Nujhar around the same time that my mother died giving birth to me. Being childless, my father invited Jelkah to live with him in his hut and look after me. It was a convenient arrangement for everyone.

'Growing up, Jelkah taught me everything and doted on me like I was her own child and, as time progressed, my father and Jelkah became lovers. Then my father became jealous of the attention I received from Jelkah. To make things worse, as I grew older, I began to look more and more like my mother. My father blamed me for her death and every day I reminded him more of her. He started to drink heavily and become aggressive not only towards me but also towards Jelkah. In his drunken stupors he abused us verbally and attacked us physically. I told you Jelkah passed away when I was fifteen. Well, it was after my father struck her too hard one night while she was trying to protect me.

'From that day on, I vowed I would escape from him and disown him as my father. Several times I attempted to escape to Nujhar. Each time I was captured, usually by Captain Chekhmar, and dragged back to the hut. My father would chain me up for several days, to 'cool off' as he put it. He kept me on slave duties cleaning, washing, cooking and anything else he demanded.'

Yarron felt sorry for Bhalar's miserable and tortured life, but he admired her courage and strength. Although she had battled through a rough upbringing, and despised her father and his offsider Chekhmar, she had not become bitter towards others. She was kind-hearted, considerate, compassionate, selfless and gentle – traits which must have been passed on from her mother's bloodline along with her beauty. Yarron sensed that Jelkah had also been a major positive influence in Bhalar's life – an intelligent and well-educated Treldarian who had known how to bring out Bhalar's best qualities.

Despite his vow not to get involved with another female, Yarron was falling in love, and, over time, he began to let down his guard, revealing his past and his real identity as well as his current mission. Over a drink one night he told Bhalar how he had become a fugitive, forcing him to change his name and identity to become a bounty hunter, as well as a sword-for-hire and how he'd made it his life ambition to track down the cut-throat Bladers and find their hiding places.

Bhalar seemed to understand how Yarron had been entranced by Khaneera Zarkwin and her beauty, and how Khaneera had manipulated him, using him to get what she wanted before tossing him aside when he was no longer useful to her cause. Bhalar reassured him he had done more than enough to make amends and be forgiven by the Ancient spirits.

'After all, Yarron,' Bhalar said, 'hmm … Yarron, that's a nice name … we all make mistakes, whether deliberate or not, and it's whether we admit them to ourselves and make up for them in the future, or deny them, which separates a good spirit from a bad one. You're a good spirit, Yarron, because you care about others and their feelings.'

Yarron was looking forward to sharing the future with Bhalar, if a future was possible. *After all, he was still a hunted fugitive.*

* * *

Back on the bridge after a sound sleep the previous night, Yarron was preoccupied with the reality they were running out of supplies and fuel. He needed to find somewhere to land within the next forty-eight hours.

While desperately searching the computer's archives Yarron discovered a sketchy navigational chart retrieved from another galaxy voyager. It highlighted two small star systems which could be reached in the time remaining. No information was given for atmospheric readings, gas concentrations, weather conditions or lifeforms. He had no choice but to take the risk. If the closest star system didn't have what they needed, they could

174

still reach the second one in the hope it would save their lives. Yarron ordered the computer to set course for the closest planet, named Kompak.

A day later their ship entered Kompak's orbit. The planet was isolated and in darkness, without a sun. It was more like a spherical asteroid than a planet. Yarron cautiously switched to stealth mode and began scanning the surface. Within minutes the computer's luminous, pale-blue screen flickered to life on his console. Accompanied by electronic blips, data began printing on the screen:

ATMOSPHERE:	NIL, UNSUITABLE FOR LIFEFORMS
TERRA FORMA:	600 MILE RADIUS, LOW GRAVITY, NO VEGETATION, NO WATER.
INHABITED:	TZURACIANS
ENERGY SOURCE:	LARGE XYTRINIUM RESERVES DETECTED IN STRUCTURES - 23 DEGREES ...LAT. 10 DEGREES...LONG.

From her position next to him in the co-pilot's seat Bhalar sensed Yarron's surprise. She maintained her silence, watching Yarron as he reasoned with the information.

Large Xytrinium reserves here? Lightyears from anywhere? Perhaps General Dakhar had sent survey teams to the Western Quadrant, looking for other planets to join the Federation and searching for Xytrinium deposits on uncharted planets. Could this be an emergency refuelling base for Tzuracian exploration ships? Had the Tzuracians established an artificial environment to survive?

Yarron couldn't believe his good fortune. He turned to Bhalar. 'This is a stroke of good luck. I think we're saved. But ...' he paused and drew a deep breath, '... we could also get ourselves into serious trouble.'

'Please explain, Yarron?' Bhalar said with a worried look.

'The good news is, I think this is a Tzuracian emergency refuelling depot. The bad news is I'm not sure whether the Tzuracians here will recognize me as a fugitive and want to arrest me. I bluffed my way in a similar situation once before by telling the Tzuracian in charge I was a Sentinel hunting down the fugitive Khaneera Zarkwin and needed their help. It worked thanks to the Ancient Spirits. But this story won't cut it now with Khaneera in prison.'

Bhalar thought for a moment before replying, 'Well I have an idea which might work.' Yarron listened intently. 'Tell them you've captured a Treldarian and you're taking me back to Terra Major for interrogation. If they know about the impending invasion, you could impress them more by telling them you've captured the daughter of the General who's leading the attack. What do you think?'

'Brilliant!' Then smiling and raising an eyebrow, Yarron added, 'Of course I'd have to clamp you in wrist restraints to make it believable. Then you'd be totally at my disposal.'

They both chuckled at the suggestion before heading for Yarron's sleeping quarters to prepare for their charade.

To help convince them he was a Sentinel, Yarron changed into his maroon Sentinel uniform and blue cape which he had kept carefully folded away for such emergencies. He shaved off his dyed black beard and moustache and placed his silver helmet on his head to hide his dark dyed hair. Then he placed his Pledge ring on his finger and tucked his staff blade into his belt. He gently clasped the restraints onto Bhalar's wrists held behind her back and swung her around to face him, kissing her passionately.

'I like what I see,' said Bhalar, admiring Yarron's changed appearance.

'Well, here we go, Bhalar. Put on a tough face as if you resent being a prisoner – just like the first time you laid eyes on me.

Show me those cold resentful eyes from when you first opened the door of your father's hut.'

'Those eyes weren't for you, Yarron,' Bhalar objected. 'They were for that snake, Captain Chekhmar, who wanted to take over from my father and own me as *his* slave.'

'I'm glad he didn't get that opportunity,' Yarron said through clenched teeth.

Yarron reasoned that if there were Sentinels on the base, contacting the Tzuracians through a holographic transmission might help to persuade them of his story. So, they returned to their pilot seats before de-cloaking the ship. Yarron pressed one of the blue crystal studs on his Pledge ring, then held his hands clasped together at his waist. He didn't have to wait long before a ghostly image of a Sentinel standing an arm's length from Yarron's body appeared in the misty haze of a projected beam of light.

The receiver initiated the conversation, beginning with a Sentinel salute. 'I'm Sergeant Syprah, 32nd Infantry, Kompak Refuel Base, Western Quadrant. Who are you and what's your business? We don't recognise your ship.'

Yarron drew breath. 'I'm Lieutenant Brekhan, 7th Squadron, Terra Major,' he said confidently. 'This ship has been modified to avoid identification as a Tzuracian vessel. I'm returning from a special mission after capturing an enemy Treldarian.' Yarron raised his arm and pointed to Bhalar who was now standing restrained, nearby. 'I'm on my way back to Terra Major to report to General Dakhar who wants to interrogate this prisoner. The matter is urgent and I'm low on fuel and food supplies.'

'Why didn't you use normal Comms to transmit your request?' the Sergeant asked cautiously.

Yarron knew the Sergeant was testing him. He hadn't intercepted any orders about transmission security, but if the message he sent from Mankro had reached Dakhar in time, it would be standard practice for the General to have limited communication to Sentinel Pledge rings.

He called the Sergeant's bluff.

'I'm using my Pledge ring as ordered by General Dakhar to ensure a secure transmission. This Treldarian I've captured is the daughter of the general who's leading the invasion on Terra Major. Can you assist me?'

There was a long pause, causing Yarron to stress the urgency with a more intense statement. 'We're *wasting valuable time*, Sergeant.'

The Sergeant acted instantly. 'Yes, Lieutenant, I understand your plight. You have permission to land in Docking Station five. I'll arrange to have you refuelled and stocked as a priority. You'll be on your way within two hours. Sergeant Syprah, out!'

After closing the transmission, Yarron and Bhalar both breathed a sigh of relief.

'First step, successful,' whispered Yarron.

They docked through airlocks into what was obviously a hermetically sealed compound lit up under high intensity floodlights. The compound contained at least a dozen huge, globe-shaped, white tanks spread out over a large flat area and interconnected with large pipelines leading into a towering structure. The other half-dozen grey buildings on the opposite side of the compound, he surmised, were used for living and sleeping quarters for those stationed on the outpost.

While Bhalar stayed on board the craft waiting for it to be refuelled, Yarron organised the loading and storage of food stores as fast as he could. He was unsure how many Sentinel soldiers were assigned to this base, but he knew that the longer he and Bhalar stayed there, the more they were at risk of being caught out and captured.

When the sergeant started to ask more questions about his secret mission, Yarron, hid his nervous tension, shrugged his shoulders and calmly replied, 'Sorry, Sergeant, it's confidential. All I can say is the information they hope to extract from the Treldarian general's daughter will be of vital importance to use against the dark forces.'

Thankfully, the sergeant seemed to accept his response and, as promised, within two hours Yarron and Bhalar were on their way with the controls set on autopilot and hyperspeed for Terra Major.

'What do you intend to achieve Yarron, when you get to Terra Major?' asked Bhalar with keen interest as they settled back into their journey. 'You know it's a place where they execute fugitives for treachery and desertion.'

'Well, I hadn't really thought that far ahead. I've been preoccupied with my Treldarian prisoner who's been quite a handful. Why don't you take my mind off it, while I leave the restraints on your hands?'

Turning to face Yarron with a big grin she replied, 'Tell you what, my handsome saviour, I'll make a deal. You work out exactly what you need to do now, before we reach Terra Major, and I'll let you have your way with me. Deal?'

'With promises like that, how can I refuse? Deal!'

'I don't have the specifics in this plan of mine, but I can share the outline I've been churning over. If you want to add anything, please do.' He looked deeply into Bhalar's eyes. 'We need to work on this strategy together, Bhalar. I don't want any harm to come to you.'

Her eyes said it all. 'I don't want anything to happen to you either. I've grown too fond of you to lose you.'

They embraced for a precious moment before Yarron continued. 'Okay, just before we reach Terra Major which will be heavily guarded, I'll transmit a holograph to Commander Dakhar to let him know I'm travelling with General Rokan's daughter who wants to defect. I'll explain that you do *not* have allegiance to the Treldarians. You wish to help the Tzuracians win this battle by giving the Sentinels inside information about the Treldarian forces.

'I'll ask for safe passage to land on Terra Major to deliver you to the Commander in Charge of Military Operations, on the condition you're given safe sanctuary. I'll ask to join the Tzuracians in the fight to help thwart the Treldarian forces. Hopefully Dakhar will agree to these terms and ensure our safety. How does that sound, Bhalar?'

Bhalar looked worried. 'It sounds to me as if you're taking a very great risk with your life. Suppose they agree to your terms, then change their mind and grab you as soon as you make ground contact?'

'They won't,' Yarron said confidently. 'A Sentinel's word is his bond, and to break the bond is to breach the Code of Honour.'

'Does this still hold in deals with a wanted criminal who deserted their ranks?' questioned Bhalar. 'You need to be sure.'

'Yes,' he replied adamantly. 'Even with wanted criminals and deserters.'

'I'm not sure whether it's foolish or honourable, or both. But if you respect the Sentinels' morals, then I agree with your plan. I just hope they do too.'

'It's settled then. Computer,' called Yarron, adopting a more optimistic outlook, 'what's our estimated time of arrival at Terra Major?'

A crackling sound was heard over the Comms followed by the synthesised voice. 'With current hyperdrive operating at maximum speed estimated time of arrival to Terra Major, is two days, five hours, thirty-five minutes.'

'Computer,' responded Yarron, 'perform a maintenance check and provide an inventory of food and fuel. Report when completed.'

'Affirmative, Captain.'

The Comms went dead and Yarron looked directly into Bhalar's eyes with a cheeky grin. 'Well, Bhalar, my part of the deal is completed.'

'Then I suppose I'd better do the *honourable* thing,' she said, smiling, 'and live up to my word, or be excommunicated. Bring the hand restraints and follow me, Captain.'

PREPARE FOR WAR

TWO days before the graduation ceremony on Tzurac, all citizens of Khazor were requested to attend an important public meeting. The leaders and more prominent members of society gathered in the main square of the Citadel to be addressed by Senator Ghalbrak, while others gathered at satellite broadcasts at multiple locations across the vast city.

Standing on the dais, Ghalbrak waited for the chattering of the crowd to subside before commencing his announcement over the PA system. Acoustically, the main square or courtyard in the centre of the multi-storied Citadel was ideal for broadcasts with high solid sandstone walls on all sides and cobblestones underfoot.

'Citizens of Khazor, thank you for attending. I welcome those who are here in the Citadel and those who are gathered at the satellite sites across the city. We are all excited about our new cadets trained on Terra Major – the newest planet to join our Federation – officially becoming Sentinel officers. All the preparations have been put in place to make their graduation a memorable occasion. General Dakhar, Commanding Chief in Charge of Military Operations, has travelled here from the Western Quadrant to oversee the ceremony personally.'

The Senator turned to indicate with his arm where Dakhar was seated behind the dais, then turned back to face the crowd. He continued in a more sombre tone. 'Unfortunately, this is not the purpose of my address today. Citizens of Khazor, I have some disturbing news.'

The crowd hushed to a deafening silence. All eyes were on the Senator.

'General Dakhar has informed the Senate of a mounting Treldarian force from the Eastern and Southern Quadrants. Be assured, our Sentinel army is being readied as I speak, and our allies are working closely with us. Together, we have plans in place to thwart any attempts by the Treldarians to disturb our peace.'

There were gasps of surprise within the immediate crowd and ripples right across Khazor. The Senator waited for them to settle.

'Listen carefully, citizens. I'm confident our planet is safe, and we should go about our business as usual. But we need to be prepared, just in case.'

The mood of the citizens had changed dramatically. All were shocked and alarmed by the news. They were restless. Several of the females in the crowd began weeping and were quickly comforted by others.

Observing their frightened faces, Dakhar stepped over to the microphone to offer words of reassurance. 'Don't be afraid, citizens. As the Senator implied, we are in control and a strong force to reckon with. We've beaten our enemies in the recent past on Planet Iota and on Terra Major. I emphasise that we must all continue with our everyday affairs while being vigilant. Have faith in the Ancients!'

Some among the citizens cheered and applauded, but Tajhira and Torri had mixed feelings. Despite Dakhar's reassuring words that Tzurac had the upper hand, they were concerned their husbands had kept knowledge of the growing threat from them.

Torri turned to Tajhira. 'Did you know about this?'

'No, did you? I'll be asking for answers from Ehrane when he gets home.'

When the crowd eventually dispersed, Dakhar headed for a pre-arranged meeting at Senator Ghalbrak's Quarters. They needed to finalise arrangements.

'Come in, General,' the Senator called out when he noticed Dakhar standing in the doorway. 'You know our Chief-Commander for the Northern Quadrant, Admiral Harzan, of course.'

'Yes,' replied Dakhar, smiling and reaching out for a mutual Sentinel handshake. 'Good to see you again, Admiral. I'm pleased you're here.'

Harzan smiled back and gave a nod as if to say the same for Dakhar. They had been cadets together at the Officers' Academy, an academy established to train those specifically chosen from the Tzuracian defence forces – Sentinel and non-Sentinel – to become officers. After graduating, Harzan had been commissioned into the air force and Dakhar into the elite Sentinel army. Both were now highly qualified and respected senior ranking officers.

'Commanders, please take a seat,' the Senator requested.

Dakhar and Harzan made themselves comfortable at the small and functional round table while waiting for the Senator to join them. Dakhar had visited the Elder on several occasions and was still impressed with how the Senator lived. Considering his senior status as the most powerful senator in the Council, his surroundings were very modest. There were no luxury items, no expensive paintings on the walls, and no highly crafted polished furniture. In fact, the room was devoid of most things a person of the Senator's age and achievements could have accumulated.

But what the room had that was quite unique was wall-to-wall bookcases with open shelves stacked absolutely full of leather-bound volumes on just about every subject known to the Tzuracians, especially law. The Senator was the wisest and most knowledgeable Tzuracian on the planet who was sought after for advice and consultation and Ghalbrak still considered that electronic storage of data was no match for applying wisdom from the accumulated knowledge of the Tzuracian mind. Dakhar knew it would be a very sad loss when the Senator's time came to an end. No-one could replace the master whom he had come to deeply respect and admire.

When he was seated, Ghalbrak spoke directly to Dakhar. His tone was serious. 'Now, General Dakhar, I've briefed Admiral Harzan, so please show us what you have. Tell me what you've planned in our defences against the Treldarian hordes.'

From his Pledge ring, Dakhar instantly projected a hologram displaying an aerial view of Khazor City and the moons orbiting Tzurac. 'What I propose Senator, is for us to position our fleet of ten warships, including my Flagship and one hundred Destroyer battleships, just above the surface on the shadow side of our first moon, Jorhan. This will be close enough for us to strike and surprise the Treldarian armada as it approaches Tzurac. The enemy won't be expecting us to come from behind and they'll be unable to detect us if our ships are in stealth mode as the Treldarian armada passes by the moon. Our plan is to intercept and eliminate the enemy armada at this point.'

Ghalbrak and Harzan were following Dakhar's plan closely.

'However, I think we should leave the remaining Destroyer battleships hidden in the underground hangars on Khazor to deploy just in case a stray Treldarian ship manages to evade our ambush and engage in dogfights closer to the surface. Khazor is sheltered by our huge, protective Dome and we're not expecting the enemy to reach the surface of Tzurac. In the unlikely event they do, our gun turrets, which are spread strategically over the entire planet, will also be ready to activate. What are your thoughts?'

'A sound strategy,' Admiral Harzan said in his mellow voice. 'But what if the enemy armada doesn't pass Jorhan and enters our star system from another direction? Won't this make it difficult to execute your battle plan? They could take us by surprise and our fleet ships may not be able to intercept the Treldarians before they attack Tzurac.'

'Good point, Admiral. I've thought about this. I expect the Treldarians will come via Jorhan as the more direct path from the Eastern Quadrant. However, if they come from another direction, we have contingencies.

'On our other two moons, Kelzhar and Wurtah, located on the other side of Tzurac, we've had satellite transceivers for deep space tracking in place since the end of the Grekadian War. These transceivers can detect and identify with pinpoint accuracy any objects travelling through our Northern Quadrant. If the enemy approaches from that direction, we'd be alerted well in advance, giving us time to relocate our fleet to the other moons and apply the same strategic moves. We also have remote, armed laser cannons hidden within the craters of all three moons, which can be activated on our signal.'

Dakhar paused allowing the others time to absorb the information.

After a moment, the Senator and Chief-Commander nodded their heads to show their satisfaction.

'Well,' said Harzan, 'you've convinced me. However, I'm going to throw you a possible scenario. What if some of the invaders' vessels manage to avoid being hit by our ships' laser cannons, as well as attacks launched by our Destroyer battleships? What if they destroy the protective Dome and land their ships on Tzurac's surface? Do you have plans in place to deal with Treldarian ground troops of super-soldiers swarming towards the city?'

'Another good point, Admiral,' replied Dakhar. 'Perhaps Senator Ghalbrak has already informed you that we've gained the support of the Urgellans?'

'Yes, he has.'

Dakhar went on. 'Five thousand Urgellan super-soldiers will be arriving in the next day or so. I intend to mobilise them in a similar manner we used in the battle on Terra Iota. This proved to be a very successful strategy. We won't have enough of these soldiers to deploy too widely. So, I'll place them in a half-mile circle around Khazor, concealed in the forests with lookouts in the tallest trees. Their green uniforms will camouflage them, and their archery skills will be invaluable.

'I'll position the Sentinels not far behind them within a quarter-mile radius, interspersed with two hundred laser cannons. If the Treldarian forces break through the outer perimeter of Urgellans, they'll face a wall of Sentinels and be trapped between our two armies – Urgellans behind and Sentinels in front. The defence walls surrounding the Citadel will be fortified with a regiment of Sentinel soldiers supported by gun turrets fully stacked with laser cannons. The Destroyer battleships will also provide air support as well as fly-over ground cover.'

The Senator, who had sat silent for most of Dakhar's talk stroking his white beard and watching with intrigue, turned to Dakhar. 'From what you've shown us, this plan of yours has been well thought out. It looks like we're well prepared. But you also told the Senate about Terra Major coming under attack simultaneously. What plans have you to protect our newest member of the Federation?'

The Senator and Admiral Harzan looked directly at Dakhar with worried expressions, waiting for an explanation.

Closing down the holograph, Dakhar made himself more comfortable in his chair before answering their concerns. 'Sirs, we know the size of the Treldarian forces attacking Terra Major. My fleet of warships and battleships should be enough to combat the Treldarian armada in the outer orbit of Earth. However, if they manage to break through and mobilise their soldiers on the surface, our two regiments of Sentinel soldiers, reinforced with two thousand resurrected Diutrons, should be adequate to deal with their armies of Treldarians and their allies.

'I've placed my trust and confidence in one of the most experienced and loyal veterans in our army, Captain Kal Zawkon. His record shows he is highly skilled as a war tactician. He's won many successful battles in the past with very few Tzuracian casualties. His knowledge of Treldarian warfare is second to none. I've appointed him acting Chief-Commander in my absence and trust him to design a strategic and effective battle plan for Terra Major.'

There was a moment's pause before Admiral Harzan cut in. 'I've heard of this Captain Zawkon. His reputation as a fierce warrior is well known throughout the ranks. I believe you've chosen the best soldier for the job, Commander.'

The Senator cleared his throat and spoke directly to Dakhar. 'Time is of the essence. As the Elder I have the authority to approve this battle plan without consulting the other senators. Therefore, if Admiral Harzan agrees with your plan, Commander, I'll sanction this operation now.'

Harzan indicated his approval and the three rose from the table, Dakhar giving a Sentinel salute to the others before disappearing out of the room.

* * *

When he arrived home later in the afternoon, Dakhar received a somewhat uneasy reception from Tajhira and Torri. Tajhira initiated the conversation as he sat on the couch beside her. She looked worried.

'So, my husband, the Treldarians are gathering again? I thought we'd seen the last of them. Why didn't you tell us earlier?'

She paused for Dakhar's response. Dakhar raised his eyebrows, but before he could speak, Tajhira cut in. 'It's terrible news. When did you find out about this? Did you know before we left Terra Major? You may have put Torri and the children in real danger.'

'Hold on,' said Dakhar, raising his hands outstretched in front of him, in an attempt to explain. 'I know it's bad news. It's a shock to us all. May the Ancients protect us. But remember, I told you in confidence on Terra Major – and I assume Kyron told Torri – there was a rumour the Treldarians might start a war with the Federation. I asked Kyron at the time if he wished to reconsider bringing his family with him to Tzurac. He said if the rumour were true, he would want his family close beside him where he could better protect them.'

Torri spoke up. 'That's true. Kyron and I decided we would want all of us here together on Tzurac.'

Dakhar continued, 'It was only late yesterday afternoon that I received a devastating holograph from Yarron, confirming the Treldarians are intending to attack Tzurac and Terra Major simultaneously, and soon. The bloodthirsty warmongers! I wanted to tell you, but I couldn't breach the code of confidentiality. You know that, as Chief-Commander, I'm obliged to inform the Senate first. They commanded secrecy and an immediate defence plan.

'So last night Kyron and I worked together till the early hours of the morning on a strategic plan to intercept any invaders before they reach us. I presented my plan to the Senate first thing this morning. It all happened so fast with no time to talk to you in private, Tajhira. I'm sorry you had to hear the first of it in a public arena, but my immediate priority was devising a battle plan.'

'Very well, Ehrane,' said Tajhira looking apologetic. 'I was so overcome with fear for all of us, including our dear friends. I'm sorry for questioning your responsibilities.'

'I well understand your concerns, Tajhira,' Dakhar said, rising from his seat and embracing her with a long and comforting hug. 'I'll not let any harm come to you or Torri and all our children.'

* * *

Next morning after arranging to see the Fleet Commodore, Dakhar left the Main Hall and went to the air base. He was escorted by one of the Flight Lieutenants to the office of Fleet Commodore Morkhan Tarhdok. The Commodore had become a permanent fixture at the Khazor Air base since graduating from the Space Academy as a Flight Lieutenant some forty years ago. He had worked his way up the ranks with hard work and dedication and was an officer well respected by his aircrew and the Tzuracian military. His knowledge of crafts and war strategies was unequalled, and he was a no-nonsense officer who didn't tolerate incompetence or weak excuses. On appearances he was hardened, with steely blue eyes which could burn through your gaze, a square jaw, straight face and solid physique. But for those who knew him well and were respected by him, the Commodore showed a compassionate heart.

Tarhdok welcomed Dakhar with a warm smile and a Tzuracian handshake. 'Good to see you again. It's been a while, Captain, or should I say, General. Congratulations on your appointment.'

'Yes, it's been far too long since I saw you last, Commodore.'

'There was urgency in your voice when you contacted me. What can I do to help?'

Dakhar presented the battle plan to the Commodore and requested he mobilise the fleets to their respective locations immediately.

'We need to surprise the enemy before they have a chance to strike. We're going ahead with the ceremony as if all is normal. As soon as it's complete, I'll take the graduate lieutenants in a Destroyer to the warships stationed behind Moon Jorhan. You can assign the remaining graduates to the Destroyer battleships based here on Tzurac. We need to maintain Comms silence once the ships are in position to prevent the Treldarians intercepting our transmissions. I'll use my Pledge ring to contact the officers on board the other warships. Are you okay with this, Commodore?'

There was no hesitation, 'Yes of course, General. I'll action it straight away.'

'Thank you, Commodore. May the Ancient spirits protect us and guide us to victory.'

STRATEGIC MANOEUVRES

YARRON was in the pilot's seat reading diagnostics from a status report on his computer screen when crackling from the Comms disturbed his concentration. A monotone synthesized voice followed.

'Captain, continuing at hyperspeed, the ship will enter Terra Major's orbit in one hour.'

Yarron responded promptly and began typing in coordinates. 'Computer, reduce our speed by half, change to stealth mode and raise shields to sixty percent. Here are our landing coordinates.'

He turned to Bhalar seated next to him in the co-pilot's chair. 'I need to send a holograph to General Dakhar to negotiate an amnesty for us. If you stay seated where you are, he'll be able to see you clearly.'

Pressing one of the blue gems on his Pledge ring, a bluish light projected onto the console and, within minutes, the ghostly image of a Sentinel appeared. As the ethereal blanket slowly dissipated, General Dakhar's silhouette emerged.

'General Dakhar,' Yarron began, 'this is Yarron Blandhar. I have a request which will benefit both of us in the fight against the Treldarians.'

There was a momentary pause. 'Alright, Yarron, you have my ear.'

'I'm *en route* to Terra Major. As you can see,' Yarron continued, pointing to Bhalar, 'I have with me the daughter of the General who is leading the Treldarian forces to invade Terra Major. Her name is Bhalar Rokan, and her father is General Rokan of the Third Legion. She helped me to escape from their base in the Southern Quadrant and she wants to defect to the Federation.

'Bhalar has valuable information about her father's strategic plans and the Treldarians' military strengths, weaponry and weaknesses. She's asking for asylum in return for this information. I trust her with my life, General, and I know she'll be of great value in helping us win this war. So, would you permit her safe passage to Terra Major? And would you also allow me to join the Sentinels on Earth as a 'gun-for-hire' in the fight against the Treldarian invasion? We both want to be of service and help in any way we can to thwart the invasion.'

Again, there was a moment's delay before Dakhar responded. 'Yarron, we've appreciated the help you've given to us previously and your dedication to our cause. However, I recall you trusting another female in the recent past – a female who betrayed all of us and, with the Treldarian Bladers, very nearly brought the Federation down. Now you want us to trust a female Treldarian? The daughter of one of their generals? Have your emotions clouded your judgment once more?' He was sceptical.

'You're right, General. I *was* fooled by Khaneera Zarkwin. But this is very different, sir. Bhalar is putting her life on the line to help us. She is carrying no equipment or weapons – she has nothing other than the clothes she's wearing. On arrival on Terra Major, you can take her into custody and question her.'

Dakhar thought carefully for a short time before answering. 'Alright, Yarron, I'll trust you again and grant you both temporary amnesty. Deliver Bhalar to acting Chief-Commander Zawkon on Terra Major and you can assist us in the battle against the Treldarian invaders. Advise us of your ship's details and I'll arrange for Commander Zawkon to meet you at the ASPECT Air base when you land. I trust in your sincerity, Yarron. Don't disappoint me.'

Yarron signed off, ordered the computer to increase speed to full hyperdrive and turned to Bhalar with a smile. 'We'll be safe,' he said confidently.

* * *

Three hours later, the Sentinel fugitive piloted his unmarked black craft onto the ASPECT Air base escorted by two of General Blake's jetfighters flanked on either side of his vessel.

Yarron was surprised by the numbers deployed to meet just two people. Commander Zawkon was accompanied by a regiment of Sentinels who were all lined up, standing at the ready on either side of the walkway. General Blake and a unit of armed Terranian military personnel stood to their rear. Yarron was pleased to see his former brothers-in-arms on a familiar planet, but he was still somewhat apprehensive about how he and Bhalar would be received.

As the two disembarked from his ship, Yarron dressed in green Urgellan attire and Bhalar in her simple Treldarian sarong, Zawkon and Blake approached them. Everyone seemed surprised to see the unlikely couple – a black-haired, would-be Urgellan in a dark-green uniform rather than a blonde Sentinel in a maroon outfit and blue cape; and a remarkably good-looking and well-shaped Treldarian woman. Zawkon had encountered female Treldarian warriors before, but as he approached the new arrivals, he was quite taken by Bhalar's stunning appearance. She was more attractive than any Treldarian female he'd ever seen. In fact, he was mesmerised by her refined features.

Shifting his gaze to Yarron, Zawkon spoke in a formal manner. 'Corporal Blandhar, I presume? You may address me as Commander Zawkon. This is General Blake, Administrator of ASPECT. We're here to escort the Treldarian female to the Citadel. General Dakhar informed me of your proposal and under the circumstances, I'll honour his decision. You've been granted temporary amnesty to help the Federation in this battle. The daughter of the Treldarian General has also been given a temporary amnesty until a decision about her defection has been made by the Senate Council. We're grateful for the help you've given us in the past, Corporal, and the vital information you've supplied. You have my word we'll not fire upon you during the imminent battle. However, be warned soldier, we can't promise your safety if you get in our way. Do I make myself clear, Corporal?'

'Yes, sir,' replied Yarron now standing at attention with respect for his superior. He maintained a straight cold face, 'Perfectly clear, sir. But I want no harm to come to Bhalar. General Rokan's daughter has come here of her own free will and in good faith. She'll tell you all there is to know about the invading Treldarian army, and I'll expect you to treat her with dignity and courtesy. Do I have *your* word, Commander Zawkon?'

Zawkon wasn't used to being spoken to in this way by a subordinate, although he realised the benefits both Yarron and Bhalar were offering the Federation. 'Yes Corporal, you have my word. If General Blake approves, you're welcome to stay on base in your ship until the invasion starts.'

The General signalled his approval by touching the peak of his cap and turned to his unit. 'Escort General Rokan's daughter to the Citadel.'

Yarron agreed with the arrangements and then turned to Bhalar with a warm smile. 'Don't be afraid, Bhalar. They'll take good care of you, and I'll see you soon.' He wanted to give her a loving hug and a parting kiss, but he didn't want to create ill-feeling or resentment by fraternizing intimately with the enemy in full view of others. 'You have the word of a Sentinel Chief-Commander. You'll not be harmed, Bhalar.'

Bhalar smiled affectionately at Yarron as the escort unit surrounded her and led her away.

Commander Zawkon ordered Yarron to re-board his ship and asked General Blake to place a guard around the perimeter.

In turn, General Blake gave a direct order to the Lieutenant standing at his side, 'Corporal Blandhar is not to leave his ship without the express permission of myself or Commander Zawkon. There are a number of Sentinels here on Earth who were on Tzurac at the time Yarron freed Khaneera Zarkwin and stole the Xytrinium formula. Although Yarron has helped us since then, and promises to do so again, many Sentinels still regard him as a traitor. So, for his own safety, and for the security of the Base, he needs to remain out of sight. I'll hold you responsible.'

The Lieutenant saluted. 'Yes sir, understood!'

* * *

Back at the Citadel, Commander Zawkon sat in a private room with Bhalar. He questioned her firmly, but gently.

'First of all, I need to know why you're asking to defect to the Federation. We need to be sure you aren't a spy trying to gain access to classified information.'

Bhalar looked at the Commander, clearly surprised at the inference. She responded calmly and confidently. 'I understand your concerns given I'm the daughter of a Treldarian general. But I'm *not* a spy and I'm *not* working for my father, or for the Treldarians.'

She went on to explain her history and circumstances, 'I've wanted to escape from my father for a long time. So, when Yarron

196

arrived on our planet, it was the opportunity I'd been waiting for. I saved his life in return for him helping me. You can confirm this with him. If I was a spy, I would've told my father what Yarron's transmission said, but I kept this information to myself. I only alerted my father that Yarron had sent a transmission so he would imprison Yarron and provide me the opportunity for us to escape together. On the night of his capture, while all the soldiers and my father were getting drunk in celebration of the coming war, I freed Yarron, and we escaped in his spacecraft. Thankfully, we made it here safely.'

While looking directly into her eyes, Commander Zawkon reflected on her story. *He sensed she was telling the truth. His Sentinel instincts told him so.* 'Alright, Bhalar, I believe you. I thank you for keeping secret the contents of the message sent by Yarron. It's imperative we maintain an element of surprise. So, what can you tell us about your father's army which could help us in our defence? How many are there? What are their strengths and weaknesses? What type of artillery do they have? And what is their plan of attack?'

Bhalar took a deep breath before answering. 'I believe my father now has an army of three thousand soldiers; one thousand Treldarians who've been made into super-soldiers from Xytrinium injections; and two thousand primitive Nujharenes who use basic weaponry and ancient firearms that use black powder to fire bronze bullets.

'They're coming with five warships and a considerable number of small crafts. They have laser cannons on board these ships, but plan to limit their use because they have limited reserves of Xytrinium. Their plan is to focus on the central points of control on Terra Major where your space fleets are stationed. My father will attempt to break through your air defences and mobilise his soldiers on the ground for a land assault.'

Zawkon interrupted, 'How would your father know the location of our central points of control?'

'Information about your planet was given to my father by a Blader called Captain Ramlok who said he'd fought with Dranz against the Federation in the recent past and conspired with the Earthling, Jackson Jensen. Captain Ramlok was the one who brought us the method and equipment to make super-soldiers.'

Zawkon cursed inwardly. It was now evident Ramlok must have escaped from planet Steiros with the Xytrinium formula before Zawkon and his Sentinels attacked and captured General Dranz and his army of Bladers. *He thought he'd eliminated any possibility of the formula falling into further enemy hands. Obviously not. Ramlok was a marked man.*

He refocused his thoughts. 'Anything else we should know about your father's plans, Bhalar?' asked Zawkon with deep interest.

'Yes, there is. After your central control points have fallen, his fleet will move on to destroy the other major cities on your planet. He intends to control all the Xytrinium reserves and take his revenge for the execution of General Dranz. The Treldarians want to annihilate the Federation once and for all, and that's why there will be a simultaneous assault by the Eastern Quadrant Treldarians on Planet Tzurac.'

Zawkon's mind was ticking over. *He knew he had only a small window of time to set things in place.*

'Thank you, Bhalar. This is most helpful. We'll need to detain you here until the battle is over. You'll be treated as our guest, and I'll arrange for you to stay in one of the guest rooms in the Citadel.'

'Thanks, Commander. You're most kind.'

Zawkon turned to one of his soldiers. 'Lieutenant, take Bhalar to one of the guest rooms in the west wing. Make sure she has everything she needs for her comfort. I want a guard posted outside her room for her safety and protection!'

'Yes, sir! Please come with me Ms Rokan.'

As Bhalar left the room Zawkon mused for a moment. *Bhalar was so naturally beautiful, both inside and out. No wonder Yarron wanted to protect her.*

As soon as Bhalar and the Lieutenant left, Zawkon went straight to General Blake's office. After settling into one of Blake's visitor's chairs, Zawkon commenced, 'Let me brief you, General, about what I've just learned …'

He finished with a plan for action. 'Bhalar confirmed her father will be focussing his forces on ASPECT and MERIC first and will then proceed to other major cities. I propose we evacuate immediately all citizens within a fifty-mile radius of New York. I'll notify the World Assembly to be prepared for possible attacks elsewhere.'

As Commander Zawkon stood to leave the General's office, he received a Sentinel holograph transmission on his Pledge ring.

'Commander, this is Captain Skarhdok. The Diutrons have been reactivated and are on their way to Terra Major with Lieutenant Hurbarq in charge. They should be arriving within twenty-four hours and Engineer Thompson is accompanying them.'

'Thank you, Captain. Are you prepared in case the Treldarians attack Iota?'

'Yes, sir. The miners and their families are all safe in the underground bunker and our defences are now in place. We're ready, sir!'

'Very good, Captain. Keep me posted. May the Ancient spirits protect you! Zawkon, out!'

He turned to General Blake. 'Be ready to off-load the Diutrons.'

* * *

In the afternoon, from his office in the Citadel, Commander Zawkon ordered the remaining fleet of six warships to migrate to the dark side of Earth's moon and maintain stealth mode – cloaked and silent, and undetectable to their enemy. Communication back to base was by Pledge ring holographs only. He directed battle stations on Earth to be manned by Sentinel units around the clock with Destroyer battleships piloted and at-the-ready hidden in the underground hangars. He directed General Blake to mobilise the Terranian troops in the planned strategic locations and to begin evacuating the city using the subways of New York. Now, the only operation left was to strategically position the Diutrons when they arrived.

He didn't have to wait long. There was a rush of activity at ASPECT in the early hours of the following morning. The three imposing Tzuracian warships, with huge cargoes on board, docked at the air base. General Blake and Commander Zawkon stood watching the enormous vessels overshadow everything on the field.

Large thick hatch-doors on the sides of each blue- metallic ship began sliding open with loud hydraulic shunting noises. Heavy metal gangplanks shot straight out from the hatches and then tilted, lowering slowly to the ground forming steep, angled ramps.

No sooner had the first side-hatch opened, than a sign of life appeared, making its way down the ramp. It wasn't a Diutron as Zawkon had anticipated, but instead a red headed, red bearded Irishman, dwarfed by the giant construction from which he was disembarking. It was none other than the jolly Grant Thompson, approaching with a huge grin and a lively step.

'Hello, Commander,' Grant called out in his strong accent as he waved, 'How'd ya be lad?'

'I'd be fine,' replied Zawkon, mimicking Grant's Irish lilt. 'What took you so long?'

'Spent too much time lookin' for dat bloody elusive pot-o'-gold, I did.'

They both laughed and shook hands.

'General, may I introduce Chief Engineer Grant Thompson, and Grant, this is General Blake, the Senior Administrator of ASPECT and the Space Academy.'

The men shook hands.

'Good to finally put a face to the name of the officer I've heard so much about.'

Then, once the 'all clear' was given, Grant demonstrated the small control module he held in his hand. As he pressed several buttons, a screen came to life on the device showing the current location, area and compass markings.

'This looks similar to the navigational guidance systems on our jet fighters,' the General remarked, looking over the Irishman's shoulder.

'Yes, General,' said Grant enthusiastically, 'I used the same principle. The program's been reconfigured so the Diutrons can recognise friend and foe. They'll only attack the enemy – Treldarian military and Kyroni warriors and anyone else who threatens them with weapons. Their infrared sensors can also detect powered weapons on the enemy. Now are we ready to start the parade, gentlemen?'

'Go ahead, Grant,' said Zawkon. 'Show us what you can do. Hope you assembled more than one controller module?'

'Are ya daft man!' replied Grant defensively, raising the volume of his voice, 'I wouldn't be lettin' these killin' machines wander too far out o' range and go on a rampage. This is the 'Master module' I have in me' hot little hands. It'll override the t'ree udda smaller controller modules I made. I'll need to instruct whoever will be usin' dese controllers 'cause they're more *bloody* complex to operate than the simple devices used for remote-controlled quadcopters or virtual reality games!'

The Commander and the General couldn't help chuckling.

'Alright, Grant, point taken. I knew I could rely on you to think ahead. Job well done! Now start the parade, Master Controller.'

The first robotic monster appeared. Weighing over two tons, it began making its way slowly down the ramp, walking on thick mechanical legs, its powerful automated arms moving backwards and forwards to maintain its balance down the steep slope. Appearing behind it, was what seemed like a never-ending line of identical machines, their heavy movements reverberating across the air base. The Diutrons looked almost indestructible with a two-inch-thick steel-plated exoskeleton fused onto another external layer of one-inch-thick Xytrinium armour.

Zawkon recalled the devastation the Diutrons had caused in the battle on Terra Iota, while the army personnel who had not encountered the machines before, including General Blake, were simply amazed.

'Strange alien engineering, but I can't wait to test them under battle conditions,' said Blake. 'If any of the Treldarian vessels are lucky enough to land on Earth's surface they won't be expecting this!'

Zawkon smiled. 'We'll give them a bit of their own medicine here and in Washington. Grant, leave five hundred on board. We need Diutron reinforcements in both locations.'

THE DARK FORCE COMETH

WHEN the Urgellans arrived at Khazor, twenty-four hours before the graduation ceremony, Commander Dakhar was there to greet them. Row by row, five thousand red-headed soldiers, dressed in dark-green camouflaged uniforms, bows strapped on their backs, pistols and blades hanging from their belts, filed out of the three warships. Once assembled on Tzuracian soil, Dakhar led them to the Citadel's main courtyard to be briefed.

Standing on the pedestal with the senators seated behind him, all Dakhar could see before him was a sea of green. He began his speech over the PA system in their native Urgellan tongue.

'Friends of Tzurac and the Federation …' He paused and took a deep breath. 'First of all, let me start by saying, we welcome and thank all of you for volunteering to help us in these grave times. We're very grateful you're joining us to prevent this dark force not only from conquering Tzurac, but also from destroying the Federation of Planets and the rest of the Universe in which we've lived in peace and harmony for over five hundred years. We're unsure about the size of the Treldarian army that is bound for Tzurac – we don't know the size of their armada of warships or the numbers of soldiers they will bring. However, we're well fortified and well-armed, and have the element of surprise in our favour. Our fleet is in waiting, ready to strike.

'We plan to destroy their ships before they reach Tzurac's outer orbit. But, if we're unsuccessful and the Treldarian enemy breaks through, we'll launch Destroyers from Tzurac to engage them. The ultimate threat to us is if they manage to destroy our protective Dome. Then, our ground troops with *your* assistance will be called upon to defend our planet.

'Captain Zawkon, who fought with you on Planet Iota against the Treldarian Bladers, has suggested we use similar tactics to defend Khazor. The plan is to position yourselves in a half-mile radius, hidden in our dense forests, using showers of arrows in the first instance to halt the enemy's advance. Any of our enemies who are lucky enough to breach this line of defence, will be confronted by an inner circle of Sentinel soldiers and be trapped between our two armies.

'Be mindful my friends, the Treldarian soldiers from the Eastern Quadrant have also been infused with Xytrinium. They'll be equally matched with your strength and agility in hand-to-hand combat. Fortunately, the enemy will be unaware of your presence until we attack. So, stay hidden and make every arrow a fatal wound. I'm confident, with your skills and experience, we'll defeat them again.

'Once deployed in your respective places in the field, I emphasize the need to maintain silence, limiting your transmissions to emergencies only. I trust your leader, Aloran, to direct you and I wish you all success in battle. May the Ancients protect you!'

Finally, raising his voice and his sword, he cried out, 'Urgellans! Are we ready to do battle and be victorious?'

Instantly a roar rose from the crowd, the soldiers thrusting their hand-held swords and bows above their heads before breaking into a war chant. It was a centuries' old battle-cry, handed down from father to son – a ritual performed by the Urgellans before every battle.

Dakhar was overwhelmed at the show of dedication and passion. *The Urgellans were clearly determined to thwart the enemies who threatened them and protect their loved ones and their homes at all costs.*

Eventually the noise subsided and the Urgellan soldiers organised themselves quickly into their own clans, indicated by the different, yet very distinctive, tartan berets they wore. They were then led by Sentinel escorts to their dedicated field locations. Everything on the ground was now set in place.

Mid-afternoon, General Dakhar received a holograph from First Officer Senior Flight Commander, Captain Lombharq, on-board the Flagship *Rhazon*, named in honour of the General's famous grandfather. Lombharq confirmed all fleet ships were in place behind the two moons with an Armonusian high priest on-board each warship to provide physical and psychic healing. Laser cannons hidden in the craters of Tzurac's three moons were also confirmed as operational.

'Thanks, Commander. I'll be joining you in a Destroyer immediately after the ceremony. With me will be six newly assigned lieutenants for deployment to the other warships as First Officers. I think we're as ready as we'll ever be to do battle. Once we're in place, it'll just be a waiting game.'

* * *

Early the next morning, just before sunrise, the Chief-Commander's household was a flurry of activity. Both Dakhar and Kyron were adding the final touches to their full-dress maroon-and-blue uniforms, with metallic silver buttons and buckles polished to a gleaming shine; sashes crisply pressed; seams on sleeves and trousers razor-straight; black knee-high leather boots mirror-shined; and their shimmering shield-capes correctly affixed over their left shoulders.

Meantime, their wives, both attired in the latest designed brightly coloured Tzuracian costumes, were also making sure nothing was out of place. They had spent most of the morning painting their faces with powders and potions and adorning themselves with sparkling jewellery. Kyron was surprised to see Torri indulging in all the feminine finery in which she was usually not interested. With her natural beauty she didn't need to emphasise her already-refined features of stunning green eyes, cute nose, soft-pink lips and long silky chestnut-red hair. *Though a touch of makeup does enhance her looks,* Kyron thought.

For the special occasion Torri was wearing an antique-gold Cartier timepiece Kyron had given to her on one of her birthdays, her gold and diamond wedding ring, diamond ear studs, and a gold bangle. She was also wearing the precious star-brooch which served a dual purpose. Dakhar had given it to her several years ago to communicate with him during their first encounter with the conspirator Jackson Jensen. *She looks stunning,* thought Kyron. *Tajhira has had a strong influence on her, bringing out more of her feminine qualities.*

Meanwhile, the three children were expending their excess energies, racing around the house and getting under everyone's feet. They were the first to be dressed in their best outfits, and were entertaining themselves with games, while waiting for their parents to finish what they were doing.

'Zuri! Ehrana!' Kyron called in a strong and fatherly tone of voice. 'No crawling on the floor or you'll get your clothes marked!'

Dakhar echoed, 'That goes for you as well, Kyrah.'

All three children were fully engrossed in their games and too excited to hear. The words evaporated into thin air as soon as they were spoken. Yet soon, all finely attired, the three children accompanied by their parents, were travelling in Dakhar's hover-transporter to the Citadel.

Light began to streak across the massive fortress as the sun started to creep slowly above the silhouetted horizon. Flickering in the soft breeze atop the high stone walls the numerous high-masted blue-and-maroon-coloured flags cast their long shadows across the grey cobbled expanse of the courtyard. Kyron could feel the excitement in the atmosphere. *Today marked the day he would be fully accepted as a Sentinel in the elite Tzuracian Army. His father would have been proud of him and his mother would also feel the pride which only a mother can have for her son.*

While Torri, Tajhira and the children headed for the main entrance, Kyron diverted to the parade ground to join the rest of his graduation class. Within minutes of his arrival, the cadets were instructed to assemble in their respective rows in alphabetical order. Standing rigidly at attention, they were inspected by their commanding officer and handed their maroon felt-and-leather graduation caps displaying on the short peaks a brass insignia of a 'Lieutenant, First Class'. Right on schedule, they proudly marched into the side entrance of the west-facing citadel wall.

Once inside the Main Hall, the graduates were seated in the front stalls, just a few paces from the podium. Behind them, their parents and many of the citizens of Tzurac filled the seats, all the way to the back wall. The audience looked resplendent, clothed in their bright and colourful fine-woven garments. They were dressed up to show off their latest acquired fashions.

Behind and to the side of them, Sentinel soldiers in full battle dress lined each wall of the room, standing rigidly at attention. Their shiny silver helmets and swords held upright glistened from the reflection of the sun's rays shining through the glass windows of the high domed ceiling and the small circular side windows on the eastern walls. Colourful banners and more flags of various sizes decorated the walls. Noise from the continuous chattering of the large crowd almost drowned out the background military music filtering through the PA system.

Turning his head around, Kyron saw the smiling, joyous faces of the throng, and amongst them he could just make out Torri and the children seated next to Tajhira, way down in the back stalls. They were looking in his direction, so he winked and nodded his head, and in response Torri gave a big grin and held up a thumb for good luck. The atmosphere was electric.

As the music stopped, Chief-Commander Ehrane Dakhar emerged from behind the long ceiling-to-floor midnight-blue velvet drapes on one side of the stage and strode onto the podium with an air of authority. He was followed by Admiral Harzan and the senators who quietly took their respective seats in the large wooden chairs towards the back of the podium. In the centre of the stage in front of them was a long table covered with a dark-blue cloth. And spread out upon it was a large number of very small dark-red velvet boxes and neatly stacked white scrolls each tied in the middle with a narrow silver ribbon.

Dakhar approached the sculptured metal pulpit to commence his introductions. The now still and hushed crowd waited in anticipation as the military music faded.

'Citizens, visitors, dignitaries, and friends of Tzurac,' Dakhar uttered in a loud voice, 'I want to thank all of you for attending this auspicious occasion. I'm aware the timing of this graduation isn't ideal while we're dealing with a potential enemy threat. However, after years of training and commitment, our cadets deserve to receive their reward and become officers in our elite army. They deserve to be recognised for their achievements.

'These are the first to graduate from a Sentinel Officers' Academy based on another planet, Terra Major. Today, these highly skilled and well-educated Sentinels will be officially inducted as officers, to serve in the Regiments with allegiance to the Federation and to uphold the Sentinel Code of Honour.'

Dakhar paused for a moment while the audience applauded. *He was enjoying the welcome relief from battle preparations.* 'I'll now call upon our Elder, Senator Ghalbrak, to help bestow the honours.'

The Senator rose from his chair and walked to the long table. He picked up one of the scrolls, acknowledged the writing on it and called in a soft voice to Dakhar.

The Chief-Commander then turned to face the seated cadets calling out, 'First Officer Lieutenant Jheron Bahtork, please step up to the podium to receive your Diploma and Sentinel Pledge ring.'

As the cadet made his way onto the stage, the Elder handed the scroll and a small velvet box to Dakhar. Standing in front of his Chief-Commander, the cadet saluted and stood at attention. Dakhar returned the salute and passed the scroll to the cadet. He opened the lid of the box to display a gold ring and gave it to Cadet Bahtork before speaking out loudly enough for the audience to hear.

'Congratulations on your achievement First Lieutenant Bahtork. This Pledge ring is engraved with your family name. Wear it proudly.'

Dakhar continued, 'Written on your graduation diploma is the Regiment to which you have been assigned. I wish you all the best for your future as a Sentinel officer.'

'Thank you, sir,' said the cadet humbly, saluting. Dakhar returned the salute, and the cadet marched to the velvet curtains on the other side of the stage to the loud applause of the audience.

The protocol continued as each cadet was called in alphabetical order to accept their diploma and Pledge ring.

Finally, it was Kyron's turn.

'First Officer, Lieutenant Kyron Tyros.'

Kyron hastily ascended the platform and presented himself to his Chief-Commander. After exchanging their formal salutes, Dakhar handed Kyron his graduate diploma and then turned to the crowd.

'This is the son of Captain Ahrmon Tyros. Kyron Tyros has returned to Tzurac from Terra Major. Many of you may not know this, but three hundred years ago after Captain Ahrmon Tyros was falsely accused of my father's murder, Ahrmon Tyros thankfully escaped to Terra Major where he started a new life with a Terranian family under the name of Rhamon Shield.

'It was only by a stroke of fate, most likely engineered by the Ancient spirits, that I discovered Kyron who was wearing his father's Pledge ring. His father had raised him in secret on Earth as a Sentinel soldier, instructing him in weaponry and martial arts. While still unaware of his heritage, Kyron graduated as a Senior Engineer from one of the Terranian Royal Colleges. It was while he was investigating an explosion on Planet Iota, caused by the unearthing of Xytrinium, that our lives crossed.

'I'm now just as proud of Kyron as his father would have been seeing him graduate as a First Officer. I've fought by his side and he's as skilled as any of the best Sentinels. I owe my life to him for his actions in saving me from what could have been a fatal wound incurred during recent events on Terra Major. Please make him feel welcome.'

Spontaneous applause broke out and Kyron stood silent and proud, somewhat overwhelmed by the warmth of the crowd's response. He could just make out Torri wiping tears from her eyes and cheeks, smiling with pride and admiration. Kyron saluted the crowd, turned and marched off the stage, diploma in hand.

The ceremonial inductions continued for half an hour. Afterwards the attendees and the dismissed cadets milled around tables of food and drink placed around the walkways of the hall.

When Kyron joined Torri, Tajhira and the children, Tajhira couldn't help but comment, 'Lieutenant Tyros, you looked so handsome and debonair up there on stage in your dress uniform, with your Officer's cap, your shimmering cape draped over your shoulder and a royal blue sash across your broad chest.'

'Thanks, Tajhira,' said Kyron humbly, feeling warmth on his face from a flush of embarrassment. 'I'm sure all the other graduates looked just as handsome and debonair.'

'No, you were the most handsome of them all,' said Torri proudly, hugging him. Zuri and Ehrana grinned with pride too as they wrapped themselves around their father's legs.

Just as Torri finished commenting, there was an almighty, thunderous noise. It was so loud it shook the whole structure of the Main Hall for several minutes. The crowd was stunned temporarily. Then they started rushing frantically in a panic towards the main exit doors, spilling out onto the outside courtyard like a torrent of gushing water. Tajhira picked up Kyrah and Kyron grabbed both his children, hauling them to his hips. Torri who was standing right behind Kyron, held onto the children's arms as they melded into the rushing crowd.

Outside, the citizens stared skyward to witness a strange rainbow colour in the outer Tzuracian atmosphere between the two moons, Kelzhar and Wurtah. There was no damage to be seen anywhere but people were yelling and screaming, fearing the worst.

Inside the Main Hall, Chief-Commander Dakhar, Admiral Harzan, and the senators were confronted by a holographic projection from the Flagship, *Rhazon*.

'Chief-Commander Dakhar, this is Captain Lombharq.' There was urgency in his voice. 'Our laser cannons on Kelzhar have just decimated a long-range missile which was carrying what appears to have been a Xytrinium warhead. No doubt you heard the explosion and saw the aftermath. The missile was fired from somewhere deep in the north-eastern Quadrant and its trajectory showed it was heading directly for Khazor. The enemy is approaching sooner than we anticipated. And obviously, they have destructive warheads on-board!'

Dakhar and his Senate were surprised and stunned by the news. 'Thank the Ancients our defences stopped the missile in time! Gods forbid they have another missile that could destroy our protective shield! Hold your positions in stealth mode. Order the crew to position themselves in their battle stations and do it quietly. Our enemies' sonar will detect any sounds we make as their armada approaches Tzurac. I'll join you as soon as I can. Dakhar, out!'

The illuminated projection dissolved and Dakhar focused his attention on the others. 'Sirs, we're under attack. We have no option but to secure our citizens in the underground tunnels for their own safety. We need to act quickly. Send a broadcast across the city. I'll alert our ground forces via the Sentinels stationed in the forests and in the Citadel. Admiral, I'll leave you to command the armies on Tzurac while I command the fleet from the *Rhazon*. We still hope to intercept them.'

'Yes, General. May the Ancients protect you!'

'Now let's move!'

Immediately, Dakhar ordered the units of Sentinels still stationed around the Main Hall to return to their posts within and around the Citadel. Then he ran outside to the courtyard. The scene was chaotic. Many still had their eyes to the sky murmuring and pointing. They were in a state of near panic.

To get the crowd's attention Dakhar jumped onto one of the three-foot-high stone walls near the entrance and fired a laser pistol several times into the air. The crowd turned their focus towards him, still murmuring.

'Attention, citizens! Attention!' he shouted. The chatter stopped and the crowd began to listen. 'We've been fired upon by the Treldarians. They sent a missile from deep in space towards Khazor. Luckily our laser cannons on Kelzhar destroyed it before it reached its target. That was the explosion you heard and saw. This was unexpected but our enemy are still some light years away and we'll mobilise our fleet to intercept them. For your safety, we need you to hurry to the underground tunnels. I urge you to move quickly. Be brave and be vigilant. Stay safe in the tunnels until we give the 'all clear'!'

As the citizens rushed off in all directions to reach the underground networks, Dakhar called out above the frenzy to his new officers. 'Lieutenants, say a quick farewell to your friends and loved ones and then report to your assigned posts. Those commissioned for the warships report back here to me.'

Dakhar strode toward Kyron, Torri and Tajhira. He held Tajhira tightly in his arms for some time without a word and then, releasing her, picked Kyrah up and kissed him on his forehead. Kyron too held his family closely around him before Dakhar and Kyron shepherded their families to the safety of the underground tunnels.

'I love you, Torri,' Kyron said gently as they departed. 'I'll be with you again soon.'

'Come with me, Torri,' Tajhira called out, 'we've no time to lose.'

Kyron turned to Dakhar with mixed emotions in his eyes. 'As your newly assigned First Officer, I'm ready for action.'

Dakhar spoke in a low whisper, 'Kyron, my friend, I know how you feel. Under normal circumstances you'd be travelling with me on the *Rhazon*. But while my fleet confronts the Treldarian armada in space, I'd prefer you to stay here on the ground. Your fighting skills will be put to a far better use here on Tzurac. You'll also be closer to Torri and the children to protect them and can look out for Tajhira and Kyrah should anything happen to me. I'm ordering you to stay here, taking my place, doing what I'd do if I were here. I have great trust and faith in you, Kyron.

'I've assigned you temporarily to Admiral Harzan. I believe he needs you more than I do in this war. You have more experience and knowledge in physical contact with the enemy. Am I right, my friend?'

Kyron looked upset and somewhat confused but after some hesitation he had to agree. He knew he was more skilled in hand-to-hand combat with Treldarian Bladers, and he'd be closer to his family on the ground.

'Yes, Ehrane, you're right.'

Dakhar leaned forward and held out his arm and the two exchanged a Sentinel handshake. No words were needed. As they looked at each other, their eyes said it all.

As Dakhar's new first officers reported back, he instructed them in a low voice, 'Lieutenant Tyros, report to Admiral Harzan in the control centre! The rest of you, follow me!'

TERRA MAJOR WAR GAMES

NO sooner had the fleet of eight warships sent by Commander Zawkon positioned themselves on the dark side of Earth's moon, than a frightening image of a Treldarian armada flashed onto the main screen of Captain Wolzhart's lead warship, *Predarus*. Five massive, black, Treldarian warships with red scorpion markings on their hulls materialised, dropping out of hyperspace on the outer rim of Earth's orbit. They were cruising at low speed in a triangular formation.

'What in the Gods' names!' the captain exclaimed. He hadn't expected a force this size so soon.

Wolzhart's past performance as a strategist had shown him to be an officer with a quick mind who was calculating and decisive under battle conditions. Now he had managed to capture the armada's image on his ship's tracking transceivers before the Treldarian fleet had a chance to cloak their ships. Although he was a veteran Sentinel pilot, with a proven record of successful battle strategies in space combat, he'd never encountered such a large force of this magnitude in such close proximity.

Wolzhart could feel his heartbeat quicken and the pulse in his temples pump stronger. Tiny beads of sweat began to weep onto his forehead and his palms felt moist. Being responsible for leading the rest of the fleet into battle, he compelled himself to stay calm and collected. He needed to slow down his now-racing mind and regain clarity. It was time for action, and he had to show confidence in front of his crew and the other commanders.

Realising the gravity of the situation, he holographed Commander Zawkon to warn him of the approaching danger.

'Yes, Captain?' Zawkon answered, noting the urgency on his captain's face. 'What news do you have?'

The captain was not your average looking Sentinel. Physically, he was of average height but very thin. His golden locks had been closely cropped and his fresh, youthful, clean-shaven face and clear bright eyes suggested a much younger person than his forty years. Yet his brow was furrowed with concern.

'Sir, the Treldarian armada with five large warships is upon us. They're currently on the outer rim of Terra Major's orbit, just passing the moon. They're travelling at low cruising speed in triangular formation. What are your orders, Commander?'

'Hold your position and stealth status, Captain,' Zawkon replied confidently. *It was just as Bhalar had forecast.*

'I'll contact General Blake and have him activate the Destroyer battleships. I'll also alert the troops to be ready for a ground attack. If the Treldarians stay in that formation, we may be able to surround them with our fleet, attacking them from all sides. If they have armed scout ships on board, we'll counterattack with the Destroyers. The aim is to keep the battle in space and prevent the enemy from landing on Terra Major. Wait till I give the order to attack. Zawkon, out!'

Zawkon contacted General Blake urgently using cabled Comms to avoid interception by the Treldarians. 'General Blake, this is Commander Zawkon.' His voice was stern.

'Yes, Commander. What's happening? You sound anxious.'

'I am. The Treldarians are here. Their five warships are already orbiting Terra Major. Ready your jet fighters and alert the Tzuracian Destroyer pilots, including Corporal Blandhar. Have them on standby waiting for my order. Put your platoon soldiers on guard. I'll inform my Sentinels in the field and have Engineer Thompson and my First Officers activate the Diutrons here and in Washington. Remember, General, although the Treldarians are here sooner than expected we can still surprise them!'

'Understood, Commander.'

In an instant Zawkon's thoughts turned to the safety of Lauren Blake who was still in the MERIC Building. *He had become especially protective of her.* He grabbed the land Comms and depressed one of the illuminated lights on the handle. His call was answered instantly.

'Good afternoon, Lauren Blake speaking. How may I help you?'

Zawkon was mesmerised temporarily by the softly spoken but official voice.

'Hello, who is this?' Lauren repeated when she received no response.

Slightly tongue-tied, he forced out his words. 'Hello, Lauren. It's Kal Zawkon.'

Lauren's tone melted the moment she heard his strong deep voice. Her reply was much friendlier, 'Good to hear your voice, Kal. Are you alright? You sound worried.'

'I'm okay. Thanks, Lauren. But I need to tell you what's happening if you haven't already heard.'

'Is there something I can do to help?' she asked sincerely.

The sound of her voice was wonderful therapy for him. Her tone was soothing, gentle and soft. It was like floating in calm waters after surviving a battering storm at sea.

'Yes, there is, Lauren. I have to confess I'm very concerned for your safety. I can't help myself. I hope I'm not too forward, but …' He stopped to catch his breath as his chest started tightening and a lump swelled in his throat. His heart was beating faster than ever. '… I've become very fond of you, and I don't want to lose you.'

There was silence on the line. Zawkon felt guilty about his confession, thinking he'd ruined his chances of getting to know more about the only woman who had ever softened his heart and charged his emotions. He was relieved by her response.

'You *are* very forward for someone who closely protects his feelings, Kal. But I'm happy you told me how you feel. To be honest, I'm also very fond of you.'

Zawkon smiled to himself. 'Thank you, Lauren.' Then he spoke with more urgency. 'The enemy is here. Do you have somewhere safe to go?'

'They're here already? I can't believe it!' Lauren was astounded. 'Yes, the ASPECT complex has a deep underground bunker, and my father can arrange an escort for me.'

'Good,' Zawkon said, feeling reassured. 'I want you to go there immediately and take with you the others in your building. I'll contact you when it's safe to surface.' His voice softened a little. 'Take care. I'm looking forward to spending time with you in the very near future, Lauren.'

'I share your thoughts, Kal. God speed and return to me safely.'

Zawkon calmed his excitement and collected his thoughts. *He needed to focus on his mission. The success of the counterattack depended on timing and execution. Everything needed to be perfectly coordinated to launch the simultaneous double strike on the Treldarian armada from Earth and from space.*

He noted the hour on his timepiece before holographing one of his unit leaders in Washington. The room illuminated and in the bluish-haze an outline of a Sentinel lieutenant appeared in full battle dress wearing his metal armour and helmet.

'Commander Zawkon, this is Lieutenant Lurtz Gharzak, First Officer, 37th Infantry.'

'Lieutenant, what's your status on the mobilization of the Diutrons?'

'Sir, the Diutrons have been installed around the World Assembly building and the senators are secured underground. My troops have been placed close to the Diutrons and are at the ready.'

'Thanks, Lieutenant. Is Engineer Grant Thompson close by?'

'Yes, sir. He's beside me just out of visual range. Mr Thompson can you come a little closer?' he called.

Zawkon had dispatched several units of Sentinels and five hundred Diutrons to Washington to defend the World Assembly. After instructing some of Zawkon's officers at MERIC and ASPECT how to control the robots, Thompson had volunteered to accompany the Washington dispatch. Although he wasn't a trained soldier, Thompson wanted to help defend Earth against the invaders. In his younger years he had prided himself on being a champion player of virtual reality war games. He was excited at the prospect of applying the skills he had mastered to the real world in a very real battle. Although he knew he was in danger of being injured or even killed, he couldn't resist the temptation, reasoning that he'd be in the protection of the elite Sentinels.

Zawkon could see Thompson moving slowly into range. 'Grant, how are you managing?'

'Very well so far, Commander. How's it goin' down there? Have those nasty buggers arrived yet?' Thompson spoke as if he was trying to rid a bitter taste from his mouth.

'Yes, they have Grant. It's time to start up the metal monsters. We need to be on guard and ready for battle. Lieutenant Gharzak, have your soldiers armed and ready. The Treldarians may attack at any time.'

'Yes, sir! Understood!'

'May the Ancient spirits protect you and your soldiers. Zawkon, out!'

Next, Zawkon contacted his officers at MERIC and within the Citadel, instructing them to be armed, on guard and to activate their Diutrons. Five hundred of the metal giants were now positioned around the Citadel; five hundred circled the MERIC Building; and a further five hundred encompassed ASPECT and its air base.

Zawkon checked his timepiece again before making a call on the land Comms to General Blake. 'Launch your fleet immediately to these co-ordinates. The Destroyer battleships are to approach the enemy armada armed and in stealth mode.'

'Acknowledged. Blake, out!'

Zawkon holographed Captain Wolzhart on the *Predarus*. 'Our Destroyers from the ASPECT Air base have been launched. Commence your attack in thirty minutes.'

'Affirmative, sir. Wolzhart, out!'

Now there was nothing more Zawkon could do but wait anxiously in the Control Room within the Citadel. He stared at the bank of screens in front of him. High-powered scopes on the moon projected telephoto signals onto the main screen. He watched the ominous black Treldarian armada silently approaching. Images were also being received on other screens from the super-sensors located on the surrounds of the ASPECT complex and MERIC Building. They displayed his ground troops and Diutrons waiting silently in their battle positions.

From the set of smaller screens, the Commander could monitor images taken by powerful micro-telephoto lenses fixed to the helmets of his First Officers in the field. History had taught Zawkon that the best defence a Chief-Commander can have, is to know at all times what is happening in every theatre of the war. Seated in his command post, he was perfectly positioned to monitor the battle in space and on the ground when it began.

* * *

Onboard the armada, the Treldarian Third Legion led by General Rokan and Captain Chekhmar in the warship, *Trigan,* were set on course for Terra Major. They were leading a force of one thousand Xytrinium-infused, Treldarian soldiers as well as two thousand, primitive Nujharenes in basic bronze armour.

The once-feeble, white-haired General was now dressed in battle fatigues like his men – a brown leather jacket over a black shirt – and sporting a sword and laser pistol. He was energised with renewed vitality and resolute.

'Everything's going to plan,' he said confidently, his voice stronger than ever.

'All good,' said Chekhmar, smiling deviously at his General from under his bushy uncombed beard and thick, ragged black hair.

They were unaware they were in for a surprise.

* * *

It seemed like an eternity for Zawkon, waiting and watching the black silhouette of the armada against the dark void. Then, suddenly, his own fleet of eight warships materialised from stealth mode and appeared from the dark side of the moon. Manoeuvring themselves into a wide surrounding semicircle, they began pounding the Treldarian vessels with laser cannon fire. Hundreds of pulsating luminous-red laser beams streaked across the expanse, finding their mark on the enemy armada.

* * *

'Where the hell! did they come from?' General Rokan cursed loudly.

His mind started to churn over the recent events on Mankro. *What had been in that transmission sent by the prisoner Armel? Who was Armel? Who had he alerted? Damn him!*

'Return fire! Prepare to disperse the scout ships!'

* * *

Green laser streaks returned by the Treldarians found their targets on Tzuracian vessels. Both sides repelled cannon fire using their protective shields. While the space battle continued relentlessly, Zawkon knew the constant pounding could not be sustained indefinitely. He was worried. Blake's fleet of Destroyers and jet fighters had not yet arrived. To make matters worse, during this exchange of firepower, the Treldarians unexpectedly launched hundreds of scout ships which weaved swiftly in and out of the flack, blasting the Fleet ships by targeting their laser fire on the vessels' thrusters.

'In the name of the Ancients!' Zawkon cursed under his breath. 'This General Rokan is a cunning rat!'

The dark space was thick with scout ships swarming like gnats and their rapid manoeuvrability avoided them being hit. Although the occasional scout ship was knocked out of commission, the Treldarian armada continued to inflict damage on their opponents. Zawkon watched in horror as one of his Tzuracian ships began belching black smoke from one of its thrusters, while still returning fire.

Then, without warning, the five Treldarian warships suddenly vanished, and in their place appeared the squadron of Tzuracian Destroyers sent from Earth.

'Thank the Gods!' Zawkon cried out. 'Reinforcements! But where the hell did the armada go?'

A dogfight ensued between the Treldarian scout ships and the Destroyer battleships with laser beams firing in all directions. It was looking more like a fireworks celebration on a 4th of July Independence Day.

To Zawkon's relief, the Destroyers' powerful protective shields easily repelled the scout ships' laser assaults and missiles. And, with their superior aerial manoeuvres, scout ships began falling from the void, trailing smoke and then burning up as they hurled through Earth's atmosphere. Zawkon punched the air, sensing victory. *They were gaining the upper hand.*

Then, 'Damn!' Zawkon yelled out loud. He was stunned to see on the other screens four of the black Treldarian ships with their red scorpion insignia materialize on the open grounds surrounding the city of New York. The instant their hatches opened, hundreds of enemy troops spewed out of them heading for the Citadel and the ASPECT complex. *The cunning rat Rokan had created a diversion with his scout ships while off-loading his soldiers for a ground assault.*

Zawkon's plan had been for his fleet of warships and Destroyers to keep the battle in Terra Major's orbit and annihilate the Treldarian armada there. He shuddered, realising the devastation the Treldarian ships' laser cannons could unleash at close range on the Citadel, the MERIC Building and the ASPECT complex.

* * *

As General Rokan and his army of rebel soldiers poured off their ships and headed for the Citadel and the ASPECT complex, they were completely stunned to see an army of huge menacing robots surrounding the buildings. Hundreds of giant mechanical monsters were advancing slowly towards them, firing into their ranks from cannons mounted on their thick solid arms. Rokan had expected to encounter Sentinels and Terranian soldiers, but this was a force they had never imagined.

'What the …!' cried Rokan.

'What are these damn things?' Chekhmar was amazed at the number and physical size of this alien army.

Rokan swore under his breath then cursed to Chekhmar, 'We've been deceived! Those liars, Ramlok and Vark, told us Terra Major wasn't well fortified.'

There was no time to think or take cover. It was all happening too fast. Torn and mangled bodies splattered with blood and burnt clothing were flung haphazardly into the now dust-clouded air. Pungent odours of burning flesh and black carbon-smoke filled the atmosphere. Blasts coming from the robots as well as the gun turrets were firing all around them, causing explosions everywhere.

Above the loud noise of screaming and blasting, General Rokan waved his sabre in the air and yelled his commands. 'Chekhmar, we'll fight to the end and take as many of them as we can! Soldiers, charge!'

Rokan and his rebel army streaked towards the Sentinels and Diutrons, sabres and swords waving recklessly while firing wildly with their laser pistols. While some of the Treldarians' laser fire struck a few of the Sentinels, felling them to the ground, laser fire and sword blades had no effect against the robots' metal amour reinforced with Xytrinium. The monstrous Diutrons marched relentlessly towards them, blasting the oncoming soldiers with their built-in laser pulse cannons while trampling on any enemy soldier who came into contact with them. The ground shook with the impact of their advance.

* * *

Zawkon could see the Diutrons were creating havoc. But he knew that once the hatches closed on the Treldarian vessels and the armada lifted off the surface, the enemy warships would unleash their might using whatever armaments they had. They would blast MERIC and ASPECT. He reached for the Comms to send an order to his fleet of warships to swoop immediately from their current positions and attack Rokan's armada on the ground.

Before he could utter a word, his fleet of ships, now numbering six in total, materialised about ten-thousand feet directly above Rokan's vessels. They released fire rapidly on the enemy ships, explosions erupting all over the black hulls of the armada. Rokan's ships had no chance to raise their shields or fire their cannons.

Zawkon punched the air again, sensing victory.

* * *

Amid the fighting, Captain Rokan heard loud explosions behind him. He looked back in horror to see his precious warships exploding. *His troops on the ground were trapped with no way of escape and he feared the worst ...*

* * *

Yet Zawkon was curious. *What had become of the fifth Treldarian warship and the other two Tzuracian warships? Had they survived the battle? He'd seen no sign of a crash landing.* While the battle raged, Zawkon holographed Captain Wolzhart for an answer.

The captain opened the transmission. 'General Zawkon,' he said, jumping to attention near his console on the Bridge. 'Is there something wrong, sir?'

'First, Captain, perfect timing! I commend you on your quick action, bringing your fleet down to blast the Treldarian vessels before they had time to raise their shields.'

'Thank you, sir, I relied on my Sentinel instincts.'

'But two of our warships are missing if I'm not mistaken. And there's no sign of the fifth Treldarian warship. What happened to them?'

'Sir, one of the Treldarian vessels escaped. Its heat sink trail showed it was heading for the World Assembly in Washington. I sent Captain Turkrahn to intercept it. Assuming the enemy warship had more scout ships in reserve, I also dispatched Corporal Blandhar in his Destroyer as an escort. I directed our other warship, which reported a damaged thruster, to return to the ASPECT Air base.'

'Good call, Captain. I'll request General Blake to direct some jet fighters to Washington. We've got a battle on the ground down here, but it appears to be going in our favour. Your priority now is to stop the remaining Treldarian scout ships from landing and bringing enemy reinforcements. Keep me posted. Zawkon, out!'

On one of the screens, Zawkon could see the Sentinels and Diutrons holding back the enemy hordes. He recognised the Treldarian soldiers by their distinctive physical features and Blader-like uniforms and could see among those who engaged in close combat that their enhanced powers were challenging his Sentinels.

Fighting alongside them were a different race of aliens, pale green in colour, using antiquated firearms and shooting arrows from small bows with some accuracy, several finding their mark on his Sentinels. *They must be the primitive Nujharenes Bhalar had described.* These aliens didn't possess Xytrinium-enhanced powers and although their numbers added clout to the enemy attack, they were easily overpowered by the Sentinels in close combat. Even the armour they wore was ineffective against Xytrinium weapons. Zawkon could clearly see there was no organised strategy being used by the invading ground forces, the enemy relying only on brute strength and numbers.

Laser cannon fire, from the Citadel and the other buildings, as well as from the mechanical monsters, was rapidly depleting the enemy ranks. Using the Diutrons for cover against flying arrows and laser fire, the Sentinels were providing a second line of defence. They were pushing the attackers back, leaving fallen enemy soldiers in their wake. The enemy had nowhere to retreat. Their warships had been destroyed and were now mangled metal monoliths, smouldering in smoke and flames.

Zawkon breathed a temporary sigh of relief. *If Captain Wolzhart can keep the scout ships at bay, we will win this battle.*

CALL TO ARMS

WITHIN the hour, Chief-Commander Dakhar was on board the *Rhazon* with his new First Officers in their respective positions aboard the other nine warships, all positioned behind the Tzuracian moon of Jorhan. If the Treldarians were travelling in the direction of the Jorhan moon, the enemy ships would soon be within Tzurac's orbit.

They were surprised two hours later when the main screen on the Bridge burst into life. A transmission from one of the transceivers on the other moon Kelzhar, delivered the co-ordinates of a large alien fleet. It wasn't travelling in the direction of the Jorhan moon. Instead, it was travelling at hyperspeed in the direction of the space void between the moons of Kelzhar and Wurtah. It was on track for Khazor.

Dakhar turned to Captain Lombharq who was standing close by. 'Damn! The enemy are not approaching via Jorhan. We need to change our position immediately.'

'Computer,' called Dakhar, 'how long before the alien ships pass Kelzhar?'

There was a crackling on the Comms intercom, followed by the computer's synthesised voice, 'Commander, at their current speed they will be passing Kelzhar in five hours.'

Dakhar responded promptly, 'And how long will it take to move my fleet, at hyperspeed, to the shadow side of Kelzhar?'

'Three hours fifteen minutes.'

'Good. Captain Lombharq, set the coordinates for Kelzhar and notify the rest of the fleet of our new destination using your Pledge ring. We leave at once!'

'Yes, Commander.'

* * *

Onboard the Treldarian Flagship, General Vark received a signal from the detonated long-range missile, launched two hours earlier from one of his warships. Vark looked satisfied, taking the signal as an indication that the missile had found its target, successfully shattering the protective shield over Khazor. Captain Ramlok was not so sure and approached the General with his concerns.

'General, I'm not sure the missile made the target.'

'Why, Ramlok? Why wouldn't it have been successful? The missile we fired earlier disintegrated the Tzuracian warship.'

'Because, sir,' said Ramlok confidently, 'by my calculations, the warhead exploded *before* reaching Khazor. Either it malfunctioned, or it was fired upon.'

The General thought for a short moment before replying. *Ramlok had been right in the past.* 'I think – well I *hope* – your calculations are wrong, Captain. But, if you're right, we have more missiles in reserve. If Khazor's protective Dome is still intact when our fleet nears Tzurac's orbit, I'll launch another. They'll be unprepared for our surprise attack. Once their Dome is destroyed, we can land our vessels and mobilise the ground troops. I want to capture Khazor intact to use as our main base in the Northern Quadrant.'

Vark sat back confidently in his Commander's Chair, while Ramlok remained silently concerned.

* * *

Dakhar's Tzuracian fleet of warships and battleships soon arrived on the shadowed side of the moon, Kelzhar, cloaking in preparation for the ambush. They waited silently and patiently, like the wild beasts on Tzurac stalking their prey.

Not much more than an hour had passed when their sonar screens sprang into life. Faint grey images, outlines of five large Treldarian warships, were now within striking distance.

Dakhar holographed a transmission to the Sentinel commanders of the other fleet ships, 'Commanders, prepare to ambush!'

As pre-arranged, half the fleet sped off in one direction, the other five in the opposite direction, each escorted by a squadron of Destroyer battleships. The two fleets traversed the moon's perimeter in stealth mode, silently emerging from the shadow on the other side of Kelzhar. They were now positioned. One in front of, and the other behind, the Treldarian armada with laser cannons aimed in the armada's direction. They were matching the armada's cruising speed, still cloaked.

* * *

Onboard the Treldarian lead warship, General Vark was shocked when Dakhar's fleets suddenly decloaked. On the main screen he could see his fleet surrounded by what appeared to be Tzuracian warships.

'Where in the Gods' names did they come from?' he cursed, his scar more visible as he grimaced. 'How did they know we'd be passing through this part of the Northern Quadrant? And why didn't the sonar echoes detect their presence sooner?'

He turned to Captain Ramlok for answers, but Ramlok shrugged his shoulders. They were both in the dark.

'I suspect the exploding missile would have warned them of our attack,' said Ramlok. 'But it's *impossible* this provided time for them to mobilise their fleet and ambush us here.' Then it dawned on him. 'Not unless they were warned in advance.'

The General and his captain glared at each other with the same thought, realising their plans had been exposed.

Vark clenched his fists in anger. 'It must have been those three cowardly deserters who attacked you and Sergeant Krag and then fled Orkharn. The Federation must have caught them as I feared.' Vark and Ramlok had no idea who the real informant was.

Vark issued immediate orders. 'Captains, raise your shields and go to battle stations!'

As 'Under Siege' alarms were activated on the fleet's vessels, Treldarian crews dived frantically in all directions through passageways now immersed in green emergency lighting, while an incessant high-pitched screeching droned on and off in two-second intervals. Many of the two thousand soldiers and one thousand Kyroni on-board clasped hands over their ears – their Xytrinium enhancements amplified the volume, causing excruciating pain.

In the midst of the chaos, the main screens flickered, and a new picture appeared in place of the Tzuracian fleet ships. It was the face of a seasoned Tzuracian Officer with swept-back fair hair and clear blue eyes and the image was accompanied by an audio signal. General Vark ordered his navigator pilot to shut off the annoying alarm and switch on the translator.

'Attention, Treldarians. This is Chief-Commander, General Dakhar of the Tzuracian Flagship, *Rhazon*. We know of your declaration of war on the Federation and your intentions. My ships could easily have fired upon you and destroyed your entire unsuspecting fleet. However, if there is honour in your military code under your Articles of War, I'm granting you the opportunity to surrender. You'll be treated as prisoners-of-war under our Sentinel code and dealt with under Federation Law. If you refuse our offer, we'll have no choice but to destroy your fleet along with all those on board. You have three minutes to respond.'

* * *

Onboard the *Rhazon*, Dakhar could see on the Bridge screen, a picture of a Treldarian Officer seated in his Captain's Chair. His hair, tied back in the familiar Treldarian style, was streaked with silver-grey, matching his moustache and well-groomed beard. The officer looked concerned, his expression emphasising a long vertical scar down his right cheek.

The screen went blank for a second, before reverting back to the scene of the Treldarian armada. Dakhar was fully aware the Treldarians had Xytrinium missiles – one had already been fired *en route* and he was certain there were more. Fearing the Treldarians might launch Xytrinium missiles on his fleet, Dakhar kept his vessels at a safe distance, allowing his fleet enough time to take evasive action if required. He knew his shields were not designed to repel the Treldarians' devastating missiles. Dakhar also knew that an attack on the enemy armada could ignite the Xytrinium warheads and wipe out every vessel within a reasonable radius. Capturing the Treldarian armada was the safest tactic not only for his fleet but also for Tzurac.

While Dakhar's mind was mulling over the situation and the minutes were ticking by, the unexpected happened. On the screen, Dakhar saw the Treldarian ships rapidly shedding hundreds of small scout ships, like angry wasps that had been attacked in their nest. The scout ships began flying in all directions towards the surrounding warships and Destroyers, and within seconds, the five enemy warships cloaked to invisibility and disappeared from the screen.

Dakhar acted immediately and clinically, calling to Captain Lombharq, 'Captain! Order all ships to raise shields to one hundred percent. Fire at will at the enemy scout ships! And send in the Destroyers to combat them!'

Then he called out to his navigator, 'Lieutenant Nhasan, can you track the Treldarian warships?'

Before Lieutenant Nhasan could acknowledge her Chief-Commanding Officer, their ship came under attack from the swarming scout ships. It was battered with continuous strikes, shaking and rattling the hull. Their ship was not the only one under attack. The scene on the screen was chaotic. Numerous dogfights had broken out between the Destroyers and scout ships, green and red lasers firing repeatedly in all directions. As the scout ships attacked, laser cannons from Dakhar's warships returned fire, rapidly blasting at the swarming vessels, hoping to dispose of them before they pummelled his ships and broke down their shields.

Dakhar recognised the strategy used by the Commander of the Treldarian fleet was very shrewd. *He had used hundreds of scout ships as a diversion to keep Dakhar's fleet occupied, enabling them to cloak their warships and make their escape with the Xytrinium missiles intact.*

His thoughts were abruptly interrupted by Lieutenant Nhasan.

'Commander, the Treldarian ships left no heat-sink trails for our infrared to detect, and they've disappeared from Kelzhar's orbit. The last faint reading from our sonar shows them heading in the direction of Tzurac.'

'Thanks, Lieutenant. Good work.'

Dakhar knew he had limited time. 'Captain Lombharq, order the Destroyers to continue fighting the scout ships. Instruct the captains of our warships to cloak, setting their co-ordinates for Khazor, with their hyperdrives on full capacity. We *must* stop the Treldarians from reaching our planet.'

Dakhar was desperate to prevent the enemy using their Xytrinium missile on Khazor's protective Dome. *If the Treldarians penetrated the Dome, nothing would stop their warships from landing on the surface of Tzurac to release their armies.*

'Yes, sir!'

The *Rhazon* and Dakhar's fleet of warships jumped into hyperspeed, heading for Tzurac.

Urgency forced Dakhar to breach protocol to contact the Comms Control Centre where Admiral Harzan was positioned. The transmission echoed loud and clear over the speakers.

'Admiral Harzan, this is Chief-Commander Dakhar. The Treldarian armada escaped our ambush near Kelzhar. It's heading for Tzurac we believe, with Xytrinium missiles on board. They'll try to destroy the Dome. Place everyone on high alert. Be ready to launch the remaining Destroyers on my command and prepare the ground troops for attack. My fleet is travelling at full hyperspeed in the hope of stopping them before they reach Tzurac. Dakhar, out!'

Lieutenant Nhasan called to Dakhar, 'Commander, we're catching up with the armada. It's now in full range of our sonar. By my calculations, we'll converge in the outer orbit of Tzurac in one hour's time.'

'Very good, Lieutenant, keep me informed of any changes.' Dakhar was focused and intense, his mind preoccupied with battle contingencies.

Within minutes, Lieutenant Nhasan called to Dakhar again, this time with some chilling news, 'Commander, the enemy has increased their hyperspeed. We can't match it. They'll arrive at Tzurac thirty minutes before we do.'

The look on Dakhar's face revealed an uncharacteristic fear – *unless his Destroyers on the ground could intercept the armada in the outer orbit, the Treldarians would have a clear shot at Khazor's Dome.* A chill went through his spine, realising his whole world was in perilous danger.

But Dakhar was a seasoned war veteran. He was determined to defeat the enemy by any means possible and he had the means, as well as a contingent strategy in mind. *If he couldn't catch them, he would outsmart them.*

He contacted the Comms Control Centre again in an instant, 'Harzan, launch the Destroyers immediately in the direction of Kelzhar! An attack is imminent. Intercept them before they fire on the Dome!'

Then he directed his Lieutenant and the Sentinel captains to stay their course, instructing them to cloak their ships and to change into stealth mode just before they reached Tzurac's outer orbit. There, they would spread out in a wide semi-circle and lay in wait above Khazor, hovering silently and invisibly in space within the inner orbit of Tzurac.

If the Treldarian armada managed to destroy Khazor's protective Dome and land their troops, he would have to rely on his ground forces to confront the enemy. But knowing the Treldarian warships would land just long enough to deploy their soldiers, his plan was to trap the armada from above as they departed the planet's surface. His fleet would be well positioned to ambush the Treldarian armada when it took to the skies. He would destroy their ships before they could raise their weapons against his fleet or Khazor again.

* * *

As the Treldarian armada approached planet Tzurac, General Vark was surprised to see the protective Dome over Khazor still intact. He turned to Ramlok and, with a wry smile, admitted Ramlok's acuity. 'Captain Ramlok, you were right. The missile didn't reach the intended target. I'm sorry for mistrusting your calculations.' He raised his voice in anger, saying, 'We'll not fail this time – not at this range.'

Ramlok smiled with self-satisfaction, knowing he'd been right, again.

As General Vark navigated his cloaked ships to hover in the high altitude over Khazor well out of range from the laser cannons on the surface below, his eyes caught action on the screen. Destroyers launched from Tzurac were speeding towards his armada. *He had to act quickly.*

Without flinching he addressed his Comms. 'Computer, lock in co-ordinates for a Xytrinium missile launch on Khazor. Load and arm the warhead missile. Fire when ready!'

Within seconds, the console on the Bridge was a mass of small and flickering, red and green, fluorescent lights. Then the lights ceased flickering, his Flagship decloaked, and the missile fired, sending a mild shudder through the ship's hull. On the main screen, General Vark observed the pale-red heat trail of the missile speeding towards Tzurac's capital city.

Watching the missile's trail dissipate as it sped closer towards Tzurac, he spoke again to the Comms, 'Computer, patch me into the other ships.'

'Affirmative, General.'

Composing himself from the excitement of an adrenalin rush, Vark started his transmission, 'Captains, the missile has been launched and is on target to destroy the protective sheath of Khazor. Once the Dome is shattered, we'll land immediately. But beware, Destroyers are approaching from Tzurac. Cloak and take evasive action! Head for the planet's surface!'

* * *

'Gods forbid!' said Dakhar, as he tracked the enemy armada approaching Tzurac. 'They've launched a missile!' *His Destroyers had been too late to intercept them.*

'Harzan,' he communicated urgently. 'Call the Destroyers off. Have them join my fleet and prepare to cloak on arrival.'

'That will leave us vulnerable, sir, without air support.' Harzan was obviously anxious.

'The enemy armada is too close for us to attack with safety. An assault on the black scorpion ships now might explode any Xytrinium arsenal they're carrying, endangering Khazor and its citizens. I'm sorry, but you're about to be hit by one of their missiles, Harzan.' A fleeting image of his family back on Tzurac flashed through his mind, though there was no time for sentiment. 'I pray it's only meant to destroy the Dome. Prepare for a ground attack and we'll do what we can from here. I have a contingency plan. May the Ancients protect you!'

* * *

The Xytrinium warhead exploded with an unimaginable intensity onto the Dome, completely obliterating it. The impact was deafening, the visuals spectacular. It was like a volcano erupting with fragmented light displaying a kaleidoscope of fiery reds, purples and yellows, rippling through black smoke bellowing into the sky and almost blocking out the sun. The ground trembled as in a high-magnitude earthquake. Buildings rattled and swayed, and all power instantly shut off. Tzurac had not experienced anything like this before.

In the underground tunnels, the Khazorian citizens – including Tajhira, Torri and the children – trembled in fear as they felt the reverberations. Most believed it was the beginning of the end. On the surface, the Tzuracian soldiers and the Urgellans hidden in the forests around Khazor readied themselves for an onslaught.

Suddenly, all the monitors in the Control Centre shut down and everything went dead quiet. Visual contact to all areas of the complex was lost. Electrical discharge from the high voltage was so intense it severed all communications.

Outside in the passageway a commotion had started up. Suddenly a Sentinel burst into the room, out of breath, followed by two guards who rushed to secure him. Seeing the Admiral, the Sentinel straightened himself, gave a quick salute and asked permission to speak, struggling with the guards now grappling him.

Admiral Harzan waved his hand in a motion for the guards to release him. 'Yes, soldier, what do you have to report?'

'Admiral,' he said with urgency, 'I've come from one of the Citadel's observation towers. The Dome has been destroyed. We've sighted five huge black Treldarian warships entering our air space and circling the outskirts of the city. We're under attack!'

'Thanks, soldier,' said Harzan. 'Return to your post and prepare to defend the city.'

The soldier saluted, turned on his heels and left the room immediately.

Harzan's head was spinning with the emergency. *He was unable to contact Commander Dakhar to forewarn him and had no way of issuing orders to organise his troops. The Comms were down and not being a Sentinel, he had no Pledge ring. The forcefields holding prisoners in their cells were shut down and he knew the escaped prisoners would soon overpower the Sentinel guards. He was faced with the prospect of an internal war within the walls of the Citadel, while trying to combat the enemy outside.*

He turned to Lieutenant Tyros who was standing behind him in the Control Room. Kyron was in shock along with the rest of them. 'Lieutenant!'

'Yes, sir,' responded Kyron on impulse. *He couldn't believe what was happening.*

'Send a holograph to Commander Dakhar updating him. The Destroyers failed to intercept the armada. The Dome has been destroyed and all communications are down. And the Treldarian ships have landed and have surrounded the outskirts of the city. Then, send a message to alert the Sentinels in the field. Take two units of Sentinels down to the cell blocks and secure the prisoners, using any force necessary.'

'Understood, sir,' Kyron replied with a sharp salute. His heart was racing with anxiety, but his mind was focused. *It was time for him to put all his training into action and prove his worth as a Sentinel officer. The lives of his soldiers and the citizens of Khazor – as well as his own family – depended on it.*

BATTLE VICTORIES

THE thermosphere above Earth was exploding with laser fire as Treldarian scout ships and Tzuracian Destroyers engaged in dogfights, weaving complex patterns as they engaged in relentless attack and defence. While on the ground, the fierce battle was raging around the Citadel and the MERIC Building, the Diutrons proving invincible.

In the Control Centre, Zawkon was on high alert, monitoring the action in all theatres of the war. He could see the Sentinels and Diutrons beating back the enemy on the ground and reports from General Blake at ASPECT sounded positive. General Blake had directed several of his jet fighters that had remained in reserve, to attack the five scorpion war ships that had landed and decimate the Treldarian armada on the ground.

Within minutes the Treldarian ships were out of commission and part of the enemy's battle plan was foiled – the attacking forces were unable to utilise the firepower quickly enough from their ships' laser cannons. Zawkon thanked the Ancients there were no remaining Xytrinium warheads on the five Treldarian warships when they were decimated otherwise all of Khazor would have been wiped out. They could only apply brute force, and their vast numbers were dwindling rapidly.

The giant Diutrons, with their highly resilient armour-plate and laser-pulse cannons, were too powerful and overwhelming, not only for the Treldarians, but also particularly for the Nujharenes. The Nujharenes' antiquated pistols and arrows proved futile against the metal monsters, and the bronze armour they wore gave no protection against laser weapons. Even the blades of their bronze swords were easily snapped by the Sentinels' superior Xytrinium-alloy blades. The Nujharenes were being cut to shreds, falling like dried stems of grain being harvested. And while the enhanced abilities of the Treldarians were proving more effective in hand-to-hand combat with the Sentinels, the advanced duelling skills and fighting techniques of the Sentinels gave the elite Tzuracian soldiers the winning edge.

To hold back the enemy at ASPECT, General Blake brought jet fighters into play. In continuous low flyovers they repeatedly dropped incendiary bombs and multi-directional sky-star shrapnel mines into the approaching hordes. Travelling at supersonic speed the pilots releasing these weapons of death from their sound-proof cockpits, couldn't hear the agonising screams or see the mangled and disfigured bodies of their enemies being blown into the air or burnt alive on the ground below.

By the time the enemy reached General Blake's mobilised troops on the wide perimeters of the Complex, the attacking forces had been reduced by half. Snipers interspersed amongst the army ranks as well as the Diutrons and using extremely high-powered rifles which fired armour-piercing projectiles, hit their mark with pin-point accuracy. Shielded behind the unrelenting metal monsters, the infantry soldiers and Sentinels were fast disposing of the invaders, leaving hundreds of dead and seriously wounded enemy soldiers in their wake.

Surprisingly, General Rokan – his white beard bloodied, his black uniform dusty and torn, and his skin scratched and bleeding from surface wounds – was still leading his remaining troops towards the walls of the Citadel. Proving to be a committed leader, he was determined to fight to the end at all costs.

With his soldiers falling around him, he turned to Captain Chekhmar, cursing, 'We must get to their control centre. It's our only chance!'

'Damn them! Damn the lot of them!' swore the foul-breathed, gap-toothed Chekhmar.

Forging forward, while trying to slip through the front line of Sentinels into the Citadel, the two Treldarian leaders took laser strikes simultaneously.

Chekhmar was thrown backwards by the force of the blast. Disorientated and temporarily blinded by the flash, his hands groped for the intense pain in the centre of his chest. He felt a gaping hole in his uniform jacket surrounded by smouldering melted material. 'Damn! I've been hit!' he yelled out as he fell heavily to the ground.

Rokan's right shoulder had also been seriously hit with a laser beam, causing him to collapse, writhing in excruciating pain. But when he saw his captain lying nearby with what was surely a fatal wound to his torso, he was determined not to let him die alone. While the battle raged all around them, Rokan, using his good arm, mustered all his remaining strength and hauled himself to his confidante's side to stay with him until the last flicker of life was extinguished from the captain's body. *He had relied so much on Chekhmar over the years.*

Chekhmar tilted his head to the side and with his eyes weeping, saw the face of his long-time General. Chekhmar managed only a weak wry smile before his eyes closed and his chest sank with his last foul breath. *After years in waiting, his ambitious hopes to take over the Third Legion – as well as the General's daughter, Bhalar – were dying with him.*

While Rokan was lying there still in partial shock, the sounds of the battle around him faded from his mind as he became consumed with sharp stabbing pain. With his shoulder throbbing and pulsing, the recent past rushed through his mind. *The Xytrinium infusion had given him a second chance with an enhanced army of soldiers to thwart his archenemy, the Tzuracians, and take control of the Universe. Yet, after thorough planning and training, it seemed his ambitions had failed. It was evident his plan for a surprise attack had been exposed long before they arrived on Terra Major. How?*

He tried to piece things together and, bit by bit, he began to make more sense of what had happened. *The so-called Urgellan, Armel, must have alerted the Tzuracians in his transmission from Mankro. Perhaps he had joined them since his escape? He must have been a Tzuracian spy.*

And what role had his daughter, Bhalar, played in Armel's escape? Had she conspired with the captive to make their escape from Mankro? Armel had been secured in binding chains and locked in an escape-proof cage. There was no other way the prisoner could have escaped, other than with the assistance of his very own daughter. She had betrayed him.

Then, three Sentinels pounced upon the bloodied and badly wounded General Rokan, hauling him roughly to his feet, and taking him prisoner. 'You're finished now, General,' one of the Sentinels cursed, 'and so is your rogue army.'

It signalled the end of the Treldarian attack on the Citadel. Seeing their General captured, their ships in smouldering black smoke and the Diutrons relentlessly advancing towards them, the remaining hordes realised their inevitable fate and raised the surrender flag. Their scout ships had been destroyed without providing them any reinforcements. It was all over, not just at the Citadel, but also at the MERIC Building and ASPECT complex.

In the Control Centre Zawkon took stock. He was relieved the ground battle and the battle in space with the Treldarian scout ships had been successfully won, but he couldn't celebrate just yet. He hadn't received word from Captain Turkrahn and Yarron about the fate of the World Assembly Building.

In fact, a serious battle was developing over the skies of Washington. As the lone Treldarian warship neared its target, the World Assembly, it dispersed fifty scout ships which were soon engaged in aerial dogfights against Yarron's Destroyer and General Blake's jet fighters. The Treldarian warship hovered menacingly over the World Assembly, readying to fire off a missile when, unexpectedly, it was hit by fire from Turkrahn's warship. The two 'locked horns' in fierce battle, exchanging intense laser cannon fire.

In the thick of the battle, fending off enemy scout ships one after another, Yarron's mind was racing. *The Treldarian warship had to be stopped at all costs before it turned its guns or a missile on the World Assembly Building.* But Yarron was aware of the risk in firing on the Treldarian warship which likely contained large quantities of Xytrinium arsenal. *It had to be intercepted now before it launched a missile and while it was still far enough above the Earth's surface to protect Washington from the damaging repercussions should there be a massive explosion.*

The Sentinel fugitive decided to launch an attack by striking at the only vulnerable area not protected by the Treldarian ship's shields. He opened his Comms to Turkrahn and the jet fighters. 'I'm going in! I'll try to disable it rather than take it out. I warn all of you to stay clear of the blast-zone just in case.'

Switching to cloaking mode, Yarron snaked carefully through the maze of swerving and weaving vessels, manoeuvring between the dogfights. His ship was struck several times by laser fire, but his shields held up against any possible damage.

With pinpoint accuracy, Yarron navigated his craft to the rear of the Treldarian warship, hoping the Treldarians' sonar scanners would not detect his invisible craft amid the congestion of aerial combatants. In minutes he positioned his Destroyer for a clear shot at the rear-mounted thrusters. *To launch his Xytrinium-armed torpedoes, he had to decloak his ship, leaving himself vulnerable to attack. Timing was everything.*

While waiting patiently and silently like a venomous viper ready to strike, he addressed the intercom, 'Computer, arm two torpedoes and set their path to the blasters on the Treldarian warship. Wait for my signal to decloak and launch them.'

'Affirmative, Captain.'

Within seconds his console screen lit up to show the torpedoes armed and ready.

Moments later the opportunity presented itself.

'Decloak and fire!'

By the time the Treldarian warship had identified the incoming torpedoes, it was too late to take evasive action. The two torpedoes hit their target starting a chain reaction of an intense electrical surge throughout the ship's hull. The black Treldarian warship exploded in a massive fireball, the deafening sound reverberating through the atmosphere.

Washington was safe from a missile attack and the effects of the explosion and so were Blake's jet fighters as well as Turkrahn's warship. Yarron was not so lucky. His ship was too close. It took the full impact. Even with his shields set for maximum resistance, his ship was catapulted and sent spinning into deep space with Yarron slumped lifeless over the console.

On seeing their mother ship destroyed, the scout ships immediately went all out to attack the World Assembly *en masse*, pursued by General Blake's jet fighters. Approaching Earth, the scout ships came under heavy attack from the jet fighters above as well as from the cannons below. A bank of computer-automated laser cannons strategically mounted on top of the building, fired repeatedly at the oncoming scout ships with pinpoint accuracy. One after another the scout ships exploded, the debris burning up as it fell to Earth.

Onlookers on the ground witnessed first the total destruction of the Treldarian warship and then the complete annihilation of the attacking scout ships. Cheers went up from the Sentinels and soldiers positioned around the World Assembly Building, though not from Grant Thompson. He was overjoyed the enemy had been destroyed, and Washington as well as the World Assembly were safe from harm. However, he could be heard cursing and swearing half-heartedly under his breath, waving his arms about dramatically and shaking his head, 'Damn, damn, damn! I wanted to test m' skills against these bloody heathens and now look what's happened!' He was putting on a grand performance. 'I didn't even get to test me' new toys!'

'Don't be too hard on yourself, Mr Thompson,' said one of the Sentinels standing close by. 'Look on the bright side. You still have your life, and you'll have some big toys to play war games back on Iota.'

'Well then,' Thompson said with a glint in his eyes, 'when you put it like that lad, I do 'ave sometin' to look forward to. Must be the luck o' the Irish, to be sure.'

On board the Tzuracian warship, Captain Turkrahn holographed Commander Zawkon. 'Chief-Commander, good news, we've thwarted the Treldarian attack on Washington. They were wiped out before they landed, thanks to the quick actions of Corporal Blandhar in his Destroyer. The battle may not have gone in our favour if not for his heroism.'

Zawkon was relieved to finally hear news of the victory. 'Thank the Ancients!' he exclaimed spontaneously. 'Tell me more, Captain.'

'With his flying skills, Corporal Blandhar annihilated the Treldarian warship without inflicting any damage to General Blake's jet fighters or our troops on the ground.' Turkrahn paused for a moment. 'Unfortunately, sir, the Corporal was too close to the Treldarian's warship when it exploded. The force sent him and his Destroyer hurtling at high velocity to the outer reaches. We've tried to contact him, but we've had no response. We searched to the outer orbit of Terra Major and haven't found any trace of his Destroyer. I believe we should award the brash young pilot a commendation, even if posthumously.'

'I'll consider that, Captain, but keep searching. Yarron turned out to be a loyal Sentinel in the end.' He paused momentarily, taking in the news. 'Have the ground troops stand down and I'll inform the World Assembly of your success. When you land, you and your soldiers take some time to regroup. Then collect the Diutrons, as well as Engineer Thompson, and return to the fleet.'

'Yes, sir, understood. Turkrahn, out!'

Zawkon was saddened by the news of Yarron's mishap, even though he didn't show his emotions outwardly. *He knew Yarron had been a deserter, but he had repented. Even with his last action in battle against the Treldarians, Yarron had shown his bravery and comradeship by putting his life at risk to save the World Assembly. Yarron was indeed a hero and now he had to give Bhalar the devastating news that he was missing in action.*

Putting his emotions aside for the time being, his first priority was matters of State. He had to inform others of the victory and arrange to re-establish order.

'General Blake, this is Commander Zawkon confirming that all's clear in Washington. Thanks to the efforts of Corporal Yarron Blandhar and your pilots, the enemy was intercepted before any damage was inflicted on the ground. Luckily there was no loss of life among our citizens. Your jet fighters will be returning soon.

I'll have my warship collect the Diutrons while you reassign your military personnel to help the citizens return to their buildings.

'I'm also confirming that we've beaten the enemy here in New York and captured the Treldarian leader, General Rokan, as well as the survivors of his army. They'll be taken to the prison cells. The Citadel and the MERIC Building are intact thanks to the fighting skills of your soldiers and the protection the Diutrons provided. They were critical to our success. I'll call my warships back to your air base to collect the Diutrons. We must retain these valuable war machines. Do you have any questions?'

'Yes, Commander. Do you want me to contact the Chief of Security, Richard Hammond, to inform him of our success and ask him to stand down his Security Officers?'

'Yes, General. Oh, and one more thing, sir,' said Zawkon in a less military tone. 'You might tell your lovely daughter, all is well, and I'll talk to her later tonight. Thank you General. Zawkon, out!'

General Blake's ears pricked up when he heard the Commander's last comment. His mind was ticking over. *Was Zawkon just being polite and respectful? Or was a romance blossoming?*

After all the tension, Commander Zawkon needed some fresh air. He strolled to the top of the tall fortress walls to survey the aftermath. Sentinels were busily ferrying wounded comrades to the infirmary, dismantling the barricades and escorting the Diutrons onto heavy-duty transport vehicles destined for the ASPECT complex. The battlefields were littered with disfigured enemy corpses which were now being quickly ferried away on troop carriers to funeral parlours, where the bodies would be cremated. Those Sentinels, as well as General Blake's soldiers, killed in action, were being transported to the Citadel's morgue to await their full military funeral ceremonies. Plumes of black smoke rising from the twisted and mangled burnt-out Treldarian warships created a haze across the surrounding landscape, mingling with the acrid odour of death. It was a heartfelt reminder of the horrors of war.

Saddened by the carnage before him, Zawkon went to visit Bhalar in her guest room. Arriving at her door, he knocked gently in case she was sleeping. Within seconds the door opened and the Treldarian beauty appeared.

'Come in, Commander Zawkon,' she said quietly and then with keen interest, 'tell me what news you have.'

'Thanks, Bhalar,' responded Zawkon in a restrained voice.

As he passed through the entry Bhalar closed the door behind him and waved her hand, directing him to take a seat. 'Would you like some tea?'

'No thanks. What I feel like right now is something stronger, but not while I'm on duty.' He paused for a moment. 'Bhalar, I have both good and bad news for you.'

Bhalar looked at him in anticipation with mixed feelings.

'We've won the battle and the information you provided us in advance of the attack was invaluable,' he announced positively.

Bhalar's face lit up with a smile. 'This is good news, Commander. I hope there weren't too many casualties?'

'Only a small number of injuries and fatalities,' he said, resting the palm of his hand against the forehead of his bowed head. 'But I need to tell you the bad news,' he said, looking into her eyes.

Sensing the news was personal, Bhalar suddenly began to panic. Her heartbeat quickened and her breathing shortened. 'Has something happened to Yarron?' she blurted out. 'Tell me he's alive and nothing has happened to him!'

Zawkon held out his hand to comfort and reassure her. 'Bhalar, I'm afraid your young Corporal is missing in action.'

The shock devastated Bhalar. 'What do you mean 'missing in action'? Have you found his Destroyer? Or has he been captured or killed by my father's army?'

Zawkon took a deep breath before answering, 'I was told he saved the day in the battle for the city of Washington. He was the hero, placing his life at risk to save the World Assembly. Unfortunately, in his brave effort to destroy a Treldarian warship, the powerful blast blew Yarron and his Destroyer into deep space. We haven't heard from him since.'

Bhalar gasped in horror, turning pale, covering her mouth and shaking her head in disbelief. 'No! That can't be true!'

'I'm sorry, Bhalar. The Federation hasn't given up searching for him and we won't. They'll let me know immediately when they find something.'

Feeling faint at the news, Bhalar composed herself and held the palm of her hand to her forehead while Zawkon continued.

'The other news is, we've captured your father. He'll be standing trial for declaring war on the Tzuracians.'

Bhalar's mood changed to one of anger as she spoke abruptly with fire in her eyes, 'Why not hang him now? He doesn't deserve a trial!'

Zawkon could sense a lifetime of resentment for what she had endured at the hands of a tyrant, having no escape and no hope for a better future. 'I understand how you must feel, Bhalar. However, we must follow protocol in keeping with the Tzuracian legal system and the Sentinels' Code of Honour. Otherwise, we're just as bad as the criminals who seek revenge governed only by their emotions. And we know well what path that leads down.'

He hesitated for a moment. 'Perhaps when things calm down, you might want to see your father before the trial? It might help you to tell him why you did what you did, to air your resentment and to justify your actions.'

They sat silent for some time before Bhalar spoke softly, 'You're right, Commander, we must remain civilised and not be ruled by hate.'

Zawkon rose from his chair and without speaking, held out his hand to her. It wasn't a formal handshake, but rather a comforting gesture to indicate his hope that all would work out for the best.

'You'll be the first to know if we hear from Yarron,' he said softly as he left the room.

WAR CRY ON KHAZOR

WHEN the aftershocks from the Xytrinium warhead explosion subsided on Tzurac, five threatening scorpion-shaped Treldarian warships landed without incident on the land surface near Khazor. Although the power was out, reports from the tower lookouts, via Sentinel holographs, flowed into the Control Room, revealing what was happening. Hundreds of enemy soldiers were pouring out of the raised hatch doors, spilling into the forests on the outskirts of the city. In the lead were Treldarians dressed in black uniforms and armed with laser pistols. They were followed by hordes of fierce and bare-chested Kyroni warriors carrying scimitars.

The obliteration of the Dome over Khazor had caused a tremendous explosion sending shockwaves over the land. These reverberations had stunned the Urgellans hiding in the forests. From their hidden positions, the army of archers had watched in horror as the massive black warships descended upon the planet through the colourful display in the skies above. Using powerful high-tech binoculars, their lookout spotters in the tallest trees were now relaying hand signals and coded 'bird calls' to the ground troops, alerting them of the advancing enemy.

On the ground the leader of the Urgellans, Aloran, gave an order to his runner to relay to all the other hidden clans the following message, 'The enemy has landed and is now stalking through the forests from all directions towards Khazor. Remain hidden and in your positions. Be at the ready and keep the silence. Strike swiftly and with stealth. If any Treldarians or Kyroni break through, let them go and wait for my signal of a flaming arrow to move in and encircle them and release a shower of arrows. The Sentinels are relying on us to help defeat these invaders. Take no hostages. Dispose of as many as you can. Remember, by annihilating this scourge on Tzurac, we are defending our families, our homes, our way of life and our own planet, Urgellan. Make your Queen proud.'

The messenger sped off, quietly and cautiously, in the direction of the other clans as soon as Aloran finished speaking.

As the invaders hacked and trampled their way through the thick underbrush using their swords and scimitars, frightened flocks of birds took flight giving away the invaders' location and speed and the directions from which they were approaching. It was obvious to the Urgellan archers these enemy soldiers had no experience in jungle warfare.

When the swarms of Treldarians and Kyroni reached small clearings within the forest in range of the archers, showers of arrows rained down on them from the skies, wave after wave. Most of the metal shafts fitted with razor-sharp Xytrinium hunting heads, reached their intended targets, easily penetrating the light body-armour worn by the rebels. The enemy soldiers fell rapidly, and by the time they reached the Urgellans' line of defence, they had lost a third of their numbers.

* * *

The remaining invading army, led by the invincible General Vark, with Ramlok by his side, slowed their pace and moved with more caution and stealth, trying to reach cover in the next patch of forest, not knowing what to expect. The showers of arrows ceased, and an eerie stillness enveloped the dark forest, like the dead calm before a storm with no bird sounds and no insect noises.

Anxiety and adrenalin, mixed with apprehension, were at a high amongst the Treldarian and Kyroni soldiers, not knowing when or from where the archers would strike again. Maintaining silence, Vark gave hand signals which were passed between the ranks, giving orders for them to spread out and fall back into smaller groups of fifty, before advancing with more stealth.

As each band crept closer, the well-camouflaged Urgellans sprang swiftly and silently from their hiding places, cutting the enemy down with their short blades and lightning-speed arrows. Then, with agility and swiftness, the silent assassins retreated back to the cover of the brush. With each approaching band, the act was repeated.

In spite of the Urgellans' efforts, almost fifteen hundred of the enemy slipped through the first line of defence, with General Vark still leading the charge, angry and more determined than ever. The scar-faced General was becoming desperate. *The Tzuracians had certainly been forewarned of the attack. He should have blasted Khazor from space once the Dome was obliterated. Regrettably, it was too late now to turn back the clock.*

He activated his handheld communicator and whispered an order back to his flagship, 'Captain Tarken, come in! Captain Tarken, this is General Vark.'

Minor static interference came through Vark's communicator before an audible voice was heard. 'General Vark, Captain Tarken. I hear you loud and clear, sir!' he said in his hoarse Treldarian voice.

Vark transmitted his frustration and anger, sounding almost frantic, 'We're being cut to pieces out here. The Tzuracians knew we were coming and prepared their defences too well. Only half our army survived the ambush. Before we advance further towards the Citadel, I want you to launch the warships and bombard the city with your laser cannons until it's razed to the ground. I want to annihilate the Sentinels and crush the Federation for good!'

'Yes, sir! Immediately. Tarken, out!' Tarken needed no second command.

Lifting off from the planet's surface, the Treldarian warships climbed rapidly to sixty thousand feet to spread the impact of their cannon fire over a wide area of the Citadel and the city and positioned their warships, ready to strike.

But suddenly, just as Tarken prepared to give the command, General Dakhar's cloaked Tzuracian fleet appeared from nowhere, surrounding them.

* * *

'Fire!' ordered Commander Dakhar. 'Give them all you've got!'

The Tzuracian fleet had been waiting anxiously for General Vark's armada to return to the inner orbit of Tzurac. This time Dakhar was offering no chance to surrender. There would be no opportunity to escape.

The impact was devastating. Although Vark's ships had raised their shields, they were unable to repel the incredible force of Xytrinium torpedoes fired at them from all directions. Powerful explosions reverberated one after another, Vark's ships disintegrating and debris littering the atmosphere.

Dakhar's warships felt the impact, even though they were positioned a safe distance away with their shields raised to full capacity. The intense explosions confirmed Dakhar's suspicion the Treldarian ships were carrying more Xytrinium warheads. *In retrospect, his decision to abort any attack on the Treldarian armada while they were landing on Tzurac had been the right one. If the Treldarians had released a warhead then, Khazor and all its inhabitants would have been decimated.*

Dakhar finally breathed a sigh of relief, knowing they had destroyed any further aerial threat to Khazor. *But what was happening on the ground? He needed to provide aerial support to Harzan's troops, and quickly.* He contacted the Destroyers' squadron leader over the Comms, 'Return to Tzurac immediately! Take out the enemy on the ground.'

* * *

From the surface of the planet, General Vark watched in horror the complete destruction of his fleet in the inner orbit above Khazor. His heart was beating excessively fast, his breathing now short and shallow, and he felt light-headed. His whole body had broken out in a cold sweat, and he screamed in agony into his coat sleeve, to muffle his despair. He had lost his faithful and long-time friend Captain Tarken, and his plan to defeat the Federation to start a new order of total domination was crumbling before his eyes.

Ramlok grabbed his General's shoulder and shook him roughly. 'We can't stop now, General. We've come too far.'

After composing himself, the General finally gave a hand signal for his troops to advance. Vark was now on a mission of retaliation. Determination to kill as many Tzuracians as he could was his sole motivation. He charged towards the Citadel, almost recklessly.

Emerging from the cover of the heavily wooded forest, Vark's army was faced with a wide expanse of cleared land. In the near distance the General could see the tall towers of the Citadel jutting out from beyond another patch of dense woodland. *If he and his soldiers could make it safely across the open expanse, they'd be able to approach the walls of the Citadel unseen, under cover of the green canopy.* He raised his left arm rigidly above his head and flicked it hard in the direction of the Citadel, signalling for his soldiers to charge across the clearing.

When a flaming arrow appeared in the sky, sent by Aloran, signalling attack, the Urgellans who were now behind Vark's army, released another heavy shower of arrows onto the exposed enemy. Many metal shafts found their mark, a number of Vark's soldiers falling to the ground, some screaming in pain, others stone dead. By the time Vark's remaining soldiers made it across the open ground to the cover of the forest on the other side, his numbers had been culled to about a thousand.

Then, filtering out of the forest from the other side and now in reach of the Citadel, the surviving Treldarians and Kyroni were confronted by a massive army of two thousand maroon-uniformed Sentinels. The Sentinel army was in the formation of two parallel rows, one line close behind the other, spreading the breadth of the Citadel's western wall. They were standing ready with swords in hand.

Surveying his own soldiers, Vark could sense their eagerness to test their might against this elite war-machine. Although outnumbered, they were determined to fight to the end. It was in their blood not to give up without a fight to the death and their spirits were lifted, knowing their enhanced strength and agility was now matched against the elite Sentinels. These Treldarians and Kyroni were warriors. To yield was cowardice – to die in glory was better than to live in shame.

General Vark raised his sword and held it aloft. As the others followed suit, he yelled his battle cry, 'Death to the Federation!' Then he lowered his sword to point towards their enemy and charged.

The rest followed, yelling the same chilling battle cry, and charging with their General as they ran, kicking up the dust underfoot. Some fired their laser pistols, others hurled grenades, and most flailed their sabres and scimitars.

Leading his soldiers at full speed, Vark could hear behind him their blood-curdling war cries almost drowned out by the sound of exploding grenades lobbed towards the frontlines of Sentinels. Buzzing green laser beams streaked past him as his warriors fired their weapons. Dirt was flying high, and clouds of dust mixed with black smoke were now discolouring the once clear blue sky, partially blocking the sun's rays. Destroyers were swooping from above, taking any opportunity to fire on his troops.

In Vark's mind, *it was 'do or die'!*

RESOLUTION

WHILE the battle raged outside the walls of the Citadel, inside, Lieutenant Kyron Tyros led his units of Sentinels towards the Low Security holding cells as ordered.

Arriving at the cells in semi-darkness, they were confronted by a bloodbath in the passageways. Some of the two hundred prisoners had overpowered the sentries, killing them and relieving them of their weapons.

Without warning, Kyron's units were fired upon by prisoners who were lurking in the shadows.

'Take cover and return fire!' Kyron commanded as he dived behind one of the cell walls.

Although the Sentinels returned laser fire, they struggled to gain any advantage. They were pinned down with no other entries or exits from the cell block.

'Sergeant, go back to the armoury, collect a dozen stun grenades, and return as fast as you can. We'll cover you!'

Kyron and his unit fended off the prisoners with laser fire until his Sergeant returned and quickly handed the stun grenades to several of the soldiers in his second unit.

'Okay, Sentinels. On my signal, throw the grenades. Before the dust settles, and while they're dazed, I'll take the first unit to the High-Security cellblock. Sergeant, seize the prisoners, secure them in one of the empty rooms, stand guard and maintain your vigilance.'

As the laser fire streaked back and forth, Kyron gave the order, 'Now!'

There was a series of loud explosions, flashes of lights and screams of pain. The prisoners were temporarily disorientated and disabled. As the Sergeant and his unit rushed to secure the escaped prisoners, Kyron and his unit disappeared down the passageway towards the High Security cellblock.

Then, as they turned a corner, Kyron and his unit were suddenly confronted by a band of highly charged criminals standing at the far end of the passageway brandishing weapons. Both sides stopped in their tracks and both leaders raised an arm signalling to hold fire.

Kyron was astonished to see his archenemy, Khaneera Zarkwin, leading the pack. His pulse quickened as did his breathing, his hand instinctively reaching for his laser staff, anticipating a duel. A vivid picture of their last encounter on Terra Major flashed into his mind. Then, Khaneera had discharged her laser pistol at point blank range in an effort to kill him and would have done so if not for Yarron Blandhar who had hurled himself into the firing-path to take the burning blast.

Khaneera had kept her jet-black dyed hair cropped short and was wearing skin-tight black leathers, obviously retrieved after her escape. A laser pistol was strapped to her left thigh, and she was wielding a Sentinel sword in her right hand. It was clear the daughter of Khane Zarkwin had maintained her lithe and athletic body.

Khaneera strutted provocatively towards Kyron's unit, making a statement of defiance to her captors. Then suddenly, without any warning, she drew her pistol and started firing in Kyron's direction. One of the laser beams struck the Sentinel standing beside Kyron in the chest and the soldier collapsed heavily to the floor.

Kyron and his soldiers dived for cover, as did the prisoners at the opposite end of the passageway.

As the criminal gang fired bursts of lasers from their crouched positions to give her cover, Khaneera suddenly leapt high in the air towards the high-arched ceiling, forward somersaulting, and landing in the opening of the passageway directly opposite. She was escaping.

'I'm going after her, Sergeant!' yelled Kyron.

'Yes, sir!' replied the Sergeant, continuing his attack.

Kyron was determined to capture Khaneera. He bolted back up a passageway which led to the surface. At the top of the stairs, he scanned the courtyard in the direction he anticipated Khaneera would be heading.

Amid the chaos in the courtyard, it was almost impossible to spot her. Sentinel squads were marching double-time in all directions. Transporters were hovering at the ready, as they were loaded with weapons and equipment for urgent dispatch to the front. And there was frantic yelling and calling as orders were issued and acknowledged.

Then Kyron caught a fleeting glimpse of a slim, darkly dressed figure charging towards a stationary hover-transporter on the other side of the courtyard. It was too dangerous to fire his laser pistol with so many bustling soldiers blocking his line of fire, and he was too far away to catch her. So, he watched as Khaneera drew her laser pistol and mounted the craft, pointing the barrel of the firearm at the transporter pilot's head. Within seconds, they were airborne.

Kyron looked frantically around the courtyard until his eyes fell on another stationary transporter with a Sentinel at the controls. He charged towards it, yelling, 'Corporal, this is an emergency!'

The driver almost jumped out of his skin when he turned around to see a desperate Sentinel officer catching his breath.

'Follow that vessel!' Kyron commanded, pointing in the direction of Khaneera's hijacked craft which was quickly disappearing over the high outside eastern wall of the Citadel.

'Yes, sir!' said the driver, as the noisy thrusters roared into life and the craft jolted forward, gathering speed and height as it lifted off from the cobblestones.

Speeding off in pursuit of Khaneera, Kyron gripped the metal safety bar at the side of the transporter to avoid being flung out.

'She's an escaped prisoner from High Security – armed and extremely dangerous,' he yelled to the driver. 'She'll kill without hesitation.'

The Corporal gulped and braced himself for the chase.

'She's heading for the air base,' shouted Kyron above the noise of the whistling wind rushing through the windowless cabin, 'most likely to commandeer one of the Destroyers.'

The driver acknowledged.

'Does this vehicle have a Comms installed, soldier?' shouted Kyron.

'Yes, sir,' the Corporal shouted back, 'all military DTCs have them.' He pressed a button on the front console which opened a small sliding panel displaying a short black handset.

'Patch me through to the air base,' snapped Kyron.

He watched the Corporal press one of the red LED buttons which lit up brightly. 'You're on speaker, sir.'

'Air base, this is Sentinel Lieutenant Kyron Tyros! Can you hear me? Please respond. This is an emergency!'

For a moment all he heard was shrieking static on the open line. Then a tinny voice, sounding as if it was coming through a hollow metal pipe, echoed on the speaker, 'This is Flight Sergeant Harbrok at Flight Control. What's your emergency, Lieutenant?'

'I'm in pursuit of an armed and extremely dangerous escaped Sentinel prisoner from High Security. Her name's Khaneera Zarkwin. She'll be approaching your air base any minute in a hijacked hover-transporter. You can't mistake her. She's dressed in black, with short black hair, and she's travelling with a kidnapped driver. They'll be entering your air space from the east. Raise the alarm and have Security on alert. She may attempt to steal one of the Destroyers. I'll soon be there.' Kyron emphasised again, 'Be careful. She's a cold-blooded killer!'

'Affirmative, Lieutenant! I'll warn the guards. Harbrok, out!'

By the time Kyron arrived at the air base, Khaneera's hover-transporter had already landed.

'Don't land too close, in case she's hiding there,' Kyron instructed the Corporal.

With his own vehicle now on the ground, Kyron cautiously approached the other transporter. He could see no sign of Khaneera, but the kidnapped driver was slumped over the console with a fatal laser wound to his head.

Kyron cursed under his breath then called back to his own driver in a low voice, 'Wait here for me and keep your head down.'

Crouching low, with his laser pistol drawn and armed, Kyron made his way on the open field towards a large hangar about five hundred yards away. He was fully alert, and the atmosphere was quiet and tense.

Suddenly the silence was shattered by loud piercing sirens broadcasting on the external PA system. Kyron recognised it as a Code Red, which usually triggered when a vessel or a building caught fire. He turned his head and out of the corner of his eye saw thick black smoke billowing from one of the administration blocks at the far end of the base. A series of deafening explosions followed.

'Khaneera!' he cursed under his breath. *It was a clever diversion to draw security personnel away from the hangars. She was as cunning as ever.*

Reaching one of the unguarded entries on the southern wall of the huge hangar, Kyron saw two lifeless sentries lying face down on the concrete floor, just inside the doorway. In the background he could hear a motorised whining sound.

Tightening his grip on his laser pistol he entered the doorway carefully, all his senses attuned. Khaneera was a hundred yards away, operating the hatch on one of the Destroyers. Pointing his pistol in her direction, he called out, 'Stop what you're doing, Khaneera! Raise your hands in the air where I can see them!'

Caught off guard, Khaneera froze and slowly raised her hands towards her shoulders as if to surrender, staring at him with piercing steel-blue eyes. Like a hissing cornered cobra and with her usual condescending smile, she spat out the words coldly, 'You'd be very stupid, *farm boy*, to fire your weapon in here with all the inflammables nearby. You could very well destroy everything, including the two of us. I'm sure you wouldn't want to make Torri a young widow, left to look after your two little snivelling pups. Would you?'

Kyron knew Khaneera was not one to surrender. She was willing to die for her cause. He watched as she slowly lowered her hands and reached gingerly for the staff-sword holstered at her belt. Kyron paused for a moment realising the only way to capture her was in hand-to-hand contact. He re-holstered his pistol and reached for his own staff-sword and activated the blade.

'Well,' she quipped in a venomous tone, 'I've been looking forward to the day I could finish the job I started, *killing you* without the traitor Yarron here to step in my way. When I've finished with you, *farm boy*, I'll be going after your family to destroy the seeds of the Tyros heritage. Are they here on Tzurac?' she teased. 'It would make it so much easier. You can all be buried together in the same cemetery plot. How quaint is that?' She detected the gold bars on his sleeve. 'Or will they give you a military funeral now you've become a Lieutenant in the elite Sentinel army?'

Kyron ignored the psychology and stayed focused. *It was like déja vous,* he thought, *facing off once more with his vengeful archenemy. He thought he'd seen the last of her when she was put away for life.*

Automatically, his nerves and facial expression changed to cold hard steel. *Zarkwin's revenge against the Tyros family had continued long enough. He was ready to do battle. He would finish this once and for all. He sensed the presence of his father's spirit surrounding him in the hangar, giving him reassurance. This would be the final battle.*

Trying to provoke Khaneera and break her concentration Kyron finally spoke, 'I think not, Khaneera. If it's to be a fight to the death, then you'll be joining your dead boyfriend, Jackson Jensen, whose decrepit remains, or should I say ashes, are stored in an urn somewhere in a dark dungeon.'

His cold words worked as expected. Khaneera's smile changed instantly into an expression of hate, her eyes glaring with rage as she charged wildly at him, waving and slashing her blade.

Kyron was ready for her, and as she swung to slice across his upper torso, he moved with a lightning reflex to the right, lifting his sword in a circular pattern then slashing his blade across her right arm as her momentum carried her forward. The cut was deep enough to rip through Khaneera's leather sleeve and leave a nasty bleeding gash on her forearm.

She winced in pain but quickly recovered, spinning around and using a backward slash aimed at Kyron's neck. Kyron was too fast and ducked in time, avoiding contact then returning to an upright position and lunging at Khaneera's stomach with the sharp point of his blade. It found its mark, puncturing her jacket and cutting her flesh. But the strike didn't slow her down. Instead, it made her angrier and even more aggressive.

Khaneera composed herself for another strike, like a coiled viper ready to spring out and sink its deadly fangs into its victim. Again, she lunged at Kyron's heart, but once more his lightning reflexes enabled him to block her thrust with his blade, allowing him to step in and elbow her fiercely to the head. He heard a faint crack and wheeling around to a frontal defence position, he saw Khaneera stagger back with blood trickling from her nose.

Khaneera quickly recovered and balanced herself into a forward stance, wiping her bloodied nose with her sleeve. Ignoring the pain and staring with steely eyes into Kyron's, she retorted, 'Just a scratch compared to the bleeding from the wounds I'm going to inflict on you. This time, Tyros, I *will* kill you!'

Kyron didn't react. He focused in anticipation of Khaneera's next move, holding his arms outstretched in front of him, both hands firmly gripping the handle of his sword. In this position he could quickly block a blade attack from any direction.

Now Khaneera changed her tactics. Clasping her hands on the sword's hilt, she raised both arms straight above her head, the sword pointing to the ceiling. Instead of rushing in, she stalked slowly towards her opponent like a cat on the prowl, with short sure-footed sliding steps until she was two sword-lengths away from Kyron. Then she moved to the side and began circling clockwise around Kyron, similar to a jungle wildcat stalking a wild animal, waiting for a split-second opportunity to strike in an instant should its prey let its guard down. Kyron mirrored Khaneera's slow stepping movements, continuing to face her front-on, sword pointed at her torso.

Several seconds passed, their concentration unbroken, eyes fixated, each waiting silently in expectation. Kyron knew he had the advantage of time. He was in no hurry to attack her. He could wait until Security arrived to take her into custody. All he had to do was fend her off, though he was aware he was confronting a desperate fugitive, who like a cornered beast, would go all out to cut him down.

Khaneera knew the longer she delayed, the less chance she had of escaping the planet and the opportunity had now presented itself to finally kill the son of Ahrmon Tyros, the Sentinel who had ended her father's career.

In a deliberate move to force Khaneera's hand, Kyron dipped his sword slightly, tightening his grip. Khaneera, who had been waiting for this subtle action, reacted with speed. She stepped forward with her left leg into a wide stance, bringing the blade down swiftly and forcibly in line with Kyron's head. Kyron raised his sword with lightning speed to counter the blow, and in the one motion stepped and swung his body to the right. His blade deflected Khaneera's, and he completed the circular pattern, rapidly sweeping his sword back towards Khaneera, slicing deeply across her left shoulder. It happened so quickly that Khaneera was unable to counteract the speed of Kyron's blade. She cried out loudly as she fell to the floor on her knees, her body numbed momentarily.

Recovering quickly from the shock, Khaneera jumped up, spun around, then sprang high into the air, twisted mid-somersault and slashed at Kyron's head, landing on her feet right behind him. Kyron was unable to block her blade but luckily, his helmet took the brunt of the blow, leaving a deep indented crease across its top. The blow left him slightly dazed but unscathed.

Before she could take advantage of her position to slash at Kyron's back, Kyron leaned forward as if to do a handstand and shot out a powerful reverse snap-kick with his right leg. It landed heavily on Khaneera's ribcage, compressing her chest. Kyron heard the cracking of several bones as the heavy kick knocked her off her feet, sending her several yards backwards, and smashing her against the thick, metal fuselage on one of the Destroyers.

Khaneera slumped to the ground, semi-conscious, her sword lying beside her and the deep wound to her shoulder oozing blood. Her breathing was loud and laboured as she gasped for air to fill her punctured lungs, now being flooded with her own blood. But even in her injured state, Khaneera managed to pull her pistol from its holster and raise it towards Kyron.

His speed reflexes kicked in. *He had to stop her pulling the trigger and igniting the inflammable gases in the hangar.* He pulled a dagger from his ankle sheath and threw it with lightning speed at his opponent. The razor-sharp double-edged blade found its target in Khaneera's neck, severing the carotid artery.

Kyron paused for a moment to gather his breath and compose himself. Then, with his staff-sword still drawn, he went over to confirm Khaneera was dead. Her cold eyes were staring blankly, and blood was rushing down her neck from the severed artery. There was no sign of breathing. He knelt beside her still body and felt for a pulse on her wrist. There was none. *Finally, it was over.*

Standing up and reaching for a rag on a nearby bench, he wiped his blood-stained staff-blade, retracted it and holstered it back onto his belt. As he did, he felt a strange vibration from his Pledge ring which glowed for a fleeting instant. The words of his father resounded from somewhere inside his head, *'You've done well my son. All has been resolved. I'm proud of you.'* Kyron's mind and heart was filled momentarily with a vivid image of his father.

Looking at Khaneera's lifeless body lying in a pool of blood, Kyron was somewhat saddened at being her executioner. He knew she had been fed mistruths about her father, Khane Zarkwin, from an early age and set on a path of blind revenge. Khane Zarkwin was a ruthless bully and not the victim Khaneera's mother had led her to believe. Kyron's father had acted in self-defence when he severed Khane's hand during practice as cadets in the Sentinel Academy – it had been a last-ditch attempt by Ahrmon Tyros to save his own life against a vicious Sentinel. Yet Khane Zarkwin had never forgiven him and had turned against the Sentinels, working in league with the Bladers to plunder Federation transporters carrying Xytrinium. And it was Khane's obsession for revenge that had led him to frame Ahrmon Tyros for murder after Rhyk Dakhar was killed by the Bladers on one of their raids. Khaneera had grown up carrying with her the hatred held by her father – it was Zarwkin's revenge.

Khaneera may have been misguided about the truth of these events, but she had also been the catalyst for the Treldarian uprising, allowing the Xytrinium formula to fall into enemy hands, rekindling the Treldarians' barbarism, and causing the deaths of many innocent lives. And, by her own hand, she had almost taken the life of Kyron's very close friend and mentor, Ehrane Dakhar, as well as his own life.

Feeling his actions were justified, Kyron was suddenly overwhelmed by a feeling of mental and emotional relief. The anguish which had been haunting him for years was gone. The threat Khaneera posed to him and his family was permanently extinguished. He imagined how relieved Torri would feel when he broke the news to her.

He wrapped Khaneera's body in a canvas sheet he found lying in a corner of the hangar and carried her back to the awaiting hover-transporter. After carefully placing the body in the back section, he boarded the DTC and ordered the Corporal to return to the Citadel.

'Is that the escaped prisoner you were chasing, sir?' the Corporal asked, nudging his head in the direction of the bundled 'passenger'.

'Yes, soldier, that's her – Khaneera Zarkwin, daughter of Khane Zarkwin, who was the Chief of Security about three hundred years ago. Unfortunately, she wasn't surrendering without a fight. So, we fought to the death. It was either me or her and the Ancients didn't favour her.'

'Well, sir, I'm glad you were the one to survive. She killed an innocent hover-transporter driver in cold blood. I think justice has prevailed.'

'Yes, Corporal, I think you're right. I need to use your Comms again to inform the Admiral of my whereabouts.'

'Yes, sir. I'll connect you ...'

'Good,' said Admiral Harzan after hearing Kyron's report. 'Commander Dakhar has annihilated the Treldarian Fleet and is making his way back to Tzurac. We're winning the battle outside the western wall and it's coming to an end.'

Kyron didn't talk for the remaining short trip. As the transporter made its way back to the Citadel, he sat quietly reminiscing about what had happened in the past and his connection with Khaneera.

* * *

In spite of the efforts of Vark's rapidly advancing army, the laser fire and flying shrapnel from the exploding grenades had little impact on their opponents. Only a handful of Sentinels had fallen, crying out spontaneously in pain from their wounds.

The Sentinels had swung their shimmering blue shield capes in front of them and lowered their helmet visors. They had maintained their formation in two parallel rows and were now marching slowly towards the oncoming rabble with their short blades drawn.

One hundred yards before the two opposing sides clashed, the Sentinel captain called an order for his troops to halt. A second later, another order was called for the first row of Sentinels to drop to one knee and the second row drew their laser pistols and fired at will. 'Cease fire!' he yelled. Two seconds later another command issued, 'First row, draw pistols and commence firing at will!' Another five seconds lapsed, and the order to cease fire was again called. At least five hundred of Vark's advancing army had fallen on the battlefield by the time the remaining rebels met with the line of Sentinels.

When the two sides eventually clashed, there was fierce hand-to-hand combat with swords, knives and scimitars. Blades clashed, lasers fired, soldiers on both sides screamed and yelled and copious amounts of blood spilled on the battlefield. Yet the resilient General Vark continued to fight on bravely as his soldiers fell around him, one after another.

From the corner of his eye, Vark glimpsed his son Tykran leading his unit and fighting valiantly against the Sentinels. For a fleeting moment, he was a proud father until suddenly cut short by a Sentinel blade piercing his solar plexus. 'Aargh!' he yelled in pain as he collapsed, holding the wound, and then fell unconscious.

Captain Ramlok, who had been by his General's side throughout, yelled a blood-curdling Treldarian curse and stepped up, trying to rally the stunned troops. 'Revenge! Take revenge!' he screamed.

The ever faithful but battle-weary Sergeant Krag rallied beside Ramlok, yet the army sensed defeat. With their leader down, it was only a matter of time before the remaining Treldarian soldiers and Kyroni warriors were overwhelmed by the Sentinels and defeated.

The Sentinels quickly secured the badly injured Vark while Ramlok kicked and screamed abuse as the Sentinels disarmed the

Blader and cuffed him. 'Damn the Federation!' Ramlok swore, 'Damn the lot of you!'

As the Sentinels grabbed Krag, securing his arms roughly behind his back, he heard his Captain's defiant words, and realised the depth of the former Blader pirate's hatred.

* * *

As the surrounds fell eerily quiet in the aftermath of the battle, Harzan called on a nearby Sentinel to holograph Dakhar. 'The battle has come to a decisive end, sir. The enemy has been defeated and General Vark and two hundred Treldarian soldiers and Kyroni warriors have been captured. Power has yet to be restored, but we've contained the escaped prisoners in one of the old metal-barred cells. We're in control again, sir.'

Dakhar was clearly relieved. 'Well done, Harzan! Thank the Gods! Inform the citizens in the underground tunnels we've won the war! But don't release them until all is safe and clear. We'll be there soon.'

* * *

By the time Kyron arrived back at the Citadel, Sentinel soldiers were already beginning to restore order from the chaos. After arranging for Khaneera's body to be placed in the Sentinel morgue, he reported immediately to Admiral Harzan who was still in the Control Room.

Kyron saluted and stood at attention, 'Sir, Lieutenant Tyros reporting.'

'At ease, Lieutenant. Are you injured?'

'No, sir, but I'll need a replacement helmet. As you can see by the large crease, Khaneera's sword remodelled it. I apologise for leaving my post, sir, but I thought her capture was a priority and I acted accordingly. Unfortunately, she refused to surrender, and we fought a life and death battle. I had no choice but to end her life before she ended mine.'

'You made the right decision. Khaneera Zarkwin was regarded as Tzurac's most hated and most dangerous prisoner. If she'd escaped in one of our Destroyers, she would have wreaked havoc on our troops.' Harzan paused before adding, 'Well done, Lieutenant Tyros! I'm just very thankful it was you, and not her that survived the ordeal.'

'Thank you, sir,' said Kyron, feeling vindicated.

'Now, Lieutenant, as my First Officer, you are to join in the mop-up operations before our Chief-Commander returns. As first priority you need to ensure our power source is re-established. We need to have the city up and running again before our citizens return to their homes.

'You'll be reassigned to Chief-Commander Dakhar upon his return. And, who knows, with your engineering background, he might have you involved in resurrecting the protective Dome. That'll be all for now, Lieutenant. You're dismissed!'

'Thank you, sir,' Kyron said, standing to attention and saluting his superior, before about-facing and marching out of the Control Room. Kyron smiled to himself with satisfaction. He felt he'd proved his worth as a Sentinel Officer and as a true Tzuracian.

THE AFTERMATH

DAKHAR was still *en route* to Tzurac with his fleet when he received news from Zawkon indicating that the battle on Terra Major was over. As the holographic image of Acting Chief-Commander Zawkon appeared, Dakhar was anxious to hear the news.

'Sir, Rokan's fleet of warships has been destroyed and we've defeated his army. The General was seriously wounded, but we've captured him along with his remaining soldiers.'

'Excellent news, Commander!' Dakhar was elated. 'We've also had success here, though not without a hard fight. The Treldarians destroyed the Dome with a Xytrinium warhead, and we had to battle it out on the ground as well as in the air. I'm about to land and survey the damage.'

'Then I'll be brief,' said Zawkon. 'The Treldarians with Nujharene reinforcements also made it to the ground in New York, but the Diutrons wiped out half the enemy's soldiers and swayed the battle in our favour – it was a brilliant strategy of yours. MERIC, ASPECT and the Citadel are all safe. And Corporal Blandhar saved Washington and the World Assembly almost single-handedly while the enemy was still in the air.'

Dakhar accepted news of the success with a smile. 'And our losses?' he asked, looking more troubled.

Zawkon shook his head sadly. 'Some of our Sentinels were killed and several injured.'

'I'm sorry to hear of the loss of good soldiers, Commander. We'll honour them with a full military funeral back on Tzurac and their families will be well looked after. Congratulations on your success, Commander. I commend your soldiers and General Blake's men as well as Grant Thompson and Corporal Blandhar.

'As soon as you're ready, begin arrangements to transport General Rokan and his remaining army back here to stand trial before the Senate. I'd like this whole episode to be resolved as soon as possible. I also want Corporal Blandhar to come to Tzurac. I'm pleased to hear of his heroism, although we have some unresolved matters to settle.'

Zawkon interjected, 'I'm sorry, sir, but Yarron is missing in action. He was blasted into the void when he fired on the Treldarian warship over Washington. We've been unable to contact him.'

Dakhar closed his eyes temporarily and a frown appeared on his brow. The news was obviously disheartening. 'I see,' said Dakhar with sadness in his voice. 'Search for him for as long as it takes.'

'Yes, sir. We will,' said Zawkon, impressed that the General shared his own concern for Yarron's life. 'And the Diutrons? Is it too soon to ask of your plans for these machines?'

Dakhar refocused and issued orders without hesitation. 'Keep fifteen hundred on Terra Major for the planet's future protection. The others can be returned to Terra Iota with Thompson.'

'Yes, Chief-Commander. I'll see to it.'

* * *

When Dakhar and his fleet finally arrived back at the air base on Tzurac, he left some of his captains and their crews to oversee minor repairs on his ships while he journeyed to the Citadel to inspect the aftermath of the battle. He was pleasantly surprised to see that, despite the obliteration of the Dome, little damage had been done to the city and surrounding buildings. Although the generators which had powered the protective Dome were totally burnt out, power had been restored temporarily to most of the inhabited structures including the Citadel.

Standing atop the Citadel, Dakhar surveyed the battlefield where the main confrontation had taken place. Amid the fallen casualties of both armies which were painstakingly being removed, he watched the war-torn Urgellan soldiers filtering back through the forests, slowly making their way across the fields towards the Citadel. Some were assisting their wounded. Others were carrying their dead comrades on field stretchers with the help of Sentinels. There was sadness in his heart for those families who had lost their young offspring to this senseless war. Condemning those who would be standing trial would not make up for the futile loss of good lives.

After returning to his office, Commander Dakhar soon summoned Admiral Harzan.

'Again, well done, my friend,' Dakhar said as Harzan entered the room. 'That was tougher than anticipated.'

'Yes, too close for comfort, sir. We could have lost this battle had we not been forewarned by Corporal Blandhar.'

Dakhar agreed. 'Yes, and I've just heard from Zawkon – we also could have lost the battle on Terra Major had it not been for Yarron's heroism in his Destroyer over the skies of Washington. Unfortunately, our Corporal is now missing in action and we're not sure whether he'll live to receive our gratitude.'

The two respected officers exchanged a knowing look, both realising just how fortunate they had been in thwarting the Treldarian invasion and winning the battles for Tzurac and Terra Major.

'And how is my First Officer, Kyron Tyros?' Dakhar asked anxiously. 'How did he fare?'

'I'm not sure what you've heard Commander, but all the prisoners escaped from their cells when the power was cut. While attempting to capture them, Lieutenant Tyros fought and killed Khaneera Zarkwin who had escaped to the air base.'

Dakhar's mind instantly flashed back to images of his last encounter with Khaneera Zarkwin. He had been seriously wounded by her dagger and Kyron almost killed by a blast from her laser pistol. He started firing questions at the Admiral. 'Is Kyron injured? Where is he now?'

'No need to worry Commander, he's in good health. He's leading his unit in the mop-up as we speak.'

'Very good, Admiral. Kyron and I go back a long way. His father and my father were the best of friends you know. I wouldn't want to lose him. So, thank you for putting my mind at rest.'

'I understand, Commander. Would you like me to send for him?'

'That won't be necessary, Admiral. I'll see him soon enough. I want you to assemble the Urgellans in the main courtyard first thing in the morning. I'd like to address them before they leave. You'll need three warships to accommodate them for their return voyage, allowing room for their fallen soldiers in the cryo-tubes. I'll prepare dispatches for Queen Tarune expressing our sincere appreciation for her invaluable support and offering our deepest condolences for the Urgellan losses.

'I also want you to arrange another warship to transport the Armonusians home – they played a minor but important role in calming and healing our troops during the battle. Continue overseeing the return to normal life on Tzurac, Admiral. If we can clear the battle ground, I think the citizens can start returning late this afternoon.'

'Yes, sir.'

* * *

IT was late that evening when Dakhar and Kyron finally made it back to Dakhar's mansion to be reunited with their loved ones. Tajhira, Torri and the children had returned from the safety of the underground tunnels only an hour earlier.

As soon as Kyron appeared through the main doors, Torri rushed to him and threw her arms around him. They held each other tightly as Torri's emotions overwhelmed her and tears began to stream uncontrollably from her eyes. Her heart was beating so fast from the joy and excitement of seeing and holding Kyron again. They kissed passionately, as if it were for the first time. No words were needed to express their joy at knowing they and their children were safe and unharmed. It was Zuri and Ehrana who broke the silence when they both pounced on their father with delight calling out, 'Dad, Dad, we love you.'

When Dakhar arrived home minutes later, he embraced Tajhira and Kyrah together, holding them tightly before reaching out his arm to Kyron to exchange a warm Sentinel handshake. 'Well done, my friend,' he said. Both were relieved to see each other unharmed.

When the reunions were over, and the children were settled into their beds, the adults all sat down together, to enjoy a much needed and soothing mellow wine.

'I needed that,' said Dakhar.

'We all did,' Tajhira responded.

'Hear, hear!' Kyron echoed.

'I believe you've got some news to share, Kyron', Dakhar prompted.

'I do,' said Kyron looking at Torri who was waiting keenly to hear what he had to say. 'I encountered Khaneera Zarkwin today. She had escaped from the prison.'

Torri gasped with surprise, almost choking on the mouthful of wine she had just taken. 'What!' she exclaimed, an image of the murderous vixen rushing through her mind.

'It's okay, Torri. I tried to recapture her and ended up chasing her to the air base where we met face to face. She had every intention of ending my life rather than surrendering.'

Torri was agitated. 'Did she attack you, Kyron? Are you injured?'

'Yes, she attacked me, but no, I'm not injured. We fought one on one. I had no choice but to defend myself and, in the confrontation, she was killed.'

Torri's fearful and anxious expression changed to relief with the news the bane of her life had finally been eliminated. 'Thank the Gods you're safe!' she said, throwing her arms around Kyron.

'I feel some guilt about taking her life,' Kyron added remorsefully, 'but it was her life or mine.'

'Don't feel bad, my friend,' Dakhar said reassuringly, 'I heard the full report from Admiral Harzan. Khaneera was set on a path of destruction, and you were following orders. In the end, Khaneera's death was best for all concerned.'

There was relief all round, knowing that Kyron and the Tyros family were now finally safe, free forever from the threat of Zarwkin's revenge.

* * *

AFTER arriving at the Citadel early the following morning, Dakhar went straight to his office to prepare official documents for the Tzuracian allies. They were soon dispatched to the Elder, Senator Ghalbrak, for his signature.

Later that morning Dakhar strolled to the Main Courtyard where the army of tired but victorious Urgellans were gathered. He carried with him the signed and sealed documents.

As he stepped up to the podium and raised both his arms, embracing the gathering, the noisy chattering of the throng died down. 'Friends, fellow soldiers, I'm elated with our victory.'

The crowd cheered, thrusting their weapons to the sky. Dakhar waited for the excitement to dissipate before continuing. 'Twice we Tzuracians have prevailed upon you Urgellans for your support in fighting our enemies. Both times you've shown your bravery and commitment to the cause. We're grateful to all of you, knowing without your help, we would have lost this battle against the dark force, bringing death, destruction and chaos to the Federation of Planets. Together, we've defeated our enemy once more and today we stand here proud, knowing we've eliminated the threat and won freedom for our families. Thank you all!'

Then, in a more sombre tone, he continued, 'I also thank those who have fallen in battle, knowing their lives have not been in vain. We will always remember them.'

Solitude fell upon the Urgellan soldiers, their heads bowed in remembrance for a silent prayer to their comrades-in-arms who would not be returning to greet their families or to share in the joy and celebration of the victory.

The stillness was broken as Dakhar called on their leader, 'Aloran, before you go, please come forward to receive a dispatch for Queen Tarune. I ask that you deliver this to her. It thanks her once again for her valued support in Tzurac's time of need and conveys an invitation for her to make an official goodwill visit to Tzurac to cement the close relations between our two planets.'

As Aloran came forward and collected the dispatch, Dakhar concluded by saying, 'Our warships are ready to take all of you back home. Transporters are waiting at the Citadel's entrance. I wish all of you a safe journey, and may the Ancient spirits protect and guide you.'

He raised his arm in a respectful Sentinel salute and to his surprise the entire army returned the salute in unison, before breaking ranks.

* * *

Back in his office, Dakhar and Harzan were seated in conference. 'Instruct one of your Units to make arrangements for our fallen comrades-in-arms to have a military send-off,' said Dakhar solemnly. 'That includes those who fell on Terra Major. Our fleet will be arriving here soon, and I'll be informing the families of those we've lost about their courageous actions in battle.'

'Yes, sir.'

'And, on another matter, has anything been done to arrange trials for the perpetrators of this bloody war?'

'Nothing yet, sir. We've been too busy trying to establish order from the chaos.'

'Understood, Admiral. Leave this one to me as well.' The atmosphere changed when Dakhar's expression hardened, as if his blood had turned cold. 'I'd like a public audience to be present when the murderous rebels are condemned for their war crimes.'

RELIEF

WHILE waiting anxiously for word about Yarron, Bhalar was granted permission to see her father and was escorted by a unit of Sentinels to the High Security cell where he was awaiting his trial. She was apprehensive about confronting him but determined to tell him why she escaped from her life of captivity and how she had grown to despise him. Bhalar wanted to remind him of his lack of compassion for her, his only daughter, and for Jelkah, the midwife who had been like a mother to her.

At General Rokan's cell, Bhalar was seated outside the forcefield facing her father and the escort of Sentinels retreated just out of earshot.

Though dishevelled and war-torn, the aged and white-bearded General Rokan stood defiantly with his arms crossed over his chest. 'So, traitor, why are you here?' he questioned bitterly. 'Surely not to gloat over my defeat?'

'No, father,' Bhalar responded with a slight tremor in her voice. She was overcome with a mix of fear, hate and sympathy, realising she had betrayed him. 'I haven't come to rejoice over your capture. I'm here to tell you why I escaped from Mankro, or more to the point, escaped from *you*.'

There was an uncomfortable silence.

'Escaped from *me*?' Rokan said sarcastically. 'After all I've done for you? I looked after you when your mother died, clothing you, feeding you, educating you and giving you a roof over your head. And you show your gratitude by fleeing? Was it you who betrayed me and alerted the enemy of my planned attack? Is this how you repay my kindness?'

'*You*, father!' Bhalar retorted, taking a deep breath and pointing her finger directly towards her father's face. 'If you think you've been kind to me, then *you've* been living an illusion!' With a look of disgust, she raised her voice, 'You treated me with no more respect than a slave. I suffered years of constant beatings, insults and intimidation. You deprived me of my freedom. I wasn't even allowed to go out of your hut and mingle with our people. A domesticated hound had a better life than me!

'It was only Jelkah who protected me and loved me like a daughter. She was the only saving grace in my life. Yet, you even took *her* away from me when you *murdered* her. She was the only one I really loved.' Her look had changed, and a tear came to her eye.

Bhalar continued, seething with anger again while her father stood silent and motionless with a blunt expression on his face.

'You were suffocating me, slowly choking the life out of me for your own selfish needs. You weren't a father to me – you were my keeper. I reminded you so much of my mother that you kept me locked up like you would a valuable painting, to gaze upon for life and take your hate out on me for her death, whenever it suited you. What a sick, selfish and callous being you are! You don't deserve to live.'

She paused for a second. 'But death would be too easy, too quick for what you've done. I'd prefer you to suffer with a life-term imprisonment, to feel what it's like to be caged up with nowhere to run, with no-one who cares. Now you've been treated with Xytrinium, it will be your torment for centuries to come. Perhaps that will give you time enough to realise what you put me through and finally make peace with your conscience.

'And yes, father, I seized the opportunity to escape with your prisoner Armel, who was in fact a Sentinel in disguise. I decoded the transmission he sent from Mankro which warned the Tzuracians of your intent to invade. Together, Armel and I secured amnesty on Earth in return for information about you and your army.'

Without waiting for a response, Bhalar rose and walked briskly away, leaving the bitter old man to mull over his daughter's words. Bhalar's confession had pricked his conscience, all too late. *Now, he had nothing and no-one to live for.*

As she paced down the passageway, Bhalar felt satisfied and relieved to have expressed the thoughts she had suppressed for so many years. Her despair had all but dissipated. *All she needed now was for Yarron to be alive.*

* * *

Ten hours after the explosion over Washington, Yarron woke in total darkness and silence, gasping for air. His head was pounding, and he was disoriented. All the ship's power systems had shut down, and with the air convertor not operating, he was quickly running out of oxygen. *He had to send a distress holograph to the Federation with his co-ordinates.*

He activated his Pledge ring and waited desperately for a response. The minutes seemed like hours before the holograph was acknowledged by Commander Zawkon.

'Commander, this is Corporal Yarron Blandhar. My ship has lost all power and I'm unsure how much oxygen is remaining. I need your help.'

Zawkon was surprised and relieved by the communication. *Yarron was alive!* But he could tell from the strained and weakened voice that Yarron was slowly suffocating from the increased carbon dioxide in his confined containment. He reacted promptly and decisively.

'Don't talk, Corporal. Save your oxygen. We have your co-ordinates now. I'll ask our search ships to undertake an urgent rescue. Keep the faith soldier and may the Ancients protect you. Zawkon, out!'

The holograph faded and Yarron was left in the silent darkness once more. Having no intention of waiting it out and playing a game of chance with death, Yarron reached for his staff-sword and pressed a partially concealed button at one end. Instantly, a blue glow projected from the tip, illuminating the cabin. Destroyers were fitted out with survival kits which contained a small cylinder of oxygen and breathing apparatus for emergencies. He hoped it would sustain him until he could repair the damage to his ship and restore the oxygen flow. Without further hesitation he went into search mode. *It would be a race against time with his life the high stake.*

Without gravity and with low oxygen, Yarron pulled himself sluggishly towards the back of the vessel until he reached the galley. The storage compartment's sliding door was sealed tight, and he needed something with which to pry it open. He pressed another concealed button on his staff-sword and a blade shot out. Using the tip of the blade as leverage, he tried to jemmy the door open in the crevice of the wall where the door slid into the cavity. He had little energy, and it was hard going.

Finally, his persistence seemed to work. The door started to give and then, suddenly, being spring loaded, it snapped fully open. Yarron's breathing was now laboured and his vision slightly blurred. He was light-headed and dizzy. Shining the pale blue light inside the compartment, he quickly located the oxygen cylinder. Data stencilled on the small blue metal tank read: 'Capacity of four hundred litres compressed: Normal respiration depletes supply in three hours. *So*, he thought, *there was limited time to get the power operational and restart the conversion generator. He hoped there was no serious damage to any of the parts.*

Strapping the cylinder to his back, Yarron donned the clear moulded face mask, turned on the valve tap and set his timepiece for a two-and-a-half-hour alarm trigger. The flood of life-giving rich oxygen was overwhelming. He filled his lungs to capacity and thanked the Ancients for the gift as his vision and strength quickly returned to normal.

With renewed energy and optimism, he ventured in the semi-darkness to the Comms centre located underneath the central walkway. Lifting the small rectangular metal grate to gain access, he floated down the narrow opening to the next level using the handrails for grip and leverage in the gravity-free environment. As he did, he had to take precautionary care not to knock the oxygen tank on his back against the compartment fixtures.

Following the massive amount of colour-coded cabling and piping which snaked its way from the front of the vessel to the rear, Yarron was able to locate the 'Diagnostics' module identified by a small red LED. It was flashing on and off in one-second intervals in the centre of a wall-mounted black cabinet. Yarron breathed a sigh of relief. The rechargeable back-up Xytrinium battery in the module was still working.

He slid the panel across the front of the cabinet to reveal a monitor the size of a console screen containing rows and rows of small chrome switches with smaller clear buttons underneath them. After flicking the switches on and off in a specific sequence, the fluorescent blue screen jumped to life and data started to print on the screen.

WEAPONS SYSTEM	OPERATIONAL	ON STANDBY
ELECTRICS	OPERATIONAL	ON STANDBY
COMMUNICATIONS	OPERATIONAL	ON STANDBY
CRYSTAL CONDENSER	OPERATIONAL	ON STANDBY
GUIDANCE SYSTEM	OPERATIONAL	ON STANDBY
GRAVITY SYSTEM	OPERATIONAL	ON STANDBY
FUEL SUPPLY	LOW	
WATER SUPPLY	LOW	
AIR SUPPLY	EXTREMELY LOW	
CONVERSION CHAMBER	MALFUNCTION	

Yarron activated all the systems showing 'ON STANDBY' by pressing the clear buttons. As each button was pressed it changed, emitting a green LED accompanied by a high-pitched electronic sound, and the screen indicated the change in status to 'ACTIVE'. It was several minutes before the noise settled down to a white noise in the background.

His priority was to repair the Conversion Chamber which exchanged the stale inert air for clean oxygenated air. He checked his timepiece. *Half an hour had lapsed already. There was no time to waste.*

The Conversion Chamber was located in the middle of the vessel on the same level behind thick insulated metal panels. These panels acted like a giant freezer by maintaining a stabilised temperature of minus thirty degrees. Now the lighting and gravity were restored, he was able to move faster through the ship. It took three minutes to reach from his last location.

On opening the door to the chamber, Yarron immediately discovered the problem. It was the cooling condenser. When the power shut off, the Xytrinium generator which fed liquid coolant to the pipes surrounding the condenser core, had also shut down, meaning there was no exchange of gases.

Yarron started to panic. The temperature of the core condenser had reached thirty degrees Celsius, and, by Yarron's calculations, it would take at least four hours for the cooling pipes to bring the temperature down to minus thirty degrees. *If the rescue mission failed to find him in time, he was in serious trouble.* This condenser was also used to produce drinking water and without it, the supply of water, which was already running low, would soon run out. *If he didn't die from lack of oxygen, he'd die of dehydration.*

As a last resort, Yarron decided to risk remaining defenceless in outer space. He addressed the Comms which was now operational, 'Computer, divert power from the systems for weapons and guidance to the cooling condenser. With the additional power, how long will it take to reduce the temperature of the condenser to minus thirty degrees?'

After a short pause, Yarron received the answer: 'Three hours and forty minutes, Captain.'

'Good, keep me posted on the progress.'

'Affirmative.'

Yarron's mind was racing. *Damn! His emergency supply of oxygen wouldn't last the distance and there was no guarantee the rescue mission would find him in time. Was there another alternative?*

'Computer!' shouted Yarron, 'Can the ship reach the planet Kompak on the remaining fuel? And how soon could we get there?'

A slight crackling was heard before the response came through. 'At current location, quantity of fuel is adequate. Two hours travel time at maximum hyperspeed by channelling all energy to the thrusters.'

Well, Yarron thought, *the good news was that he was still in the Western Quadrant. The gamble was whether he would reach Kompak before the oxygen in his small tank ran out. He had to decide immediately. Every second counted.*

'Computer, re-divert energy back to the Guidance System and set co-ordinates for Kompak. Get the ship there now!'

'Affirmative, Captain.'

For an instant, everything went quiet. Then the ship's lighting changed to red emergency. Yarron heard the muffled sound of the thrusters and felt the mild vibration of the vessel's hull. He also experienced the shift in the orientation of the ship until it stabilised and started to move. The change to hyperdrive was subtle and being below deck, the visual effect from the light-streaks of stars couldn't be seen. Even so, Yarron knew he was on his way to planet Kompak.

Returning to the Bridge, Yarron activated his Pledge ring. The holographic reception came in clearly, depicting Zawkon.

'Commander, it's Corporal Blandhar again.' This time he looked and sounded stronger. 'I've decided to try and reach Planet Kompak in case the rescue party doesn't reach me in time. If I can make it there in two hours, I'll have just enough oxygen to sustain me.' He paused before adding, 'If I don't make it, please tell Bhalar how much I love her.'

Zawkon knew Yarron needed to conserve his oxygen, so he responded with a brief acknowledgement, 'Thanks, Yarron. I'll pass your message onto Bhalar, though I sincerely hope you make it back to tell her in person. I'll redirect rescue teams to your new co-ordinates. Zawkon, out!'

* * *

After issuing new orders to his search party, Zawkon went directly to see Bhalar in her guest room.

'Come in,' said Bhalar as she opened the door. She looked somewhat forlorn and expected the worst.

'Bhalar,' he said kindly, 'I just wanted to let you know we've heard from Yarron.'

289

Bhalar's expression was suddenly one of hope and anticipation. 'What have you heard, Commander? Please tell me he's alive!'

'He's alive, Bhalar, but only just. He's low on oxygen.'

Bhalar couldn't help herself. She rushed to Zawkon and hugged him in relief. 'Thank you, Commander. Thank you.'

'He's not out of danger yet, Bhalar. However, I think he has a chance. He asked me to tell you he loves you.'

REWARD

WHEN the Tzuracian warship from Washington finally docked back at ASPECT with its cargo of Diutrons and Sentinels – and of course, the colourful Irishman, Grant Thompson – General Blake advised Thompson that the fifteen hundred Diutrons at New York were to stay behind.

'What do ya' mean the metal monsters are not bein' loaded on the ships?' responded the red-headed Irishman adamantly, directing his question to General Blake.

'Chief-Commander Dakhar has spoken with Commander Zawkon about his plans for the Diutrons. You'll need to speak to Zawkon directly.'

'Alright, I'll go an' see him now and sort this out!' Grant stormed off muttering, 'Damn nuisance!' to himself. After resurrecting the Diutrons and overseeing their success in battle, he felt as though they were his personal responsibility to look after back on Terra Iota.

Zawkon was in the Citadel waiting quietly and patiently for news of Corporal Blandhar when his silence was shattered by the Irish engineer who barged through the door, his arms thrashing about.

'What do ya mean lad, tellin' General Blake we're not loadin' the metal monsters aboard the ship! I want to get back to me' base on Iota and dis is delayin' me' departure.'

'Calm down, Grant,' Zawkon insisted, 'there's more to this. Please sit down while I explain what our Chief-Commander has in mind.'

Surprisingly, the hot-blooded Irishman did as he was told. He calmed down, the red blush on his cheeks dissipating as he sat open-mouthed.

'Commander Dakhar asked me to pass on his heartfelt appreciation to you and your colleagues for resurrecting the robots in time for our defence. And he asked me to commend you personally, Grant, for your bravery as a volunteer civilian.'

The Irishman was speechless. He sat there staring into a void with a huge grin on his inflated head.

Zawkon let him wallow in the high praise for an instant before bringing him back to reality. 'So, my friend, did you want to say something to the Commander?'

'No, no. Not at all,' Grant spluttered in his humble Irish lilt, 'Jus' t'ank him for me, will ya?'

'Alright, but there is something else our Chief-Commander wants from you.'

Grant sat quietly with his eyes widened and his ears pricked.

'Commander Dakhar wants to leave fifteen hundred Diutrons on Terra Major for the Earthlings' future protection and he wants you to take the rest back to Planet Iota for the colonists' security. He also wants you to return to Terra Major annually to maintain the 'metal monsters'. This means you'll be able to visit your family and relatives here every year. What do you have to say to that, Grant?'

'Holy blessed Mother of Jesus!' Thompson blurted out excitedly. 'Me Christmases 'ave all come at once. I'll be delighted.'

'Good. I'll pass this on to the Chief-Commander and I'll let General Blake know when you'll be returning to Terra Iota.'

'Tanks very much lad. I'll be goin' now.'

With that, the happy Irishman rose from his chair and broke into an Irish jig, singing a joyful Gaelic tune as he departed Zawkon's office. It was his way of showing good humour.

* * *

Three hours had passed with no word from Yarron, or the rescue party, and Zawkon was becoming anxious. *Had Yarron met an untimely end?*

He was about to transmit a holograph to Yarron when the Comms suddenly sprang to life from the transceiver on his desk.

'Commander Zawkon, this is Flight Lieutenant Lordhark from the Search and Rescue party.'

Zawkon held his breath momentarily, expecting the worst.

'Yes, Lieutenant. What news do you have?'

'We've located Corporal Yarron in the outer orbit of Kompak. He was barely alive when we boarded his Destroyer, and we found him just in time. We placed him in a medivac capsule to monitor his symptoms while transferring him to the base camp on Kompak. He's now in the Recovery Room for observation. The Med Officer says he's lucky to be alive and it was only his Xytrinium enhancements which saved him. Do you want us to bring him back to Earth once he's been cleared to travel?'

Zawkon breathed a quiet sigh of relief. 'Yes, Lieutenant. Have the rescue team return to Terra Major with Corporal Blandhar once he's recovered and bring his Destroyer with you. Zawkon, out!'

* * *

On this occasion, Zawkon's visit to Bhalar's room was more pleasant. He was happy to deliver the good news, and, for a second time, Bhalar rushed to him, hugging him. 'Thank you, Commander. Thank you.' She was overwhelmed.

* * *

It was an interminable wait for Bhalar until the Search and Rescue Party finally arrived back at the ASPECT Air base with Yarron and his Destroyer. After the debriefing was completed, an anxious Bhalar was escorted to Yarron's ship to be reunited with her precious partner. The door closed behind them, leaving them to embrace …

After several hours of mutual indulgence, the pair were resting, wrapped content in each other's arms, when Bhalar turned to Yarron with a question, 'So what do you have in mind for the future?'

Yarron sighed deeply. 'I know I want to be with you, although I'm not sure if that will place you in danger. I have no home to return to and no safe haven as far as the Federation's concerned – they're still hunting me as a fugitive.'

They were quiet for a moment.

'Well, I have an idea about our future together,' Bhalar said. 'It's only a thought, but it might work to both our benefits.'

'I'm listening,' he said with keen interest, running his fingers gently through her hair.

'My father will most likely be executed or thrown into prison for the rest of his life for the crimes he's committed.'

'Yes, go on, I'm all ears. But what's that got to do with our future?'

'Well,' she said with more optimism in her voice, 'under Treldarian law, I would inherit all his property and assets. So, we could return to Mankro and live in my father's hut. I know

I'd be accepted back into the village, particularly with you, an Urgellan warrior, as my partner.' She laughed about his identity. 'The villagers will be thankful they're no longer living in fear of my father and his army.'

Yarron thought for a while, contemplating the possibility before responding, 'It sounds like a very good idea as long as we don't have to worry about the Federation finding our sanctuary. I need to know the Federation's intentions once they remove my amnesty.'

No sooner had he finished talking than the Comms erupted into life, disrupting the meditative moment. 'Corporal Blandhar, this is General Blake. Sorry to disturb your reunion, but Commander Zawkon wants to see both of you in his office at the Citadel, immediately. Oh, and he doesn't like to be kept waiting. Do you copy?'

'Yes, General,' said Yarron hesitantly. 'We'll come straight away.'

Reluctantly, they simultaneously sprang out of the warm comfortable bed, dressed hurriedly, Yarron in his Urgellan greens, and kissed each other passionately. Bhalar could sense how anxious Yarron was, not knowing what fate lay in store for him.

'Well,' he said with a shallow smile, 'I guess this is the day of reckoning. We'll know soon what our future will be. Don't worry, Bhalar, whatever happens you'll always be in my heart. I fell in love with you from the moment I first saw you standing at your father's door. Stay strong.'

She squeezed his hand. 'You'll always be in my heart, too. I'll be with you in spirit wherever you go. We're soul mates destined to be together.'

Stepping down the gangplank of his Destroyer several minutes later, the rogue Sentinel and his female partner were confronted by six armed Sentinels. Yarron felt quite vulnerable not being allowed to carry weapons while under 'house arrest'. The rogue Sentinel was now at the mercy of the Federation and was relying on Dakhar's promise of him being under an amnesty of safety while on Terra Major.

After performing a body search and confirming they weren't carrying any concealed weapons, the pair were escorted to a troop carrier and driven to the Citadel to face whatever consequences awaited them. A short journey brought them into the courtyard of the Citadel, and they were marched to Commander Zawkon's office.

Zawkon was seated at his desk when a hard rap on the door interrupted his concentration. 'Enter!' he called out.

The door swung open, and the Commander was confronted by the traitor-cum-hero, Yarron, and his Treldarian partner, Bhalar. There was no welcoming smile to greet Yarron. The Commander's face bore a stone-cold expression. The atmosphere was tense and for a short moment, both said nothing until the silence was fractured by the sharpness of the escorting Sentinel's voice.

'I've brought Corporal Blandhar and Bhalar as you requested, sir!' the Sentinel blurted, saluting respectfully.

'Thank you soldier. You're dismissed,' said Zawkon in his authoritative tone of voice. 'Close the door behind you as you leave.'

Zawkon waved a hand, indicating for the couple to take a seat. Still feeling apprehensive, Yarron made himself as comfortable as he could in the chair, with Bhalar sitting close beside him.

'So, Yarron,' Zawkon began sternly in a lowered voice, stroking his thick blonde beard in contemplation, 'you've returned alive.'

'Yes, thank the Gods and your search party'.

'Commander Dakhar is pleased with your recent performance, as am I. We're indebted to you for your actions over Washington.

However, we can't ignore the fact that you have a dark history. You were an elite Sentinel who stole Tzurac's precious Xytrinium formula for the love of a treacherous female accomplice, Khaneera Zarkwin. With Khaneera you were instrumental in passing the formula to Treldarian Bladers, enabling an attack on Earth and Terra Iota. You're a fugitive the Federation has been hunting for the last two years.'

Feeling uncomfortable and guilty, Yarron remained silent. He understood the Commander's hostility.

Zawkon continued, emphasising his next words, 'We usually execute treacherous deserters.'

Yarron took a gulp and sank lower in his chair while Bhalar bit her tongue, restraining herself from defending Yarron until she heard more. *She hadn't expected such a cold reception.*

Then Zawkon's demeanour softened, and a rare smile covered his typically stern face. 'However, in spite of your serious crimes, I have some good news for you.'

Yarron sat up from his inclined position and listened more intently while Bhalar relaxed and breathed more freely.

'Chief-Commander Dakhar and the Tzuracian Senate have taken into consideration your efforts to redeem yourself – assisting the Federation by exposing the hideouts of the remaining Bladers, alerting us to the recent Treldarian attack and acting heroically in an effort to save Washington and the World Assembly. They believe you have atoned for your sins and earned the forgiveness of the Ancients.'

Yarron and Bhalar exchanged relieved glances.

'Corporal Blandhar, you've been requested by our Chief-Commander to travel to Tzurac. One of our warships will be leaving Terra Major within the next few days with our captives, General Rokan and his surviving handful of soldiers. The plan is for you to accompany the warship as an escort in your stolen

Destroyer. I've been told that, on Tzurac, you are to accept your official pardon before the Senate. Will you be ready, Corporal?'

Yarron could hardly believe what he was hearing. In recognition of his efforts over Washington, he thought the Federation might have given him a three-day head start before commencing the hunt for him again. *An official pardon was unexpected, indeed overwhelming.*

Yarron jumped up from his chair and responded with a formal salute. 'Thank you, sir! Thank you. Yes, I'll be ready.'

'But what about Bhalar?' he added.

Zawkon smiled even more broadly. 'Bhalar has been permitted by the Senate to defect to Tzurac. She's been granted permanent asylum wherever she travels within the Federation. I assume Bhalar will be travelling with you, so I'll inform General Blake of the arrangements. Now soldier, you're dismissed.'

'Thank you, Commander.' Yarron was still somewhat overcome with gratitude.

Bhalar rose from her seat with a huge grin on her beautiful face and went straight over to Zawkon, giving him a hug. 'Thank you, thank you so much.'

Although feeling slightly embarrassed in front of his subordinate, the typically formal Captain returned the hug. 'No need to thank me, Bhalar. I simply told the Senate about the vital information you gave us, and they recognized how important your assistance had been in stemming the attack. You'll be given your official citizenship papers when you arrive on Tzurac. Now you should both leave and get ready for your departure.'

The couple were numb with surprise as they left the room.

Back on board the ship, Yarron fetched a bottle of Terra Major's strong alcohol – Whiskey' it said on the label – which he had been keeping safe for a special occasion. Pouring a little quantity into two glasses, he offered one to Bhalar, while raising the other. 'Bhalar, you're looking at a soldier who's been given a second chance. The Ancients must have forgiven me.' They clinked glasses and savoured the moment.

'Here's to no more running, hiding and looking over your shoulder,' said Bhalar, raising her glass and toasting again.

'Yes,' Yarron said, 'and here's to you being free to travel throughout the Federation … and spend your life with me.' His words melted both their hearts. They put their glasses down and kissed with passion to seal their future together …

The following morning the two glasses of unfinished whiskey were still where they had left them on the table the night before.

* * *

Over the next two days Zawkon arranged for the Treldarian and Nujharene prisoners to be transferred to the High Security cells on board one of the warships. He also organised accommodation for the deceased Sentinels in cryo-chambers for the long trek back to their home planet.

Zawkon had been instructed to remain on Terra Major for the time being and was sad that he would be missing the military funerals of his courageous comrades-in-arms. On the other hand, he'd have time to visit Lauren Blake and find out how deep their mutual feelings for each other had become. Lauren had awoken emotions in him that had been dormant throughout his military career. His recent acquaintance with Bhalar showed him the depth of her love and affection for Yarron, strengthening his own desires to seek a stronger bond with Lauren.

In fact, he was completely taken by Lauren, and she seemed very interested in him. Just thinking of her, made him feel weak at the knees. Was this love? So many poems and songs had been inspired by the feelings of those who had succumbed to this powerful, invisible attraction. He had witnessed soldiers do extraordinary things under this potion of passion and had never quite understood why. To him, it hadn't made sense ... until now.

He soon contacted Lauren, bringing up the visual on his desk screen as she answered. 'Hi Lauren, things have finally quietened down after these torrid events.'

'How nice to hear your voice again, Kal.' Lauren's voice was warm and enthusiastic, and she looked smart and refined in her familiar tailored suit and black-rimmed glasses.

'I wonder whether you might have time to join me for dinner tonight?' he asked somewhat hesitantly. Although he'd spoken with Lauren several times, and they had admitted a fondness for one another, they had yet to experience an intimate evening together in private. *Would she want to share time with a battle-scarred veteran? He hoped so.*

'I'd *love* to join you,' she said, admiring his strong physique and strength of character.

That evening was to be the beginning of a beautiful and long-lasting relationship.

HOMECOMING

DAKHAR was in his office when he received an incoming holograph from Terra Major. 'Yes, Commander Zawkon, what do you have to report?'

'Sir, Corporal Yarron Blandhar has been found alive. He needed urgent medical attention but thankfully he's now recovered. He's fit for duty and will be travelling back to Tzurac with our fleet commanded by Captain Turkrahn. They departed Terra Major today.'

Ehrane acknowledged the good news, dipping his head.

'The fleet has General Rokan and his surviving soldiers secured on board as well as cryo-tubes bearing the Sentinels who were killed in the battle. Corporal Blandhar is travelling with General Rokan's daughter and is among the Destroyers escorting our warships. They should arrive on Tzurac within the next ten days.

'Oh, and I've relayed your commendations and orders to Grant Thompson who is delighted and thankful for the arrangements concerning the Diutrons. He'll be departing today for Terra Iota with the five-hundred robots on board.'

'Thank you for the update, Commander. Dakhar, out!'

* * *

That afternoon, Kyron returned to the Citadel to inform both the Admiral and Commander Dakhar the repairs to the Xytrinium generators were completed and full power to the city had been restored.

While Kyron was in Dakhar's office, the opportunity presented itself for the Chief-Commander to discuss with Kyron the schedule for their return to Terra Major.

'Kyron, now that you've graduated to a Lieutenant, First Officer, and the battle with our enemies has come to an end, the time will soon come for you and your family to return home to Earth. I'll be leaving on my Flagship when the trials have been completed.'

Before Dakhar could continue, Kyron spoke, 'Ehrane, my friend, do you think the Senate will let you return to Earth now you've proven yourself such a worthy leader on Tzurac? And how will Tajhira feel about leaving her family and friends again? Won't she be a little upset?'

'Thank you, my friend, for considering our feelings about leaving Tzurac, but I'm sure Tajhira has resigned herself to staying a little longer on Terra Major, particularly since she and Torri have become such close companions. As for me, I must go where my orders send me. Besides, you and I have grown close, and I would miss you as well as Torri and your two lovable children. So, unless I'm told otherwise, I'll be returning to Terra Major as Commanding Chief of the Western Quadrant with you as my First Officer.'

Kyron smiled in agreement.

'And what about you, Kyron? You haven't yet had the chance to catch up with your extended family here on Tzurac and find out more about the Tyros ancestry. And you haven't yet visited our Grand Library containing the complete history of our planet. I'm sure you'd like to spend more time here.'

Dakhar could see his junior officer contemplating what he'd said and paused, waiting for his response.

'Well, I know Torri is keen to return to her work at MERIC – she doesn't want to leave her management role in Lauren Blake's hands for too long. Perhaps if you delayed your departure for another week or two, I might be able to do all the things I'd planned to? Maybe you could tell the Senate Tajhira is expecting another child and it would be unwise for her to journey the long distance in her condition at present.'

Dakhar almost fell off his chair. He was shocked and bewildered. 'What! Is she? Do you know something I don't, Kyron?'

'No, no. Calm down my friend. I was only joking,' Kyron said, covering his mouth with his hand to suppress his chuckle. 'I was simply trying to make some excuse for you to delay your departure.'

Dakhar reclined in his chair, composing himself. 'I'm not sure if I appreciate Earthling humour,' he quipped.

* * *

En route to Tzurac, Bhalar noticed Yarron becoming more and more unsettled as they neared their destination. He began calling out aloud in his dreams and waking up in cold sweats.

Over breakfast one morning, she couldn't refrain from saying something to him, 'Yarron, I don't mean to interfere, but you need to tell me what's happening.'

'What do you mean?' he snapped defensively.

'Well, you've lost your appetite and you're restless at night. Is there something I can help you with? Is it me you're troubled about and our future together?' she asked affectionately.

'No, Bhalar,' he said reassuring her. 'It's nothing to do with you. I want us to be together, no matter where we go. I love you.'

'Then what is it? Please tell me. I'm worried and I want to help.'

Yarron sighed deeply and buried his head in his palms with his elbows still resting on the table. Then he slowly raised his head and stared through Bhalar, as if watching his life unfold before him.

'I'm feeling anxious about returning to Tzurac. I have a black mark against my name for being a traitor and breaking the Sentinels' Code of Honour. I stole the Tzuracians' most guarded secret which had been kept for over a thousand years and, I aided a highly dangerous prisoner to escape from a security cell I guarded for over two years. I stole the Destroyer battleship in which we're travelling. But worst of all Bhalar, I betrayed my mother's trust. I deceived her and my conscience won't give me peace. Her career and our family name were ruined because of me and that's something which cannot be repaired, no matter how much penance I do.'

He fell silent, tears welling up in his eyes.

Bhalar went to him, cradled him in her arms and spoke softly. 'Listen, we've all made stupid mistakes which we regret, mistakes which have caused hurt. But you're a good soul. If you didn't have a good heart, you wouldn't be feeling guilty and wrestling with your conscience. You've told me about the things you've done of late for the good of the Sentinels and the Federation, as well as for the Universe. I believe you've more than atoned for your past mistakes. And, as for your mother, I'm sure she'll find forgiveness in her heart. It's what mothers do when they love their children.'

Yarron was amazed by Bhalar's insight and wisdom. *She was someone with special qualities. She had a deep understanding of the nature of people, especially him.*

That night, Yarron had the deep unbroken sleep he'd been missing for so long. He woke the following morning feeling exhilarated. The heavy burden he'd been carrying for a long time had gone and once more his mind had the clarity of a Sentinel. He felt more confident to face the Senate – and his mother.

*   *   *

The following day, the convoy of space crafts from Terra Major finally reached the Khazor Air base, arriving with a thunderous roar. Noise from the huge warship and five Destroyer battleships temporarily frightened some of the citizens of Khazor who thought they were being invaded again by a second wave of Treldarian warships. But order was quickly restored.

Yarron's distinctive black ship with the modified features was nestled in amongst the other Destroyers which docked towards the rear of the huge hangar. From his ship's Bridge, he watched on the main screen the Treldarian captives disembarking from the warship in the front area of the docking bays. Two units of Sentinels, weapons at the ready, surrounded the lowered drawbridge, as the prisoners, two hundred of them, were herded into a three-line formation, their wrists bound behind their backs, and their legs restricted by short ankle chains. Still clothed in their dusty blood-stained black uniforms, they appeared fatigued, dishevelled and unkempt. Yet they still retaliated aggressively when shoved back into line by the Sentinels.

Yarron's body jerked backwards in surprise when he recognised the officer standing rigid at the head of the pack.

'What's the matter?' asked Bhalar who was standing behind him.

'It's your father, General Rokan!' he exclaimed.

Bhalar leaned over his shoulder and peered at the screen. 'Yes, so it is.' Her voice was uncharacteristically sour. 'Perhaps the Senate will see true justice done and deal him the punishment which befits his crimes?'

'The crimes against you, Bhalar? Or the crimes against the Federation?' Yarron asked, turning to face her and raising an eyebrow.

'Both. The Universe has a way of keeping the balance. It's just a matter of time.'

Yarron agreed. *Bhalar was right.*

Turning back to the screen, he watched the prisoners as they were marched out of the hangar and bundled into armoured and window-barred transporters.

JUDGEMENT DAY

NEXT morning, on the day of the trial, the Senate Chambers filled with citizens as units of Sentinel soldiers took their positions around the interior walls of the Chambers. Bhalar had been granted permission to watch the fanfare and was amongst the crowd in the gallery. For his own protection, Yarron had been escorted to the Chambers by two Sentinel guards and was seated in one of the observation booths just behind the elevated bench where the senators would be seated. From this position he could see in almost all directions through narrow dark-tinted horizontal windows.

Perusing the faces of the Sentinels lined up against the wall of the Chamber, Yarron recognised many of his comrades from his old Regiment. As his eyes wandered, he let out a muffled cry when he saw the figure whose life he'd saved on Terra Major nearly two years ago – it was Kyron Tyros in the full-dress uniform of a Sentinel, now with the gold insignias of an officer on his collar and cuffs.

Yarron watched intently as the Master of the Chambers entered through a side door and paced swiftly to the front of the Chambers. Standing before the noisy gallery of citizens, the

Chamber Master stamped his golden rod heavily on the stone floor three times. The loud echoes reverberated off the high ceiling of the ancient structure.

'Silence!' he called. 'Silence in the Chambers!'

Within seconds, the noisy muttering amongst the audience ceased. In the silence, the anxious crowd watched with curiosity as the five legal senators, including the Elder, Senator Ghalbrak, filed into the room and took their respective positions on the elevated semi-circular bench. Chief-Commander Dakhar had joined them and was seated to one side.

When all were composed, the Elder signalled the Chamber Master with a wave of his hand. Bowing his head to the senators, the Master struck the floor once and called, 'Bring in the accused!'

Through the lower side entrance on the gallery level, a unit of six Sentinels surrounding two Treldarian soldiers in shackles marched out to the front of the Chamber and stood before the senators. Loud murmurings from the gallery stabbed the stilled atmosphere.

'Silence!' the Master shrieked, causing the crowd to stop the noise instantly.

Senator Ghalbrak subtly waved the Sentinels to stand behind the Treldarians, still at full alert, and the Senator commenced his address to the gallery.

'Good citizens of Khazor, you are all here today to witness the sentencing of the two Treldarian Generals who stand here before you – General Vark of the Eastern Quadrant and General Rokan of the Southern Quadrant. This is not a trial to decide their guilt or innocence. They're not here to plead their case. No, they're here to be sentenced for their crimes against the Federation – for attempting to destroy the democracy which has taken so long to establish. Their intentions were to annihilate the Sentinels with total disregard for the lives of the innocent and to subjugate Tzurac and Terra Major. They wanted to become dictators through chaos and enslavement. The penalty for these heinous crimes is ...' He paused for effect and, leaning forward and glaring, spoke harshly and deliberately, '... *execution by lethal injection.*'

There were murmurs throughout the audience and Bhalar expressed a silent sigh of satisfaction.

'As for the remaining soldiers,' the Senator continued, 'they'll have their Xytrinium enhancements neutralised and be sent to serve life imprisonment on work-farms in the penal colonies in other galaxies.'

He turned to the two Generals. 'Do you have anything to say before I send you to your holding cells?'

Vark and Rokan remained silent, their heads bowed. Rokan was motionless, absorbed in his self-inflicted destruction, unaware that his daughter, Bhalar, was among the crowd witnessing his trial on Tzurac. Then Vark lifted his head momentarily, his eyes searching the room. He had gambled his empire and lost all. But was his son, Tykran, among the prisoners to be tried? Had he survived the battle? He'd had no sign or word of him. Vark scowled at the senators, and then lowered his head, accepting his fate. As leaders, both Treldarian Generals knew the consequences of defeat.

After some deliberation, the Elder spoke again, 'The executions have been scheduled for two days' time. Guards, remove these prisoners from the Chambers and return them to their cells.'

As the two Generals were marched from the Chambers, whisperings started up amongst the crowd. Ghalbrak waved to the Master of the Chambers, and, in response, the Master slammed his metal rod onto the stone floor once more. After the third strike, the Master again commanded silence. The gallery hushed and all eyes focused on the senators. Ghalbrak rose from his chair and called to the Master, 'Bring in the rebel Blader, Ramlok!' before resuming his seat.

Two Sentinel guards entered from the side door, struggling with the resistant prisoner who was also shackled at the wrists and ankles. They forced Ramlok to stand, reluctantly, in front of the raised podium. Ramlok's appearance was very different from his fellow Treldarians. His uniform was dusty and half unbuttoned with his sleeves rolled up to his elbows. His unkempt and matted long hair was no longer tied back into a groomed ponytail, but instead hung raggedly down to his shoulders. The copper-skin on his face was leathery and noticeably scarred and his sunken eyes had a crazed look in them.

Still seated, the Elder addressed the captive. 'Captain Ramlok, you've been brought before the Senate to be sentenced for your crimes against the Federation. The citizens of Khazor have a right to know about the serious crimes you have committed.'

Senator Ghalbrak reached for a scroll on the bench and began to read, 'For many years as a Blader pirate serving under your leader, General Dranz, you plundered Tzuracian transport ships, mercilessly killing Sentinel soldiers and pilfering our Xytrinium cargo. You and your rebels also attacked other spacecraft, stealing their goods and chattels, and sometimes their ships, raping the female passengers on board, and enslaving the male passengers and crews. You then conspired with the Treldarians in the other Quadrants of the Universe, giving them the stolen Xytrinium formula to enhance their armies, and inciting them to go to war against the Federation.'

The Senator threw the scroll onto the bench with disgust, taking a deep breath. He was visibly angry. 'And you have the audacity to call yourself a soldier!' he said with a raised voice, pointing his finger at Ramlok. 'You're a hypocrite, and nothing more than a murderous barbarian. What do you have to say for yourself prisoner before I sentence you?'

With piercing eyes, the rebel Ramlok retaliated, 'You're all dictators!' he shouted. 'The Federation has deprived the Treldarians of their freedom ever since the Grekadian War. You wanted to keep the Xytrinium all to yourselves and rule the other planets. You all deserve to die!'

Without warning Ramlok lunged towards the raised bench and threw himself headlong at the Senator, only to be brought down by two laser shots fired by the Sentinel guards standing behind him. The gallery members jumped to their feet screaming as the prisoner slumped to the floor, fatally wounded by one of the laser blasts which struck his head.

For an instant as he lay there, Ramlok's life flashed before him and the final image he took with him to the afterlife was the vision of the Ludaxian beauty Shanowah reclining in the hot baths of Orkharn – *he would never know whether she was genuine or just another painted lady*. The lifeblood of the soldier, who had been sent on a mission by General Dranz, and had single-handedly mustered a major Treldarian uprising, was extinguished. The last of the so-called rogue Bladers had met his fate.

The Chamber Master slammed his metal rod onto the stone floor to quell the now noisy crowd. 'Order, order in the Chamber!' he shouted. 'Be seated! Everyone, be seated!'

Shaken and slightly bewildered, the senators and Dakhar, with his blade instinctively drawn, slowly returned to their seats. Nothing like this had ever happened before in the Chambers.

When Ramlok's body had been removed and some semblance of decorum was re-established in the Chamber, the trial eventually continued.

Senator Ghalbrak stood to make another request. 'Bring in Corporal Yarron Blandhar.'

Kyron flinched in surprise. He hadn't expected Yarron to set foot on Tzuracian soil again. Some of the Sentinels were also taken by surprise, the expressions on their faces showing animosity towards the traitor. Kyron could sense the tension growing in the ranks. There was also a disturbance in the crowd, the undertones increasing in volume.

Once again, the forceful clank of metal reverberated throughout the hall, accompanied by the loud order of 'Silence!' from the Master.

Stepping out from the lower side entrance, escorted by the two guards, Yarron nervously approached the high bench and stood at attention, facing the senators. He could hear the whispers in the gallery behind him, the occasional words of 'traitor' and 'dishonourable' being quite audible. *Would the Federation break their promise? He had seen the punishment they had dished out to the previous conspirators.* Thankfully, his mind was put to rest when he saw Chief-Commander Dakhar and Senator Ghalbrak smiling in his direction.

Picking up a scroll, the Elder began to read, 'Citizens of Khazor, for those who may not recognise this Tzuracian standing before me, I will introduce you to him. This is Corporal Yarron Blandhar, a once-elite Sentinel who brought dishonour on himself and his family when he deserted his Regiment and aided another dishonourable Sentinel to escape the life sentence she was serving. Her name was Khaneera Zarkwin.'

The crowd muttered.

'To make things worse for himself, and for the Federation, this Corporal stole our precious Xytrinium formula and saw it passed to the Treldarians for use in wars against us. For these crimes alone, he deserves the death penalty.'

Bhalar gasped, placing one hand over her gaping mouth and the other on her tightened chest. She could feel the rapid palpitations of her heart. *This can't be happening,* she thought. *They've broken their word, their promise, after Yarron returning in good faith. Was this a trick to lure him into their trap, giving him a false sense of hope?*

Yarron was also floundering. *What have they done?*

Their fears were instantly waylaid when the Elder continued, 'But I have it on good faith, as told by my Chief-Commander and, from what I've witnessed myself, that Corporal Yarron Blandhar has earned clemency.'

There was a hushed murmur around the room.

'After realising the error of his poor judgement, Yarron has been a valuable voluntary informant for the Federation for the last two years. He took it upon himself to track down the Bladers and provide us with the locations of their sanctuaries and their cohorts. Almost two years ago on Terra Major, he placed his own life at risk to save the life of our newly graduated Lieutenant Tyros. And now, without his forewarning of the impending recent attacks on Terra Major and Tzurac, as well as his quick strategic manoeuvre to thwart a Treldarian warship over Washington, the Federation would have been badly defeated. We believe Corporal Yarron Blandhar has suffered enough, living with the guilt of his major mistake and trying to atone for this.

'Therefore, the Senate has decided to give Corporal Yarron Blandhar a full pardon for his crimes and a formal discharge from the Sentinels. He will be banished from Tzurac for his own protection. However, we will allow him to keep his Sentinel Pledge ring and Destroyer should we ever need his assistance again.'

Smiles appeared on both Bhalar's and Yarron's faces as the crowd came to terms with the news.

Rolling up the scroll in his hand, Ghalbrak asked Yarron to step forward. But, as Yarron reached out to clasp the scroll, one of the Sentinels standing in line with the others on the left wall of the Chambers, rapidly drew his laser. Pointing it towards Yarron, he yelled 'Traitor!'

A split second before he released a round of laser fire, Kyron leapt to cover Yarron's back, his quick reflexes allowing him to use his shield-cape to deflect the laser blast. The offending rogue Sentinel was instantly disarmed by the Sentinels standing beside him and restrained before being ushered quickly from the Chamber.

As they regained their balance, Kyron turned to Yarron. 'I guess this makes us even, wouldn't you say?'

'Yes, my friend. Thank you,' he said sincerely, as the two Sentinels smiled and exchanged a look of mutual respect.

The Chamber Master silenced the noisy gallery once more and Senator Ghalbrak invited Yarron to speak. 'Yarron Blandhar, do you have anything to say?'

Yarron was lost for words, thankful for the pardon but unsettled by the animosity of the rogue Sentinel. 'Thank you for your forgiveness, sirs. I'm most appreciative, although with your permission, I'd like to ask for one more favour.'

Somewhat surprised by Yarron's response, the Senator replied, 'You want more?'

'Yes,' said Yarron timidly, 'because I'll not be returning to my home planet ever again, would it be possible to have one last audience with my mother before I leave Tzurac?' *Yarron had received the forgiveness of the Senate. But would his mother forgive him?*

Ghalbrak turned to face the other senators to gauge their reaction before turning slowly back to Yarron. 'Yes, I'm sure this can be arranged.'

He signalled for the Chamber Master to empty the Senate Chambers and for the last time, the Chamber Master stamped his rod on the stone floor. 'The trial has ended. Citizens of Khazor, please vacate these Chambers.'

* * *

Two days later, as decreed by Senator Ghalbrak, the execution of the two Generals, Vark and Rokan, was conducted. It was not held as a public execution: The Senate considered the sight of someone being put to death by lethal injection was not a pleasant experience for the citizens of Khazor and they were loath to subject the people to more reminders of the horrors of war. They had been through enough terror, seeing their city under siege and witnessing the gore of those killed in battle. Instead, this was a private affair behind closed doors.

However, out of courtesy and respect, the senators invited General Rokan's daughter to witness her father's execution, hoping this would bring final closure for her. Although Bhalar was at first reluctant to attend, she finally agreed with the senators it would put her mind to rest.

On the day of the macabre event, Bhalar, with Yarron beside her for support, was escorted by Sentinel guards to a small sound-proof theatre with no windows and dim lighting. The Senate members including the Elder Senator Ghalbrak were already in attendance, some dressed in their representative robes of purple and others in red. The audience was seated facing a glass panel designed for one-way viewing only; they could see what was happening before them, but those on the other side saw only a dark grey wall. The other three walls in the room were draped in dark-blue velvet which gave an atmosphere of reverence.

They were no sooner seated when they observed Generals Vark and Rokan being led by four Sentinels into the room on the other side of the glass panel. Both were cuffed at the wrist and their legs restricted with ankle-chains. They were placed in the two high-backed black padded chairs.

While two Sentinels stood rigid behind them, the other two Sentinels pressed brightly lit red buttons on the side of the chairs. This action rapidly released two narrow illuminated strips of light which shot out from the sides of the chairs, one wrapping across the chest and arms, pinning the subjects against the back of the chairs, and the other wrapping itself across the prisoners' shins, forcing them tight against the base of the chair.

By now Bhalar was feeling slightly uncomfortable with mixed emotions and Yarron, who was holding her hand, felt her grip tighten. He turned in her direction. She was staring straight ahead with fixed intensity.

'Are you alright, Bhalar?' he whispered with concern.

'I will be when this is over.'

Although Bhalar never wanted to see her father again in her life, she was apprehensive about witnessing his death. *She would have preferred he spend the rest of his life in prison suffering the same cruel entrapment she had experienced, where nobody cared about him and there was no escape, isolated in hopelessness, with his life being drained day after day. Maybe then he would find remorse in realising what he had done to his only daughter and beg for the Gods' forgiveness?*

Senator Ghalbrak who was seated beside Bhalar, noticed her uneasiness and spoke softly to her, 'Bhalar, there's no need to fret, they'll feel no pain. The lethal injection they receive will act like a sedative, sending them into a deep sleep from which they'll never awaken.'

'Thank you, Senator. He deserves to be punished, although I believe death is the easy way out for him.'

She continued to watch the face of her white-haired father as it changed from the familiar hateful look to a more relaxed expression, his eyes closing slowly as the fluid from the administered lethal drug coursed through the General's veins. For a fleeting moment, his softer expression reminded her of the father she had once loved as a little girl. Within seconds her father's life was gone forever as was the life of the ruthless Vark beside him.

Bhalar sighed with relief. *She was happy and yet sad at the same time for losing the only father she knew – a father who had once loved her but had grown to despise and mistreat her.* Tears began to stream involuntarily down her cheeks.

Yarron placed his arms around her shoulders and held her tightly to comfort her. As she rested her head on his shoulder, he could sense how she felt. There was no need for words to be spoken.

* * *

Two days later, Yarron, with Bhalar by his side, was escorted to his mother's quarters to make amends. He was anxious as the Sentinel escort knocked on the door of the apartment. Bhalar squeezed his hand in a gesture of support.

As the Sentinel stepped back out of sight, the door opened to reveal a grey-haired woman who had aged considerably since Yarron saw her last. 'My son, I've been expecting you,' she said softly, maintaining her distance. 'You look well. Come on in and bring your friend with you.'

'Thanks, Mother,' he said, tears welling in his eyes, 'it's wonderful to see you again and to introduce you to Bhalar, the woman I plan to live with for the rest of my life.'

'You're very welcome, Bhalar,' said Yarron's mother, acknowledging Bhalar and directing the couple to a seat on the nearby couch.

As Yarron sat down facing his mother, he searched her eyes for acceptance. *He knew he had ruined her career as one of Tzurac's chief scientists when he stole the formula from her laboratory.*

'I had to see you and ask for your forgiveness. I made a grave error of judgement in deceiving you and I've regretted it ever since. I've tried to redeem myself with the Sentinels and they've pardoned me, but can *you* ever find it in your heart to forgive me?'

For an awkward moment his mother hesitated. Then, with a subtle smile, her eyes moistened. She reached for his hand and held it. 'You have a good heart, my son, and I'll always love you. I *was* deeply hurt by your actions, but I'm relieved to learn your true colours are now shining for all to see.'

Without another word, mother and son rose and embraced, knowing this would be their final farewell. And as Yarron and Bhalar departed, his mother hugged Bhalar tightly, whispering, 'Please take care of my precious son.'

'You have my word,' Bhalar promised, 'and he has my heart.'

LIFE CHANGE

AFTER making peace with Yarron's mother, Yarron and Bhalar were now nearing the orbit of Mankro. Their journey had been long and thankfully, uneventful. *En route* the two travellers had learned a lot about each other's history, their childhood to their adulthood, their likes and dislikes and what they wanted in the future. Their bond had grown stronger day by day.

Yet there was something on Yarron's mind which had begun to worry him, and Bhalar sensed it. She was not one to procrastinate, so she confronted him.

'Okay, Yarron, you need to tell me what's worrying you now. I've been observing your moods while we've been travelling, so don't try to hide it. You've been wrestling mentally with something, and it has become noticeably worse as we get closer to my home. Please tell me what it is and let's see if we can resolve this together.'

'Alright, Bhalar, you're right – there's something on my mind. I'm concerned about how your people will accept me after what I did to their soldiers, forewarning the Tzuracians about the surprise invasion by the Treldarian army. They may string me up, or worse! I know you were glad to see your cruel father get what he deserved, but will your people feel the same way? Will they hate me for betraying your father and his army?'

To Yarron's surprise, Bhalar broke into laughter.

'Why are you laughing?' he asked. 'This is serious. I'm in mortal danger! It's no laughing matter.'

Bhalar composed herself. 'You have no idea, do you? My people lived in fear of my father and his army. The soldiers were brutal towards the villagers. The villagers were more like slaves than free citizens, working hard to feed the army, making their uniforms while tolerating their sexual abuse. The villagers never came to rescue me from my father because they would have been executed. The day you arrived at our camp their hopes, like mine, were raised at the possibility you might have been our saviour. And they were right.

'They'll welcome you with open arms when they learn the General has been executed and the soldiers imprisoned. They'll never have to live in fear again. You've won their freedom and they'll be beholden to you.'

'Even if they find out I'm a Sentinel? Or was, I mean.'

'That would be even better. Because they'd know you have the backing of a military force which can liberate them from tyranny. So, Yarron, you no longer have to pretend you're something you're not. No more hiding in shadows and talking in whispers. You're free to be who you truly are. I like you as the Urgellan, Armel,' she said, stroking his once-black hair that was now revealing signs of its natural colour, 'but I have to say, I'm looking forward to seeing you as a blonde-haired Sentinel.'

'Well,' said Yarron, looking relieved, 'you've made me feel more comfortable. Only there's one other thing you need to be aware of.'

'Oh, what's that? Don't tell me you have another lover?' Bhalar teased.

'No, Bhalar. You're the only one in my life and my future and you know it. My only regret is that you won't be there for us to grow old together. Remember, with Sentinel blood, I'm destined to live to a very ripe old age.'

Bhalar laughed out loud once more.

'That's not funny. I don't want to live hundreds of years without you!'

'Don't worry, my love. You needn't think you were going to get rid of me that easily, do you?' she retorted. 'Without my father knowing, I managed to persuade the Blader Ramlok to inject me with the Xytrinium formula when he was infusing the Third Legion. I swore him to secrecy by promising him a share in my father's wealth if the General should be killed in battle. Deep down he was still a pirate, and I wasn't going to be forced into my father's army.'

Yarron was stunned. 'Is that true?' A wide smile came over his face.

'I've kept my new-found strengths well hidden, to protect both of us. But who knows,' she said, 'I might be a better match for you than you imagine next time we practise our martial arts. And I may even outlive you!'

* * *

Several days after the trial, Chief-Commander Dakhar was summoned to appear before the Senate Tribunal. On entering the chambers, he was confronted by ten senators seated at a long bench with glass jugs of water and matching goblets placed at given intervals along the length of the bench. Senator Ghalbrak waved his arm in the direction of a vacant chair located at one end of the bench, indicating for Dakhar to take the seat.

After seating himself comfortably, Dakhar faced the others with a somewhat puzzled look. *Had something gone wrong? Or was he to receive new orders which might affect his future?*

Senator Ghalbrak spoke first, 'Welcome Commander Dakhar. Thanks for coming so promptly. We've not had the opportunity to discuss the outcome of the war and your involvement. The Senate is grateful for the way you conducted yourself and the strategies you implemented to thwart our enemies. The Tzuracians never imagined our Dome could be destroyed and leave us at the mercy of our attackers – we thought it was impenetrable. Yet even without the protection of the Dome, you saved the day and we, the Senate, are in your debt.'

Dakhar relaxed.

'Your time on Terra Major has proven to be valuable in establishing good relations with the Terranians and a solid satellite base for further exploration into the Western Quadrant. However, we think now would be the right time for you to relinquish your position there and focus on the future of Tzurac.

'Commander Dakhar, we'd like to offer you a position as a Senator on our council. We know you have the wisdom and experience to contribute to the administration of Tzurac, as well as the diplomacy needed to steer the Federation into a successful future. What do you say to this, Commander?'

Dakhar was taken by surprise and needed a moment to gather his thoughts. He poured himself a goblet of water, taking several gulps before responding. 'Well, Senators, I'm overwhelmed by your confidence in me and humbled by your offer. You've offered me a great honour and privilege.' He spoke with calm confidence.

'I come from a long line of soldiers with a military background, over eons of time. Like my forefathers, it's in my blood to fulfil my destiny as a Sentinel. So, as much as I like the idea of becoming a senator, I believe it wouldn't be long before I'd be yearning to return to my roots, to my Regiment and comrades-in-arms.

'I've earnt the respect of my soldiers who would follow me anywhere, at any time, to lead them into battle, no matter what the consequences. This is loyalty above and beyond the call of duty. If I were to relinquish my position now, I feel I would be deserting my soldiers. I have a lifelong obligation to my soldiers who believe in me, respect me, and have faith in my judgement as a leader and strategist. Therefore, Senators, with the deepest respect and my most sincere appreciation, I must decline your offer.'

The senators had not expected this response, but they were moved by Dakhar's convictions. They turned to one another trying to discern each other's thoughts and eventually all responded positively.

Noting the satisfied expressions of the other senators, the Elder spoke on their behalf. 'We can hear your passion and dedication to the military service, and we respect your decision. Therefore, we want you to continue in your commissioned role as Commanding Chief of Military Operations in the Western Quadrant and return to Terra Major.'

'Thank you, Senators, I appreciate your wisdom,' Dakhar said. 'I do however have one request. If possible, I'd like to delay my return to Terra Major by one month, leaving Captain Kal Zawkon to act as the Chief-Commander until then.'

'May we ask why, Commander?' asked Ghalbrak, somewhat surprised.

'My First Officer, Lieutenant Kyron Tyros, needs time to meet his close relatives here on Tzurac. It's his first visit to our planet and his plans were disrupted by the unexpected action of the last few days. He needs time in the Grand Library to learn more about the history of his home planet and his heritage. His father, Captain Ahrmon Tyros, would have wanted this.'

Ghalbrak looked to the other senators, sensing their support. 'This is an unorthodox request Commander, but under the circumstances, you have our permission.'

'Thank you, Senators, much appreciated.'

* * *

Later that day, just before the evening meal at Dakhar's house, Ehrane asked Kyron, Torri and Tajhira to sit with him on the couches in the family den.

Puzzled, Tajhira was the first to speak up. 'What's this all about, my husband?' she asked inquisitively.

'Well, I wanted to tell you something before you hear it indirectly from other sources.'

All three waited anxiously in anticipation.

'I've been invited to become a senator on the council.'

'Wonderful!'

'Well done!'

'That's amazing!'

Excited at the wonderful news, they voiced their congratulations all at once.

Dakhar grinned in appreciation.

Kyron had mixed feelings, though he chose not to display them openly. His mind was unsettled, and his thoughts turned to mild despair. *It would mean he and Torri, together with their children, would be returning to Earth without his best friend and mentor – the 'brother' he'd never had.*

He looked at Torri who seemed to be having similar thoughts. *Her best friend, Tajhira, would not be coming back to Terra Major.*

Their thoughts were interrupted as Tajhira stood up. 'I'll fetch the wine so we can toast the new appointment.'

Dakhar gestured for her to sit. 'No, my love, don't do that just yet. There's more.'

'More?' she questioned with surprise.

Dakhar waited until Tajhira had reseated herself. 'I've declined the offer,' he said, smiling, 'and here's why …'

At the end of his tale, Dakhar turned to Kyron and Torri, 'So,' he said, 'I'll be coming back with you two in a month's time, and I hope Tajhira and Kyrah will also be coming with us.'

Although slightly disappointed at the news Ehrane was turning down the honour of being a member of the Senate, Tajhira understood her husband's commitment to his Regiment. She also had her own news to share. She patted her stomach gently, saying, 'I only hope I'll be able to travel in this condition.'

There was a moment's interval before shock of the news sank in. Dakhar jumped to his feet and rushed over to his wife to hold her. 'Are you telling me we're expecting a new brother or sister for Kyrah?'

'Yes, Ehrane, I am. You've had so much to worry about recently, I didn't want to burden you and I've been waiting anxiously for the right moment to tell you.'

'This is wonderful news!' said Ehrane, hugging and kissing her with excitement.

He turned to Kyron, saying, 'So much for your Earthling sense of humour' and chuckling at their private joke.

Kyron laughed too as he reached out to congratulate his friend with a vigorous Sentinel handshake. And Torri, smiling fondly, came over to Tajhira to hug her and kiss her on the cheek.

'Now we can open the wine and celebrate,' said Ehrane, reaching for the wine bottle and filling their glasses. 'Here's to our life change.'

'And here's to our continued partnership as Sentinels of Tzurac, General,' said Kyron, toasting again. 'Thanks for asking the Senate to delay our return voyage to Earth and for ensuring our two families will stay together.'

Torri and Tajhira raised their glasses and shook their heads in full agreement as Kyron continued, 'You're such a true friend, and I thank you deeply.'

'We'll always be true friends Kyron, just like our fathers were, and our families will be close friends too. Now, shall we call the children from upstairs and share the good news?'

GLOSSARY

ALORAN	Chieftain Leader of Urgellan clans.
ANCIENTS	Revered warriors of the past who founded Tzuracian Civilisation.
ANKROD	One of the three moons orbiting Dunkor in the Clavistoq Star System. Inhabited by primitive barbaric hunter-gatherers.
ANKRODIANS	Primitive barbaric hunter-gatherers from Planet Ankrod.
ARMEL	Fictitious name used by the Sentinel Yarron Blandhar while pretending to be an Urgellan.
ARMONUS	Planet in Northern Quadrant, Grekadian Domain.
ARMONUSIANS	Inhabitants of Armonus. Peace- loving spiritual monks who possess healing powers.
ASPECT	Earth's Aero Space Exploration, Colonisation and Transportation program.
ASRAM	Capital city of Planet Urgellan.
BHALAR	See Rokan, Bhalar.
BHARKAZ	Treldarian capital of Planet Orkharn.
BLADERS	Treldarian army deserters turned mercenaries who refused to sign the Federation of Planets Treaty after the Grekadian War.

BLAKE, LAUREN	Daughter of General Blake (ASPECT) and acting administrator of MERIC.
BLAKE, MALCOLM	General in charge of ASPECT.
BLANDHAR, YARRON	Fugitive Sentinel Corporal who helped Khaneera Zarkwin escape from prison on Tzurac with the Xytrinium infusion formula.
BREKHAN	Lieutenant, another fictitious name used by Yarron Blandhar.
CHEKHMAR, GLOBAK	Treldarian Captain, 3rd Legion, Southern Quadrant.
CITADEL	Tzuracian military complex.
CLAVISTOQ STAR SYSTEM	Southern Quadrant, containing the dead Planet Dunkor with three orbiting moons: Mankro, Ankrod and Nujhar.
DAKHAR, EHRANE	General, Commanding Chief of Military Operations, Western Quadrant.
DAKHAR, KYRAH	Son of Ehrane Dakhar.
DAKHAR, RHAZON	Grandfather of Ehrane Dakhar. Distinguished General who fought in the Grekadian War.
DAKHAR, RHYK	Ehrane's father.
DAKHAR, TAJHIRA	Ehrane Dakhar's Urgellan wife.
DESTROYER, (CLASS 10)	Tzuracian fighter craft with stealth and cloaking capabilities. Weapons include laser cannons and Xytrinium torpedoes.
DIUNON	Volcanic planet in the Grekadian Domain, Northern Quadrant.
DIUNONS	Inhabitants of Diunon. Small red devilish-looking creatures.
DIUTRONS	Eight-foot high, remotely controlled robots, built by the Diunons. Made with reinforced Xytrinium armour plate and armed with laser pulse cannons.
DRANZ	General, leader of the Treldarian Fifth Legion from the Northern Quadrant.

DTC	Division Transport Carrier. A low altitude Tzuracian hovercraft powered by magnetic propulsion.
DUNKOR	A dead red planet in the Clavistoq Star System, Southern Quadrant.
EHRANE	See Dakhar, Ehrane.
FEDERATION OF PLANETS	An alliance of the planets Tzurac, Treldar, Kyronis, Armonus and Diunon made after signing a peace treaty following the Grekadian War.
GLANTOS	One of the five planets in the Orkharnian Star System.
GLANTOSIANS	Inhabitants of Glantos. Small hairy grotesque creatures who live underground and mine Xytrinium for the Treldarians.
GREKADIAN WAR	The interplanetary Great War over control of Xytrinium which took place over five hundred years ago.
HAMMOND, RICHARD	Chief of Security at the MERIC Building, Earth.
HARBROK	Flight Sergeant, Flight Control Centre, Tzurac's Khazor Air base.
HARJAR	One of the three Kyroni who confronted Yarron (Armel) at the bar on Krima.
HARZAN	Tzuracian Admiral, Commanding Chief of Operations, Northern Quadrant.
JELKAH	Bhalar Rokan's stepmother, deceased.
JENSEN, JACKSON	Deceased son of Samuel Jensen. Conspirator in MERIC.
JENSEN, SAMUEL	Founder and former CEO of MERIC, now deceased.
JHAMARZ	Sergeant, 33rd Battalion. One of the Treldarian assailants who attacked Ramlok and Krag in the alley at Bharkaz.

JORHAN	One of the three uninhabitable moons orbiting Tzurac.
KELFAS	Elderly leader of the Nujharenes.
KELZHAR	One of the three uninhabitable moons orbiting Tzurac.
KHAZOR	Capital city of Planet Tzurac.
KIKEN	Leader of the Diunons.
KOMPAK	Small planet in the Western Quadrant used as a refuelling depot for Tzuracian exploration vessels.
KRAG	Treldarian Sergeant, 25th Infantry Battalion on Orkharn.
KRIMA	Planet of corruption on boundary of Eastern and Southern Quadrants.
KULBARK	One of the three Kyroni who confronted Yarron on Krima.
KURDARQ	Military female Councillor in General Vark's War Council on Orkharn.
KYRON	See Tyros, Kyron.
KYRONI	Warriors from Planet Kyronis.
KYRONIS	One of the five planets in the Federation of Planets.
LAUREN	See Blake, Lauren.
LHANTAR	Tzuracian senior Senator involved in military arrangements for Terra Major (Earth).
LOMBHARQ	Captain, First Officer, acting Commander of Tzuracian Flagship *Rhazon*.
LUDAX	One of the five planets in the Orkharnian Star System.
LUDAXIANS	Inhabitants of Planet Ludax, including very beautiful females.
MANKRO	One of the three moons orbiting the dead Planet Dunkor in the Clavistoq Star System

	in the Southern Quadrant. Home of General Rokan and his Treldarian army.
MANKU	Novice priest on Armonus.
MERIC	Mining and Engineering Resource Industrial Company, founded by Samuel Jensen.
MORZHAN, PYRHAM	Senior Tzuracian Senator, Legal Fraternity. Emissary to Planet Armonus.
MURZAK	Tzuracian Colonel, Red Star Regiment.
MYZEK	Lieutenant, 33rd Battalion. One of the Treldarian assailants who attacked Ramlok and Krag in the alley on Orkharn.
NHASAN	Tzuracian Lieutenant. Navigation Officer aboard Flagship *Rhazon*.
NUJHAR	One of the three moons orbiting the dead Planet Dunkor, Clavistoq Star System.
NUJHARENES	Green-skinned inhabitants of Nujhar.
ORKHARN	One of the five planets in the Orkharnian Star System, Eastern Quadrant. Home of General Vark of the Treldarian Second Legion.
PLEDGE RING	Gold holographic communication ring engraved with the Sentinel's family ancestry.
QUADRANTS	The four compass divisions of the known Universe.
QUEEN TARUNE	Beautiful ruler of Planet Urgellan.
RAMLOK	Treldarian Lieutenant in Dranz's Blader army of mercenaries. Later a Captain in General Vark's Second Legion, Eastern Quadrant.
ROKAN, BHALAR	Daughter of General Rokan.
ROKAN, JELZAD	Treldarian General, Third Legion, Southern Quadrant.
SARKAN	One of the three Kyroni who confronted Yarron at the bar on Krima.
SHANOWAH	Seductive Ludaxian female in the hot baths at Bharkaz.

SHIELD, KYRON	Also known as Kyron Tyros.
SHIELD, RHAMON	The name taken by Kyron's father, Ahrmon Tyros, after escaping to Earth.
SCOUT-SHIPS	Small Treldarian spacecraft used for battle and for reconnaissance.
SENTINEL	Elite soldier of the Planet Tzurac with enhanced powers and a 400-year lifespan.
SKARHDOK	Tzuracian Captain stationed on Planet Iota.
STEIROS	Volcanic planet used as Treldarian sanctuary in Northern Quadrant.
SYPRAH	Tzuracian Sergeant in charge at Kompak refuelling depot.
TARHAZ	Treldarian soldier of 3rd Legion accompanying Yarron on Ankrod.
TARHDOK, MORKHAN	Fleet Commodore at Tzurac's Khazor Air base in charge of all space vessels.
TARKEN	Treldarian Captain in General Vark's Second Legion.
TARQ	Master, High Priest on Planet Armonus.
TERRA IOTA	Planet several light years from Earth in Western Quadrant, being mined for Xytrinium by MERIC.
TERRA MAJOR	Earth, Western Quadrant.
TERRANIANS	Earthlings, humans.
TERRA UPSILON	Underground penal colony from where Jackson Jensen escaped with his henchmen.
THOMPSON, GRANT	Irish engineer on Planet Iota.
TORRI	See Tyros, Torri.
TRELDAR	Original planetary home of the Treldarians and a reluctant member of the Federation of Planets following the Grekadian War.
TRELDARIANS	Descendants of the inhabitants of Planet Treldar including soldiers of the Second and Third Legions.

TRIGAN	Treldarian warship commanded by Captain Chekhmar, Southern Quadrant.
TURKRAHN	Tzuracian Captain of warship over Washington.
TYROS, AHRMON	Sentinel Captain, known on Earth as Rhamon Shield. Kyron's father. Deceased.
TYROS, EHRANA	Daughter of Kyron and Torri.
TYROS, KYRON	Also known as Kyron Shield. Son of Sentinel, Captain Ahrmon Tyros.
TYROS, TORRI	Wife of Kyron, formerly Torri Madison.
TYROS, ZURI	Son of Kyron and Torri.
TZURAC	Planet in Northern Quadrant where the Sentinels come from.
TZURACIAN	Inhabitants of Planet Tzurac.
URGELLAN	One of the planets in the Grekadian Star System and member of the Federation of Planets ruled by Queen Tarune.
URGELLANS	Inhabitants of Planet Urgellan.
VARK, KHURAM	Treldarian General, Second Legion, Eastern Quadrant.
VARK, TYKRAN	Lieutenant, son of General Vark.
VEXAR	Capital of Planet Kyronis.
VOLHARDTZ	Tzuracian Senior Senator, Law Fraternity, emissary to Urgellan.
WALKARM	Urgellan Captain of the Royal Guards.
WAR COUNCIL	Located in Orkharn's capital city, Bharkaz, with ten military members.
WOLZHART	Tzuracian Captain commanding the lead warship *Predarus*.
WORLD ASSEMBLY	Earth's controlling administration body on world affairs located in Washington.
WURTAH	One of the three uninhabited orbiting moons of Tzurac.

XYTRINIUM	Most volatile powerful blue crystal in the known Universe.
YARRON	See Blandhar.
ZARKWIN, KHANE	Deceased Tzuracian Chief of Security, Khaneera's father.
ZARKWIN, KHANEERA	Vengeful Sentinel daughter of Khane Zarkwin.
ZAWKON, KAL	Tzuracian Captain. Acting Commanding Chief of Military Operations of Western Quadrant, Terra Major.

* * *

About the Author

In the early fifties I emigrated from England to Australia as a youngster with my "ten pound pom" family. I spent my boyhood and teenage years reading Marvel and DC comics and followed all the sci-fi TV series of Star Trek, Lost in Space, Dr Who and Time Tunnel. Then, in my adulthood, I watched sci-fi movies including Star Wars, Battlestar Galactica, and Star Gate, and continue to watch new release sci-fi movies. I have always loved English literature and started writing romantic poetry, graduating to my first non-fiction book in 2003. After retiring from a career of forty years in the public service, I am now writing full time and applying my past martial arts training and my interest in science as well as science fiction, to write believable and exciting sci-fi stories. Readers from Amazon Books who read my first sci-fi novel published in 2012 "Sentinels of Tzurac –Terra Major Under Threat" have asked for more in the space opera adventure and I have now made the series into a quadrilogy.